W9-BXU-602

DESTINY

ALSO BY TOM LOWE

A False Dawn
The 24th Letter
The Butterfly Forest
The Black Bullet
Blood of Cain
Black River

DESTINY

A NOVEL

TOM LOWE

K

Kingsbridge Entertainment

Library of Congress Cataloging in-Publication Data

Lowe, Tom 1952-

DESTINY / Tom Lowe – 1st edition
ISBN: 1503099938
ISBN-13: 9781503099937

1. Isaac Newton—Fiction. 2. World War II—Fiction. 3. Bible prophecies—Fiction. 4. Chartres Cathedral—Fiction. Title: DESTINY

DESTINY is distributed in ebook and print editions. Printed books available from Amazon.com and bookstores.

First Edition: February 2015. Published in the U.S.A. by Kingsbridge Entertainment.

ACKNOWLEDGMENTS

*T*his novel is a bit of a departure for me. After writing six Sean O'Brien mystery/thriller books, I wanted to take a shot at writing my first stand-alone novel. I had an idea gnawing inside me that involved a side of Isaac Newton that isn't as widely known as his scientific discoveries. Newton spent more than fifty years of his life combing the Bible for codes – for prophecies. Did he succeed? And if he did, what did he find?

More than 250 years after his death a chest containing Newton's unpublished and lost papers was found and opened. In 1936, the papers and manuscripts were sold at auction in London. Who bought the papers, and what did Newton's final notes reveal? And how, collectively, might these lost pages speak to our times?

What if they could speak volumes because Newton was searching for codes that might shine a long light into future events – events of today and tomorrow? Newton helped explain *gravity* --- but could he do the same for humankind and our *destiny*?

On this page is the part of writing that I enjoy the most because it's where I can thank those who've helped me. A HUGE thank you to beta readers Cassie Turner, Darcy Yarosh and Helen Christensen. Great job! I tip my hat to my phenomenal production team at Amazon which includes: Carina Petrucci, Kandis Miller and Brianne Twilley.

A special thanks to a special person … my wife Keri. She's an excellent editor with a savvy insight into human nature. Her skill-set includes a dry sense of humor that is particularly vital when married to a guy who often starts a sentence with, *"What if?"*

And finally to you, the reader. Thank you very much for taking a seat at the campfire. If you're a new reader of my work, welcome. If you've been on the journey through our Sean O'Brien novels, I hope you enjoy this story and find it as fascinating as I did when I first thought, *"What if?"*

For Christopher Lowe

"What is man in nature? He is nothing in relation to infinity, all in relation to nothing, a central point between nothing and all—and infinitely far from understanding either. The ends of things and their beginnings are impregnably concealed from him in an impenetrable secret. He is equally incapable of seeing the nothingness out of which he was drawn and the infinite in which he is engulfed."

- Blaise Pascal, 1659

"While we look not at the things which are seen, but at the things which are not seen. For the things which are seen are sequential, but the things which are not seen are eternal."

- 2 Corinthians 4:18

ONE

LONDON, ENGLAND – 1936

No one knew what was in the old trunk. It had been locked for more than 250 years. But in 1936, the trunk was about to be opened, and in a few days its contents would be sold to the highest bidder. For more than two centuries, the trunk was stored in a back room deep in the bowels of a home owned by the Earl of Portsmouth's family. The trunk, a shade of tarnished silver, had been moved to the Sotheby's building on New Bond Street in London where a locksmith kneeled, probing the rusty lock.

The Sotheby's auctioneer, a balding man with sagging eyes, wiped a handkerchief across his perspiring upper lip. "How much longer?"

The locksmith grunted, his slender fingers twisting a pick inside the lock. "This chest has been bolted since 1727. I can't open two-and-a-half centuries in a few seconds."

"The auction is in two weeks."

"Whatever's in here could have bloody turned to dust."

"The trunk looks secure to me. Perhaps its contents are fine."

There was a sound, ancient metal releasing its grasp. The locksmith grinned. "Got it!"

"Please, open it."

A rail-thin photographer for the London Times finished a cigarette, crushing the butt in an ashtray. He advanced the film in his camera, stepping closer to the trunk. "I hope there's something worth photographing," he said, flicking a speck of tobacco from his tongue.

The auctioneer said, "The trunk is heavy. There's definitely something in there."

The locksmith nodded, using a chisel to pry between the top of the trunk and the base. "Get the other side."

The auctioneer leaned down, gripping the left side of the trunk.

"On three," said the locksmith. "One…two…three."

Both men carefully lifted the lid. Under the flickering light from the incandescent bulbs, the men could see thousands of papers, all handwritten, stacked in the trunk.

"What's that?" asked the locksmith.

The auctioneer's hands trembled as he pushed his glasses up the bridge of his nose. He leaned closer and read from one paper. "This, my friend, is a treasure."

"Doesn't look like gold to me."

"Perhaps it's more valuable than gold."

"A lot of old papers. They even smell musty."

"These are not a lot of musty-old papers. They are the unpublished works of Britain's greatest scientist, perhaps the most brilliant mind the world has ever known. These are the secret papers of Sir Isaac Newton."

"Newton? Why were they hidden? What's in 'em?"

The auctioneer touched the notes, all stacked high in the trunk. With shaking hands, he lifted out some of the papers, the ink dark brown, originally written using a quill pen. The odor of aged papers, as if opening an old cellar door, crawled out of the chest where it had been trapped for centuries. The auctioneer read silently for half a minute.

"Oh my."

"What is it?" asked the photographer, lifting his camera.

"Oh dear."

"What?"

"This *is* incredible."

"What does it say?" asked the locksmith.

The auctioneer didn't answer. He scanned the aged handwriting, lifted a few more pages from the trunk and read, his hands pale in the soft light.

The photographer said, "Hold the papers up, and I'll snap a photograph."

The auctioneer looked up from the pages, his eyes filled with delight. "Although these are the unpublished works of Britain's greatest scientist, he was apparently much more than a scientist."

"What do you mean?" asked the photographer.

"Newton seems to have had a lot to say about God."

"What would a scientist have to say about God?"

The auctioneer said nothing. He set the papers down and lifted another one. He released a low whistle, his eyes narrowing.

"What is it, Mr. Kinsley?" The photographer scribbled notes.

"It looks like Newton was extracting passages from the Bible. He's writing about mysterious fires. He mentions the Book of Revelation and the Books of Daniel, Matthew, Ezekiel and Isaiah. He seems to have been comparing something. He's writing about alchemy and scribbles something that seems to spell the words *Philosopher's Stone*."

"What in bloody hell is that all about?"

"I don't know. Maybe it will take a scientist, or a man of God to understand these. Newton seems to have been both. Now it's my task to try and catalog these by subject, and there are a lot of words written here. The question is: What is it that Newton is trying to say, and is there anyone out there smart enough to find the answer?"

The photographer nodded. "All right, Mr. Kinsley, stand to the left of the ol' trunk and hold up some of those papers."

The auctioneer held papers in both hands, looked toward the camera and smiled. The camera's flash engulfed the room, capturing a time capsule originally written by a man who understood the meaning of time and space more than anyone on earth.

TWO

VIRGINIA – PRESENT DAY

*P*aul Marcus stood on the wooden front porch of his old farmhouse as twilight crept up, the pecan grove filling with buttery light. He sipped a cup of coffee, watching his wife and daughter ride their two horses in from the pasture. He could hear them laughing when Buddy, their border collie, ran in front of them, barking, as if he were ordering the horses to follow his lead to the barn.

Marcus rested his six-foot frame against a post on the porch where hanging baskets, the size of beach balls, sprouted petunias dripping with burgundy and snow white petals. The breeze blew in from the west, awaking the wind chimes, delivering the scent of burning pecan shells and pine straw from his neighbor's property across the road. A four-day growth of beard on Marcus's angular face made him look older than his thirty-seven years. His hazel eyes trapped the green of the pines and the deep sapphire of the Blue Ridge Mountains in the distance.

When he stepped off the porch, a red-tailed hawk lifted from the aged oaks in his yard, soaring above the tree line and over the millpond in the center of his sixty acres. He walked down to the small barn and pasture. A split-rail fence his grandfather had built sixty years earlier separated the barn from the front and backyard of the old home. Honeysuckles wrapped their leafy tendrils around the fence posts, the pale yellow blooms throbbing with honeybees.

The distant whine of a semi-truck straining to climb the mountains was lost when cicadas began chanting in the grove and crickets chirped from the cool underbelly of the barn. The sunset played hide-and-seek with leaves and limbs sauntering in the breeze, causing the old oaks to be painted in deep shadow one moment, then turning a golden light.

"Daddy, I got Midnight to run fast! Mommy and I galloped most of the way home," said Tiffany, pulling a strand of dark hair behind one ear. She grinned, her green eyes radiant in the light, a dusting of freckles across her cheeks, her small hands at ease holding the reins.

"She did great," Jennifer said, dismounting.

"That's my girl." Marcus stepped up to the horses to help his daughter down. "It won't be long before you have Midnight jumping."

"Yep, that's what I told her on the trail today."

"What'd she say?"

Tiffany grinned, dimples popping. "She just nodded her head."

"Okay, lead her to the barn. We'll get the saddle off and give Midnight a rest."

"Are we still going for ice cream after supper?"

"It's Friday night, of course."

"Yes!" Tiffany smiled and walked her horse to the barn.

"She's a natural with animals," Jennifer said.

Marcus turned toward her, the wind shifting, teasing his wife's chestnut brown hair. Her caramel eyes were playful in the twilight, full lips wet and warm, sensuous as the sunset. Jennifer's hair was drenched in light, a quiet radiance of love swelled from her eyes, palpable as the glow of dusk. Even after ten years of marriage, Marcus's desire, his yearning to be near his wife only grew.

He felt an allure, an attraction mysterious as the pull of a magnet, drawing him close to her. The sun dropped below the tree line, squeezing pumpkin-colored beams through strands of trees, the speckled patterns displayed on the side of the faded red barn.

"They've arrived," Jennifer said, pointing behind Marcus. "It's the first firefly I've seen so far this year. They add an impressionist painter's touch to a summer's eve."

"When I was a kid, I filled one of my grandmother's canning jars with fireflies. I did that one time, and they were dead the next morning. Never caught one again."

"Hope you gave them a respectable burial." She grinned and touched her horse. "We'd better get Midnight and Lightning cooled down and into their stalls."

The old barn smelled of hay, horse sweat, manure, and oil cans. They unsaddled the horses, walked them a bit before taking off their bridles, brushing them while Buddy searched the stall for a mouse he chased from behind a wooden toolbox. Marcus looked toward the far entrance of the barn and could see the full moon slowly rising above the valley, mountains awash in a bone-white glow.

— • —

After eating ice cream cones at the Creamy Delight in downtown Warrenton, Marcus and his family started home, just as a dark cloud tumbled over the moon.

"Feels like it's gonna rain," Jennifer said, buckling her seatbelt.

Marcus started the car. "Weather forecast said no chance of rain until Wednesday."

The back roads across the mountains were similar to driving through a black tunnel deep in a deserted coal mine. There were no lights in the distance. The night grew darker with the approaching storm.

"Daddy, I'm cold," said Tiffany from the back seat.

"I'll adjust the heat to make it warmer. And, you can wrap up in my jacket."

The raindrops were large and falling in flat globs—the noise against the roof and windshield sounded like hands smacking the car. The rain fell with such intensity that Marcus couldn't see but a few feet beyond the front bumper, headlights unable to penetrate the wall of water.

"Maybe we should pull off the road," Jennifer said, touching her shoulder strap.

"Where? The only place I can think of is County Line Road, and that's at least two miles away. I'll put on the emergency flashers. Hope no one hits us from behind."

Thunder crashed with the ferocity of two speeding freight trains colliding. Lightning exploded, severing the limb off a tall pine—the burst of light illuminating the mountains in a half-second strobe of white light. Marcus blinked hard for a second, trying to scatter the green spots trapped in his retinas, floating above his hands on the steering wheel.

"I'm scared, Mama."

"It's okay, baby. We'll be home soon. Daddy knows these roads well."

Marcus gripped the wheel, straining to see through the windshield, the full bore of the wipers doing little to move the torrent of water pouring over the car. Then, as quick as the storm arrived, the rain slacked, the wipers now easily pushing the water off the glass. Marcus eased his grip on the steering wheel. He could hear his wife release a deep breath, stress lifting from her chest. "That was unnerving," she said.

They drove quietly for a half-mile, fog climbing up from the valley and creeping across the road. Jennifer crossed her arms. "This weather is weird, strange. Paul, look over there. Someone's trying to change a tire."

Marcus's headlights panned across a newer model car parked on the side of the road. They could see the figure of a man, bent over, trying to jack up the car. "Slow down, honey," Jennifer said. "That poor man seems alone. It looks like he doesn't have a flashlight. Maybe we should help. He could be elderly."

"I don't recognize the car or the person."

"Well, we don't know everybody here anymore. A lot of new families are moving to this part of Virginia. Even your grandfather was a newcomer to somebody at one time."

Marcus drove up behind the car and stopped. The man had his back to Marcus's car and continued adjusting the jack without turning around. The flashing emergency lights filled Marcus's car with a pulsating maroon blush that had a peculiar ambience to it. He watched it reflect from his wife's eyes for a moment. "Hand me the flashlight in the glove box. I'll see if I can help."

Jennifer found the flashlight, giving it to Marcus. She watched the man. "Why isn't he looking our way? We're not that far from him."

"I don't know. Like you said, he could be an older man."

"I have to go to the bathroom," Tiffany said.

"It won't take long. Daddy's just going to see if that man needs some help."

"Lock the door behind me," Marcus said, putting the transmission in park and getting out. The rain was now a mist. He switched on the flashlight and walked toward the parked car. The man crouched next to the left rear wheel, wearing a dark coat, hood covering his head, his back to Marcus. Thunder rolled in the valley and lightning crisscrossed the sky, the Blue Ridge Mountains a backdrop of mauve and dark purple.

Marcus felt something wasn't right. He could see that the man's car wasn't lower at one end because of a flat tire. The man slowly stood and turned around, the hood of his raincoat pulled forward over his head, face cast in dark shadow, fog rising out of the valley and crawling toward them.

"Thought you could use some light," Marcus said, shining the flashlight on the tire. It was perfectly inflated. The jack wasn't engaged under the truck.

"You're a good Samaritan." The man's voice sounded distant, and it carried a dialect he didn't recognize, perhaps from living in different places.

"In this weather, figured you could use help," Marcus said, keeping the direct glare of the light toward the man's feet. "You don't have a flat. What's the trouble?"

The man said nothing for a moment. He reached inside his coat pocket, pulled out a small cigar and lit it. A red flame illuminated unblinking black eyes. Even in the dark, Marcus could feel the apathy, the veiled contempt from the man's eyes.

"Trouble?" asked the man, the ruby tip of the cigar burning, the smoke mixing with the fog. "I believe you're the trouble."

"I'll be on my way." Marcus backed up, not turning around, his senses acute. He could hear drips of water against the car, ticking of the engine, a diesel moaning over the mountain, and a gentle but fragile sound in the night—his daughter's sneeze.

THREE

"What's Daddy doing?" Tiffany asked, straining to see out the front windshield

"It looks like he's talking with the man, honey. Maybe the man's okay and doesn't need your father's help."

"But why's Daddy walking backward to our car?"

— —

The man tossed the cigar into a pothole near the shoulder of the road, the hiss from it resembling a snake in the night. "I'm the contractor."

"What?" Marcus stopped walking.

"Preventative maintenance."

"What are you talking about?"

The man grinned, a vein of lightning in the distance ensnared in his hard, black eyes. He reached inside his jacket again. Marcus thought he was getting a second cigar.

He got a pistol. "I'm just a hired gun, brother," he said, grinning. The small black revolver looked surreal in the glow of flashing red lights and fog swirling around them. Marcus saw the flash, bright white and a burst of crimson gas.

It was as if he had been hit in the chest with a sledgehammer.

As he fell, he heard a long, painful scream from Jennifer, and the terrified cry from Tiffany.

9

He fell on his back, rain cold against his face, heat of his blood seeping into his shirt, pooling toward his naval. The man stepped over Marcus, water and road grit falling from the man's shoes onto Marcus's face.

"Paul!" *Bam. Bam.* The shatter of glass.

A whimper and Tiffany's scream. Daaaaddddy! *Bam.* Silence.

Marcus could hear his breath coming in thick gurgles, the slapping of his car's windshield wipers, gears of a semi-truck downshifting and approaching in the distance.

The man walked back to Marcus, squatting down. He lit a thin cigar, smoke curling and rising up under the hood covering the man's head. He sat on his haunches, rain dripping from the slicker onto Marcus's face, the smell of burnt gunpowder and tobacco in the air. He rocked slowly while squatting, puffing the cigar, watching the life seep out of Marcus. His small mouth curled into a predator's grin. He whispered. "Die! You *hear* me? You're dying now…a slow damn death I thought I would have the pleasure of watching, but someone's coming."

The white of the high beams from a semi truck raked over the mountaintop. The man looked in the direction of the oncoming truck. Then he stared down at Marcus, lights coming closer. Marcus looked up, smoke dissipating from under the man's hood and his face. He had thin lips. Arched dark eyebrows. The eyes were black as coal, unblinking and appraising Marcus—a butcher inspecting a cut of beef. He pulled out a knife, sinking the blade to the hilt on the left side of his Marcus's chest.

Marcus felt the blade tear though muscle, cartilage, nerves and ribcage bones. The pain was white hot, searing. The truck was coming closer. The man stood, stepping over Marcus to pick up his wet cigar from the pothole. He ran to his car.

Marcus stared up into night sky. There was a separation in the clouds, as if dark curtains were slowly pulled open. Stars pulsed with a secluded and lonely presence. He raised his hand, blood dripping down his arm. "Jen… Tiffany…." His voice was a whisper. Sweat rolled from his face, his heart thrashed, sputtered, slowed and tried to jumpstart, his life draining away. He dropped his hand back to his chest the same instant a meteor carved a fiery trail across the heavens and faded into the blackness that engulfed him.

— ▬

Marcus sat straight up in bed. Sweat pooled in the center his chest, some of it dripping down his sides. Thunder rumbled and lightning illuminated his bedroom, painting the room in half-second shades of coppery color. For a moment, Marcus felt as if there was no air in the room, the oxygen sucked out, stale and bone dry. Heavy rain roared across the pastures, pelting trees and engulfing the old farmhouse.

Marcus breathed deeply, his heart hammering, jaw muscles sore. Since Jennifer and Tiffany's death, his dreams ridiculed and haunted him. Some dreams were sweet scenes of his family, only to be juxtaposed with grisly, visceral riddles, dark images of Tiffany and Jennifer's bodies shot in the head. Others were of people he did not know and had never met. None of it made sense. People and places he didn't recognize and no dialogue. Only snippets of violence, like poorly edited movie trailers, projected in an incoherent speed deep in his subconscious.

Marcus closed his eyes for a moment and sat on the edge of his bed. *Did God have nightmares? If so, did he share them?* "What a stupid thought— maybe I'm losing my damn mind," he mumbled.

Buddy whined, getting up from the cushion where he slept in a corner of the bedroom.

"It's okay, boy." Marcus stood and walked to the kitchen. He filled a glass with ice, took a bottle of Belvedere vodka from the freezer and poured two inches over the ice.

He went into his daughter's bedroom, turned on the lamp and simply stood there. The room was as she'd left it, almost like she was coming home. The bed unmade, stuffed animals at the foot of it. Posters of Justin Bieber and Taylor Swift on the wall next to a signed picture of Kelly Clarkson. A vertical bulletin board held tacked pictures of Tiffany and friends at a skating rink, horse shows, and a school trip to Williamsburg. Several blue ribbons from equestrian competitions rimmed the board. On her nightstand was a picture of Tiffany and her mother making Christmas cookies. Another photo was the three of them playing with Buddy in the yard, autumn leaves in the background.

Marcus felt a lump in his throat. He blinked back tears and shut off the light. He entered the family room and sat in a leather chair. Buddy lay down at his side. He scratched the dog's head. "I'm turning you into an insomniac, too. Sorry, Buddy. But there's no greater friend to have in a storm than you." Marcus sat there and sipped his drink. He watched the rain falling beyond the stretching light from the front porch. In the distance, lightning cast the Blue Ridge Mountains into silhouettes of ancient humpbacked, purple dragons that slumbered quietly through the ages.

—▪—

The sun was only a hint behind dark clouds two hours later when Marcus called the local police department. "Detective Russell, any new leads?"

"No, Mr. Marcus. Nothing new since you called last week?"

"I call every week because no one from your department calls me."

"That's because we don't have anything new to tell you. I'm sorry."

"It's been almost two years."

"Sometimes these things take more time. Something will break."

"Detective, it only breaks when you break it. Every day that goes by the leads grow colder."

"We had very few leads to start with, and nothing points in the direction of the killer. I assure you, we're doing the best we can." He sighed into the phone.

"That's not good enough."

"I'm hanging up now, Mr. Marcus. I understand your frustration, but—"

"But what! Some sick bastard killed my family. My wife and daughter are gone, forever. Do you know what it's like to lose your family…not to a car accident or disease, but to another human being who made the *decision* to brutally end their lives?"

"I'll call you if anything further develops."

"Before you hang up on me, Detective, I promise you I will make it develop."

"That would be a mistake, sir."

"The mistake is to wait for somebody to do your job—"

The detective disconnected. Marcus slowly lowered the phone from his ear. He reached out to touch a framed photograph of Jennifer and Tiffany, which stood on the kitchen counter. In the picture, they were feeding hay to the horses, the evening sun soft against their faces, wide smiles and laughing eyes. The glass over the picture was cool to his fingertips. "I'll find him…."

Marcus walked out onto his front porch and watched storm clouds descend over the mountains, darkening the valley and bending the treetops. A strong gust blew in from the west, shaking the wind chimes into a frenzy of sound and a string-puppet dance. Marcus stepped off the porch just when a second commanding gust blew in, catching a great horned owl in its squall. The owl fought the wind's grasp. It beat its wings, flying to within a few feet of Marcus, one wing almost grazing his face. The owl's unblinking yellow eyes stared at him for an instant, resembling two gold coins shining from the dark heart of a tornado.

FOUR

JERUSALEM, ISRAEL

Jacob Kogen stepped back from the whiteboard, capped the marker in his hand and stared at the equation. At age sixty-eight, he was recognized throughout Israel as brilliant, the most dynamic mathematician in the nation. Students from around the world, those with a deep interest in engineering, science, space travel, and physics, took his classes. Today, he worked on a problem no one, not any of his colleagues at the Hebrew University of Jerusalem, had been able to solve.

He looked down at the handwritten notes drafted meticulously almost three centuries years earlier. "What were you trying to say, Mr. Newton?" he mumbled, his tired eyes rising back to the long equation across two thirds of the board. Jacob's pale, narrow face reflected deep thought, a suggestion of internal quandary swirling in a mind wired to solve problems. His brown corduroy jacket hung from his lean frame, white hair uncombed beneath the kippah he wore on the back of his head. His eyes were the blue shade of swimming pool water, white eyebrows wild and tangled as barbed wire.

The phone on his desk buzzed. "Yes," he said, picking up the phone without taking his eyes off the whiteboard.

"Dr. Kogen," said the receptionist, "I know you asked not to be disturbed, but I have a call from Paris. The woman's name is Gisele Fournier."

"Did she say what she wants?"

"She says she has a gift for the university library. Shall I put her through, sir?"

"Yes." Jacob lowered his eyes from the whiteboard, answering the call.

14

"Professor Kogen," the voice had a slight French accent. "My name is Gisele Fournier. My grandfather, Philippe Fournier, attended a Sotheby's auction in London. I think it was in 1936. He purchased some papers from the estate of Sir Isaac Newton."

Jacob felt his pulse kick, the phone now warm in his moist hand. He gripped tighter. "Yes, yes—what do you have?"

"I'm not sure, really. My grandfather died. Before his death, though, he asked that we donate the papers to your university library because he read how you were searching for some clues possibly from the Bible, yes?"

"Correct. For years we have been researching the Newton papers we received from the Yahuda collection. We knew some were missing from the Sotheby's auction in 1936. Maybe these are the lost Newton papers."

"Perhaps you would find interest in adding these to your collection."

"Oh yes, indeed, thank you. This is most generous of you. Perhaps the papers you have in your possession will give us some of the answers we have been seeking to find. Is there a cost associated with the acquisition?"

"It is a donation—a gift. I will send them to you."

"Thank you, Miss Fournier. You are most generous."

"Professor?"

"Yes?"

"My grandfather was a religious man, a good man. He dealt in antiquities and art sales. He believed he had purchased something very extraordinary...so extraordinary that he did not wish to sell it or even let others know it was in his possession."

"I see. Did he offer any clues?"

"He read his Bible trying to learn what it was. He thought Isaac Newton had discovered something that he, Newton, took to his grave. As a little girl, I remember being at my grandparent's house one summer night. My grandfather, after consuming a bottle of wine, was going to destroy the papers. He finally sealed the boxes and placed them in the attic. If you find something in these papers, something that has meaning, please tell me, and I will share it with my grandfather in my prayers."

"Of course. Miss Fournier, I will give you our shipping number. Can you send these overnight? Perhaps these papers are the missing puzzle pieces."

FIVE

Jacob Kogen paced the atrium in the Hebrew University of Jerusalem Library, glancing through the glass door every minute or so. He saw his restless image in the reflection from the glass, almost like a weary traveler staring back at him.

The morning sun rose over Jerusalem, shimmering off the parked cars, chrome winking in the parking lot. Jacob thought about what Gisele Fournier had told him—the papers might have been one of the last things Newton wrote, because they were dated ten days before the famed scientist's death in 1727. The rumble of a diesel engine broke Jacob's thoughts. A FedEx truck stopped near the outdoor fountain pool. The driver wore dark glasses and shorts. He carried an electronic tablet on top of the cardboard box, perspiring as he entered the library.

"Over here," said Jacob. "In this room. Please put it down on the table." The driver followed Jacob into a small room lined with bookshelves and textbooks. The lighting was soft. The room carried the musky scent of very old paper, cloth and glass cleaner. He lowered the box to a wooden table. "It's for Jacob Kogen"

"I am Jacob. I'll sign for it."

The driver nodded and left as a younger man entered. "Is that—?"

"Yes! Yes, it is," Jacob said. His hand trembling, using scissors to open the box.

Samuel Bronner, broad-shouldered with dark rimmed glasses, raised his thick eyebrows. "Perhaps the remaining pieces to the mystery, Jacob?"

"We shall see." He lifted the old papers from the box. "They have the ancient bouquet of time. Written so many years ago." He lowered the hand-written notes down to the table, pulled out a chair and sat. He read silently for half a minute, his index finger, knotted from arthritis, tracing the words as if he were following a treasure map. Then he looked up, over his bifocals, his pale eyes now bright and alive. "These are indeed from the hand of Sir Isaac Newton."

"Do you think somewhere in there Newton found what no man has found before—the hidden prophecies of God?"

"If it is God's will. He may have allowed Newton, perhaps the greatest mind ever, to find the cryptograms of our forefathers, and maybe the fate of our children, our world, too."

"We have had many of Newton's papers since Abraham Yahuda donated them to the library and university in 1969." Samuel touched his mentor on the shoulder. "I hope we can find something new here. However, perhaps even Newton, as smart as he was, could never understand all that is woven through the earliest texts."

Jacob glanced at the pages faded after centuries of storage, the dark ink from the quill pen legible as the day when Newton wrote the words. Jacob said nothing, his eyes shifting through the sentences, glancing in the margins at the rows of numbers. His lips pursed, and he made a low whistle.

"He wrote quickly," said Jacob, his voice above a whisper. "The man who invented calculus filled the margins of each page to their maximum. He appears to have written the equations very fast. What if his mind outdistanced his own hand while he deciphered codes pouring over verses from the Bible? He thought there was truth, an ancient wisdom in the world, first delivered in scriptures, and that knowledge was lost."

Samuel grunted, shifted his weight and looked at the papers. "It is believed Newton spent fifty years of his life trying to decode the Bible, and now we're trying to make sense of his final papers. I don't want to sound pessimistic, Jacob, but what if he never succeeded? How can we interpret Newton? Since Einstein, there probably has been no greater scientist than Newton. He figured the laws of gravity, but he may never have discovered hidden prophecies in the Bible, if they do exist."

Jacob smiled and looked up at his friend. "Samuel, would you mind making us some tea? I want to look over these documents. I'm longing to get in front of the whiteboard with a marker. I hope there is reason in these notes to do so."

Samuel pushed his glasses up on the bridge of his nose. "Tea sounds good."

There were dozens of pages all handwritten in sentences of varying length. Some staccato. Disjointed. A few words were twice underlined. Some had exclamation points. Jacob read each word. He jotted down notes on a legal-sized paper. He murmured when he found something he recognized, his unkempt eyebrows lifting. He read aloud:

"Daniel, whose visions concern the things prefigured in the law, is bid to enclose the vision of the ram and goat. This again in his last vision where the angel comes to show him what is noted in the scripture of truth. He is to enclose the words and seal the book. This book of the scripture of truth sealed in the hand of God that is understood by him alone. It is written within and on the back side, within by hidden predictions of things to come, on the back side by open allusions to things past. The lamb now comes to receive and open when the prophecy is called the Revelation of Christ which God gave unto him, being a Revelation or opening of the scripture that has been sealed."

Samuel returned with two cups of steaming tea. He set one down, careful not to get it too close to the old papers. "You look mesmerized. Find anything?"

Jacob was silent, reading the last few pages, his eyes locking on three words jotted in the margin, under a calculus equation. He sat back in his chair, his stare distant, and his thoughts far beyond the small study. "Newton went to his grave believing the Bible held truths beyond the obvious. Imagine if he'd had a computer. What would he have found or what did he find in the scriptures?"

"You are a great mathematician, Jacob, your colleagues are some excellent statisticians, and yet we only surmise Newton was on the verge of fully interpreting Bible prophecies. There is only a single box of papers here. Can they tell us what thousands of words before those have not revealed?"

"They already reveal something I have never before seen."

"What is that?

"Look at this." Jacob pointed to a name in a margin beneath the numbers:

Born 1972 A.D.

"Newton wrote a man's name, and he jotted down the words prophet with a question mark after it. He wrote: *'and in the year 2015, this man will accept a noble prize for healing the sick....'* I believe he meant the Nobel Prize for Medicine."

"Nobel Prizes began in the early 1900's. That would have been at least 175 years *after* Newton died."

"Maybe this is the first Biblical prophecy Newton actually found."

"Why?"

"Because I've read the list of winners for this year's awards. The ceremonies are in December, but the winners are always announced this month, October. In medicine, it is an American, and he has the same name Newton wrote in the margin, Paul James Marcus."

Samuel scratched above his left eyebrow, leaning closer. "May I see?"

Jacob pointed to the name in the margin of the final page, Newton's handwriting is small, yet precise.

Samuel said, "It can't be the same man. It's impossible."

"Perhaps. But something in my heart tells me it is the same man. My heart also tells me it may be difficult to speak with this Paul James Marcus."

"Why would that be?"

"Because he is declining to accept the Nobel Prize for Medicine."

SIX

VIRGINIA

Paul Marcus walked alone though the cemetery on the outskirts of Warrenton, Virginia. It was cool, the October skies a deep blue, a campfire scent in the distance, and autumn leaves ripening with colors of gold, orange and cherry. Some fluttered down as he walked. He didn't bother to knock them off his shoulders. Marcus carried two bouquets of flowers.

It had been more than a month since he was last here. For Marcus, it felt like a lifetime. He remembered somehow fighting off shock, rising to his feet, stumbling to his car, and pushing his hand through shattered glass to unlock the doors. Jen had been shot once through the forehead, but Tiffany was still alive, barely, her body curled in the fetal position, moaning, hair matted with blood. He cradled her in his arms, *"Daddy…it's so dark. I'm cold, Daddy…. "*

"Hold on, baby…help's coming, Tiff…. " He kissed her pallid cheek, softly sobbing, the tears flowing down his unshaven face. Then his world went dark again.

Marcus pinched the bridge of his nose approaching the graves. He stood at the two gravestones, both side-by-side. The inscription on the left read:

Jennifer Marcus
Beloved Wife and Mother
1974 - 2012

Marcus looked at the headstone to his right.

Tiffany Marcus
You are forever missed
2001 – 2012

He placed one bouquet on his wife's grave and the other flowers next to Tiffany's headstone. Marcus stood there alone, lonely, in the stippled light that filtered through the oaks. The afternoon sun was radiant, like spun gold, as it spilled onto branches still heavy with autumn leaves.

He watched a squirrel hide an acorn in a secret place under the grass, which was turning brown from an early frost. A robin fluttered from a nearby old oak, hopping across the ground. *Life all around in a place of the dead. The world turns. Seasons come and go.* Somehow he was supposed to rejoin the orbit. *Bullshit.* What was he expected to do with his own life when the two people he loved with absolute resolve lay in front of him beneath six feet of Virginia earth?

He looked at the graves as a gust of wind blew through the trees. The breeze tugged at the leaves, many releasing their hold on the branches, wind-surfing around marble headstones, then departing when another draft scattered them across the cemetery.

"I miss you both so much," Marcus whispered. "It's not the same. Nothing is. I know I'm supposed to move on, to *live* life. That's what you always said, Jen. And, Tiffany, that's what you did in the short time you were here. I learned a lot from the two of you. Now, with what I've learned, I don't have you here to share it. Isn't that what this side of the grave is all about? What's the purpose, the meaning, if not that? And now that doesn't exist." Marcus looked up, his eyes drifting back to the headstones.

"Mama Davis is not doing too well either. She had a fall, sprained her ankle, and her blood pressure shot up. I'm going to visit her again tomorrow. I'm not sure which is more bruised, though, her arms from the fall or her ego."

The temperature dropped, and Marcus could feel the brisker, drier air coming in from the northwest, out of the mountains.

"Tiffany, Buddy's doing fine. He's a little heavier. The vet tells me I have to stop sharing cheese pizzas with him. I guess Italian food isn't part of a border collie's diet." Marcus licked his dry lips, his eyes watering. He could see the Blue Ridge Mountains arching in the distance beyond the fiery tree line. An eagle flew just above the tallest pines and called out, beating its wings, sailing over Marcus.

His cell phone chirped, the sound somehow foreign in place of bird-song and the fussing of squirrels playing hide-and-seek with acorns. He lifted the phone from his belt. *Unknown.*

He ignored the call, looked at the graves before him. "They want to give me an award for breaking a genetic code that will help regulate the electrical signals for the heart. I'm so sorry I couldn't have helped you, Tiff. I love you both—my heart aches all the time for you."

Marcus' cell chirped again.

Unknown.

Marcus thought about simply tossing the phone harder than he had ever thrown a football, throwing it into the valley below him, the depth already pocketing with afternoon shadows. *Maybe it was someone calling from the assisted living center about Mama Davis.* He answered.

"Mr. Marcus?"

"Who's calling?"

"My name is Jacob Kogen. I am calling you from Jerusalem."

"How'd you get my number?"

"That's not important, what's important is how I got your name."

"What are you talking about?"

"I teach mathematics at Hebrew University of Jerusalem in Israel. Also, I have been researching papers donated to the university library in 1969. The papers were written by Sir Isaac Newton."

"Why are you calling me?"

"May I meet with you?"

"Why?"

"We recently received a second donation—some of Newton's lost papers, ones he'd worked on for many years. He was a great student of the Bible. Newton was convinced the secrets to our future lie in our past, or maybe in the Book of Revelation. He went to his grave trying to decode the information in the Bible, and he may have succeeded."

"What does that have to do with me?"

"In one of the last papers Newton wrote, he added a name of a man who wouldn't be born for another 273 years. He added your name, Mr. Marcus. Perhaps Isaac Newton was handing the torch to you, maybe to solve something he could not. The question now is—what will you do with it?"

Marcus said nothing. He lowered the phone for a moment and stared up at the canopy of yellow, ginger and red leaves.

"Mr. Marcus, are you still there?" came the metallic voice from the cell phone.

Marcus raised the phone back to his ear.

"I'm here. Look, I'm sorry, there's a mistake. I'm not your guy. It's a fluke."

"Isaac Newton didn't create flukes, as you call it. He was a man of science and religion, and he believed the two did not and could not exist apart. But in his lifetime, even he had great difficulty pulling them together."

"I have to go."

"Please, Mr. Marcus, simply examine the information, the documents. All of your expenses will be paid. I don't know how to say this more sincerely than what my heart is telling me. Please, bear with me and allow an old man a moment. What if you found something that could add immense value to our world? If you don't examine the data, you'll go to your grave never knowing what was there, and how you might have helped."

"Helped? I'm *really* the wrong guy."

"What if you weren't selected by Newton, Mr. Marcus? What if God chose you? Could you, would you, refuse the request?"

"God? I've only made two requests to God in my life. Both denied, and I'm standing in front of them. I'm standing in front of the graves of my family—my wife and daughter—so don't talk to me about God. I have to go."

"Please, don't hang up. I'm very sorry for your loss. Mr. Marcus, we believe Newton came closer than any human to unlocking the layers of text and passages in the Bible. Imagine if you discovered some prophesies that could literally shine light onto our world, a world often too dark."

"What are you talking about?"

"Conceivably, at this point in time, the insights Newton labored to unlock centuries ago were not ready to be revealed—their lock impervious to a key. What if now the time is closer?"

"Closer to what?"

"To God's plan."

"Who the hell *are* you?"

"I am who I said I was, and everything I've told you is true."

"And I'm ending this call."

"Before you do, Mr. Marcus, I beg you to consider something I want to leave with you. If you are the successor to Isaac Newton, if you are chosen by God to unlock a biblical prophecy and you walk away, what would it mean?"

"Not a damn thing."

"Possibly, however, if you are the one, the person chosen to reveal something from the Bible that might have a wonderful influence on our world, and you turn your back—the world becomes far worse because of it…and you *know* it because you did nothing, could you rest at night?"

"This has gone far enough."

Marcus disconnected. He glanced down at the graves of his wife and daughter. Even in the chill, he felt a drop of sweat roll between his shoulder blades. He looked to his right, the valley an undulated dark sea of trees, copper and red leaves tossing in the wind, blurring into a horizon of purple mountains against the backdrop of indigo sky.

He turned from the graves and headed to his car, the only sound in the cemetery was the crunch of his boots through the dead leaves.

SEVEN

TEL AVIV, ISRAEL

Jacob Kogen had been in the building only once in his life. It was more than twenty-five years ago when the mathematician was making a name for himself. It was then that he was summoned to meet with the field ops director of Mossad, Israel's intelligence agency. The former director had retired; he was replaced with a man Jacob had never met, but knew of his persuasive global moves to keep Israel safe.

Jacob easily located the nondescript offices of Mossad north of Tel Aviv. He was cleared by security and told to wait in the adjacent lobby for an escort to take him to the office of the director.

"Professor Kogen," said a young man with a wide smile, extending his hand. "I'm Ira Schultz. Although I didn't attend Hebrew University, I'm in awe of your reputation in theoretical and quantum physics."

Jacob smiled. "Don't believe everything you hear. I still have a difficult time balancing my checkbook."

"Somehow, I think you can handle it. Please, come with me. Mr. Levy is ready to see you."

Jacob followed the intern to an elevator leading to a top floor filled with a labyrinth of halls and floors. The director's door was partially closed. The intern knocked softly.

"Come in."

"Nice meeting you Professor," said the intern, walking away.

Jacob entered the office. It was filled with photographs on the walls. Many depicting the director in his career as a military officer before he joined the Mossad. He also was seen posing with Menachem Begin, Yitzhak Shamir, and Ariel Sharon.

One old photograph caught Jacob's eye. It hung directly behind the man's chair. The black and white picture was from World War II, and the image was that of two dozen people, all dead, lying shoulder-to-shoulder in a muddy trench. Two men stood near the trench. One was a German officer pointing a Luger pistol at an emaciated man. The man showed no sign of fear on his dirty and, yet, defiant face.

"The gentleman about to be shot was my father," said the director.

"I'm sorry."

"I keep it there as a reminder of what happened, how it happened, and how it shall never occur again. Please, sit Professor." Nathan Levy, the field ops director of the Mossad, had a heavy face and large eyes the color of black onyx. He had the discreet baggage of a man who'd seen tragedy, but kept an impression of optimism on a face marked by time and decisions involving life and death.

Jacob said, "I understand. Israel cannot afford to lower her guard."

Levy grunted. "Your work has helped define and perhaps refine some of our nation's best scientists. Physics has always been rather abstract to me. Although I must admit, there's no deception in numbers. They don't lie."

Jacob smiled. "Why did you want to see me?"

"Do you really believe the name you discovered in Isaac Newton's notes, Paul Marcus, is the American who is declining a Nobel Prize?"

"Absolutely."

"You know, Professor, it may be a coincidence."

"Newton didn't spend too much time dealing with happenstance."

"I heard that a good scientist begins with things coincidental and attempts to prove a definitive relationship, or perhaps none at all."

"Are you referring to my years studying the Newton papers that Abraham Yahuda willed to the National Library?"

"You are a great mathematician, Jacob, but what have you proven?"

"We've proven that Newton was most definitely on the cusp of something."

Levy half smiled. "But you cannot tell me what our adversaries are planning."

"Newton was fluent in Hebrew and Latin. Discovering biblical prophecies was his real passion, a passion he had to hide before his death."

The director said nothing, his eyes drifting from Jacob to a window overlooking the Sea of Galilee. "You received Paul Marcus's phone number. Have you spoken with him?"

"Yes. He didn't believe it was his name I found penned in Isaac Newton's hand."

"An old acquaintance at the CIA, a man I worked with, who lived in Syria, Jordan and Israel for almost twenty-five years, gave me a small bit of Marcus's background. Perhaps there is something to the name you found on Newton's notes."

"What is that?"

"Paul Marcus grew up on a farm in Virginia. He was a gifted football player, as a young man he played for the University of Michigan. Academically, his high school college scores were extraordinary, especially in mathematics. He learned languages easily. His talents caught the eye of recruiters at the CIA where he worked for two years. Marcus, however, was more intrigued with breaking codes rather than catching spies, so he moved over to NSA. He broke an exceedingly difficult code that exposed some movements by al Qaeda."

"How?"

"Marcus figured out how to substitute words, symbols or numbers for plain text. A single symbol could, in fact, mean an idea or a short message. The code the terrorists created consisted of words chosen out of dialects from Iran, Saudi Arabia, Syria, Afghanistan, Pakistan, Yemen and Lebanon. Local street jargon was inserted with the words either before or after them. The finished message was hidden in Islamic religious passages."

"Most impressive."

"But Marcus's job at NSA ground to a halt after ten years."

"Why?"

"He'd been married to a woman he knew from college. They had a child, a girl, during the time he was at NSA. When his daughter was about eight, she was diagnosed with heightened arterial fibrillation. Marcus quit NSA and joined Hughes-Johnson Medical where he worked almost nonstop for three years. The result was that he cracked a type of gene therapy that could be used to stabilize false electronic signals sent through the hearts of those suffering from a type of ventricular arrhythmia. One of those suffering was indeed his daughter. She died right after Marcus had found the results he was seeking."

"Killed from heart disease?"

"No," Levy paused and glanced at the picture of his father on the wall. "She was murdered. His wife was shot and killed at the same time. Marcus was shot, stabbed and left for dead, but somehow he survived a wound that severed his aorta. Medics say he was without a heartbeat for at least two minutes. Miraculously, his heart started beating again, when he was clinically dead. His brain was oxygen deprived, perhaps for too long a period. Regardless, he returned to an empty home and a job he'd decided to leave right after his gene code proof-of-concept was demonstrated."

"He was robbed of the chance to see if it would have restored his daughter's health."

"Yes. Marcus left Hughes-Johnson within a month after breaking the genetic code to the mystery of the human heart. He was out of sight until the announcement of the Nobel."

"Do you think Marcus will travel to Jerusalem to meet with me?"

"If the man has no interest in traveling to Stockholm to pick up the most prestigious prize in the world, he may not be inclined to travel to Jerusalem."

Jacob looked at the photograph on the wall, the fearless face of the man about to be killed. "Maybe I could convince him to come by appealing to his scientific interests."

"You're more likely to get him if you tell him there's something in those divine notes that will help find the person responsible for the deaths of his wife and child."

"But I don't know that."

"He doesn't either. To catch a fish, put bait on the hook." Levy slid a folded piece of paper across his desk.

Jacob reached for it. "What's this?"

"The address for Paul Marcus. Send him plane tickets."

EIGHT

VIRGINIA

*B*uddy sniffed the morning air and followed close behind Paul Marcus, walking from his restored farmhouse to the barn. A chill hung over the October morning in Virginia, the autumn leaves sprinkled with heavy dew, traces of wood smoke coming from a neighbor's house a quarter mile away.

"C'mon, Buddy." Marcus lifted a bale of hay from his pickup truck and entered the stables. Buddy barked once, the dog's breath a puff of mist in the cold air. Marcus set the hay down and approached the two horses, both in adjacent stalls. He pulled out two carrots and gave each horse a snack.

"You ladies staying warm? Ready for some exercise?" One of the horses snorted.

Marcus smiled. "I thought so. We'll open these doors and let you run around some, what do you say?" He unlocked the stalls and led the first horse to the stable door.

"Go on, Midnight." The horse trotted off toward the pasture. He followed with the second horse. "You too, Lightning. Go play." Buddy gave quick chase, the horse ignoring the small dog with eyes as bright as the fall colors. Buddy abruptly stopped, a movement catching the dog's attention. Marcus watched the horses in the pasture; his thoughts drifting back to his wife and daughter trail riding.

Buddy barked.

Marcus looked in the direction Buddy had turned. Someone was coming.

Slowly, a black SUV moved down the long driveway. The windows tinted dark. As the car came closer, Marcus could hear the sounds of acorns crushing against the gravel he'd long ago spread over much of the dirt drive leading to the house.

Buddy paced and barked again.

"It's okay, boy. I have a feeling I know who's behind those darkened windows. But this is the first time I've seen him make house calls. Maybe it's got something to do with the fact I wasn't up to a visit."

The car pulled to a stop beneath a lofty oak, its red and yellow leaves dusted with frost. The lone driver got out. He wore a black suit and a mid-length grey coat. The man placed his hands in his pockets and smiled as he approached Marcus. He had intense, dark eyes that reflected the cloudless blue sky. He was in his early sixties, smooth face, African-American. The man flashed a wide smile, somewhat like Denzel Washington.

"Hello, Paul."

"What brings you all the way out here?"

"You brought me out here because you chose not to come into DC."

"I've paid my dues. Ten years at NSA was enough."

Bill Gray nodded. He looked at Buddy and then at the horses grazing under the pine and maple trees. "But it's not every day that Secretary of State Hanover asks for a meeting, per the president. And it's not even once in a lifetime that someone turns down the Nobel Prize."

"I've told you why. I have no interest in that. It's a prize, and I wasn't seeking a prize trying to help my daughter. I was looking for a cure. I was trying to save her life. I failed. The discovery for Tiffany was more by default than perseverance. I can't accept a prize for that."

"You didn't cause Tiffany's death. Someone else did. I know that doesn't lessen the impact of what happened, but it's her life that gave you the opportunity to do what you did. The award is in recognition of that."

There was a distant echo of a rifle firing somewhere in the hills. One of the horses whinnied. Buddy turned a half circle, his eyes following a chipmunk.

Gray said, "Must be the beginning of hunting season. All Secretary Hanover asks is that you reconsider the award. What you and your team did is nothing short of a miracle breakthrough. Since the president is up for the

Nobel Peace Prize, it wouldn't look too great if one from the home team didn't show."

"I'm off the payroll. Have been for a few years now."

"I hear your work is done at Hughes. You were relentless, and your results showed it. A lot of people will live longer because of what you discovered."

Marcus said nothing.

Gray nodded, his eyes following a red-tailed hawk. "Anything new on the police investigation? New leads, maybe?"

"They don't even have a suspect."

"Somebody knows something. It's just a matter of time. Look, Paul, I'd appreciate it if you'd reconsider the Nobel award. Ceremonies aren't until December. Give it some reassessment, all right?"

Marcus nodded. "I can't see anything changing because—"

"Please, just reconsider. Maybe something will happen to change your mind."

"I have some work to do."

"Sure…are you going to keep the place here?"

"It's my home, Bill."

"I just know how much Tiffany and Jennifer enjoyed the horses, the life you had as a family out here." Gray paused and nodded. "Loneliness is like a cancer. It's internal, and the heart is the first organ that turns black. I'm sorry for your loss, but I also don't want to see you isolate yourself."

"Do you know what it's like to bury your child, to bury your entire family?" Marcus started toward the stables.

"Paul…just one more thing."

Marcus turned around.

Gray cleared his throat and wiped his nose with a handkerchief. "I received word that there have been some inquiries about you from the Middle East."

"What are you talking about?"

"Israel, specifically. Longtime allies with us, of course. However, the Mossad has been known to become, shall I say, *curious* from time to time. Seems someone there is inquiring about you. They may have seen your file. There's nothing compromising in it, of course. It is basic background information, and nothing about your cryptography skills. So, I wonder why the Israelis would take an interest in you suddenly; and if they have, who else might be looking at what they're investigating?"

"I have no idea."

"As you know, one of the greatest threats this nation faces is cyber-sabotage—malware. Our guys tell me the right cyber worm can wriggle into systems, such as complex software, launch an attack, physically cripple a facility and never fire one bullet or bomb. This intense damage could be inflicted on a nuclear facility or even the power grids to the nation's cities. Imagine *that* damn scene. The good side of the story is there are very few people with the skills to figure the coding and algorithms to make those little buggers become miniature destroyers, considering the internal damage that they can do. It's like an apple when a hungry worm gets in there; you pretty much toss the whole apple away. Would you consider returning to NSA? You were the best we had. Damn, you were the best I ever had."

"No thanks."

"You wouldn't be doing freelance work for anyone, would you, Paul?"

"What are you saying?"

"Everyone has to eat. If you're turning down Nobel Prize money, maybe it's because you're earning it from somewhere else."

"All the years we worked together, I thought you knew me better than that."

"It's a different world now. Cyber-sabotage is the new warfront, but there are very few soldiers who can even read the battle charts. Those who can will be highly paid, especially when billions of dollars are to be made or lost."

"It's time you went back to DC."

"I'm sure you'd let me know in the event anyone casts a hook your way. See you around, Paul." Gray turned and walked to the SUV with windows dark as coal dust.

A crow called out, flying over an adjacent cornfield. Marcus watched the crow grow to a tiny speck in the distance across the field, long since harvested. Under the bright sky, the twisted and bent cornstalks cast crooked shadows—an army of dark, broken stickmen retreating over the Virginia hills.

— —

The guards were in place. They patrolled the front gate of the oceanfront villa on the Mediterranean Sea. The sun had been up more than two hours when the Syrian general, a handsome man with an angular face and dark eyes, took his coffee and newspaper to a balcony spot by the sea that had a clear view of the water. The general sat in one of the lounge chairs, shook open the paper and sipped Turkish coffee from a small cup. He wanted to relax after spending a week in North Korea.

The luxury yacht off shore attracted no attention from anyone in the neighboring villas. The yacht was one of many that would pass by that day. But it was the only one with an assassin on board.

The general took a second sip of dark coffee. The balmy air felt good coming off the sea, the smell of salt and the warmth of the eastern sun cleared his sinus.

The assassin opened a small, tinted window on the port side of the yacht. The captain, wearing wrap-around sunglasses, kept the speed at six knots on the flat morning sea. The ocean's surface was as smooth as the blue felt on a billiard table. Through the crosshairs in the high-powered rifle-scope, the killer watched the general reading the paper one hundred meters away. A bikini-clad woman refilled his coffee, rubbed his chest and kissed him on the mouth. The general grinned, an erection rising in his jogging pants. He glanced toward the sea just as the yacht came in view. He used his left hand to shield the sun from his eyes.

The .30 caliber bullet hit the general in his left eye. The round shattered his sunglasses, exiting out of the back of his skull, leaving a spray of blood against the woman's white bikini.

— —

Paul Marcus awoke in a profuse sweat. He had fallen asleep on the couch in his living room, Buddy lying on the rug in front of him. The front door was open, a soft, cool breeze coming through the screen door, the smell of pine needles in the house, a half moon rising over the mountains. Marcus went into the kitchen and filled a glass with water. Buddy followed him.

"You need to pee, Buddy?" Grabbing a hooded sweatshirt from the coat tree, Marcus walked out the screened door and onto the front porch. Buddy followed him outside, trotted off the porch to an oak tree and lifted his leg. Marcus lowered himself into a wicker chair and sat in the dark. Buddy returned and lay down beside him. They watched bats catching insects under the moonlight. Marcus heard the distant cry of a freight train winding across the mountains, a nightingale singing in the oaks, a soft drop of a single yellow leaf falling from a tree onto the porch step. He looked at the hanging baskets and thought of his wife.

"We'll need to take Jen's flowers into the barn in case we get a heavy frost." Marcus scratched his dog on the head, stood and poured the remaining water into a hanging basket. "Buddy, do dogs dream? I'd trade a nightmare for a boring dream any night. Mama Davis used to talk about 'the handwriting on the wall.' Something she quoted from the Bible. Is there some crazy handwriting on the wall for you and me, boy? I'm told the Israeli intelligence has my bio. You know that means somebody else does, too. Is it because I said no thanks to the Nobel folks, or because a long-dead scientist allegedly wrote my name on something? If he did, is that the handwriting on the proverbial wall? If it's there, does it say anything about the man who killed Jen and Tiffany?"

NINE

*T*wo days later, Paul Marcus left shortly after daybreak to drive into Manassas to buy groceries, oats for the horses and paint for the barn. He stopped at the Ashton Diner, took a seat in a booth where he ordered coffee from a fifty-something, blonde waitress who had penciled eyebrows drawn high over her wide, brown eyes.

"Special this mornin' is a country omelet with Virginia ham, diced potatoes and toast or biscuits. All for six bucks. Coffee comes with it, hon."

Marcus smiled. "Sounds good. Biscuits, please."

She wrote down the order, nodded and left. Marcus opened the Washington Post on the table. He scanned the headlines, stopping on page two where he read the caption:

Syrian General Assassinated at Seaside Villa

The story, the description of the man's assassination, resurrected the dream Marcus had buried. The article indicated that it was believed General Abdul Hannan had recently returned from North Korea where he had toured that nation's nuclear facilities. The reporter quoted anonymous sources as saying the general may have been one of those in Syria leading the efforts to build nuclear weapons.

The heavily guarded villa had kept penetration away from the front of the estate. An approach from sea wasn't expected, especially coming from what a groundskeeper next door identified as a luxury, high-speed yacht.

Marcus finished the story and punched keys on his cell phone. Bill Gray answered on the second ring.

Marcus said, "It's Paul. Why did you want me to meet with Secretary Hanover?"

"Did you change your mind?"

"How quickly can you set up the meeting?"

"Let me make some calls. What changed?"

"Events of late."

"Care to elaborate?"

"Maybe it's nothing more than a gut feeling, some kind of hunch."

"Okay, I'll go with that. Call you later."

——

Secretary of State Hanover met Paul Marcus in a small conference room adjacent to her office. Merriam Hanover was a career politician. She'd held positions as a U.S. Senator and governor before the president tapped her to become his first appointment after taking office three years ago. She was in her late fifties, dressed in a crisp, dark red suit, graying hair worn up, and eyes that beamed with vigor. A gold eagle pin with a ruby eye and a large pearl in its talon graced her lapel, giving her a rich and stately appearance.

"Thank you for agreeing to meet with me. I hope you like tuna fish," she said as her assistant delivered two lunches of tuna on salad with sides of fresh fruit.

"I do like tuna. But I find myself eating less of it. The world is catching them quicker than they can repopulate."

"Then, I'm sure you'd be interested to know that the president is proposing a fishing ban on numerous species that are facing extinction. Our challenge, of course, will be to get the cooperation from nations like China and Japan."

"The president has my support, for whatever that may be worth."

"It's worth a lot. Paul, you're recognized internationally for your work that resulted in a greater understanding of gene therapy in fighting heart disease. I assure you, your support will help."

Marcus said nothing.

"I heard the reasons why you aren't in a rush to accept the Nobel Prize for Medicine. I hope you'll reconsider."

"Then you understand my reasons for declining the award, Madame Secretary."

"Please, call me Merriam. I *do* understand your reasons. And I am so very sorry for the loss of your wife and daughter. As you know, the president is the recipient of the Nobel Peace Prize, and you are the only other American honored in an award ceremony that the entire world watches closely. It would be in the best interest of everyone if things went well."

Marcus ate in silence for a moment. The ticking of a grandfather clock in the corner was wrapped in the slight whirr of warm air blowing through the vents.

"Paul, your discovery was a medical breakthrough that's going to help people around the world. Please don't undermine the award by refusing to accept it. If nothing else, the money you receive can go to a foundation in your daughter's name to help other children with life threatening heart ailments. The president has asked me to convey to you our intent to offer a matching grant from the National Science Foundation. I hope you will consider the grant."

Marcus looked out the window to traffic moving across C Street, the sky steel gray. He met the secretary's eyes. "Although I don't feel that I've earned it, I'll give it consideration, and I appreciate the president's offer of a grant, although I can't accept it."

She smiled. "Thank you for you willingness to think about it."

"As I reconsider it, I'd like to know what you can tell me about the assassination of a Syrian general, Abdul Hannan."

Secretary Hanover said nothing, her eyes flat.

"Do you know who was behind the assassination?"

"No, why do you ask?"

"Was I invited here for you to encourage me to go to Stockholm to accept the prize, or does this have something to do with what I learned last week?"

"What is that?"

"Bill Gray suggested this meeting with you. He'd driven all the way out to my place in Virginia to tell me he's heard some chat, some inquiries about my background. Allegedly coming from somewhere in Israel. Does our meeting here today have overtures of that?"

"No, I assure you, it doesn't."

"Do you know more than I was told?"

"I don't. Although, I'm glad you brought it up. Israel is one of our closest friends. They may have a competing Nobel laureate." She grinned.

"I don't think that's it."

"Oh, why?"

"I got a call from a man who identified himself as Professor Jacob Kogen. He called me from Jerusalem. He's a mathematician at a university there. He said he'd recently received some lost papers apparently from a private collection."

"Lost papers? What kind of papers?"

"From Isaac Newton."

"*The* Isaac Newton, the long dead scientist?" She smiled, head tilting.

"The same. Kogen said he had other papers from Newton, and he's convinced that Newton was trying to decipher something concealed in the Bible."

"What do you mean, concealed?"

"He said some kind of biblical prophecies."

"I can see how that would interest Israel or any nation, for that matter."

"Kogen asked me to help him."

"How?"

"To look at the Newton papers to see if I might find some clue, some way to decode whatever it was that Newton was trying to find."

"What was he trying to find?"

"That's a good question."

"Then you don't know if he found it." The Secretary of State held his gaze. "Will you accept his invitation?"

"I don't know."

"Paul, if you do find something that's hidden in the Bible, something of interest to Israel or any nation in the Middle East, I hope you would tell us."

"At this point, I have no reason not to."

"Good, then we wouldn't have a reason to be suspect of this situation."

TEN

Marcus left the State Department, stepping into bright sunshine and the cavernous blue skies of October in Washington, D.C. He walked down the street, entered a parking garage and headed to the elevator. There was the sound of a car door shutting and hard heels coming from behind a row of cars. "Paul Marcus, it *is* you."

Alicia Quincy pulled her purse strap onto her shoulder and smiled. She walked toward Marcus. Her dark hair was pinned up, pearl earrings and matching pearl necklace accentuating her long, slender neck. She had full lips and dark eyebrows that arched with her wide smile. "How have you been? I mean, I haven't seen you since the funerals." Her voice dropped an octave, smile melting. "I'm sorry. How *are* you doing?"

"I'm okay. It's good to see you, Alicia. Are you still at NSA?"

"Starting my tenth year in November. I heard you left Hughes-Johnson not long after—" She gripped the purse strap, knuckles white. "Not long after the funerals."

"Yeah, I did."

"I read a story on the Post's website about you turning down the Nobel Prize. That takes conviction, especially after the president's nominated for the Peace Prize."

"It seems to have evolved into something political, and I never meant it to be."

"In this town, everything's political."

Marcus paused and studied her sapphire blue eyes for a moment. "It's really coincidental, you know?"

"What is?"

"The two of us right here…running into you in this parking lot. It was just a couple of days ago when Bill Gray, your boss, stopped by my farm. Now you're in a parking garage. What are the odds? What would the numbers say?"

Marcus could see confusion move over her face. She raised an eyebrow. "I'm meeting a friend for lunch. I didn't know Bill went to see you. Can I ask what it's about?"

Marcus held a steady, unblinking gaze on her eyes for a few seconds. "It's about some inquires someone's been making concerning me."

"I'm not familiar with this. What inquiries and who's making them?"

"Gray says Israel, probably the Mossad. But it's never only one intel agency. The ears and eyes are everywhere. You know that. If they're asking stuff, others are listening."

"That's odd. Is it in some way related to the Nobel Prize thing?"

"Funny, because that's just what the Secretary of State asked me today."

"You were there?"

"Secretary Hanover was specific in asking me to reconsider the Nobel award. I think Israel, ostensibly the Mossad, is more interested in checking me out because a professor at the Hebrew University in Jerusalem wants me to examine some documents."

"What kind of documents?"

"He says they're from Isaac Newton. Some papers apparently lost for a couple centuries. They were found and delivered to the university. The professor says Newton wrote my name in the margin before his death."

"Your *name*? Centuries before your birth?" Alicia smiled, her hand relaxing on the purse strap. "Newton the scientist is Newton the *prophet*? Come on."

Marcus blew out a breath. "Yeah, that's what I thought—a bit too far-fetched. This guy, a professor of physics, was insistent. He says Newton spent the majority of his life trying to decipher codes in the Bible, trying to come to terms with…" Marcus paused, his eyes following a piece of paper blowing across the floor of the garage. "This professor wants me to come to Jerusalem and see if I can pick up where Newton left off. Maybe see how close the world's greatest scientist came to unlocking the secrets of the Bible like he unlocked some of the universe. It may be a wild goose chase, but..."

Alicia's eyes filled with animation. "But, what?"

"Nothing."

"This is exciting. Where did Newton leave off? What did he find? What was he searching for? You're talking about a legendary scientist doing biblical research. I've never heard about that side of Newton. Lost papers now are showing up on the steps of a noted research university, and you getting an invitation to look at possible biblical coding. Wonder what you might find?"

"Nothing, because I'm not going."

"Why? You were so good with encryption, so good at being able to look at the big picture, the whole of something, and then see how components might be used to communicate a message. Maybe there's something in these Newton notes. Aren't you just a little curious, Paul? I would be."

Marcus felt his jaw line tighten, his scalp stretch, a vein behind his left eye pulse. "I'm curious, and I'm anxious, too. Look, I have to get back to the horses. It was good seeing you, Alicia." He walked toward the elevator and pressed the button. As the doors opened, he turned toward her. "I hope it was coincidental. Give Bill Gray my regards."

Alicia stood there a moment while the elevator doors closed behind him. She looked down at the tips of her painted toenails protruding through the opening in her shoes, then blew out a long breath and turned to walk away.

━ ━

Marcus exited off the I-66 freeway and followed the Mill Road toward his home. He looked in his rearview mirror and saw a black Ford Explorer in the distance. He eased his foot off the gas pedal and slowed without touching the brakes. The driver in the Ford seemed to maintain an equal distance.

Marcus caught movement out of the corner of his eye. He came to a quick stop. Two deer darted across the road, their white tails raised like caution flags, instantly absorbed into the sea of autumn leaves. Marcus accelerated, but still giving the driver in the Explorer time to come closer. He could see that the driver wore dark glasses, white windbreaker and drove with one hand. His other hand held a phone.

Marcus resumed speed. He was less than a half-mile to his home. He glanced in his rearview mirror. The driver seemed to slow, giving at least thirty yards between the two cars. Marcus considered driving by his home and cutting back.

He quickly turned into his drive and slowed to a crawl. Marcus kept his eyes on the mirror while the car passed, the lone driver turning his head toward Marcus's home. The man in the car continued driving.

Marcus pulled up next to his home, got out and unlocked the front door. Buddy greeted him, turning in half circles, his short tail blurring.

"Bet you could use some outdoor time."

The dog scurried past Marcus and trotted to the front yard, cocking his leg next to a persimmon tree. As he relieved himself, a Fed-Ex truck lumbered up the driveway toward the house. Buddy, leg hiked, managed to cough out a single bark that sounded more like a howl.

The driver slowed to a stop. Marcus approached the truck. The driver nodded, getting out of the truck with a package and a digital signature board.

"Hi, are you Paul Marcus?"

"Yes."

"I have a package for you." He handed Marcus the pad for him to electronically sign his name. The driver petted Buddy. "My brother had a dog like this. She could catch eight out of ten Frisbee tosses. Here's your package. Looks like it came from a place I've always wanted to visit."

"Where's that?"

"Jerusalem. Have a good day." The man climbed in his truck, cranked the diesel and followed the circular drive back to the road.

Marcus walked up to his front porch, sat in a rocker made from red oak, and opened the package. He found a letter and a sealed envelope. Marcus read the letter while Buddy sprawled on the wooden porch beside his chair.

Dear Mr. Marcus:

I spoke briefly with you last week. My inquiries are not intended to be intrusive. However, if I did not try to contact you, I feel as though, in some way, I am not doing as God may have intended. Now that I am the recipient of the Newton papers I mentioned, I feel certain that you are indeed the man Newton was referring to shortly before his death.

My contact information is enclosed on a separate page. I believe you, too, will understand the depth of what is at stake. Perhaps we will never fully grasp the significance of the words or even manage to pluck them from God's agenda. I am not a young man, and before I find my final resting place on the Mount of Olives, I feel an obligation to seek you. If you choose not to answer the call, perhaps that, too, was meant to be. However, if you will look at a copy of a page from Newton's hand, and still profess no interest, so be it. But in God's name, I reach out to you. I think we all do.

Most sincerely,

Jacob Kogen

Marcus slid the second page from behind the letter. It was a photocopy of handwritten notes that were written in small, precise penmanship. Marcus scanned the words, his eyes searching for anything between the lines, something that was less obvious as he read. He followed Newton's handwritten words, the prose making reference to passages from the Book of Daniel.

'Daniel was in the greatest credit amongst the Jews, till the reign of the Roman Emperor Hadrian and to reject his Prophecies, is to reject the Christian religion. For this religion is founded upon his Prophecy concerning the Messiah.'

Marcus finished reading the page and his eyes narrowed on the handwriting in the lower right corner:

Daniel was given the visions from God to be continued by the visions conveyed to the Apostle John. Those revelations will be made

43

whole by those who are yet unborn, but chosen, and according to the visions seen by Daniel and John, the final deliverance of the word shall be given to Paul James Marcus, who, in the year 2015, is awarded a noble medal for healing.

Marcus felt a chill move through his body. His throat was dry, hands trembling while holding the letter. The sun broke from mauve clouds, framing the dark purple mountains in a nimbus of orange. Marcus looked up to see a screech owl fly toward the valley below the farm. The sudden rustle of a cool breeze drew his attention to the multitude of leaves dancing across his porch, giving hint of an early winter. He opened the envelope, his brow tightening when he read the destination.

Marcus held a one-way plane ticket to Jerusalem.

ELEVEN

The next morning Paul Marcus parked his car in the lot of Mayflower Assisted Living, which was located outside of Fairfax. He entered the facility and walked through the atrium, the smell of bleach and roses shadowed him making his way to the reception area. He was told his grandmother had just finished her breakfast in the courtyard. Marcus followed a middle-aged nurse supervisor who led him down the hallway to the terrace. Her large inner thighs caused a swishing sound each time the polyester uniform rubbed together. She pointed to a woman sitting in a wheelchair.

"It's kinda cool outside, but your grandmother insists on bein' out here. She's got her favorite sweater on, and we make sure she isn't out here too long."

"Thank you." Marcus left the nurse and walked toward his grandmother.

Mama Davis sat by herself. Speckled sunlight broke through canopies of red and yellow leaves in the oak and mulberry trees. The old woman turned toward the warmth from the sun. Her face was aged and wrinkled but yet radiant. She closed her eyes and listened to the breeze in the boughs. A cardinal chirped and flittered through the limbs while two squirrels played hide-and-seek around the base of an oak tree.

She wore her white hair pinned up, a touch of pink powder on her cheeks. She held a cup of tea in both hands and opened her eyes to Marcus.

"Good morning, Mama Davis."

The old woman smiled. Marcus bent down and kissed her cheek. "Oh, Paul, my dear, Paul. I didn't know you were coming. I'd have fixed my face, had I known."

"You never need make-up. You're a natural beauty." Marcus smiled and stood.

"Pull up a chair and let's visit."

Marcus slid a wooden rocking chair next to his grandmother and sat down. She patted him on the knee. "I wonder if you're getting enough to eat. You're looking a little on the thin side. I worry about you…have ever since Tiffany and Jenny passed."

"I'm fine. And I'm eating well. Even Buddy likes my cooking."

She closed her eyes for a moment. "I miss that sweet dog. How is he?"

"Buddy's great. The question is…how are you doing? The nurse said your blood pressure has regulated, but how's that ankle?"

"Getting better. This old body is pretty resilient—I'll be good as new in no time. Where I'm having trouble is…I miss my little home and your farm, too. I make friends here, but just about the time I get to know them, who they are and how many grandkids they have, they pass away. Harold Snyder, you remember him from your last visit, Paul?

"Yes."

She nodded. "Well, he died right here on the patio in his wheelchair two weeks ago. The help thought he'd fallen asleep, but I knew better. His chest wasn't moving up and down." She glanced at the cloudless sky and was silent for a moment. Then she looked directly at Marcus. "You're troubled. I can feel it. You've been gifted to see and feel things, so what's going on?"

"Then, why couldn't I see the deaths of my family, maybe do something to stop it?"

"We can only see what's revealed to us, Paul. Tiny cracks, these little places where just a drop of God's paint is shared within a canvas big as the universe, show up and shed light on things."

"I want Jen and Tiffany's killer revealed."

"He will be." She held a resolute gaze on her grandson.

"I came here to let you know I'm thinking about going overseas for a little while."

She nodded and looked at the squirrels darting through the fallen leaves, her eyes marred with cataracts and yet filled with truth. "Are you going over there to accept the Nobel Prize?"

"No. If I go, it would be about something else."

"What's that?"

"A professor who works for a university in Jerusalem believes my name is connected to an old document left behind by Isaac Newton. The professor said Newton wrote my name in his papers near the time of his death. And he thinks I can pick up where Newton left off and crack or reveal some things Newton was working on when he died."

"So this professor believes your name is connected to Newton. That's interesting…through math, science, prophecy? What was Newton working on?"

"Sounds weird, I know. Apparently, Newton was researching biblical prophecies. More specifically, whether events were or are foretold in the Bible. I'm not sure there is a connection, only that some Israeli professor claims it's my name in Newton's notes."

"I believe some events are God's providence. He opens them through his prophets. My goodness—let me collect my runaway thoughts. Okay, there were people like Ezekiel, Daniel, Jeremiah, Solomon and others. Jesus gave us prophecy, too. Are you going?"

"I haven't decided."

"Go, Paul. You've been gifted. Go to Jerusalem. Maybe you can help make known God's plan, if that's the way it's supposed to be."

"If all is known, or planned in some kind of divine providence, what's the use? We'd be as insignificant as pawns on some chessboard."

Mama Davis sipped her tea, choosing her words carefully. "I believe it is all part of a larger picture we won't fully understand until it's disclosed to us." She held her eyes on Marcus and then touched his right hand. "The discovery you made figuring out how to adjust the life spark in a human heart was revealed to you through your gifted talents and some help."

Marcus smiled. "I'll let you know what I decide." He stood to leave, bent down and kissed his grandmother's cheek.

"Do you have to go now? You're the only visitor who comes to see me—in person that is." She winked and smiled wide. "I miss you, Paul."

"I miss you, too, Mama Davis. I have to get back to let Buddy out."

She took both of his hands in hers. Marcus could feel her very slow heartbeat.

"Listen to me, grandson. I'm old, and I've lived a long life. The older I get, the more I do know that there is a grander picture. I can't explain that awful thing that happened to Jennifer and Tiffany. But God didn't *cause* it."

"And he didn't prevent it."

"But you are still alive. Why? You'll see, Paul, God will work it into good."

"Without them, what the hell does that mean, good?"

The old woman was silent for a moment. "You figured out how to fix hearts. It's my prayer that you'll figure out how to fix yours, 'cause your heart is buried in bedrock deeper than the Blue Ridge Mountains."

"I have to go." Marcus paused, the rustle of wind growing stronger in the trees.

She nodded and lowered her eyes for a moment, licking her bottom lip. Then she looked up and took in the full measure of her grandson. "I feel that you hold God responsible for the deaths of Tiffany and Jennifer. You will only see what will be revealed to you. When that happens, trust in a higher power—have faith—because it will be returned to you."

"What are you saying? I don't believe in—"

"Listen to me, Paul. He wouldn't have chosen you if you couldn't do His will on earth."

A brown leaf fluttered down from a tall oak, settling in Mama Davis's lap. Marcus looked at it. "What if God's dead as that leaf?"

"When you go to Jerusalem, if your desire is to prove God is responsible for what happened to Tiffany and Jennifer, you will leave with nothing. But if you open your heart to our Lord's calling, you will see through the glass stained by evil, see through the dark places."

"I'm not sure what you mean, Mama Davis."

"I think you will in time. Your grandfather used to say the difference between an intelligent person and a wise person is the choices he or she makes for the good of others."

Marcus leaned in and kissed his grandmother on her forehead. "Goodbye, Mama Davis. I'll let you know what I decide. I love you."

"I love you, too. Be careful, Paul. There's something in my heart that's whispering disturbing things. I just can't hear it well enough, yet."

TWELVE

Under a cloudless, blue October morning sky, Paul Marcus walked to his barn to feed the horses. Buddy stopped for a moment, sniffing tracks a raccoon had left during the night. In the chill of the air, Marcus could smell wood smoke from his neighbor's chimney a quarter mile away. It was Sunday, and beyond the chirping of a cardinal, he heard bells from the Shiloh Methodist Church in the distance. His mind shifted to the cemetery behind the old church where he had buried his wife and daughter.

Dressed in jeans, a flannel shirt and a denim jacket, Marcus turned his collar up in the cool air, and continued walking through yellow leaves dusted soft white from last night's frost.

Buddy followed him into the barn where he watered and fed the horses. Within a minute, the sun crept over the valley, the shafts coming horizontal through the open barn doors, illuminating the bales of hay and stalls with a crimson glow.

"Good morning ladies," Marcus said, opening the stalls. "How's everybody doing? Ready for some pasture time?" He led the horses to the door. They trotted off, Buddy giving chase for a moment, turning his head back toward Marcus as he ran. "No, Buddy! It's too early for a game of tag. Let the girls have some quiet Sunday morning time." Buddy stopped and padded back toward the barn, his eyes bright from the short chase.

Marcus took an ax from the barn and began splitting wood against a round piece of the heart of pine. He split the first log into two parts, tossed them on a woodpile next to the fence, and was raising the ax over his shoulders when Buddy growled. The dog's keen eyes had picked up movement down at the end of the long drive.

"What's got your attention, boy?" Marcus looked in the direction. A blue Honda car came up the drive, leaves scattering, acorns popping. A cardinal stopped its morning song and the church bells faded into the background. Marcus could see that a woman was behind the wheel.

Alicia Quincy parked under a large oak near the house and got out of her car. Buddy ran in the direction of the parked car. Marcus walked toward her, ax still in his hands. She smiled and petted Buddy while he sniffed her black jeans. She wore a thick-weave, beige sweater, her dark chestnut hair pinned up, minimal makeup. The crisp air gave a brushstroke of light pink to her high cheekbones. "Good morning," she said, smiling. "Do you usually greet a woman with an ax?"

Marcus smiled and set the ax against a tree. "I was chopping firewood."

"I've always loved border collies. What's his name?"

"Buddy."

Alicia petted Buddy on his neck and shoulders. She looked up at Marcus. "I guess you're wondering what I'm doing out here on a Sunday morning."

"The thought crossed my mind."

"I remembered all the years you worked at the agency before going to Hughes to help Tiffany. I know how damn *hard* you worked. I can't forget the funerals for Jennifer and Tiffany. Just down the road, I passed the cemetery behind the church and remembered it was a day like this, the leaves changing, winter approaching."

Marcus said nothing for a few seconds. "Why'd you come out here, Alicia?"

"Maybe because I didn't like the way our conversation ended in the parking garage, or maybe because I didn't sleep well last night. I wanted to start over, if possible, and not have suspicions between us. It's important to me."

Marcus nodded and smiled. "Okay. No problem."

She smiled and took in the property, her eyes drifting to the horses in the pasture. "This is a lovely home. I recall you telling me your grandfather had bought it years ago."

"But he kept it in better shape than I'm doing. Barn needs a new coat of paint."

"When you make coffee, do you boil it on the stove in one of those tin coffee pots, you know, the blue ones with the white spots on them?" She grinned.

"It's a drip machine. Would you like a cup? I just put on a pot."

"I'd love a cup."

"Please, come in."

"Can we drink it out here on the porch?"

"Sure." She followed him inside and into the kitchen where Marcus poured steaming coffee into two large ceramic mugs.

"Your home is warm, comfortable."

"Jen did all that. I haven't touched a thing since…since she was killed."

"We've all followed the case. No arrests yet, right?"

"Not even any suspects, so I'm told. How do you take your coffee?"

"A little cream and a touch of sugar."

He fixed the coffee and handed a cup to Alicia. He could smell her perfume, the trace of a flowery shampoo lingering in her thick hair. He felt something stir deep inside his chest. "Let's sit on the porch," he said, walking to the front door.

Alicia followed him, stopping to look at a framed picture hanging on the wall. The image was of Marcus, Jennifer and Tiffany on a ski trip, mountains of snow in the background. Alicia blinked a few times, exhaling a deep breath, wrapping both hands around the cup.

"That was our last vacation together—Telluride."

"Such a beautiful family."

They stepped on the porch and sat in large, white wicker chairs with plump cushions on the back and seat. Buddy lay down on the oak wood porch. A blue jay fluttered from the trees, chirping, as a robin hunted for insects in the grass, which was still coated silvery white from frost.

A breeze puffed across the yard, scattering leaves and making music with the wind chimes on the porch. Alicia looked at the chimes and smiled. "If you decide to accept the Nobel Prize, it'd look good on that mantle inside, above the fireplace."

Marcus sipped his coffee. He watched a red leaf flutter from an elm tree. "You sure Secretary Hanover didn't send you out here?"

Alicia shook her head and laughed. "No, she did not, and no one from the agency asked me to come here either. Although I'm sure Bill Gray would love for you to come back to your old job. You mentioned Secretary Hanover, I want to ask you something."

"Okay, what is it?"

"Do you remember me telling you about my sister, Dianne?"

"I remember her picture on your desk at work. I remember that her husband was one of the people killed when the jet crashed into the Pentagon on 9/11."

Alicia looked down at her coffee cup before raising her eyes up to Marcus. "About two months ago, her only child, my niece Brandi, was hiking in the eastern border region of Turkey. She and her boyfriend, Adam, were there working for the Peace Corps, teaching school in the area. Iranian border guards arrested them for allegedly crossing into Iran. Paul, they're holding them as U.S. spies. They're just kids, both barely twenty."

"I heard about the arrests. I didn't make the connection because of the difference in last names. What's being done to free them?"

"They've become poker chips in an international game. Tehran wants the U.S. to release four people we're holding in exchange for the release of Brandi and Adam. It's going nowhere." Alicia pushed a strand of brown hair behind her ear. "My sister...Dianne went through hell after the death of her husband. Now, it's this horrible kidnapping, and that's what it really is, a damn kidnapping. Dianne is at the breaking point. I can't imagine what Brandi and Adam are experiencing."

"It wouldn't be smart for Iran to hurt them or treat them inhumanely."

"What's smart in this crazy world anymore, Paul? The Iranians could falsely convict them and issue the death penalty. We're desperate. Maybe you could do something."

"Me? What could I do?"

"I'd read that the daughter of Ali Assimi, the head of Iran's Revolutionary Guard, has a heart condition maybe similar to what affected Tiffany. Maybe you could look into it and offer some advice."

"Alicia, I'm not a doctor. I managed to figure a way to help doctors prevent ventricular arrhythmia in some hearts by subjecting the heart to intense electromagnetic impulses that help the heart regulate itself. This can provide a new option to the practice of ablation surgery, which destroys tissue in the heart muscle to regulate the electrical circuit."

"Since you know Secretary Hanover, maybe you could ask her to try to expedite their release."

"I'm not sure how much pull I have."

"She and the president want you to accept the Nobel Prize. That's a lot of pull."

He looked at her a moment, the sound of church bells coming up through the valley. "I'll speak with Secretary Hanover."

Alicia smiled. "Thank you. I've been thinking about the stuff you mentioned concerning your contact from the Hebrew University in Jerusalem and the newly discovered notes from Isaac Newton. This could be a tremendous opportunity for you, Paul. What if Newton left behind something?"

"What do you mean?"

"I did a little research on the man, Sir Isaac."

"Find anything new?"

"For starters, he definitely had a most beautiful mind. Three hundred years later, we're still using his math to fly rockets and satellites. He was a hybrid kind of scientist. Apparently, the science stuff was the least of his interests, the theological material, the *why we're here, the living a life of meaning,* kind of thing was what drove him and pushed his buttons. Not well known, eh? But he thought the answers were in the Bible, and it's believed he wrote more than a million words on the subject."

"Maybe he has a condensed version somewhere on one piece of paper."

Alicia smiled. "After a little digging, I found that Newton was very interested in a supreme knowledge or *absolute* knowledge."

"Does it exist? Can absolute in anything be demonstrated?"

"Newton researched the ancient Greeks, Romans, Egyptians, Babylonians, and people like Copernicus, da Vinci, Plato and Archimedes—looking for some kind of secret or handed-down ancient knowledge, maybe to help him understand or research the Bible. What if he found something?"

"Then why don't we know about it? He left us calculus, the theory of gravity and motion. Why wouldn't he have left that, too?"

"Maybe he found something too frightening or too large for the world to fully grasp. The theory of destiny certainly would be a bigger concept than gravity to comprehend. He could have taken it to his grave, or like you say, left it on a slip of paper. Maybe he needed more time to prove it. But unless we know what to look for, the world might never have an answer."

"A million words can create quite a haystack."

Alicia scratched Buddy behind the ear. "Go search for the needle in the haystack. I have a feeling that if anyone on earth can find it…it's you."

"What I care deeply about finding is the man who killed my family."

Alicia was silent.

Marcus looked out across his property, the breeze tinkling the wind chimes, an unseen rustle in the trees, his eyes filled with thought. "Now that you've told me about Brandi and Adam, I'd like to see them set free before some sadistic Iranian court sentences them. Alicia, if I go to the Middle East, I may need someone like you…no, I may need *you* to help. Your computer skills, your research, your hacking talents are uncanny. We may be in for some cyber archeology, digging into places no one since Isaac Newton has ever looked."

Alicia turned her body toward Marcus. "I'll help where I can."

— —

The next day Marcus placed a call to Bill Gray and asked, "Are you on a secured line?"

"Yes, Paul. What's going on?"

"When you drove to my place, you said there's been chatter about me. I'm willing to travel to the Middle East on the agency's behalf to see what the interest is all about. I'll be bait, and I'll have the perfect cover. But I'll only do it if Secretary Hanover and the President work to immediately free Alicia Quincy's niece and her boyfriend from an Iranian prison."

Gray said nothing for a moment, his breathing perceptible in Marcus's ear. Then Gray said, "Why the sudden interest on Alicia's niece and boyfriend?"

"Because, right now, it seems like the right thing to do."

"Your intentions are in a good place, but, and please don't take this personally, you're not a field agent. They could eat you alive over there."

"Yes or no, Bill?"

"We won't negotiate overtly. It sets a bad precedent. But we'll use every resource behind the scenes to free them."

"Okay."

"Are you certain about this? Paul, you sure as hell know there's a big difference in code breaking behind the remote safety of a computer compared to face-to-face mind games with the enemy. You haven't been trained in-"

"Sometimes the most efficient engagement in the art of war is done with a Trojan horse."

"All right, it's your ass on a very dangerous international line. We'll deny your existence should the shit hit the fan. If you're discovered, you're alone."

"This agreement stays between us. Alicia's not to know."

THIRTEEN

Early Saturday morning, Paul Marcus zipped up his suitcase and walked to his front door with Buddy at his side. Marcus set the bag down and squatted to rub Buddy's head. "You keep an eye on this place, okay. No chasing the horses, especially Midnight. You know she's not genetically wired for a game of tag." Buddy wagged his tail and cocked his head. "Our neighbor Amber will come by twice a day to walk and feed you and the girls. Be a good boy. Hell, just be yourself."

Buddy let out a slight whimper. Marcus stood, smiled and locked the door on his way out. The air was cool. He walked to the barn and looked toward the Blue Ridge Mountains. A blanket of fog rested on the shoulders of the ancient mountains, the peaks visible, craggy stone heads above the shroud. Daylight stole its way between the dark and the fog, the direction of the sunrise as obscure as the base of the old hills.

A whippoorwill called out into the cool morning air. Marcus walked inside the barn and approached his horses in their stalls. He stroked their necks and said, "I'll miss you ladies. Stay strong." He kissed them both on their foreheads, turned and went up the yard to his car.

As Marcus unlocked the car door, an acorn fell from one of the oak trees, popped off the hood and rolled to a stop in the driveway. Then all was quiet for a long moment as he took in his surroundings. He heard one of the horses snort and whinny in the barn. A rooster crowed somewhere in the black of the valley. Marcus thought of Jen and Tiffany. Sadness, cold and dark as the bottom of an abandoned well, filled his heart.

He needed to think, to plan for what he was about to do. He drove the back roads in the direction of Dulles International Airport. Fog crept across the road, the car's low beams punching through the sheet of rolling white. The sun labored to climb above the tree line, a lit torch flickering in the mist and casting the tall pines in cloaks of blood orange.

Marcus drove across the bridge over the Shenandoah River, the mist twisting in slow pirouettes rising from the river's belly. He thought about his grandmother, the worry building in her eyes. Marcus could still feel her frail and slow pulse in the palm of his hands, could hear her voice deep in the well of his submerged thoughts.

"There's something in my heart that's whispering disturbing things."

Marcus pinched the bridge of his nose and pictured Buddy running after the horses. Since the deaths of Jennifer and Tiffany, Buddy and the horses were all that remained for him. He hoped his trip would be short.

His analytical, scientific side told him the person's name Isaac Newton had written in the notes was nothing more than a striking coincidence. But something pulling deep in his chest left him with an aftertaste of uncertainty. He had always been an ardent admirer of Newton's genius. *What if Newton had discovered something really big? Maybe it was something too great to have been revealed then or now. If so, what would it have been, and why would Newton have hidden it?*

At this point in his life, the place called the Holy Land had no meaning. He wondered if it ever really did. His father had little use for organized religion as his only church experiences had come from Sunday morning prayer in the Salvation Army after a week of binge drinking. His mother had been the opposite. Quoting passages from the Bible that she used to justify her own prejudices. God became her security blanket and then a shield, holding up her defense of all things that she found fault with, all things that didn't parallel her grasp of the world. Both parents had been killed in a house fire.

Did they find a better place after life?

Marcus tried not to dwell on an afterlife or the after death. The current life was complex enough. He reached Dulles International Airport at few minutes before seven a.m. His flight was in ninety minutes. He parked, cleared security and bought a cup of coffee, waiting to board. When his seating section of the plane was called, Marcus began to board. He glanced back over his shoulder before he entered the covered ramp leading to the plane. For a millisecond, Marcus thought a man dressed in a gray sports coat with dark blue pants was watching him. But the distance was too great. Maybe the man had been looking at the clock above the entranceway to the plane.

Maybe not.

— —

About an hour and a half later, Marcus landed in New York. He, again, had an eerie feeling of being watched. Just before Marcus boarded his international flight, he turned and briefly connected eyes with a man in a plaid shirt and jeans. The man abruptly turned and walked toward the expanse of windows in the terminal where he watched a jet touch down, looked at the time display on his cell phone and punched in numbers.

"He's leaving now. Flight's for Tel Aviv."

The voice on the phone said, "As anticipated."

Within a few seconds, the jet carrying Paul Marcus thundered down the runway, gained altitude, circled to the east and became a black dot on the horizon.

FOURTEEN

TEL AVIV, ISRAEL

Marcus cleared customs and pulled his carry-on bag through Ben Gurion International Airport, located outside Tel Aviv. He walked past the massive columns erected from the polished marble floor to the ceiling, past dozens of uniformed security forces, and past a fountain that seemed to shower water from a skylight cut in the ceiling to a pool directly below. He watched the sunlight refract through the falling water, sending bursts of rainbow colors across the marble and over people dining near the water. He looked at his watch and adjusted the change in time.

Marcus made his way to Bank Hapoalim where he exchanged dollars for shekels. He followed signs to the arrival area, stepped from the cool of the air-conditioned terminal into the heat of the morning in Israel.

Marcus looked for the rental car signs when a white van pulled up next to the curb. The driver got out and approached. An unkempt reddish beard sparsely covered his youthful face. The clothes seemed to hang on his lanky frame. He wore a black kippah on the back of his head. Wide smile.

"Welcome to Israel, Mr. Marcus. My name is Elam Mandel. I am here to take you to Jerusalem, to the hotel. Professor Kogen asked me to drive you."

"How did you recognize me?"

"Professor Kogen described you well."

"I've never met him."

"Maybe he has a picture of you."

"I don't think so."

Elam smiled. "You are to receive the Nobel Prize for Medicine so your picture is available. Maybe Professor Kogen got it from the Internet. Here, let me take your bag. I work as an intern in the Hebrew University."

He reached for Marcus's small suitcase, lifted it to an empty seat in the van and said, "Please, get in. The journey is not too long."

Marcus sat on the passenger side in the front. The driver put the engine in gear and began driving east, traveling on Highway 1—the road to Jerusalem. They drove in silence for a few minutes. Soon, the hotels and commercial buildings near the airport bowed out of sight and the barren landscape appeared.

Marcus looked at the countryside, and he thought about its history. Rusted and discarded armaments, military relics from wars past, were still there. They dotted the landscape as if aged soldiers were lost in time and anchored in weeds, rocks, and forgotten battles. It was a rolling backdrop where hostilities held the country hostage and armies left scars that still cut to the bone of the land.

"Will you have a chance to explore Israel, Mr. Marcus?"

"No, this should be a short visit."

"Too bad. There is nowhere else in the world with the unique history that you can discover here. May I ask, what is it you do? Medicine I suppose? Are you a doctor?"

"No. I guess I'm between careers."

"I understand. The American economy is not what it used to be. Perhaps you can find work here. I would imagine that being a Nobel winner looks impressive on a resume, yes?"

"I wouldn't know."

"While waiting for your plane to arrive, I read a little about your accomplishments. I spend more time on my tablet than I do reading papers in the coffee shops. To break genetic codes is like unlocking deep secrets sheltered in the human body. How do you train for such a thing?"

"In my case, it was a career change brought on by my daughter who was ill."

"I hope your efforts help make her well."

Marcus said nothing.

"Are you a scientist now?"

"No."

"What do you do?"

"I have a small farm."

"A man of the soil." Elam grinned. "Maybe you are here because a possible ancestor of yours was here."

"Ancestor? What do you mean?"

"History is my major. We are traveling on part of what was called Israel's Burma Road during the war."

"Which war?"

"The 1948 siege of Jerusalem. This road allowed convoys through to Jerusalem. Had they not made the journey, the remaining Jews in the city would have starved to death or been forced to surrender. An American helped build the road. I assume you know his name, maybe you are related to him."

"Who?"

"His name was David Marcus. Is this a coincidence or a relative?"

"No relation."

Elam shrugged. "He was so important in the war that Ben Gurion, our former president, named David Marcus as a general in the Israeli army. He was the first general in two thousand years. Imagine that, an American as our first general."

"What happened to him?"

Elam released a deep sigh, his dark eyes scanning the land. "He died here. Probably around your age."

"How'd he die?"

"It is most tragic. He did not live to see peace he'd worked so hard to achieve. Six hours before the cease-fire, in the village of Abu Ghosh near Jerusalem, Marcus left his quarters at night. He told someone he couldn't sleep. The night was cold, so he wore a white sheet around his body as he went for a walk. Maybe he looked like a ghost. An armed sentry, a young Jew, saw a man in what appeared like an all-white robe coming closer. In Hebrew, he called for him to halt. Marcus spoke, but the guard didn't seem to understand, and he killed him. David Marcus was a great man, and today he remains an important figure in the history of Israel. He opened this road to Jerusalem." The driver grinned. "I wonder what roads your genetic research will open for the world."

The van reached the top of a small hill, and Jerusalem waited below. Descending down a twisting road lined with an old stonewall, Marcus watched Jerusalem appear like a vast mirage scattered across the land. The rocky hills were dotted with cedar and date palm trees. As they came closer to the old city, the sun reflecting from the Dome of the Rock made it look as if a torch was smoldering in the distance.

—▪ ▬

Marcus thanked Elam for the ride and entered the lobby of the Mount Zion Hotel, the Damascus Gates to the Old City nearby.

Marcus took in the lobby, narrowing his attention down to the tuxedoed piano player softly playing Gershwin's *Summertime* near the ornate bar where guests were being served pastries, sandwiches, coffee and wine. There were dozens of overstuffed couches and chairs with people clustered in intimate circles, sipping drinks and laughing, discussing events in one of the oldest cities on earth.

One man sat alone, and he didn't glance up from his newspaper when Marcus approached the reception area.

"Yes sir," said the desk clerk, smiling, his dark hair neatly parted.

"I'd like to check in. Name's Paul Marcus. I have a reservation."

The clerk typed the keyboard, nodded. "Although your room is prepaid, we will need your credit card on file for incidentals."

"How long is the room prepaid?"

"Um…looks open-ended, sir. Your room has a balcony and a nice view of David's Tower, Mount Zion and the Mount of Olives. And, you are within walking distance to the city's main cultural, historical and religious sites."

Marcus smiled. "I've had a long flight, how far is my walk to a bed?"

"Not far, sir. Take the lift to the fourth floor. Your room is on the right when you exit the lift."

"Thank you."

Marcus stepped to the elevator. The man sitting alone in the lobby folded the London Times in his lap, sipped a cup of tea and watched the elevator doors. Marcus rode alone to the top floor. The man reached inside his coat and took out a phone. He punched in a number.

"He's here." The man nodded. "Yes, I understand."

FIFTEEN

The next morning, Marcus took a taxi to the Hebrew University of Jerusalem Library and abruptly stopped when he entered the front door. The stained glass windows were like none he'd ever seen. He stood in the cool of the lobby and stared at the far wall. The stained glass rose from floor to ceiling, three separate panels at least thirty feet wide. The primary colors were blood red, blue and chalk white. But it wasn't the colors that caught Marcus's eye—it was the images, abstract yet distinct in shape and form. Floating planets. Half-moons. Symbols of the universe layered with what looked like a page of Hebrew text.

There were three rows of theater-style seats in the lobby. Five people sat in the front row, looking at the mammoth glass as if it were a motion picture screen.

"Many consider it Ardon's finest work."

Marcus turned around, and Jacob Kogen smiled, his pale face filled with vigor. Red and blue light filtered through the images on the stained glass and reflected off his glasses.

"Mr. Marcus, I'm Jacob Kogen. Welcome to Jerusalem! Welcome to Israel. I trust you slept well and that your journey yesterday with Elam was comfortable?"

Marcus smiled. "Yes. It's my first time, but somehow I feel as if I've been here before. Maybe it's because I've seen so much of this city on television and in pictures."

"Indeed." Jacob glanced to the stained glass. "I would imagine you haven't seen that artwork before, however."

"No, I haven't."

"The artist was Mordecai Ardon. Many consider this his masterpiece. After he painted the glass, Ardon dedicated the windows to Isaiah's vision of eternal peace. He used his talents to paint scenes from the Hebrew text found in the Kabbalah."

"I wasn't aware there were scenes in the Kabbalah."

Jacob chuckled. "Not in the literal perspective, perhaps, but in the spiritual one." Jacob pointed to the painting in the center. "Here, Ardon, following the Kabbalah, seemed to be visualizing God as the all-encompassing force, controlling everything in reality. All the world's forces descend from this upper power. Some of these we know, such as gravity and electricity, but the insight of the Kabbalah speaks of higher powers that remain hidden to us. They may have remained hidden to Isaac Newton as well. What if Ardon captured them in there? What does the story on the glass tell us?"

Marcus said nothing. He studied the images, the sun rising beyond the windows, changing their color and look. The people seated in the front row stood, snapped a picture of the stained glass and left the lobby for the parking lot.

Jacob said, "I've seen people, especially those who have traveled a great distance, sit here for hours, mesmerized, viewing the art. Come, Mr. Marcus. Let me show you our research room. I can't tell you how thrilled we are to have you as our guest."

"Don't get your hopes up. This science is a branch I've never seen or done."

The room was near the back of the library. It was a deep area filled with white boards, computers, plasma screen monitors, filing cabinets and ancient manuscripts, many under glass. Two people, a man and a woman, sat at computer screens and typed on keyboards. They scarcely looked up as Jacob escorted Marcus to the far side of the room, stopping next to a long table filled with file folders. In the center of the table was a cleared area with a single folder, magnifying glass and a gooseneck lamp.

Jacob said, "This is where my colleagues and I have spent the last few weeks analyzing what we believe are the last of the lost Newton papers. We have hundreds of Newton's work scanned on digital files. I photocopied the one with your name and sent it to you."

"It may be my name, but it doesn't mean it's me. I'm not the guy Isaac Newton had in mind when he wrote it."

Jacob smiled with his eyes and gestured to a chair next to the table. His face ignited with hope, his eyebrows arched, and lights from the computer screens trapped in his blue eyes. "Please, sit. Let's talk."

Marcus sat and Jacob pulled up a chair in front of him.

"Mr. Marcus, may I call you Paul?"

"Of course."

"Paul, please call me Jacob. Your name, Marcus...were you raised Jewish?"

"No. My father's parents practiced the faith. They died when I was a child. My father became religious when he was drinking, and he was definitely non-denominational. My mother was the opposite. She could quote scripture but couldn't communicate."

"Where are your parents?"

"They died in a fire. I was young, thirteen. I was raised by my maternal grandmother."

"I didn't mean to pry. It'll become quite obvious to you that Isaac Newton was a deeply religious man. He believed he was appointed by God to interpret, not so much the Bible, but the prophecies planted in it. Sort of like seeds. Newton wanted to harvest them for the good of mankind. Maybe he did."

"I have no illusions."

Jacob smiled. "You will have any and everything here at your disposal. You can begin, if you want, by going over the latest file, the lost papers. There are twenty-four pages in it. Through the years, we've received lost pages from Newton's papers that were auctioned in 1936. A Biblical scholar, Abraham Yahuda, gave the majority to us after his death in 1969. What you see in front of you showed up last month."

"Where'd it come from?"

"Paris. A woman made the donation. She's the granddaughter of a Frenchman who was at the same auction in 1936. I have been using the whiteboard near the table to see if any of the new papers can add pieces to the step code we've used. We originally began with the Torah, the first five books of Moses. Hebrew is read from right to left on the page. We remove all spaces from the words, leaving a continuous string of letters. We have tried dividing this into sections and rows of letters, and then using an equidistant letter spacing sequence, ELS, correlated to Hebrew calendars and Biblical events to see if we could unlock information. We choose a starting point with any letter, skipping numbers, using intervals of seven, fourteen or twenty-one spaces, going forward for positive information, and backward for negative codes."

"What have you found?"

"One example is the names of seven rabbis written in code a thousand years before their births."

"Do these codes predict the future?"

Jacob smiled. "That's the challenge. To research codes in the Bible, you need to insert information, known information. But, for the future, thus far, it has been impossible to extract information because we don't *know* the future."

"Have you found any relation to the ELS model and numerology, or for that matter, theology?"

"No, not yet. Although, in poring over Newton's papers, he seemed obsessed with the Books of Daniel, Ezekiel, Isaiah, Matthew, John and Revelation. He was using math he invented, calculus, and early quantum physics to apply to the Bible."

Marcus looked across at a long mathematical equation that took up two thirds of the large whiteboard in front of the table.

Jacob said, "Would you care for some refreshments, tea or water?"

"No thanks."

"Then you'll excuse me for a minute. My plumbing isn't as robust as it once was." Jacob grinned and left the room. Marcus stood back for a moment to take in the entire board. He studied the partially finished hypothesis. Then he stepped forward, picked up a black marker and began working the problem.

SIXTEEN

A woman in the back of the room looked over her computer monitor, her mouth opening to form an O, her eyebrows arching. She got the attention of her male colleague and pointed toward Marcus who stood with his back to them in the far section of the room, working the problem.

Marcus locked on each progression in the equation, his hand grasping the marker and moving with decisive, bold strokes. He closed his eyes for a moment, opened them and wrote non-stop for the next thirty seconds before replacing the cap on the marker. He backed away a few steps to take in the entire whiteboard and the series of steps he used to bring the problem to a conclusion, to a solution. Marcus sat down.

The woman lifted her cell phone to snap a picture of the whiteboard. She leaned closer to her colleague and whispered. "Do you think he's solved it?"

The man's eyes were trying to follow the numbers. He didn't seem to blink for a long moment. Then he said, "I have no idea."

Jacob returned. He glanced at the whiteboard, his face filling with wonder, his eyes tracing the sequence and conclusion to the problem. He said nothing for a half minute.

"Are you sure?" he asked Marcus, his voice just above a whisper.

"I'm sure that's the solution, but that's as far as my skills can take it."

"That's far enough. The hypothesis has been there a month. A dozen of the best mathematicians in Israel and elsewhere have tried to bring forth a conclusion. No one did until now. Do you *know* what it may mean?"

"What?"

"The postulate opens doors that may bridge mathematics and the cosmos. Do structures that exist mathematically also exist in the physical sense? Newton explored the premise. The postulate, now perhaps a theorem, is an extension of his notes."

"But it *proves* nothing, really." Marcus placed the marker back on the easel.

"Please, sit down, Paul. I'm a little weak in the knees after seeing that."

"It's numbers. Just numbers and beyond measurement, they don't mean—"

"No, it's more than that. I doubt if there's another person on earth who could do what you did in the time I went to the bathroom. I believe you are Isaac Newton's heir. Newton's gift was legendary. One day, the great mathematician, Johann Bernoulli, on a quest by the Royal Society in London, brought a problem in physics to Newton. The postulate was to determine the curve of minimum time for a heavy particle to move downward between two given points. This challenge had baffled the most famous eighteenth century mathematicians of Europe for almost a year. Bernoulli left the problem with Newton in the afternoon. Later that day, after dinner, they returned to Newton's home, and he had solved it."

"Please, don't compare what I just did to anything Newton accomplished. We're still using his math to launch satellites. I might have a grasp on math and ways to approach encryption, but I couldn't hold a candle to guys like Newton or Einstein. As much as you want it to be, I'm not the guy whose name is on the paper Newton wrote."

"Your humility is gracious, but your discovery in gene therapy for heart disease places you in an area in which less than a measurable percent of the world will ever go. I believe Newton used science and theology to come as close to prophecy as humanly possible. And I think he was right about another thing—you. The Paul Marcus in his papers and you are the *same* man. Now, I'm convinced of that. At the end of Newton's life, you are the man he predicts would carry on the research. Please, open the folder in front of you. That, Paul, is the first step."

SEVENTEEN

Ten hours later, Marcus still pored through hundreds of Newton's papers that had been scanned and filed under the *Theology* heading in the computer file. Marcus drank a pot of coffee and filled two legal pages with notes. He turned down offers of food, absorbed in the world of Isaac Newton, while working and reworking mathematical equations that Newton had begun or finished in the pages.

For much of the time, Jacob Kogen left Marcus alone and ordered that no one disturb him while he was studying the Newton papers. An hour after sunset, Jacob quietly entered the room. Marcus was staring at the computer screen, and then he glanced down at the original pages left in the last file.

Jacob said, "Paul, you must be famished. You haven't eaten all day, turning away offers of nourishment, and you're not a small man. I hope you don't fall out of the chair when your sugar level dips lower than a cold winter's night in Jerusalem."

Marcus looked away from the computer screen and focused on the professor's expectant face. Marcus's eyes were beginning to flush, red near the irises. He leaned back in his chair.

"What have you found?" Jacob asked, folding his hands in front of him.

"Look, this is all fiction to me. My religious convictions and knowledge of the Bible are flat. Isaac Newton studied this stuff for years. I can't gain a footing on a guy at that level."

"But Newton never had the tools you have at your disposal."

"The first conclusion I'm drawing is I'm not your man. Never thought I was, but you offered a trip to a place I hadn't seen, and I wanted…"

"What did you want?"

"Nothing. It's not important. I think you've wasted your time on me."

"I respectfully disagree. Please, then, try to look at it as a science project."

Marcus closed his burning eyes for a moment and said, "This is like hieroglyphics, really. I'm wondering if Newton lost it somewhere in all this analysis. There seems to be a certain psychosis to the science."

Jacob nodded. "At one point in his life, he had a nervous breakdown. It's evident in a letter he wrote to John Locke."

"It's apparent here that he was so deep in calculations that his mind must have been swirling, especially since he didn't have computers or calculators. He had to devise his own new math and computations to figure the time references between the books in the Bible. There are more words and references in Newton's writing than I would have thought one man could write, especially by hand."

Marcus looked down at the papers scattered across the desk. "One thing that seems evident to me is coming from this last file of papers you received."

"Yes, and what is that?" Jacob leaned forward.

"I'm beginning to see how there may be a pattern here."

"What kind of pattern?"

"I'm not sure. Using the computer, I can quickly cross reference many of the topics Newton wrote about. I'm seeing interesting correlations from the Book of Ezekiel, Daniel, Isaiah, John, Matthew and Revelation."

"In what areas?"

"A continuation, if you will. It's almost like the events that Ezekiel spoke about, were picked up again by Isaiah, Daniel, Matthew, and finally by John in Revelation. It's as if we're looking at the pieces to a large jigsaw puzzle that expands thousands of years, events, people and places—hidden links to what was…what is…and what might become."

"Become? What is that picture looking like?"

"I don't know. It's going to take me more time, a lot more time than I scheduled here, and I don't know if I'll get any further than what I'm stumbling across now."

"You can stay indefinitely, work out of the library or the university next door. We will underwrite your efforts."

"Why?"

"Pardon?"

"Why is this so important to you?"

Jacob deeply inhaled, glancing at the whiteboard and back to Marcus.

"The scientist in me is curious about what the greatest scientist of all time might have found in the Bible. The heritage in me, the DNA of Israel flows through my veins, and in that respect, I would like to know whatever may be available."

"You know the past, the history. So I'd assume you are talking about one thing—the future. Specifically, the future of Israel."

Jacob smiled, his eyes soft. "Perhaps that can never be told. But if it were possible, maybe not the prophecy, but the probabilities, then we can be better prepared."

Marcus smiled. "I thought that was what religion was all about, always being prepared for whatever life tosses in your face—faith. Do faith, free will and fate contradict each other?"

"Please allow me to buy you dinner. I have a favorite restaurant close to your hotel."

"I'll save this file on the computer, and I'll save it to my flash drive, too. I want to do a little homework with it." Marcus inserted the drive, punched the keys, his eyes following the sequence of the computer shutting down.

It was then that he spotted it—between a single blink of his eyes.

Marcus stopped, leaning closer to the screen. His fingers flew across the keyboard, watching the numbers and data.

"What is it, Paul?"

"What kind of security does the library have on its system?"

"I've been assured that it's some of the best."

"You need better than the best."

"I don't follow you, why?"

"Because you've been hacked."

EIGHTEEN

WASHINGTON, D.C.

Deep inside the secure confines of the National Security Agency outside of Washington, D.C., encryption analyst, Alicia Quincy, stared at her computer screen. Her dark hair was pinned up, blue eyes locked on the images. Ron Beckman, pointed face, military haircut in a dark suit, stood next to her. She looked at the time on the screen: 12:15 p.m. on the east coast of America.

"Are you sure it's Paul Marcus on that computer?" asked Beckman.

"Most likely. It's consistent with his skills. He's running numbers, decryptions, on the machine. I can't tell exactly what he's doing, but the data is definitely coming from computers within the Hebrew University Library, and he just shut down."

"What kind of decryption?"

"I recognize the pattern, but I don't recognize the source."

"Does he know we've breached their system?"

"I don't know. If he caught on, we wouldn't know it immediately. Remember, Paul helped with some of our internal security codes before his daughter became sick. I have a weird feeling in my gut doing this. It's like we're invading his privacy, especially after what happened to his family."

Beckman's eyes looked hard as steel. "Alicia, there is no such thing as privacy when it comes to national security. You can't have privacy and security, too. You know that. We're just doing another job we've been told to do."

"Who said for us to watch Paul Marcus and why? Is it because he told the Nobel Prize people thanks but no thanks? Or is it because he's doing decryption in Israel?"

"I'm not sure. It comes from high up."

Alicia was quiet a few seconds. "The CIA's doing fulfillment, and we're doing the tracking. Maybe Paul pissed off somebody with that Nobel Prize deal. He was always such a damn good guy, the real deal. What's going on?"

"We're not here to speculate. That's where this line of questioning ends." He turned to leave.

Alicia watched him stroll through the cavernous room filled with computers, international maps and plasma screens displaying video and cyber tracks left by people across the nation and the world.

— —

Marcus and Kogen finished a late evening meal in a small Lebanese restaurant a few blocks from Marcus' hotel. After paying the bill, Marcus insisted on walking back to his hotel. The night was cool. He wandered up Jaffa Street with the walls to the Old City on his left. Lights inset at the base of the ancient stonewall wrapped it in soft yellows. Skeletal trees, having shed their leaves, cast crooked shadows against the wall.

Although exhausted, Marcus was in no hurry to get back to the hotel. He wanted time to walk and think. He thought about the delicate hacking of the computer while he had worked. Who was behind it? CIA? The Mossad? Someone else? Why?

Three bearded men, orthodox Jews dressed alike in black, two wearing Fedora's, strolled past him, the men in a heated discussion. Tourists were still exploring the Old City at night, a time when the clank of bells faded with the gray twilight and many street vendors stowed away charms and souvenirs they sold from displays set up on rugs.

Marcus walked toward Jaffa Gate, the trace of grilled lamb, garlic and coffee still clinging in the tranquil evening air. Globed streetlights cast pasty sheens across the stone walkways. Marcus looked toward the Tower of David and the Citadel, both immersed in the golden glow of lights. A yellow cat darted into one of the narrow cobblestone side streets and ran until it was lost in the labyrinth of stone set two thousand years ago.

Marcus entered the ancient city through Jaffa Gate, walked down David Street and then stopped. It was nearly deserted. A few tourists strolled by, heading out of the Old City. Pockets of amber light lit some of the buildings and the closed shops. Marcus simply stood and took in the street that he knew would lead through the heart of Jerusalem, from the Tower of David to the Western Wall.

He noticed a small wrought iron enclosure with two tombstones to the left, almost hidden beneath trees. He walked toward them, wondering if there were inscriptions on the graves.

He heard a sound. A forced whisper, a muffled threat, somewhere in the shadows of tombs and stone carved from bedrock—a mugging. Marcus could turn around and walk back to his hotel, or he could walk toward danger.

NINETEEN

A cloud parted and the Old City was immersed in soft moonlight. Marcus stopped. He listened without turning his head. Then he cut his eyes in the direction of the sounds. An old man was trapped like a frightened animal in the corner of the ancient crypt. A younger man held a knife to his victim's throat and demanded money. The attacker's back was to Marcus. He looked around. No one. Marcus slipped off his shoes and walked in his socks toward the mugger and intended victim. Now he could hear them clearly.

"The pouch! Where is it old man?" demanded the mugger.

"In my store! In the safe."

"I see you take it every Monday. Today is Monday! Where is it? Tell me or I'll slaughter you like a lamb! No cameras over here. Nobody will know." He pressed the blade against the side of the old man's neck, an inch from the carotid artery. Blood trickled down the aged skin, a blossom of red forming on his white collar.

Marcus was less than twenty feet away. Moving silently.

The old man saw Marcus approaching. He didn't allow a response to register in his eyes, quickly looking back at his attacker's face.

The mugger said, "Lift your jacket! You hide it in your belt. Lift it!"

"He's not going to lift anything," Marcus said, now less than fifteen feet from the attacker.

The man whirled around. His face filled with disbelief at what he was seeing and hearing. His breathing was fast. Chest expanding. Sweat rolling down his forehead. Pupils dilated wide as cats' eyes at night, adrenaline and cocaine flowing in his system.

"Don't do it," Marcus said evenly. "Just go. Walk away."

"Gimme your wallet asshole! And that laptop! Now!"

"I'm not going to do that."

The man sneered. To the old man he shouted, "Keep back!" Then he shifted his weight. Crouching, he gripped the knife, his right hand swaying.

Marcus lowered the laptop to the ground, never blinking, never breaking eye contact with the man holding the knife. He stepped closer to the mugger, the man's eyes wider with disbelief. "You sound American. This will be where you die. Right here! Tonight!"

"Just turn and walk away." Marcus said, stepping closer.

There was laughter in the distance. A group of tourists entered through Jaffa Gate. The mugger looked toward them, his face twisted in disgust. "Screw it, man!" He turned to leave, glaring at Marcus. "You weren't even scared, dude. That mistake will get you killed in this country." He used the index finger on his left hand and moved it across his neck as if it were a knife. "Next time." Then he turned and ran, the alleys swallowing him as if he entered a dark catacomb.

Marcus approached the old man. "You're bleeding. Let me see."

"It is only a scratch," he said, taking a clean, white handkerchief from his pocket and holding it against the cut. "Thank you. Thank you, my friend. And thank God. My name is Bahir Ashari. You are?"

"Paul Marcus."

"Thank you, Paul Marcus. You saved my life. I am indebted to you."

Marcus smiled. "No, you're not. I'd like to believe, if the situation was reversed, you'd do the same for me."

Bahir smiled. "I would like to believe that as well. But I'm not sure I could. I saw your eyes when the man faced you. I saw no fear. None."

"I was pretty far away."

"Not that far." The old man's croaky voice with the Arabic inflection sounded as if it came from another age. He stepped closer, out of the shadows and into the light. He wore a dark Nehru jacket and pants. A week's growth of silver whiskers on his weathered face caught the light. "How did you see us so far from the center of the street?"

"I didn't see you. I saw those graves first. Then I heard you, or at least I heard him threaten you."

Bahir's eyebrows rose. "Most people don't see them, especially at night."

"Pardon me?"

"The ancient tombs. To most, they go unnoticed. I am waiting for my grandson to bring the car to carry me home. He telephoned and said he ran out of fuel and had to walk to a petrol station. I've been here about two hours after I closed my shop. Maybe two hundred people have walked by. You are the only one who stopped at the graves."

"Who's buried there?"

Bahir smiled, his eyes opening wider. "It is believed these are the graves of the men who designed and built the very walls that surround the Old City. They were commissioned by Suleiman, the Ottoman ruler, in 1538 to build the granite walls."

"How'd they die?"

"Murdered. Killed by the sultan, it is said, because the men failed to include Mount Zion and David's tomb within the walls." Bahir chuckled. "Suleiman must have had some respect for the architects because he buried them here near the entrance to the gate, which legend says every conqueror of Jerusalem will enter. Why did you stop in the night when so many never see the tombs?"

"I don't know."

"Do you need directions?"

"I was just taking in the night air and sort of wound up here."

"If you are headed for the Western Wall, it's about five hundred meters straight down David Street. Jewish Quarter is near it. The Muslim section is the area to the north of the Dome of the Rock. The Christian Quarter is to the north of where we now stand."

A group of teenagers, laughing and singing, walked by heading east on David Street. An organized church group followed them, a dozen people with matching blue T-shirts. In white letters and numbers across the front of each shirt was: *John 3:16.*

Their leader, a man wearing a baseball cap backwards, bull neck and a girth that strained the shirt said, "Okay, everybody, we'll make a night stop at the Church of the Holy Sepulchre for pictures only."

When the group left, Bahir said, "Anything you need to know about this place, please ask me. I've lived here all my life, and I have seen many, many things. My coffee shop is called Cafez, right down David Street. I give you my card." He lifted his jacket and pulled a small leather pouch from a band under his coat. He unzipped it and handed Marcus a business card. "Please, come by. You have free coffee and conversation for the rest of your life." He grinned.

Marcus smiled. "Thank you."

"You are American, yes?"

"Yes."

"You do not look like a tourist."

"How can you tell?"

"I see thousands of them, each week, from all over the world. You are here for something else, business perhaps?"

"Yes, business."

The old merchant smiled. "I imagine this business is of interest to others, possibly?"

"Why do you ask?"

"Because the time we've been speaking, a man has stood back under the arch at Jaffa Gate, smoking a cigarette and trying not to give the impression of watching you."

Marcus looked toward the gate when a man turned and walked away. He was cast in silhouette as a small car shot through the entrance and pulled up closer to where Marcus and Bahir stood.

"Ah, here is my grandson."

Marcus nodded.

The old man opened the passenger side door. "We can provide you transportation to wherever you are staying. Perhaps the man we saw had his eye for that computer bag you carry. Possibly it is something else, yes?"

"I doubt he was watching me."

"Which hotel are you staying?"

"The Mount Zion."

"It is very close to us. Please, get in and we will make your journey easier."

"I appreciate the offer, but my hotel is a short walk."

"Please, sir. Forgive the concerns of an old man. Although this is a holy city, it still is one of the bloodiest cities on earth. Let us drive you to your hotel. Trust me on this, my new friend."

TWENTY

Marcus set his laptop on a table in his hotel room, opened the mini-bar and poured two ounces of vodka over ice. He walked onto the balcony facing the Tower of David. The tower, Citadel, and the entire walled city were unmoving in pockets of golden light, ancient stone and shadows captured in a surreal postcard image.

Marcus thought about Bahir Ashari, the man he'd just met—maybe saved his life. There was radiance in the old man's eyes that Marcus couldn't recall seeing in anyone's eyes since Jennifer's death. Soft but filled with sparkle. Wise yet playful, but, more than anything, there was tenderness. *I've lived here all my life, and I have seen many, many things.*

He sipped his drink and stared at the Old City and its blanket of white light against brown stone. Marcus thought about the Newton numbers and how, by adding events in the Jewish new years and fitting the puzzle pieces tighter, they were beginning to reveal something. Was it a prophecy Newton pulled from the Bible, information related to the Jews return to their homeland? Maybe it was part science and part luck, he thought. What, if anything, would the entire puzzle tell? Prophecies, if they existed, now had little relevance from Isaac Newton's time. *What would be from this day forward? How do I look for them when there was no data, no clues to feed into the Biblical timeline?*

The moon rose above the Tower of David, and the inky sky filled with the shimmer of stars, opaque light falling on the stone shoulders of the Old City as if the light floated down from the heavens. Marcus finished his drink, opened his wallet and stared at the photograph of his wife and daughter. Beautiful smiles. Beautiful hearts.

"I miss you both more than I can tell you."

Lost. Gone forever. His eyes watered looking at their faces. At that moment, they seemed farther away than the ancient city that lay to the east of him. He wiped his eyes and placed his wallet back on the table and looked beyond the Old City to Mount Olive in the distance. Marcus felt a deep sense of loss, utter loneliness. The chilly breeze filled his pores, depositing a mood of solitude in his heart darker than the universe high above the Old City.

The buzzing of his cell phone on the table beside him sounded odd in the silence of the night.

No caller ID.

He hesitated for five rings and then answered.

"Paul, this is Alicia Quincy. How are you?"

"I'm okay. Are you calling from Washington? What time is it there?"

"Yes, it's almost five. Close to midnight in Jerusalem. Did I wake you?"

"No, not at all. It's good to hear your voice. Anything new with your niece?"

"Talks are moving at glacial speed. My sister's on anti-depressants."

Marcus said nothing.

"You know, Paul, I'd be fired for telling you that NSA is watching you. It's all bogus. I have your back because it's the right thing to do."

"Are you on a secure line?"

"Yes."

"I'm here doing research, that's all—nothing to do with encryption or covert code-breaking. Put that in the damn report and tell Bill Gray to shove it where the sun doesn't shine."

"I haven't seen Bill. I believe it comes from somewhere else. The CIA is following someone's inquiries. Even Ron Beckman doesn't know."

Marcus was silent.

"Whatever you're doing over there, it has caught the interest of someone. I'm not sure who that someone is, but it's got far-reaching tentacles."

"One of the computers I was working on in the university was hacked. Did it come from NSA?"

Alicia said nothing for a few seconds. "Yes, but I see you caught it quickly. We couldn't get through the second wall."

"Is the hacking continuing?"

"Not to my knowledge. But that doesn't mean the agency isn't curious about how you're working with Israel. The primary reason is the Internet chatter in certain Middle Eastern circles. Blame it on your new celebrity status, the Newton papers, the Mossad's interest in your files, or most likely, your talents to create or detect cyber-sabotage. The combination of it all, not to mention the timing, certainly would make some people in high places very curious about you."

"Why are you risking your job to tell me this?"

"Because you worked here. You're one of *us* for crying out loud! Some of us spoke at the funeral for Tiffany and Jennifer. You're trying to intercede on my family's behalf to help my niece, Brandi." Her voice became strained, words weighted with sadness.

"Thank you for telling me. Are you okay?"

There was another pause. Marcus could hear Alicia exhale. "Dad has pancreatic cancer. It's not good."

"I'm sorry to hear that."

"Like everything else in his life, he's taking it in stride. My father is an amazing person. It's never been about him. It's always about how he could make it better for me or my sister…or Mom. Or anyone, for that matter."

"Maybe I'll get a chance to meet him." Marcus heard a sniffle.

"Goodnight, Paul."

"Thanks for calling, Alicia." As she disconnected, Marcus gripped the balcony railing and watched lightning flicker above Mount Olive. A dark storm in the eastern skies stalked over Jerusalem, moving in silently then erupting in thunder and blocking light from the heavens.

TWENTY-ONE

*F*or the next week, Marcus reported to the library and worked twelve-hour days poring through Isaac Newton's papers. To further protect the computer where Marcus was doing his research, the university and the library's IT department added firewalls, changed passwords, created a dummy clone and rerouted access.

Marcus still had reservations.

"To catch a mouse, you have to set a trap," he mumbled, layering in decoy emails and fake subject lines. In one he wrote: Physicist Abromov's arrival from Moscow to Tel Aviv pending transfer... "Come get the bait," he whispered.

Then he began reading through the countless words that Newton had written, hypothesizing and leveraging dialogue and text from the Bible into repeating patterns. The further Marcus dug, the more fascinated he became with what Newton had discovered in the ancient passages. He was becoming even more impressed with Newton's remarkable gift. He started to think that somewhere in the math, parables, early calendars, iconic imagery, and puzzling symbols, that maybe there were hidden predictions to be found.

The more Marcus uncovered, the exhaustive science and Newton's fastidious attention to detail—the scientist's ability to find, correlate and understand the connections from Old Testament script with events in the New Testament, was beyond the capacity of anyone he'd ever known. It became apparent that Newton was seeking an innermost set of laws—the secrets to an intricate plan weaving together three-thousand-year-old cryptograms.

Late in the afternoon on the fifth day, Marcus wasn't sure if he was beginning to hallucinate or if he was starting to see something rise to the surface of the massive amount of text. He had a dull headache, but he didn't want to stop working. He used every mathematical and decoding skill he'd honed to figure the equations and examine the science from the hand of Newton. Marcus scrutinized how Newton brought forth data from the movement of the planets, the equinoxes, lunar and solar eclipses, and the biblical events in alliance with prophecies that seemed to fit into sequential patterns from the Old Testament to the New Testament.

Marcus tried to find momentum, a nexus that drew sequences into a central theme of what those actions meant at the time they happened and how they may have an influence on things yet to happen. He rubbed his temples and read Newton's words aloud:

"'The prophecies of Daniel are related to one another, as if they were but several parts of one general prophecy, given at several times. The first is the easiest to be understood, and every following prophecy adds something new to the former. The first was given in a dream to Nebuchadnezzar, King of Babylon, in the second year of his reign, but the King forgot his dream. Then it was given again to Daniel in a dream, and by him revealed to the King.'"

Marcus sipped room temperature tea, read from the batch of Newton's handwritten papers in the folder, and then returned to Newton's words that had been scanned, filed and displayed on the plasma screen in front of his work desk.

'In the next vision, which is of the four beasts, the prophecy of the four Empires is repeated, with several new additions; such as are the two wings of the Lion, the three ribs in the mouth

of the Bear, and the four wings and four heads of the Leopard. Also, the eleven horns of the fourth Beast, and the son of man coming in the clouds of Heaven, to the Ancient of Days sitting in judgment.'

"How are you doing?" asked Jacob Kogen, entering the room. "Anything more, or is it getting increasingly difficult to make sense out of it as you proceed?"

Marcus looked up from the screen, his eyes burning. "Newton's genius was off the charts. His skill at using mathematics, astronomy, multiple types of calendars, connected to three thousand years of biblical history, and his ability to link it with a margin contingent on whether he was working in Hebrew, Greek, Armenian or Roman calendars, is beyond human comprehension. His grasp of how the events of the Bible seem to fit in a set of moveable laws is astounding."

"Moveable?"

"As in over the course of time and human events. Through the timeline, from central Europe, Greece, Egypt, Rome, Babylonia and the rest of the Middle East, it's like looking at one enormous chessboard. The players: kings, queens, bishops, rooks, knights, and pawns, are all given opportunities to play the game with a set of tenets. But, as in chess, it too often becomes a real war; and the lust for land, power and conquest tosses out the rules. The prevailing set of laws that Newton seems to have been uncovering—the symbols, language, and subtext that he's finding from book to book in the Bible, are the buried cornerstones in the Old and New Testaments."

"What kind of laws?"

"I don't know yet."

"God's laws, perhaps."

"That's apparent in Newton's writings. Also, he spent years studying alchemy, and I've been reading many of his papers on the subject."

Jacob smiled. "Turning lead into gold, the Philosopher's Stone, perchance?"

"I don't know."

"Many alchemists, maybe Newton included, are thought to have died from the effects of mercury poisoning because the elixirs they consumed, the substance of transforming lead to gold, they believed might give them lives stretching into a second century. Some scholars suggest that the transmutation of lead into gold is metaphoric for the transmutation of the physical body with the goal of attaining immortality."

"What do you know about the Emerald Tablet?"

Jacob raised a bushy eyebrow. "Why do you ask?"

"Because Newton mentions it in his papers on alchemy. He even interpreted the writing."

"Many have interpreted it. No one alive knows who really wrote it. The brief text could go back to the ancient Egyptians, Hermes perhaps. Many describe it as a short, truth-seeking list that offers insight into the balance of the universe, especially in the area of natural laws."

Marcus read from the screen. "Newton offered his own interpretations. He listed them from one through fourteen. He writes that the first thing the Emerald Tablet says is that all the rest of what it says is true. The other things include this:

"That which is below is like that which is above. This does the miracles of one thing only. The sun is the father and the moon is the mother. The wind has carried it in its belly, and the earth is the nurse. The father of all perfection in the world is here. Its power is absolute if it is converted into earth. Its force is above all, for it vanquishes every subtle thing and penetrates every solid thing... and so the world was created."

Jacob interlocked his fingers across his stomach. "What are you thinking?"

"Newton seemed to be trying hard to bring the metaphysical, spiritual and physical into one caldron, turn up the fire and see what it boils into."

"How about his decoding, anything there? Such as using the ELS coding we found in the Torah? These have proven that biblical prophecies are real, as in revealing the names of some prominent rabbis centuries before their births."

"If you have enough text in any book, *War and Peace*, for example, using the ELS codes, picking sequential letters, can fit whatever you feed into them. You must get more specific."

"What do you mean?"

"That's the question, and I'm hoping I might find the answers, at least some of them, from Newton."

"He may have written more than a million words on theology alone."

Marcus stared at the screen, the white light burning into his unblinking eyes.

Jacob said, "You're tired, my friend."

"Yeah. I'll dump this to a flash drive and work on it from my hotel."

"If you find something, please call me. I don't care what time it is. Understand?"

"Yes."

"Oh, I almost forgot. I've arranged to have a rental car for you. It's a blue Toyota in the car park outside. Taxi rides get old." Jacob handed Marcus the car keys. "Goodnight, get some rest. Your eyes look like they hurt."

"Thanks for the car."

It was almost 9:30 p.m. when Marcus parked in a lot across from the hotel and walked into the lobby. His body was drained, but his mind couldn't disengage from the possibilities of what Newton could have discovered if he'd had the resources of a computer. He checked his watch for the time back in Virginia and made a call.

"Amber, how are Buddy and the horses?"

"They're fine. I rode Midnight yesterday. Hope you don't mind."

Marcus smiled. "Of course not. They need to be ridden more. Ride them anytime you want. Look, I need to stay a little longer over here, okay?"

"No problem. How's the Holy Land?"

"I haven't had time to visit much of it."

"Take lots of pictures. You sound tired."

"I'm working long hours. There should be plenty of food for the horses. If you run out of food for Buddy, I'll reimburse you."

"That's fine. How long do you think you'll stay there?"

"I'm not sure. I'll call you as soon as I get a better handle on the timeframe."

— —

Marcus couldn't remember the last time he overslept. But it happened, and it happened when he most needed to be up and out of the hotel. He looked at the bedside clock: 1:00 p.m.

How did Saturday arrive so quickly?

He sat up, on the edge of the bed, using the palms of his hands to wipe the lethargy from his eyes. *Focus.* He thought about what he'd learned the past few days in Israel and how Jacob's intrigue had turned into admiration, his new BFF and cheerleader. But, how could Marcus score points in a bold new game where nothing was a consensus, an axiom—nothing was a given because no one on earth, except Newton, had reached that level? Marcus wondered how he could use math or science to prove theorems not provable by any known, conventional way.

Maybe he couldn't, but he'd try. And, he'd try hard. He thought about that as he took a long, hot shower, ordered coffee and sat down to his computer to work. And he didn't stop for five hours.

After 6:00 p.m., he went into the city to get some fresh air—to clear his head and find good food. He drove the small car through the streets of Jerusalem, cautious not to hit disoriented, camera-toting tourists stepping in front of his car. He thought about the decoding—the roadblocks. *What am I missing?* Marcus whispered, "The sun is the father and the moon is the mother." *Newton, you used your own theory of gravity to calculate the position of the moon to reconstruct the Judean Calendar. You explained and proved Daniel's prophecy of seventy weeks by doing it. What else?*

His mind turned over combinations of codes, ways to interpret, maybe translate and decipher some meaning out of what was frozen. For Marcus it was like watching a block of ice melt around an object, hoping the speck in the center of the ice is a pearl. He lost track of time driving. Rain began falling. Marcus searched the controls trying to find the wiper switch, finally engaging it. The blades smeared road dust with the heavy drops of water. Through the grime, Marcus read a road sign:

Abu Ghosh 7 Kilometers.

Where the hell am I? In the falling rain, Marcus didn't recognize anything.

TWENTY-TWO

ABU GHOSH, ISRAEL

Lightning flickered in the low lying black clouds resembling flames behind the door of a blast furnace, licking the threshold and edges to escape. Marcus pulled off the road and up to a gasoline station. He looked at the car's gauge. Almost full. He locked the doors and jogged through the rain to the porte-cochere over the front of the small store. A man stood near the door. He had close-cropped dark hair, late-forties, shoulders that stretched his Army uniform shirt, an unlit cigarette in the corner of his mouth. His pale blue eyes beamed. "Hell of a night," he said.

"Sure is," Marcus nodded, noting the soldier wore the rank of colonel.

"Gotta pump your own gas here."

"Back home, too."

"Where you from?"

"Virginia. How about you?"

"New York, Lower East Side. Are you buying any smokes?"

"Don't smoke."

The man smiled. "I ought to give 'em up. If you're lost and looking for directions, I can help. I've been here awhile now. My information's free. Inside, could cost you the price of a soda pop." He grinned. Mist blew in from the rain and wilted the cigarette. The man took it from his mouth, his eyes watching the lightning run through the hilly terrain. He turned back to Marcus. "Are you lost, pal?"

"I'm trying to get to the Mount Zion Hotel near the Tower of David. I've been driving around, got lost in thought and wound up here."

"Bud, you absolutely got turned around. Look, I have no idea where the hotel is, but I can damn sure find the Tower of David. It's right next to Jaffa Gate."

"My hotel is within walking distance from there."

"Good. I'm trying to get to the Central Bus Station on Jaffa Road. It's less than a mile before the Old City. If you don't mind, I could use a ride on a night like this."

Marcus looked at him a moment. His thoughts replaying the night his wife and daughter were killed when he stopped to help a man. *"Die! You hear me? You're dying now…a slow damn death…the pleasure of watching…."*

"Are you okay?"

Marcus stared at him, stared at the insignia of the eagle on his uniform. "Yeah, I'm fine. Sure, let's go. You can be my GPS."

The man grinned, tossed the duffle bag over his shoulder, and followed Marcus to the car. "No problem."

Marcus unlocked the doors. "Put your bag in the backseat. C'mon, get in or you'll get soaked."

The man sat on the passenger side of the front seat. Marcus pulled up to the main road. "Which way?"

"Turn to your left, and we'll be going southeast. I'll get us there. Name's David, what's yours?"

"Paul."

"I had a good friend named Paul."

"Where's he today?"

"Killed. He was a good soldier and a great man. Paul went in with the first wave of paratroopers. That was a helluva fight."

Marcus said nothing for a moment, the wipers slapping the rain off the windshield, the car traveling beneath cones of light from the street lamps. He glanced over to the man, his face streaked in moving shadows from the rain against the windows. "Was he a family friend?"

"You could say that—we grew up together."

"Are you here on leave? I don't recall any U.S. troops stationed in Israel."

"Yeah, but I'm passing through." He felt for a cigarette in his pocket. "My last smoke got caught in the rain." He looked down at a lighter in the palm of his hand. "Maybe this is finally the time to give 'em up."

"Smart move, Colonel."

"You spotted my bird, huh?"

"It's not hard to see."

Lightning traveled across the sky in a horizontal burst, the flash reflecting off the lighter. "Is that a Zippo?" Marcus asked. "I haven't seen one quite like that since my grandfather used a similar lighter around the farm."

"Best lighter ever made." The colonel rubbed his thumb across the roller, sparking the wick, and he stared at the flame for a moment, the fire dancing in his eyes. Then he snapped the top shut, the smell of lighter fluid in the Toyota. "So, Paul, what brings you to this land?"

Marcus slowed for a pothole. "I'm here to research passages from the Bible."

"You don't have to travel all the way to the land of Zion to do that."

"Maybe not, but there's a lot of research information at the university and the library here."

"Sometimes you might learn more about the Bible by walking this land. Get out and toss a net where the apostles fished. Look across the same valley were King David watched the sun set. Walk the roads, fields and towns where Christ walked. That way the stuff that's in the pages can have more meaning. But what the hell does a soldier like me know? Not enough to get out of the damn rain." He chuckled and wiped a drop of rainwater from his arm. "You got a wife back in Virginia?"

"I used to."

"Divorced?"

"No, she was killed."

"I'm sorry to hear that."

Marcus said nothing.

"Meaning no disrespect, but you don't have the look of a man who lost a wife in an accident. You have the look of a man who lost a wife because someone took her life."

"What kind of look is that?"

"The kind I've seen on the battlefield in the eyes of some men. Not so much fearless as it is they have nothing to fear for…including their own lives. This is a helluva time to swear off smokes."

Marcus drove silently through the rain, swerving to miss another pothole. The colonel laughed softly and said, "When I first came here, the damn roads were all like that, potholes everywhere. Some of the roads were dirt or gravel. We have our own Burma Road here, too. Not like that seven hundred mile snake of a road in China. The Burma Road here is still unpaved. It makes for a good walk on a Sunday morning."

"I'll remember that."

"Take a left at the next intersection. We're not that far from the bus station and a lot closer to the Tower of David." He set the lighter down. "Tell me, have you found something in the Bible that you can hang your hat on, something that resonates in your gut, or better yet, in your heart?"

"Most of what I'm doing is trying to put puzzle pieces together. I think there are a lot of missing pieces. Maybe that's the way it's supposed to be."

"Could be. Funny thing about that kind of stuff, though. The more that's revealed to you, the more you begin to feel in awe or sort of privileged in some way. Information is knowledge, and that's power. A spiritual journey—that's the power I'm talking about. I often wonder if that spiritual versus worldly battle raged in people like da Vinci. Solomon had so much revealed to him that after a while maybe he got tired of listening to those who didn't know a damn thing. But he sure gave us a lot to think about in Proverbs. Wisdom comes from finally realizing and admitting how damn little you know."

Marcus smiled. "So you've got it figured, right?"

"Maybe. Not that I'm any more enlightened than you. But when you sit back down and look at that picture puzzle you spoke of, think of this: God knows so much more than David, Solomon, da Vinci or Einstein. But He still listens because *we're* just discovering it. Pal, that's gotta be real love. Hey, that's my stop up ahead. You can let me out at the curb. Rain's slackin' up."

"I can pull in closer."

"No, don't bother. A little fresh air before I catch the bus would be good. Sometimes it's crowded. Sometimes just a few folks are riding it."

"Where are you headed?"

"Jordan. I can get out here."

Marcus stopped the car and the man pulled his duffle bag from the back seat. "Much obliged," he said waving. "Hey, I didn't catch your last name."

"Marcus. Paul Marcus."

The man grinned. "Maybe we're kin. We have the same last name."

Marcus put the car in gear and pulled away, he looked in his rearview mirror and the colonel was standing there, unhurried, holding his bag, his gaze following the car. Marcus glanced down to turn off the wipers. He looked up again in the mirror and the colonel was gone. He stared at his watch. It had stopped, 9:29 p.m.

Then he remembered the story his driver had told him the day he was picked up at the airport—the story of David Marcus.

TWENTY-THREE

A half hour later, Paul Marcus was back in his hotel. He parked the Toyota, reaching over to touch the floor mat on the passenger's side where the man's boots had rested. It was damp, a trace of mud on the floorboard.

In his room, Marcus replayed much of the conversation he had with the mysterious colonel. *Who was he?* Marcus started toward the bathroom, but stopped when he caught the blink of a tiny red light on the phone. He lifted the receiver and played the message: "Paul, this is Alicia. I tried to reach you on your cell. It was as if the signal went nowhere...only heard a white noise kind of sound, like the distant roar of water. I couldn't send a text either. Call me."

Marcus looked at the clock on his nightstand: 12:05 a.m. He pinched the bridge of his nose, his body drained. He reset his watch and called Alicia. "I just got your message."

"Is it a late night for you in the old country?" He could hear the smile in her voice.

"A strange night is more like it."

"The longer you're over there, the stranger it might get."

"What do you mean?"

"Some things are going on in Iran, and for that matter, Israel, Pakistan and India that has our attention. Syria is near the top of the list."

"What things?"

"We have reason to believe some cyber-attacks will or are being released against the Iranian nuclear effort. To infiltrate the Iranian nuclear grid with a malware worm, it's all about coding. For Iranian officials to stop it, it's all about decoding."

"Why are you telling me this?"

"You know why, Paul. Number one, I don't know of anyone who's a better cryptographer than you. The Israelis know it, which means so do the Iranians, Syrians, Pakistanis and even India's intelligence. Toss in Russia and China for good measure and you have the ingredients to a Pandora's box." She dropped her voice. "The second reason is that I *care* about what happens to you. Be careful, please."

"Do you think the only reason I'm in Jerusalem is because the Israelis brought me here under the guise of examining the Newton papers? But all along their real reason is they want me to encrypt a cyber-worm or to keep the Iranians from figuring out how to stop one?"

Alicia signed. "We don't know that—I don't *know* that."

Marcus blew out a pent-up breath. "All I've been doing is working and reworking possible cryptograms from what Newton wrote in reference to what he found in the Bible. There's nothing else, Alicia. Nothing. Trying to make sense of references from Newton's papers to passages in the Bible is like earning doctorates in history and religious studies."

"You sound so tired."

"It's been a long day—a bizarre day."

"Want to talk about it?"

"That's like asking me if I want to talk about losing my mind."

"What happened?"

"I'm not sure. Can I ask a favor of you?"

"Absolutely."

"Check out the background of a guy named David Marcus. He's a bird colonel, Army. Originally from New York. Manhattan, maybe."

"Is he a long lost relative of yours?"

"I don't think so."

"Did you meet this guy?"

"Maybe, if that's his real name. I gave him a ride tonight to the bus station. But I don't think that's where he was really headed."

Alicia laughed softly. "You want me to do a background check so you can see if this guy's lost?"

"No, it's not that. It's something else…"

"It's what, Paul?"

"I'm not sure what to make of him or the conversation I had with him. I'll tell you about it when I get home. In the meantime, see what you can find on this guy."

"No problem. I'll have his life story, right down to his last credit card transaction. Is there anything else?"

"Yes, but I don't want to impose any more than I have. I don't like asking for—"

"Please, Paul…just ask. If I can do it for you, I will."

"My grandmother, Mama Davis, you met her at the funerals."

"I remember."

"I've tried calling her a couple of times. Each time she's been asleep. The assisted living home, The Mayflower, isn't too far from the District. Maybe you could stop in and check on her for me, if you don't mind."

"I'd be happy to visit her. Tomorrow is Sunday. I'll ride out there. Is there something you want me to let her know?"

"Tell her things are going well in Jerusalem, and I'll have some good stories to share with her when I get home."

"What else? I sense that's not your entire message."

"You can say…you can tell her I love her, too."

"I will. Get some rest. Goodnight, Paul."

Marcus walked to the bathroom, turned on the shower, stripped and stood under the hot water with his eyes closed. He let the downpour pulsate against the back of his neck, events of the day, especially the last few hours, swirling around him like gnats in his brain. *Was it hallucinations? The mud was real.* After showering, he slipped into a T-shirt and boxer shorts and poured a small bottle of Belvedere over ice.

Marcus sat in a chair on his balcony and watched the traffic and pedestrians move under the lights around the Old City. He sipped the drink; his eyes burned. He refused to think about the mysterious colonel, Marcus's thoughts focusing on the decoding—the roadblocks.

What am I missing?

The full moon appeared over the Tower of David, resembling a bone china plate hanging against the black sky and casting Jerusalem in brush-strokes of amber.

Marcus whispered, "The sun is the father and the moon is the mother." He swallowed the drink, his eyes intent, watching the rising moon. He whispered. "Newton, you used your own theory of gravity to calculate the position of the moon to reconstruct the Judean Calendar. You explained Daniel's prophecy of seventy weeks by doing it."

Marcus opened his laptop computer and inserted the flash drive. He keyed in letters and numbers and watched the screen. He mumbled, "That which is below is like that which is above. It may not have originated in the Bible, but it's telling me where to *look* in the Bible."

TWENTY-FOUR

O n Monday morning, Paul Marcus entered the university library and paused at the stained glass mural in the lobby. He looked at the symbols in the three panes of glass, his eyes coming back to the center panel. He thought about the view of the wall around the Old City he'd seen from his hotel room. The lower portion of the painting depicting what appeared to him to be the wall around Jerusalem.

A librarian walked by carrying books in her arms.

"Excuse me." Marcus pointed. "The painting in the center, is the lower portion the walls of Jerusalem?"

The woman smiled. "Some people believe that. The artist, Ardon, I don't think he ever made that clear. Others believe the images are of the Dead Sea Scrolls, Isaiah specifically, second chapter, second verse."

"What does it say? Do you know?"

She shifted the weight in her arms. "Yes, because I've been asked that question dozens of times. The passage reads: "And it shall come to pass, in the last days, the Lord's house shall be established on top of the mountain. It shall be exalted above the hills, and all nations shall flow unto it."

"The last days?"

"Yes."

Marcus continued to study the stained glass, the rising sun giving the colors a subtle feel of movement causing the images to change slightly in the morning light.

The librarian smiled. "Another part of the text on the window mentioned another prophesy in Isaiah. You can see it painted on the panel to the right. The shovels and things, Ardon visualized how weapons, like spears, will be turned into gardening tools when nations stop the wars." She paused, watching Marcus stare at the colors and illustrations on the glass. "Is there anything else, sir?"

"No, no thank you."

She stepped around Marcus and walked across the large room, the soles of her hard heels the only sound in the lobby.

—▪—

Marcus had been at the computer in the university library for five hours cross-referencing Newton's handwritten notes when he stopped and re-read a page.

'The ancient solar years of the eastern nations consisted of 12 months, and every month of 30 days: and hence came the division of a circle into 360 degrees. This year seems to be used by Moses in his history of the flood, and by John in the Apocalypse, where time, times and half a time, 42 months and 1260 days, are balanced. Matthew 24:36 says about that final day or hour no one knows, not even the angels in heaven, only the Father. The number, 603,550, from Numbers 1:46 —represents the sum of all the children of Israel... every person. To follow is to read Daniel and Revelation as one.'

Jacob Kogen entered. "I'm not sure you look rested."

"Didn't sleep very long. I may have found something."

"Oh, what is it?"

"I think Newton believed, as do many people, the symbols used, especially in the Book of Daniel, represented nations. For example: the bear for Russia. The lion for what is possibly today's Iran, Iraq and Syria, the leopard representing Turkey, Palestine, Libya and Egypt. The ten-horned beast is possibly China. He calls these nations beasts and uses the wording from Isaiah, Jeremiah, Corinthians, and Daniel to produce an accurate timeline of the shift of powers in Europe and the Middle East through much of the last three thousand years."

"Understood."

"Newton is trying to bridge a hidden link between at least a dozen books in the Bible, but seven in particular—Daniel, Ezekiel, Isaiah, Matthew, Numbers, John and Revelation. Maybe even a lesser-known series of writing from Enoch, Noah's great grandfather. There's a reference to Enoch, apparently walking with God without dying. Enoch was believed to have been 335 years old then. Was it some kind of elixir, a fountain of youth, or was it divine intervention? The book of Ezra gives the year of the decree to rebuild Jerusalem as being the seventh year of Artaxerxes, found in Ezra 7:7. Newton's broad knowledge of ancient history meant he'd be familiar with the name, Artaxerxes Longimanus, the Persian king, and to place the decree in the year 458 BC. Newton's deep understating of gravity allowed him to compute it."

Jacob leaned closer in his chair, his eyebrows arched. "How?"

"To Newton, Daniel in a vision with the angel Gabriel, referenced seventy weeks from a certain point in time, to the rebuilding of Jerusalem and the crucifixion of Christ. Newton thought the prophecy meant seventy weeks of years, or rather 490 *years*. He used his own theory of gravity to calculate the position of the moon in ancient times to reconstruct the Judean calendar to find the year in which the day of the preparation for Passover fell on Friday. Then Newton computed the crucifixion date as either AD 33 or 34. When the Enoch calendar is used, then the separation of the two dates completes exactly seventy weeks of years to the very day."

"Amazing, the riddles are slowly being revealed. This timing provides a strong witness of God's prior awareness of both dates, and of the accuracy of the Book of Daniel. It is one thing, Paul, to prove the precognition of

God that may be a given for many people, but how does the Bible reveal the future? Are the codes there?"

"I don't know. Newton seemed to struggle with those things that could be some kind of divine providence and those things which man might know. The conflict found in the interpretations."

"Some kind of divine providence—of course, you still doubt."

"I've been a scientist for a long time."

Jacob nodded. "So was Newton. What do you mean by conflict in interpretations?"

"Maybe even Newton couldn't reach beyond a certain point, a *human* point, to grasp the depth of a timeline that contains both the history and the future of mankind."

Marcus pointed to the papers scanned and displayed on the plasma screen in Newton's handwriting. "But one approach is taken from Newton's interpretation of the Emerald Tablet."

"What approach is that?"

"Newton writes that one of the canons in the tablet says *'that which is below is like that which is above.'*"

"How do we construe that?"

"Gravity. Newton knew it is an invisible force that exists between all objects. We don't really know what gravity is—we know only how it *behaves*. It's a universal power, above and below. We can't feel the sun's gravitational force on us, yet Newton knew it's the power that keeps the earth from flinging off into a black hole. In context of the areas Newton concentrated in the Bible, let's look at the power, the force, of that which is above is like that which is below."

"Paul, my old head is spinning. What do you mean?"

"Why develop skip codes to troll for words when you can be more specific with the subjects? It's like looking for diamonds. Using satellite imagery and topography testing, the geologist knows the surface ore and the strata beneath it. If he or she mined far enough, there could be diamonds. You find areas in the Bible, such as passages that Newton focused on, the Books of Daniel, Ezekiel, John, Isaiah, Matthew and Revelation, and you examine the surface text, find specific parallels. What's beneath the surface? If you can drill far enough, maybe you'd find buried messages that correlate with the exterior text."

"Using what methodology?"

"The code, whatever it is, must share the setting, the subtext, in which it is written. If not, it's tossed out as hit-and-miss junk, like computer spam. The spacing must be narrow so when the words intersect, they must relate to the encoded word. Look at it as if you're standing on a riverbank on a bright summer day. The reflection of the clouds may float on the surface one minute. The next second, you may see butterflies hovering over the water, their colors reflecting from the river. Then you might see the reflection of trees off the waters. With Newton's knowledge of history, he was trying to associate biblical and historical events into definite pools, in both the historical and futurist context with the foundations—the cornerstones floating at the surface, the prophecies somewhere below those images on top."

"So how do we peer below the surface?"

Marcus smiled. "At one time, the Greeks used glass bottom buckets to look for sponges beneath the water in shallow areas. We have to find that bucket. I think I know how."

"I'll order food to be delivered." Jacob left the room.

Marcus nodded and keyed in words, his fingers popping the keyboard like a fighter throwing fast punches.

Marcus held his breath for a long moment. He watched the words paginate across the screen like letters in a hybrid crossword and Sudoku puzzle locking into place. He let out a low whistle, glanced up from the screen at the empty room and continued. Reading the words, the adrenaline flowed into his system. "Okay, Isaac Newton, let's see what you saw."

TWENTY-FIVE

*J*acob entered the room with two plates wrapped in plastic. "Chicken, rice, tomatoes, olives and figs. Hope you have an appetite."

"Thank you."

Jacob smiled. "When you were working on a cure for heart disease, did you starve yourself then as well?"

"Watch this."

Jacob set the plates on a desk and looked over Marcus's shoulder at the screen.

"What is it?"

"It's a prophecy presumed written by John on the island of Patmos more than two thousand years ago."

"Book of Revelation?"

"That's the start. So much is allegorical in Revelation that you have to look at the entire ancient history to decipher the meaning, and who knows if we'll ever really understand the history and future, or come to terms with it when the chapters begin and end. The number seven is the place I began for trying to decode. I divided it in half to narrow searches and lessen the chance for error. So the decoding is using the number three and a half, or 3.5. John writes that two witnesses are given the power to prophesy 1,260 days, or exactly 3.5 years according to the Hebrew year of 360 days. The witnesses are killed and their bodies lie in the streets of Jerusalem for 3.5 days. The woman clothed with the sun is protected in the wilderness for 1,260 days, or 3.5 years. Gentiles walk the holy city for forty-two months, or

3.5 years. The beast is given permission to continue for forty-two months, again 3.5 years.'"

"I follow you."

"Using this information, I entered data about the enormous oil spill in the Gulf of Mexico, the BP catastrophe, I didn't include a date. Between Genesis, Revelation 8:8, passages in Daniel and Isaiah, I found this. Look at the screen. *'The lamb's wound shall yield blood and water. Then the beast will breathe out a mountain of fire over the waters of the gulf. The sea will glow and become scarlet, as if the ocean filled with blood – destroying life in its path.'*"

Jacob pushed his glasses further up the bridge of his nose. He stood and crossed his arms. "What are the mathematical chances of the letters spelling this as we view it?"

"One in seven million, give or take."

"What else might we find?"

"I haven't tried decoding for future events, primarily because I'm not sure what to look for, but I did key in data to see if President John Kennedy's assassination was mentioned."

"Was it?"

Marcus typed for a few seconds. The screen changed, filling with letters and numbers. Then he hit two keys and a series of letters were highlighted. He deleted the others around it.

"No, President Kennedy's assassination wasn't mentioned. But the death of his son, John, was. It reads: *'Son of Kennedy will fall from the sky in explosion and fire, plunge to death.'* That seems to indicate Kennedy's plane may have caught fire, maybe exploded. Was it from a small bomb placed inside it? If so, that means it wasn't an accident? And, if it wasn't an accident, who would have wanted him dead and why?"

— ·—

Jacob Kogen entered his university office and locked the door behind him. He pulled at the business card, flipped it over, and read the number to the private line handwritten in red ink. He made the call.

"Hello, Jacob," said Nathan Levy, field ops director of the Mossad.

"I have yet to grow accustomed to being greeted on the phone before I speak when I make the call."

"What do you have?"

"I'm calling you because I am not sure what to make from a revelation made by Paul Marcus in his research with the Newton papers and the Bible."

"Has he found something of concern to Israel?"

"The man is brilliant, perhaps what he's—"

"Please, professor, I have a meeting to prepare for."

"I am suggesting that Newton left more than anyone knew then or now. Paul, however, seems to understand the depth of the Bible that Newton penetrated, and he has dug farther. In doing so, he found information that seems to foretell the death of President Kennedy's son, John."

"That was an unfortunate day. When did he stumble across this information?"

"Earlier today."

"What did the information reveal?"

"Only that Kennedy's plane would fall from the clouds in a fire or explosion."

"An explosion, are you sure?"

"Yes."

"Is there an indication as to how it may have happened?"

"No, nothing."

"What else?"

"That's all. I am praying that we will find hidden information dictated by God that would help prepare Israel for a safer future."

"Send to me all the information that Paul Marcus is discovering."

Nathan Levy disconnected.

TWENTY-SIX

Marcus carried his notes and laptop from the university to his parked car. He thought about the deciphered, jumbled information he'd stumbled upon from his translations. *The Kennedy connection—was it real? Was it happenstance? Why this revelation? And why now? And how did Newton come up with my name—if it is my name?*

"Can I give you a hand getting that in the car?"

Marcus turned around. The man was a silhouette, standing alone in the lot, the sun setting far behind the Jerusalem Academy of Music and Dance across the street. "Remember me, Mr. Marcus? I was the one who met you at the airport."

"Yes, yes I do. Elam Mandel, right?"

The man smiled. "Yes. Please, let me take some of the load while you find your car keys."

"Thanks." Marcus kept his laptop, but handed him a box of papers while he opened the car trunk. He put the laptop inside, and Elam did the same with the box. "I haven't seen you since the morning you met me at the airport."

"I stay pretty busy with school and work. How are you coming with your research?"

"Good, I think." Marcus glanced around the parking lot. "Look, Elam, that day I rode in with you...you told me about a guy, an American soldier who became an Israeli general back in the mid-to-late forties."

"Yes, he was David Marcus. You share the same surname, of course. What about him?"

Marcus blew out a long breath, his mouth now dry. "You said he was killed. Where did it happen?"

"Near Abu Ghosh. He was killed by a single shot from a lone sentry because David Marcus didn't know the password in Hebrew. It was a very unfortunate accident. Why do you ask?"

"Just curious. Are there parts of the Burma Road in Israel that are unpaved today?"

"Yes, the most scenic parts."

——

Marcus parked his car off the side of the road and followed a sign marking the red trail of the Burma Road. He started walking the narrow dirt road, which seemed more like a goat trail, scraped and carved long ago from the ribs of the hilly terrain. Boulders, some large as small cars, others the size of watermelons, were strewn along the rough path.

As he climbed, Marcus could see the changes in topography, the sway-back hills to the north, the Judean Mountains to the east. He continued to go up a steep hill, his leg muscles tightening, his heart pumping, lungs sucking in air scented from lilies and cedar.

When he reached the summit, he stopped and stood on an outcropping of ancient rock. Far below, he could see how the trail descended in a series of S curves dotted with native shrubs and cedars. Marcus simply stood and felt the breeze blowing across the basin from the west where the sun was melting into an indigo Mediterranean Sea. The valleys and meadows were textured in shades of olive green, dark lime and emerald. Flowered quilts, woven in white and lavender lilies, draped the sides of the hills.

Marcus sat on the rock, his feet dangling over the side, his thoughts on the recent events, contemplating the *meaning* of it all—if there was a meaning. *What will I find here? Am I supposed to find something? I can't even find my family's killer.* He closed his eyes. A gentle wind from the sea came across the valley, the air cool against his face. He opened his eyes. The setting sun cut through a cloud, painting the hills and valleys in hues of harvest hay, sea green and jade. His senses were suddenly very acute—the sound of birds in the trees, the hum of a bee in the flowers, the scent of almonds and olives from a field below him. He felt his heartbeat slowing, an absolute tranquility moving through his body, stillness, and a presence he had never experienced in his life until now. *In this moment in time—why?*

He missed the mountains of Virginia, and he missed Jennifer and Tiffany, terribly. In a slow motion replay of his life, he could see their faces as they rode the horses, the wind in their hair, the laughter—their sweet, pure laughter. He missed the fragrance of shampoo in Jen's hair, and the way she would lock her arms around him in the kitchen when he made coffee on Sunday mornings. He remembered holidays with his wife and daughter, carving pumpkins, eating ice cream, the summers on Virginia Beach.

Marcus drew in a deep breath as two sparrows alighted upon a date palm. They chirped and flittered among the palm fronds, then the wind changed and the birds flew to a huge rock less than ten feet from him. The larger of the two sparrows had a red berry in its beak. It fed the berry to the smaller bird and then preened its feathers. The largest bird flew, turned quickly and perched on a granite rock next to Marcus, tilting its head, watching him. He could see the golden pin drop of sunset in the sparrow's dark eyes. After a few seconds, the bird chirped and flew from the rock, the smaller sparrow flapping its wings and following. Marcus watched them fly west toward the crescent of golden sun slipping into the vacant copper sea.

TWENTY-SEVEN

Early evening on the next day, Marcus headed into the Old City on foot, exploring and observing, to better grasp hold of the synthesis of the place. Tourists and pilgrims roamed David Street in packs led by scripted tour guides. Marcus stepped around a tour group and made his way down the historic street, stopping once to read the address on the card the old man had given him the night of the attempted mugging.

Was I being followed now?

He walked beneath stone arches leading to small shops filled with silk scarves, oriental rugs, copper pots, hookah pipes, guitars, ouds, flutes, Kiddush cups and enough wooden crosses and other souvenirs to represent almost every religion on earth.

He stepped quickly inside a shop, glancing into a decorative mirror with a direct reflection of the street. He could see no one watching or following him. He pulled his phone out of his pocket and placed a call to Alicia Quincy's mobile phone.

Marcus said, "Look, things are unraveling over here faster than I thought. Hell, at this point, I don't know what I thought anymore."

"What do you mean, Paul?"

"I've found coding or passages in the Bible that seems to indicate some kind of prophecy of events."

"Such as floods and national disasters?"

"The manmade kind."

"Manmade—how?"

"For starters, the BP oil disaster in the Gulf."

"What does it say?"

"It's allegorical, but I think there's enough information to connect it to the disaster in the gulf."

"Are you sure you're not reading or misreading between some dusty old lines in the Bible written by dustier old men?"

"It also indicates that President Kennedy's son, John, would die in a plane crash."

"What? You found information in the Bible that prophesied John Kennedy Junior's death in a plane accident?"

"That's *exactly* what I mean. If this is accurate, it may not have been an accident. I remember the official reports indicating there was no explosion and that the plane just dropped out of the sky. Reports specify that Kennedy was at fault."

Alicia was quiet a moment. "Who would do it? Who would have wanted him dead? Where do you go with this information?"

"I don't know who would do it, and I don't have a lot of information to do anything with it, either. The revelations are short, but yet they have enough meat on the bone to chew."

"Could the hacker or hackers have found out about this?"

"I don't think so. You're sure NSA isn't trying to hack, right?"

"Not at the moment—I'd be the first to know. Is anyone else aware of what you're learning?"

"Yes, a teacher at the university, Jacob Kogen. He believes there's further information in these notes or in the Bible that might direct the fate of Israel, and the world, for that matter."

"Paul, what can I do?"

"Let me know if anyone from the agency is sniffing further. Also, see what you can find on a Syrian general named Abdul Hannan."

"Is he currently in Syria?"

"He's dead."

"So is the guy you wanted me to run a background check on, David Marcus."

"Dead..."

"Since June, 1948. He was killed in some weird friendly fire, according to a report that wasn't easy to find. David Marcus was an American colonel, a guy who took a leave of absence and then volunteered for the Israeli military under the name of Michael Stone. He was a tour de force during the war and the subsequent evolution of Israel becoming a state. He was shot in the line of duty, allegedly due to a mistaken identity."

"Does the report indicate how many times he was shot?"

"Hold on…yes. He was shot three times. Why?"

"Three? That's weird. Alicia, does it say where David Marcus was assigned during the war?"

"Some of the stuff that really stands out is what he did in Germany. He was in charge of figuring out how to sustain and keep alive the millions of people starving in the areas liberated by the Allies at the end of the war. To drive a nail in the Nazis, Marcus was the guy in charge of planning the way the Nuremberg Trials would be operated, including the international legalities of possible death sentences for those found guilty of war crimes. My guess is David Marcus was a hero to many, and a despised authority to Nazi sympathizers."

Marcus listened to her. He said nothing.

"Paul, you said that you met someone with this name, right?"

"I spent an hour in the car driving him to Jerusalem in a wicked thunderstorm."

"Maybe that's why I couldn't reach you, atmospheric conditions."

"Alicia, something is happening over here. Something I can't explain scientifically. Can you check to see—?"

"I have to go. Someone is coming down the hall." She disconnected.

Marcus continued walking, locating the coffee shop, Cafez, at the end of Hakari, a side street near the Western Wall. As he came closer, the scent of dark coffees and burning tobacco met him. A half dozen people, mostly men, sat in outdoor chairs under cabanas long since faded from heat and rain. Two pokerfaced men smoked Turkish unfiltered cigarettes and sat in metal folding chairs playing a card game called Basra.

Arabic music came from a battered speaker bolted to the exterior of the small shop. Marcus moved past the shop and bought a newspaper a few doors down and read the headlines, a story about the upcoming elections for the prime minister in Israel, and the campaigns for primary elections in the United States.

Marcus walked back to the coffee shop and entered. The old man, Bahir Ashari, recognized him. He stood at the rear counter and grinned. "Welcome, my friend, Paul Marcus. I thought I might see you again."

Bahir came out from behind the counter, his olive face beaming. He wiped his hands on a white towel. "What kind of coffee you like, American? Turkish? Greek? Lebanese? I grind the beans fresh for you."

Marcus smiled. "American's fine. That way, I can drink more of it."

"Yes, it is so. Not too strong. I do sell some occasionally…to tourists mostly."

Marcus looked around the small shop. There were a dozen tables, a few worn couches and movie posters from American films on the walls. Two college-aged students, a man and a woman, sat at a table near the window, backpacks beside their chairs. There was one small table with two chairs in the far corner. Marcus gestured toward it.

"Can I sit there? I may be here for a while."

The old man beamed, leading Marcus to the table. "Sit, please. I told you the coffee and conversations are free for life. However, since I am much older than you, drink quickly my friend."

"Do you have Internet connection?"

"Yes, of course." He raised his shoulders. "My grandson works here on the weekends, so he insisted we have this Internet. No wires, eh. People play with their computers and drink. Business is good. Life is good. Even with your computer, I see you bought a newspaper."

"It seems to go well in a coffee shop."

"Yes, but many things in the newspaper are not good. I get your coffee now."

Marcus opened his laptop, setting it on the table. He took his seat, reaching in his pocket and removing the two flash drives. He plugged one in his laptop and waited for data to load. He began to plow through layers of coding, tracking the IP address of the hacker. Marcus reversed the information, keyed in data and waited. He watched numbers loading. He scribbled the numbers on a piece of paper.

A man entered the store. The man, face rutted and the color of a horse saddle, went to the counter where Bahir greeted him and took an order for coffee and baklava.

Within a minute, Marcus began keying and cross-referencing passages from the Bible. He pulled and translated from the Hebrew Bible, the Torah, and King James, searching for the right combination of words to enter. He stared at the screen, unblinking, his mind racing, turning over patterns, unseen links, looking for the subtle signs in three thousand years of stories, languages, prophecies and symbols.

Marcus glanced around the coffee shop. There were only a handful of customers still seated, some reading newspapers or Internet-connected tablets. A few hunched over laptop computers. His thoughts raced. *If there's handwriting on the wall about Jen and Tiffany, I want to see it.* He took a deep breath and keyed in the names of his wife and daughter, performed multiple cross-reference searches, decrypted verses from various books in the Bible, crunched numbers, years, and allusions to time and space.

And Marcus waited.

TWENTY-EIGHT

"**T**his is fine American coffee with a touch of Middle Eastern flavor," said Bahir, delivering a cup of steaming coffee to the table and proudly setting it in front of Marcus. "Please, try it." He gestured with a slight bow at the waist.

Marcus sipped the hot drink. "It's good, thanks." He looked at the screen where the data concerning his wife and daughter loaded and fully assimilated. Nothing. Nothing but jumble. He blew air out of his cheeks, ran a hand through his hair and glanced at the newspaper article about the election of the Israeli prime minister. He keyed in the prime minister's name, age, and locations the article said he would be appearing in Israel. Then he watched the screen.

Bahir grinned, a gold cap visible behind his left eyetooth. "You are not pleased with your computer, yes?"

"It's not the damn machine. It's the data or lack of it that doesn't produce results. It's sort of a Russian roulette or spin of the wheel."

Bahir grunted. "I am a man of my word, this will be the first of many coffee cups I fill for you. In my shop, your cup will always runneth over. You were my guardian angel, and it is something I will cherish until the end of my days. If you cannot be very bored by the conversation, musings of an old man—one who grew up here in the streets of Jerusalem, I would be delighted to share that with you as well."

Marcus sipped the coffee. "That sounds like a fine trade to me. Just give me a few minutes. I'm sort of in the middle of something and—"

"Ah, yes, yes. No problem. You are working. Your computer is a window, perhaps a little unclear and you are searching for a good view."

"Something like that, yeah."

Bahir chuckled. "The computer is smart, but is it wise? Would Solomon have used this electronic brain to solve the challenges, the riddles of his time? I think not. He could compute the honor of a man in one look. It was a gift from God, the same God who allowed Solomon to live in his temple while here on earth. The temple that was above in heaven, planned by the hand of God and built below paradise, less than one hundred meters from where you sit."

"Not much of it's left."

"Perhaps. At least not to the eye."

"What do you mean?"

Bahir grinned, his eyes crinkling in the corners. "What does your computer tell you? Does it think?"

Marcus shook his head. "It's only as good as the information it receives."

"Information can come like tracks in the sand—some are easier to see than others, especially after the wind blows. You are a good man, Paul Marcus. Very few people would do what you did when you stopped the man who held a knife to my throat. I feel that there is a larger reason your journey has led you back here."

"Back? I've never been to Israel before this trip."

Bahir shrugged. "Perhaps. It is only a figure of speech."

"I'm only here because I'm researching the Bible."

"What do you hope to discover?"

"I don't know."

"What do you *want* to discover, what is your desire?"

"Something that's very personal to me."

"Most who come here have studied the Bible or the Koran. Is there somewhere in Jerusalem you care to see based upon your research?"

Marcus looked at the laptop screen. He sat closer in his chair, his eyes scanning the words. He said nothing.

"What is it you see?"

"I'm not sure. It reads that *'on the tenth, an assassin will fire upon the prime minister in the plot of the weeping angel.'* " Marcus cut his eyes to Bahir. "Where's the plot of the weeping angel?"

"I have seen many tearful angels. They have been in gardens all over the world."

"Maybe this one's a little closer to home, right here in Jerusalem. I need to make a phone call."

"Of course." Bahir walked to the coffee bar and greeted a customer who came through the door.

Marcus dialed Jacob on his cell. "Jacob, I've been digging deeper, much deeper into the Newton notes. I believe Newton *did* have a line on how to tap the Bible for a look into the future."

"What do you mean?"

"I have reason to believe the prime minister of Israel is going to be assassinated."

"What?"

"The prime minister!"

"When? How?"

"Maybe the tenth. I have no idea how. There's a vague reference to it in decryption I unpeeled after taking some words from a newspaper story about the prime minister and then transposing them with similar wordage I found between Daniel, John and Revelation."

"What did it reveal?"

"Here's what it disclosed, *'on the tenth, an assassin will fire upon the prime minister in the plot of the weeping angel...'*"

Jacob said nothing for a few seconds. "The tenth? This month? Where is this plot of the weeping angel?"

"I don't know."

"That's all it says?"

"Yes."

"Paul, if you feel there is great legitimacy to this...this prophecy, I will make calls immediately. The authorities must be alerted. Wait a minute, you said the tenth, correct?"

"Yes."

"I heard a radio report on the way to work. It indicated the prime minister is in Washington on Tuesday. That's the tenth! He'll be meeting with your president."

TWENTY-NINE

*F*ifteen minutes later, Jacob Kogen received a return phone call from the Mossad field ops director, Nathan Levy. Jacob told Levy everything Marcus had said to him. He added, "If this discovery is true, then this one thing alone is priceless for Israel. To prevent an assassination attempt on the prime minister, coming from a biblical source, is unprecedented in the history of the world. It will *prove* Divine Providence. Lastly, it confirms Paul Marcus is indeed the successor to Isaac Newton and Newton's great struggles to discover the depth of God's plan."

Levy grunted. "You are proceeding to conclusions long before there is any substantive information or evidence, Professor. I have the prime minister's travel itinerary on my desk." There was a pause and papers shuffled. "The prime minister will join the president to place a wreath at the Lincoln Memorial in Washington, D.C. to commemorate the end of the American Civil War a 150 years ago."

"President Lincoln, like former Prime Minister Rabin, was killed by an assassin's bullet. I remember seeing a famous drawing that an American newspaper cartoonist did of Lincoln after President Kennedy was assassinated. It portrayed Lincoln sitting in that big chair at the Lincoln Memorial with his face buried in the palms of his hands, weeping. Many Americans thought Lincoln was an angel for preserving the nation at the time of the American Civil War. Maybe this is what the reference to the *weeping angel* means. You *must* prevent the prime minister from making that appearance."

"Professor Kogen, I will personally speak with the prime minister. I will alert our security as well as the American Secret Service, too. However, this trip has been planned for quite some time. There's substantial international media in attendance, and significant political and public relations gains to be achieved by having the prime minister participate in the observance. The prime minister has, upon occasion, said he would like to be remembered by the people of Israel like the people of America remember President Lincoln. The reference was to an American president who kept the nation together while championing the rights of its people. It would be an embarrassment to keep him away from this symbolic affair now, especially at a time when Israel could use more international support. Regardless, between our security and what the Americans bring, the area around the Lincoln Memorial will be quite secure."

"Remember, Nathan, they flew a jet into the Pentagon, a mile from the Lincoln Memorial."

"The information you have provided will be taken into serious consideration, extreme safety precautions will be in place. Now, Professor, I have a meeting to attend."

＊＊＊

Kogen called Paul Marcus. "I have alerted our top security authorities. They are taking this seriously, but I don't know what obvious action they will seize."

"What do you mean by obvious action?" Marcus asked. "The only action that matters is to keep the prime minister from laying the wreath at the Lincoln Memorial. If the term weeping angel is analogous to Lincoln, this could be horrific, and played out live on television and the Internet."

"Can you dig further in the coding and come up with anything more definitive, something that might indicate from where the threat is coming?"

"Look, Jacob, I'm lucky to have had this much revealed. I don't know if it's correct or makes sense. But I do know that I can't casually stand by and say nothing."

"Maybe there is someone you can call…someone where you used to work that might have some influence on your president. He could cancel the event at the memorial and there wouldn't be much suspicion. He might fake stomach flu or simply say the schedule was overbooked, and they will lay the wreath at another time."

Marcus closed his eyes for a moment, heat building across his broad shoulders, jaw muscles tightening. "Why do I have a feeling that you, and the authorities you just mentioned, know more about me than you're suggesting?"

"Because you're included in the very elite group of Nobel laureates, much of the world knows more about you because they're curious. Nothing more, Paul, I promise you. Please, do you have someone you can call, someone to make aware of what you have discovered?"

Marcus exhaled. "I'll make the call."

"And I'll buy you dinner tonight. I will pray that you can bring good news to the table."

"I will bring my laptop to the table because I have found something else."

"What?"

"Something that Isaac Newton knew about Israel."

Marcus looked at his watch to gauge his time before meeting Kogen and then called Alicia Quincy. Surprised by her raspy voice, he said, "Did I wake you?"

"No…yes, it's okay. Sorry I hung up on you so abruptly this morning." Her voice sounded lower, filtered through vocal cords closed with sleep. "I went to the office to catch up on a few things and left because I had a migraine. When I got home, I took a couple aspirins and laid down…guess I must have dozed off for a bit. So, two calls in one day—are you okay?"

"Yes. Alicia, I don't know what the hell's happening over here. The more I decipher, the more puzzling some things are becoming."

"What do you mean?"

"I have reason to believe there will be an attempt made on the life of the prime minister of Israel when he meets with the president Tuesday at the Lincoln Memorial."

"Where'd you get this? Did you decode it? Are you sure?" She sat up in bed and looked at the digital numbers on her clock: 11:59 a.m. "You're telling me there will be an assassination attempt on the prime minister?"

"I don't know! I just know this information is coming from multiple layers of decoding. This is what I'm getting: '*On the tenth, an assassin will fire upon the prime minister in the plot of the weeping angel....*'"

"Plot of the weeping angel—what the hell does that mean?"

"I don't *know* that either. Jacob Kogen, a professor here, remembered a poignant drawing, one that ran in newspapers and on the wire services. It showed Lincoln at the memorial, crying after President Kennedy was assassinated. Alicia, talk with Bill Gray. Have him alert the Secret Service, FBI, Homeland Security, and the CIA for that matter. Try to stop this thing from happening."

Alicia ran her hand through her hair and pushed a pillow behind her back for support against the headboard. "This is getting weird, Paul. No, it's getting damn scary. You've pulled information on the BP oil spill, John Kennedy Junior's plane crash and now this about the prime minister. How can we explain this, a freakin' prophecy, to people who won't see how notes from a long-dead scientist and passages from the Bible can be used as a warning? They'll think you're acting like some kind of *psychic*. That's gonna be received with rolled eyes, at best—"

"I don't care how it's received if we can do something. The president and prime minister will lay that wreath at the memorial Tuesday at 10:00 a.m. Please, rattle some cages. I don't give a damn whether they think I'm psychic. If it saves a man's life, they can call me anything they want. Tuesday is only a few days away."

THIRTY

Jacob Kogen and Paul Marcus sat at a table in the corner of the small restaurant, candles flickering from multi-colored glass vases in the centers of tables. No more than eight diners remained in the restaurant at 9:00 p.m. Many of the guests had finished eating and were lingering to enjoy after-dinner drinks.

The men ordered and waited for their food. The waiter poured each man a glass of wine from a bottle of chardonnay he brought to the table.

"Thank you," Jacob said, as the waiter draped a white napkin around the neck of the bottle, nodded and left. A candle, in the only mauve vase in the room, burned in the center of their table, its soft light drifting over Jacob's face in lavender brush strokes. "I am still trying to grasp how you uncovered the threat on the prime minister's life. I've prayed that the authorities will heed the warning and cancel the ceremony. All we have is a reference to the tenth, an assassin, and the plot of the weeping angel. The prime minister receives many threats on his life, no doubt. I wish we had something more definitive."

"This isn't a *threat*. This is a revelation or some bizarre prophecy, and it doesn't get too damn refined. No more than a riddle is clarified. I don't know if it's your prime minister or the prime ministers of Britain, Croatia, Canada or Bulgaria for that matter. But your guy is the *only one* meeting with the President of the United States on the tenth. If the Lincoln statue is the weeping angel, a betting person might say the odds are weighted in the direction of your man."

Jacob watched the candle flicker in the vase, his fingers interlocked, and his mind sifting through the information. "Assuming the ceremony is cancelled, we may prevent an assassination. However, if it's cancelled, we'll never know whether this forewarning, this horrible act, was imminent or bogus. But the issue isn't proving or disproving, it's preventing a death."

"It's about stopping a *murder*. Maybe this is part of the reason, hell, it could be the whole damn *reason* you brought me over here. If this information can save his life, anyone's life, it's worth it."

"You did this decryption off-site because you are still concerned about hackers, correct?"

"Yes."

"We'll purchase a brand new, never out-of-the-box computer for you and keep it off the intranet and Internet. There's no reason for someone to penetrate the library's computer firewalls. Most of our information is free, and much of it is accessible online. Why would someone want to hack into our system?"

"Professor, who have you told that I was going to be here?"

"What do you mean?"

"From what I could gather, it looks as if the system was hacked specifically to follow the computer that I was given to work with, which is yours, correct?

"I am the primary user."

"Who knows I'm here?"

"Our staff, of course. The research on the Newton papers is nothing covert. Until the recent donation of the lost papers, it's been on-going since 1969. Technology is all that has changed. Now, of course, your vast skills add to the mix."

"To most people, my skills are confined to the reason I was selected for the Nobel Prize in medicine."

Jacob leaned forward, resting his elbows on the table. The headlights from a passing car shot a harsh light momentarily in the restaurant. "Reading the news about the Nobel Prize, I became aware of who you were, and when I read the name Paul Marcus in the last batch of Newton's papers, I assumed it was no coincidence. All that Newton got wrong was the way he spelled *Nobel*, referring to it as the '*noble prize*.'"

"Someone in your intelligence agencies has been looking into my background."

"How do you know that?"

"Because it was brought to my attention *before* I even left the states."

"By whom?"

"Someone I worked with at one time."

"You have a high profile. Our nations are best allies. I'm sure any inquiries are in our mutual best interests."

"Jacob, if you expect me to pry secrets out of Newton's work, I expect there will be no secrets between us."

Jacob raised a glass of wine. "To no secrets among friends."

Marcus lifted his glass in a toast and sipped the wine.

"How long can you stay, Paul?"

"I'll soon have to get back to my farm in Virginia. Neighbors are watching our dog and horses."

"Our? Do you jointly own them with someone?"

Marcus stared at the candle a moment. "I used to own them with my wife and daughter. Since their deaths, their murders, it's just me."

"Was the person who committed these atrocious crimes ever found?"

"No."

"I'm sorry for what happened to your family. Are you going to decline the Nobel Prize because of the tragedies in your life?"

"That's part of it."

"Which part?"

"It's the most important part. I wasn't raised to accept gratuities for something I really didn't earn."

"You are a brilliant man, Paul. You cracked the code to heal sick hearts. Yet your own heart is not so well. It grieves. Time is not the healer. Love, both given and received, is the medicine."

"You sound more like a rabbi than a scientist."

"The scientist in Newton calculated codes, and, as you said, events in the Bible are not unlike a jigsaw puzzle. But the theologian in Newton believed it could really be done. He believed he was actually *picked* by God to interpret his writings."

"God's writings were penned by man."

"And, in many cases, uttered by God."

"I have no illusions. I'm not a biblical scholar. I don't know what this information about the prime minister or even John Kennedy Junior means. I don't know what else is hidden in there. I feel that the more I find, the greater grip the information has on me."

"How do you mean?"

"I might slip and fall into a concealed hole, but it doesn't make me an archeologist. I'm not an anthropologist, a forensic investigator, or even a data analyst. But if I find this information, what does it signify? Is it truthful, accurate? Or is it coincidental? I feel if it's laid in my lap, it's up to me to do *something* with it."

Jacob grunted. "Of course, and I see you have your laptop. You mentioned sharing something else with me."

Marcus set his laptop on the corner of the table. "It'll take a minute."

Jacob smiled and stood, setting his napkin on his chair. "I'll use that minute to find the men's room. The last time I went to the bathroom, you solved a problem no mathematician in Israel could solve for months. I can only imagine what awaits me upon my return."

THIRTY-ONE

Jacob Kogen returned to the table as the waiter finished refilling the wine glasses. Marcus waited for Jacob to sit, met his eyes and said, "I want you to understand that I don't have any illusions about why I'm here. If I do find something more, something about Israel, what if it's nothing you can use?"

"Use? What do you mean?"

"If you are looking for a biblical prophecy that might help Israel claim all of the West Bank, it could all be a mirage."

"Or, Paul, it might be a vision. This has nothing to do with politics."

"Everything has something to do with politics. It's inbred in us like an incestuous hand-me-down curse that's as much of our genetic cell-base as evil. We can't scrub the smell out of our pores, even if we wanted to."

"My dream is one day the spirit of God will cleanse the hearts of mankind."

"My dreams are darker—like seeing the shooting of a Syrian general, shot on the beach in Cyprus. I'm sure you heard about it."

Jacob didn't blink for a long moment. A woman in the far corner laughed at a whispered joke. A paddle fan overhead whirled. "I read about it, why?"

"Because I think I saw it or something like it in a dream, maybe a nightmare, and I don't know why. Maybe it's connected to the prime minister."

"Perhaps it all ties in with your name in Newton's papers. Some kind of plan, if you will."

"My plan is to return home soon." Marcus took a long drink from his wine glass.

"I'm sorry you don't believe in the inherent goodness of man."

"Do you, especially after all the crap the Jewish people have been through?"

"I have to believe, because I trust in the good and love of God. Yes, there's wickedness, but I like to judge that it's overshadowed by good. The scientist in Newton understood the higher force. He said it was what put the planets in motion. I think Newton believed that with his heart, and his intellect."

"It may be easier to explain gravity than the force you mentioned."

"They are both unseen but yet felt."

Marcus said nothing.

Jacob smiled. He sipped his wine as the server brought two plates of fish and steaming vegetables. "This restaurant serves fish that were swimmers in the Sea of Galilee yesterday and even this morning. Bon appétit. Now, please show me what you have on your laptop."

"It's on my flash drive." Marcus plugged in the flash drive and worked the keys, stopping, eyes boring into the screen and watching. He ate silently while the processor crunched coding.

Jacob said, "This could be dessert."

Marcus said nothing, his eyes following the computations on the screen.

"What do you see?"

Marcus looked above the screen, meeting Jacob's eyes. "I'm not sure, but it might be one prophecy Newton uncovered in the Bible."

"Please, tell me what you see."

"Newton used the Hebrew calendar to figure timelines and events. Based on information he pulled between seven books of the Bible, basing much on Daniel's prophecy of seventy weeks, he calculated something no one knew. According to what I'm seeing here, Newton decrypted numbers that indicated the redemption or return of Israel would happen in 1948, and he made that prediction two-and-a-half centuries before it happened."

Jacob stared at the screen, then looked away, the candlelight dancing across his spellbound face, marvel in his damp eyes as moisture welled. His hand trembled reaching for his wine. "You have already made your trip worthwhile. You do have a gift. One day I hope you will realize who gave it to you."

THIRTY-TWO

The building sat alone. It was a Georgian-style mansion with the look of a quaint embassy on R Street in the heart of Washington, D.C. Poplar trees nearly obscured the building from the street. An ornate wrought iron fence encircled the property. Cameras were mounted inconspicuously around the exterior of the building. Satellite dishes sprouted on the roof in positions not visible from the street.

An underground garage, manned by armed guards and electronic surveillance, offered secure entrance and exits for men who were arriving in bomb-proof, chauffeur-driven luxury cars. The building was wired with a sound-masking system, emitting a blanket of white noise throughout the structure. The 20,000 square-foot mansion was renovated and secured with meticulous attention to security and subtle extravagance. It had thirteen opulent, executive offices with adjoining bedrooms and bathrooms.

In a secluded and secure conference room, they met. They were the most exclusive group in the world—the nexus of a club so secretive that the outer circle did not know the inner circle even existed.

They were thirteen disciples of global commerce, power and government—the brotherhood of the billionaires. All men. All in positions of great influence in international business and political positioning. They were the heads of multinational banks, worldwide private equity groups, insurance corporations, governments—the regulators who controlled the ebb and flow of money and power.

Most of the men had graduated from colleges and universities where their great, great grandfathers attended. The inherited acceptance and tuition, long since funded by bloodlines and trust fund cornerstones, was set as soon as the ivy-covered campus buildings bore their surnames like brands. Their contributions to these Ivy League schools also helped ensure the public's perception of family dynasties as benefactors to hallowed institutions of higher learning and research.

They entered the room wearing suits of armor—charcoal greys and blacks, hand tailored and woven from the world's finest fabrics. "Good morning, gentlemen," said Alexander Van Airedale. "Please, be seated."

The walls of the conference room were the hue of dark honey burled walnut, thick cut and polished. A four-by-six-foot plasma screen was built into one of the walls. A world map displayed on the screen, small amber lights marked capitals, such as Paris, Washington, London, Rome and Tel Aviv.

Alexander Van Airedale, early seventies, neatly parted silvery hair, took his seat at the head of the table. The other men, most of them older than fifty, sat around a conference table made from rare African Blackwood.

Van Airedale sat erect, icy blue eyes locked beneath his thick silver eyebrows. "Let's move to our immediate concerns, gentlemen. Please turn to the agenda on the first page."

Each man opened his folder in silence, the soft whisper of air blowing through a vent. Van Airedale put his glasses on and said, "Turkey is in need of pruning. Its branches are getting a little too unwieldy. We're sensing some unpleasant developments that might have roots going back to the damn Ottoman days, at least before the Ottoman Stock Exchange was established in the seventeenth century. What is the market capitalization of listed Turkish companies, Jonathon?"

Jonathon Carlson was the youngest in the group, fifty-three, short dark hair combed straight back. Face tanned from a long weekend on his 212-foot yacht, SOVEREIGNTY, lying in Bermuda. He said, "Market cap is just shy of one hundred fifty trillion."

Van Airedale nodded. "Russia's commonwealth states, its CIS, are pumping billions into Turkey. Now the country's first nuclear power plant will be built by Russia on Turkey's southern coast. How will this shape our interests there?"

A man with cotton white hair spoke. "We can expect to lose money, unless we secure a percentage in the proposed oil and gas line."

"How will this impact our interest in Tupras?" asked Van Airedale.

"It won't, at least until the power plant is built. Then we could see a drop in revenue."

Van Airedale adjusted the folder in front of him. "It seems as if part of the deal is now more than an economic partnership; it's becoming a political partnership as well. Moscow is sending more people into Syria and Gaza to meet with Hamas. The bankrolling of ISIS is cutting into our energy-based revenues."

Carlson flashed a marauder's smile. Bone-white, perfect teeth against a deep tan. "Our interests in the Middle East may become threatened if there's more interference in Israel, particularly the Palestinian issue."

"If—" Van Airedale said, his wiry eyebrows arching, nostrils flaring, "if Russia has been making money supplying weapons to Syria and Iran, then we have a capital infusion going on, and that would be huge. If the bear decides it's in the best interest of the motherland to build a nuke plant in Iran, then we will have to make some drastic arrangements. We'll involve China."

Carlson said, "They're already involved since they hold a trillion in U.S. Treasury securities making it the biggest lien holder of American debt."

Another man at the table said, "In these intelligence notes, the Russian president is quoted as saying that Gaza is facing a human tragedy and Hamas cannot be ignored."

A man at the far end of the table, the oldest in the room, a touch of cataract forming in his left eye, stirred his black coffee with a silver spoon. He leaned forward and cleared his throat, sagging flesh hanging from his neck quivering, tiny blue veins under his alabaster skin. "A lot of this garbage is fueled by the constant stream of information on the damn Internet. A mobile phone beaming video, a Facebook or Twitter campaign, can change world opinion. Israel doesn't get it or won't accept it. Stubborn."

Van Airedale nodded. "Order is achieved from chaos. Look at Syria." He half smiled. "Darwin said it best when he wrote that it's not the strongest of the species to survive. It's not the most intelligent. It's the one who can foresee change and adapt to it. As our forefathers knew, change brings order. World order generates productivity, stability and drives the global economies."

A man with thin, pale lips and thick glasses said, "Since we're on the issue of Israel, let's segue down to the last agenda item, if we can. I've been curious about this since I received the update list last night."

"What's your curiosity, Nathaniel?" Van Airedale asked.

"The agency indicates an American, not just any American citizen, but one that's up for the Nobel Prize for medicine, Paul Marcus, is in Jerusalem. Marcus also worked for more than nine years in the National Security Agency. He's reported to be working in some closed-door capacity at the university and with one of its top mathematicians, Jacob Kogen, also known to have direct ties within the Mossad. What I want to know is this: What's a former U.S. cryptographer, a top code breaker, doing there? Who the hell's he working for, and what are *they* trying to achieve in the Middle East?"

"He's said to be working for the Hebrew University on a biblical research project, something to do with deciphering notes from Isaac Newton as it relates to the Bible."

"That sounds like pure bullshit," Carlson said, his eyes darting around the room.

Van Airedale nodded. "Whether there's any truth to the university research story or not, we do know he's been inquiring about the assassination of Abdul Hannan in Syria. That's one of the reasons his name is listed here for discussion."

"Inquiring to whom?"

"Secretary of State Hanover, for one."

"What was his line of questioning?" asked Carlson.

"We're told he asked her if she knew who was behind the elimination of Hannan."

A dead silence fell over the room.

"Did she reveal this information?" asked Carlson.

Van Airedale shook his head. "No. The conversation was secretly recorded. We've long since planted listening devices in Madame Secretary's office." His grin melted, and he said, "But on a much more urgent matter, we have word that Paul Marcus has uncovered some information in his *research* indicating that JFK Junior's accident wasn't an accident."

The men mumbled and exchanged glances as the oldest member asked, "What kind of information?"

Van Airedale deeply inhaled and leaned forward. "Something to the effect of Kennedy's plane exploding before its unfortunate dive into the sea."

The table of men all seemed to grumble at once, some of them shifting weight in their European-crafted chairs. "Finally, gentlemen, Marcus seems to have knowledge about a planned attack on the Israeli prime minister's life."

"There must me a breach somewhere!" shouted Carlson. "We have to find and eliminate it."

"Agreed," said Van Airedale. "We'll see exactly what our Nobel winner knows before he accepts what may be his final prize on earth."

THIRTY-THREE

O n Monday morning, Paul Marcus turned on the computer in the university library and keyed in the files. He was alone in the room. He looked at his watch, his thoughts racing. *Tomorrow morning, in Washington, the president and prime minister would be laying the wreath at the Lincoln Memorial unless the ceremony was cancelled.*

Marcus watched the files load, and he looked for signs of hacking.

"Let's see if the mouse took the bait," he whispered. Marcus looked at the dummy files he'd labeled and encrypted. "The seal is broken, but the genie is still in the bottle, so I can find your prints." He punched the keyboard, fingers moving fast, looking at the door across the room. "Just connect the cyber dots…and it'll lead you to their source." He inserted a flash drive in the computer, downloading the source codes to the IP address of the hackers.

Marcus glanced at his watch, put a second drive in the computer and downloaded the files he had concealed, the ones the hackers could not find. Within forty-five seconds, he had the files on his flash drive and the drive in his shirt pocket.

Jacob Kogen entered the room. "You're in early today."

"Not sleeping too well. Sort of goes with the territory. Biblical prophecies can have that effect on you."

"You have made remarkable progress, Paul."

"What have you heard about the event at the Lincoln Memorial? Has it been cancelled?"

"I placed a call to the prime minister's office again this morning. He, of course, is in Washington. However, I spoke with his assistant chief-of-staff. He says the prime minister has been thoroughly briefed but is reluctant to ask another country to call off their ceremony or to cancel his requested participation just because, and I'm quoting here, a 'premonition some biblical researcher had.' He said he appreciates the warning but believes Washington is providing more than ample security."

"The Lincoln Memorial is out in the open, just like the damn Pentagon."

"Perhaps your people can persuade the president and—"

"And…what? Premonition? Jacob, that's pure bullshit! It's not the president's life that may be in danger." Marcus paused. "That is unless an assassin is planning to take out both of them. The ceremony is tomorrow. This afternoon I'm calling the states again. Maybe Alicia has rattled cages and opened some eyes."

"Alicia?"

"She's a friend." Marcus searched online for information about the Lincoln Memorial ceremony. "I don't see a story about the wreath ceremony at the memorial tomorrow. Maybe she *did* rattle some cages." Marcus leaned back, his neck stiffening.

Jacob sipped a cup of tea and then nodded. "God provides the tools, and you have been swinging the hammer like a master builder."

"But I feel like I can't get a grip. It's as if I'm trying to walk in quicksand. The more I struggle, the farther it pulls me in. The nature of deciphering is that of removing the layers, searching for the wormholes. But, when it comes to prophesy, events yet to happen, I can't tell if it's in the Bible because I either don't know what I'm looking for, or I haven't found it yet."

"You already have uncovered information that no other human has found. You revealed a code that indicted the death of President Kennedy's son, John, was foretold."

"But was the death an accident? That's what I don't know."

"If it wasn't, what do you do?"

"I don't know that, either."

"Maybe, like an Oedipus enigma, it will reveal more in time."

"I came here to disprove I'm the guy Isaac Newton jotted down in his notes."

"Is that really why you came? Well, you have done the opposite. You are handpicked by God to reveal the meaning of the words that bridge events from the Old Testament to the New Testament and finally lead us to prophecy in the Book of Revelation."

"Lead us? Are you trying to say I'm the guy God picked to tell everyone when the end of the world will come?"

"What if you are?"

"That's absurd."

Jacob folded his arms across his chest. "Think about it, Paul. What if you have no choice? If events like the death of a president's only son are in the Holy Scriptures, what else is in there? What if you are the only living soul on earth who can reveal what our Lord wants told for the world?"

"That's way beyond my grasp or pay grade." Marcus punched a few keys and watched the screen for a moment. "Newton seems to have believed that an ancient knowledge, some kind of sacred wisdom, was part of a chain that started somewhere during the time of people like Moses to King Solomon to Aristotle and so forth. Newton writes that Solomon's philosophy is found in the dimensions of nature, but also in the sacred scriptures, as in Genesis, Job, Psalms, and Isaiah, among others. He says God made Solomon the greatest philosopher in the world. Newton even went to immense lengths to draw the dimensions of Solomon's Temple, not from some old images, but from ancient text. I'll bring the image and his notes up on the screen."

Jacob pushed his glasses higher on the bridge of his nose and studied the image. "What does it reveal?"

"Let's see."

THIRTY-FOUR

*P*aul Marcus keyed in data and watched an illustration form on his computer screen. He said, "Newton had to translate and transcribe Hebrew from Kings in the Hebrew Bible into English to put together an image. I think he believed there was something to be found—some threshold in Solomon's Temple to follow what would lead to a mathematical resolution. He's noting here that the temple's measurements given in the Bible are numerical problems, related to potential solutions for the Greek number *pi* and the volume of a sphere, such as earth and our place and proportion to it."

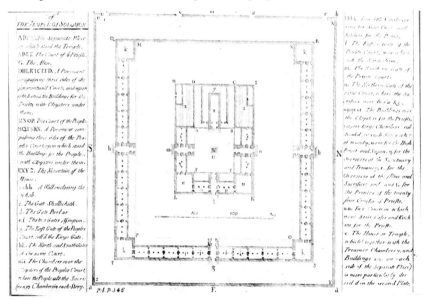

Jacob studied the image. "But *pi* is a pure number with no real measurable dimensions, meaning that it is simply a number without physical units."

Marcus nodded. "Exactly! So Newton was searching for clues, maybe measurements from Solomon's Temple, which might shed more light on all of this. But why did he focus on the temple?"

"Possibly, because there are many who believe in a sacred geometry—the cubit measurements used for the temple and other buildings."

"What's sacred geometry?"

"In essence, the temple may have been designed by Solomon, but it was inspired by God, and his hand was the primary architect, the one with the pencil on some ancient drawing board. The Holy Temple, and its dimensions, could be part of God's plan."

"Or man's plan, at least a fraternity of some of the smartest. Maybe Newton believed there was a common denominator between the ancient writings and the early architecture. What if Newton believed these men, people like Ezekiel, Moses, Daniel, Solomon and others, had hidden their knowledge in a multifaceted code? Maybe some figurative and mathematical language that, if ever interpreted, would reveal a deep secret—a knowledge of how the natural world works in tandem with the spiritual world."

Jacob grunted. "Perchance Solomon's Temple and other ancient buildings in the area were set with a divine cornerstone that supports a foundation of God's love."

"Yet, the temple was destroyed. Not once, but twice."

Marcus glanced over at Jacob, who placed his glasses in his shirt pocket and stood straighter, his shoulders round from poor posture. "Maybe it will rise once again."

Marcus stood. "I can't work here. Not on this computer. Someone is going to great lengths to watch me. I'd like to know who, and I'd like to know why."

"I thought our IT department rectified that."

"They tried, but the hackers are very good. I need to work off site."

"Where will you go?"

"Don't know. Someplace where what I'm doing can't be tracked."

"Does that place exist?"

THIRTY-FIVE

Marcus left the university in his rental car and drove through Jerusalem en route to the Old City, his mind calculating time zones and the possibility that time references could be a plant, a Trojan, to throw off a potential hacker. He looked at his watch, and made a call to Alicia Quincy's cell phone. "Has the ceremony at the Lincoln Memorial been cancelled?"

"Not yet. I don't know that it will be. I spoke with Bill Gray. He didn't exactly dismiss it, but he didn't see a lot of weight considering the fact you found it decoding Bible verses. You know Bill. For him, it's getting measurable, quantifiable data. It's always about intel information that comes from people and their political agendas, that sort of thing."

"Is he there now?"

"I'll check. Paul, what the hell's going on?

"I ran reverse coding from a hacker. The hacker sent in a Trojan, I baited it, and caught him on the return trip."

"I'm almost afraid to ask what you found."

"Because of the time reference, I suspect it's from a geographical source not too far from me. Can you run an IP trace on a secure Internet line?"

"You know that all NSA's lines are secure."

"They're secure from the outside. They're vulnerable from the inside."

"Where are you going with this, Paul?"

"If someone here in the Middle East is interested in my research, who is it and why? If it's someone else, who are they and where are they?"

"Have you found more than what you shared with me?"

"I could be on some kind of wild goose chase. The numbers don't lie. But, because I'm transferring them from Hebrew to English, I don't know if the letters and numbers I'm corresponding with are accurate. I don't know if these jigsaw puzzle pieces left by Isaac Newton and a dozen long-dead prophets are real or…"

"Or what?"

"Part of some bigger picture that may not be measurable by any scale we know. Whatever it is, apparently, this has caught the attention of people who believe I might find something, or that I might reveal some secret."

"Be careful."

"I don't know who I can trust."

"You can trust me. I have a lot of unused vacation time, and I've always wanted to visit the Holy Land. Maybe I can come there and help you with this."

Marcus said nothing for a moment. He stopped and waited for a group of tourists to cross the street at a traffic light.

"Paul, are you there? Sounds like your phone's fading. Can you hear me?"

"I can hear you."

"Did I say something I shouldn't have said?"

"No, no. I was just thinking…thinking about why I'm over here."

"You said it was by invitation from the Hebrew University of Jerusalem. Didn't you want to prove it isn't your name in Newton's notes on the Bible?"

"That's part of it."

"What's the other part?"

"It's complicated. At least I think it is."

"Do you want to talk about it?"

"Not now." Marcus drove, heading for Jaffa Gate. Out of the passenger window, he watched two black helicopters fly above the Judean Mountains. "I need to go."

"I understand. But I'm a damn good listener. Since you're overseas, you may not have seen the article in today's New York Times. It was about you."

"What did it say?"

"It's a story about the Nobel Prizes and how you were the only one MIA, still not officially on the roster to accept the prize. The reporter wrote that she'd tried to contact you for a comment, but friends and neighbors had no idea where you were. I guess it's hard to vanish off the radar when you're supposed to be a Nobel Prize laureate. Are you still planning not to accept the prize?"

"That's the plan."

"The story went on to say that your absence would be the proverbial fly in the ointment as an embarrassment for the president in his winning the Peace Prize."

"I'm sure the president will do just fine."

"You told me something earlier that doesn't align with your decision."

"What's that?"

"You said Isaac Newton wrote that a Paul Marcus is awarded a noble medal for healing."

Marcus said nothing.

"Is *awarded*, that seems to mean you not only won it, but you accepted it too. Did Newton know, or see something you haven't?"

Marcus felt the muscles in his shoulders knot. "Did you find Bill Gray?"

"Hold on, I think he's in the director's office."

"Interrupt them. Put Gray on the damn phone."

"Paul, I can't barge in there and tell him you're demanding to talk with him."

"Sure you can if you tell him the president's life is in danger."

Alicia released a long, slow breath. "Oh, boy. Okay, hold on."

Marcus drove through traffic, winding around sightseeing buses and taxis trolling for tourists. In thirty seconds, Bill Gray's voice came on the phone. "Paul, how's the president's life in danger?"

Marcus knew he was on speakerphone and his conversation was being recorded. "If the president's standing next to the prime minister tomorrow when the wreath is set in front of the Lincoln Memorial, he could be in the line of fire. If there's an attempt on the prime minister's life, there could be one on the president's, too. Or the president may be hurt or killed by being in the wrong place at the wrong time. The Pentagon calls it collateral damage."

Gray cleared his throat. "Paul, listen to me. This is really wild speculation based on the information you provided Alicia. We're taking appropriate action to spend more of the taxpayer's money to add additional precautions."

"Bill, save the money and cancel the damn ceremony…or, at the very least, back the prime minister out of it."

"Paul, this is Les Shepard." The director's voice was deep, almost guttural. "I never personally had a chance to offer my condolences for the loss of your wife and child. I can only imagine the stress you must have been under, combined by winning the Nobel Prize, almost by fluke. Your world goes from one extreme to the other—polar opposites. It's enough to make a man bi-polar, if you'll excuse the pun. The White House is not going to cancel the ceremony on the basis of some disclosure you stumbled upon in the Bible. It has no real connection to the prime minister or the ceremony to take place tomorrow. We do appreciate your concern, though. Maybe it's time you pack your bags in Jerusalem, come back home and get some much needed rest."

"So you're ignoring this?"

"No, we're deciding not to *overreact* to it. Now, I have a meeting to conduct. Paul, I hope you won't discount my suggestion to come back home and get some rest."

The line disconnected. Marcus held the cell phone to his ear, his mind racing. He pulled over, parked on the side of the road near Jaffe gate, opened his wallet and found the card Secretary of State Hanover had given him. He turned it over, memorized her private number and made the call.

THIRTY-SIX

After three rings, a woman answered the phone. Marcus didn't recognize her voice. She said, "Department of State, may I help you?"

"Yes, my name is Paul Marcus. I met with Secretary Hanover recently. She gave me her private number and said I should call it directly if I needed to reach her."

"Please hold, Mr. Marcus."

It was almost a minute later when Secretary Hanover came on the line. "Hello, Paul. How *are* you?"

"I'm fine, Madame Secretary. I'm calling you from Israel."

"How is your biblical research going?"

"It's a little overwhelming. I'm not sure how to say this, so I'll just say it."

"Please, Paul, what is it?"

"The president's life may be in danger."

"What do you mean?"

Marcus told her and added. "I wouldn't call you with this information if I hadn't tried channels at NSA."

"What response did Director Shepard give you?"

"He thinks I'm under stress, thought I needed rest. Secretary Hanover, I'm a scientist, not a psychic or somebody who dabbles in paranormal matter. I don't know if this warning is authentic or not. I believe too much is happening over here for me to ignore it. You have the president's ear. I just want him to be made aware of the possibility. It's his event, and he can cancel it."

"He's constantly reminded of the possibility of a fatal encounter. It comes with the job. I will tell him that we spoke. I'll urge him to consider the plausibility of what you're saying. In view of your impressive record as a cryptographer and a medical researcher, I feel he has every reason to believe you wouldn't offer this warning if you didn't think it was credible."

"Thank you."

"Paul, last we spoke you were going to consider accepting the Nobel Prize. Have you made up your mind?"

"I've been so swamped over here I haven't put a lot of thought into it."

"Time is of the essence now. I hope you will decide to accept it. Not because of the president's interest, but for yours. Don't feel guilty because the result of your work couldn't reach your daughter. It will reach the daughters and sons of many people the world over, and it's because of you. We are very grateful to you."

Marcus was quiet a moment, a tour bus roared by as he rolled up the window in the Toyota. "Thank you, Madame Secretary. There's something else. The niece of a friend of mine was one of the two people captured by the Iranians for allegedly crossing the border between Turkey and Iran. It's bogus. Can you tell me how close we are to getting them out?"

"Bill Gray brought your concerns to me. Unfortunately, it's not as close as I would like. We've had near daily negotiations with the Iranians. I'm sure you know they want the release of four terrorists in exchange for the freedom of two graduate students who were picking berries in a mountainous area where the border is poorly marked at best."

"My friend's niece is in failing health. She's diabetic and is in need of medical attention. I don't ask people for favors...but I am now. Please negotiate hard for their release."

"We're doing everything possible to reach an accord and get them back home. The unfortunate angle on this is our relationship with Iran, a terrorist state. It's no different than negotiating with terrorists, something this nation overtly does not do. We're hoping the publicity—the public outcry, will be the leverage we need."

"What happens if it's not?"

"I don't know. It's obvious that the Iranians are holding the couple as hostages. The president is very pragmatic. He does not and will not negotiate with terrorists."

"Maybe there's another way to gain the release of these kids."

"How, Paul?"

"Play cards with the Iranians. Put the chips on the table. Find something the Iranians want and dangle it in front of them. Keep it covert so the rest of the world doesn't think the president's cutting a deal. The Iranians look like they're being good guys, all concerned with the girl's health. They save face, and we get Brandi and Adam back. It can be done. It's a poker game; we can win."

"The chips on the table—what are *these* chips?"

"There has to be something more important to them than their request for some terrorists. As Secretary of State, you're in a better position than I am to know what to use for stakes in playing this game. Even if the chips are part of a deception and the Iranians don't win the hand, we can. The U.S. has done it before. If it's not common knowledge, the general public won't be aware that any negotiations were on the table. In the end, it would be hard for the Iranians to look bad if they get kudos on an international stage for a humanitarian release given for health reasons."

"We don't have any chips to put on the table."

"Yes, you do."

"Paul, I'm being summoned by the White House. It's urgent."

THIRTY-SEVEN

WASHINGTON, D.C.

A crowd, estimated to be more than seven thousand people, watched as the long, black Cadillac limousine made its way slowly down the National Mall in the direction of the Lincoln Memorial. The limo, flying the American flag on the left and the presidential seal flag on the right, was flanked by two black SUV's filled with Secret Service agents. Metro police on motorcycles led the procession. More black cars with government agents followed in the rear.

"There he is!" shouted a teenager to her boyfriend in the crowd. "The president waved at *me*!"

International television crews, perched on risers near the Lincoln Memorial, trained their cameras on the convoy. The signals, beamed to satellites, were carried live on television and the Internet to the world.

Inside the limo, the president turned to the prime minister and said, "We couldn't have asked for better weather. It brought out a nice-sized crowd."

The prime minister smiled. "I see many happy faces out there. It's good, but not surprising, considering the long history of our nations. I appreciate your invitation to be here today. I actually have a picture of President Lincoln in my office."

"I do as well." The president grinned.

"Did you know that President Lincoln was a friend of the Jewish people and did something in his term to prove it?"

"What was that?"

"I read that during the Civil War, General Ulysses Grant had issued an order to remove the Jews from states where his forces had taken hold— states such as Kentucky, Tennessee and Mississippi. When President Lincoln heard what had happened, he immediately rescinded the order. It truly is an honor to be here today."

— —

Alicia Quincy stood in the media room at NSA headquarters and watched the ceremony play out across a dozen fifty-inch plasma screens. Some were direct feeds from the television networks. Other images were coming in live via satellite, the pictures crystal clear from an altitude of two hundred miles above Washington.

Bill Gray, tie loosened, sleeves rolled up on his thick forearms, sat on the edge of the conference table, arms folded, watching. Technicians switched between cameras in real time, all video instantly archived on their server's hard drives. Four other cryptographers and two field agents were in the room.

They watched the president make a few remarks about the Lincoln Memorial and how Abraham Lincoln knew how to make difficult choices for the overall good of the nation. He read a few lines from the Gettysburg address and spoke of the eloquence and insight from Lincoln's words.

The prime minister was introduced and began speaking, citing the symbolism between Lincoln's struggles with a divided nation and the divisions in the Middle East.

Secret Service agents were everywhere, and they were the ones that were easily identifiable, dark glasses, suits, and eyes watching everything except the president and prime minister. Plainclothes agents filtered through the crowd, looking for any sudden or out of character moves. They had blocked all boat traffic in the Potomac River directly behind the Lincoln Memorial. Vehicle traffic was closed on the Arlington Memorial Bridge, Ohio Drive, and Independence Avenue. Two helicopters hovered, each about a half mile away in opposite directions of the ceremony. Two fully-armed F-22A Raptor Air Force jets circled high above the crowd.

— —

Marcus sat on his desk in the Hebrew University Library and sipped a cup of black coffee, watching the ceremonies at the Lincoln Memorial on his computer screen. Jacob Kogen nursed his usual afternoon cup of tea and sat next to Marcus while the event unfolded.

"So far so good," Jacob said. "I went to the wall to pray last night."

Marcus stared at the screen, almost not blinking. "It looks like the prime minister is ending his speech. He'll join the president to carry the wreath up the steps. This is where they'll both be the most vulnerable."

Jacob stood, folded his arms and said a silent prayer. "Paul, if they are both harmed...killed, it would be chaos, and one of the world's greatest tragedies."

— —

The prime minister concluded his remarks, and then the president invited him to help carry the wreath. Two helicopters circled. Secret Service agents moved through the crowd. A mockingbird warbled from a cherry tree while the prime minister and president carried a large wreath to a stand on the top step of the memorial, near the statue of Lincoln. More than thirty federal agents and dozens of uniformed police officers stood in front of the barriers that kept the crowd at bay. Officials had reminded the gathering that pictures from cameras or phones would not be allowed due to security concerns. Everyone complied.

Everyone...except one man.

He was tall, standing a foot over most of the crowd. He stood behind three people who pressed against the wooden barriers. The man lifted a camera above his head and pointed it toward the president and prime minister as they climbed the steps.

"One o'clock!" shouted an agent with dark glasses.

— —

In NSA headquarters, Bill Gray stood from the desk. Alicia Quincy hugged her arms; suddenly, she was cold.

"An incident!" Gray said, stepping closer to a plasma screen. "Take satellite seven!" The images on the screen switched to an overhead of the crowd.

— —

Marcus leaned closer to his computer. "They have somebody!"

"Does he have gun?" Jacob asked.

"Looks like it's a camera."

"Thank God."

— —

In less than ten seconds, two agents had the man's camera and were walking him to a spot near the reflection pool for questioning. He was held there as the president and prime minister set the wreath on the stand to the applause of the crowd. Using a wireless microphone, the president said, "Let the vision that President Lincoln had for people of the United States, his vision for peace, expand around the globe and touch the hearts and minds of the people everywhere. Thank you all for coming. The prime minister and I wish you a great day and a safe and enjoyable time here in Washington."

Within seconds the Secret Service had the two heads of state in the limo and began a procession to the White House.

— —

Marcus leaned back in his chair and let out a breath. He stood and looked at his watch. "I'm glad that's over. I guess the data was wrong, or that's not the right prime minister...or it's all something else. I'm just glad they're okay."

Jacob nodded. "You did what you thought was in the best interest of those men. Imagine if you'd done nothing and something tragic had happened. Let's find some food. I burned my allotment of calories for the day just watching those proceedings."

"If you don't mind, I'll take a rain check, I still have a few things I need to do."

In the secure building on R Street in Washington D.C., Jonathon Carlson sat alone in the conference room, the ceremony at the Lincoln Memorial ending on the large plasma screen, the images replaced by two Fox news commentators on camera. Carlson hit the remote button, the screen fading to black. He picked up a phone on a secure line and made a call to Moscow. As the call connected, he sat back in his overstuffed chair and smiled. When the former president of Russia came on the line, Carlson said, "I trust you saw, all went as planned. They had a massive security presence at the Lincoln Memorial. Israeli security was everywhere. Paul Marcus sounded alarms. Next time, they'll fall on deaf ears."

"The Arab states will soon be eating out of our hands, especially Syria. The plan of our fathers is coming together."

THIRTY-EIGHT

It took Marcus a few seconds for his eyes to adjust to the dim lights when he entered the Cafez coffee shop. A half dozen customers huddled around small tables and talked, some playing cards, others playing games on tablets and laptops.

"Welcome Paul," Bahir said, walking around the bar to greet him. "No one has claimed your table this hour. If they had, I politely would ask them to move for you."

"No need for musical chairs." Marcus smiled and took a seat at the table and turned on his laptop.

"You want American coffee, yes?"

"Yes. Thanks."

"From the first time I saw you to now, you had your computer with you. Do you take it to the bathroom, too?" Bahir grinned.

"No. I set some boundaries."

"I will get your coffee. Baklava, too? Made today."

"Okay."

Marcus keyed in passages from the Bible, broke sentences from plain text into numbers, scribbled notes on a legal pad and continued to plow deeper into codes—not of past events, but possible prophesies of the future.

"Here's your coffee," said Bahir, setting a mug on the table. "May I join you?"

"Sure."

Bahir grinned, pulled out a wooden chair, and sat across from Marcus. "Does your machine, the one with the window into the world of the wide web, bring you good fortune?"

"Right now this computer seems more like a time machine. Maybe it's because I'm using it in Jerusalem with all the layers of history here."

"Does it show you the account, the history of things to come?"

Marcus looked up from his coffee cup, gauging the old man's dark and playful eyes. "Where'd you hear that term, history of things to come?"

"Probably as a child. We recycle our pasts in Jerusalem." Bahir smiled and leaned forward in his chair. He rested both hands, palms down, on the table. "That night you approached the man with the long knife, you had no fear in your eyes. I could see it. Do you not fear your own death, my friend?"

"I don't dwell on it much. Not anymore."

"When a man loses his fear of death, he loses his zeal for life. The certainty of death gives life deeper meaning." He raised his shoulders, eyebrows arching. "Evil, like a leech, needs the blood of good to thrive. Good needs nothing but the present and a human host. Life is to be lived in the moment. For me, it is the time I am sharing with my family and friends. Has there been a recent loss in your life?"

Marcus stared at the steam rising from his cup. "My wife and daughter were killed. I buried them at the same time."

"How did they die?"

"They were murdered. Shot to death at night after I'd stopped to help a man change a tire. I couldn't help them."

"I am saddened to hear this. Did they find the person responsible?"

"No."

Bahir looked away for a second. "You are searching for the killer, yes?"

"Yes."

Bahir was quiet.

"I was left with my grandmother, our horses, our dog, and a lot of extreme dreams I don't understand."

"I believe something else died that night."

"What?"

"Your spirit. I feel it does not long for the taste of sweet air. It will not survive in the emptiness of the past, and it is not guaranteed a journey into the future."

Marcus drank his coffee and said nothing.

"Forgive me, Paul, it is not my intention to be intrusive. A man cannot run from his past because it travels with him. But we can learn not to give evil a room for rent in our minds. We can never escape from an oncoming train if we continue to tie ourselves to the tracks of past injustices. That man watching you the other night at Jaffa Gate, is he tied to your past?"

"I don't know who you saw. Maybe he wasn't following me."

"If he is not connected to your past, he could be predestined to cross with your future."

"But then we're not supposed to know that stuff, are we? Isn't that reserved for someone else? A lot of things are happening right now that I can't control. A month ago, if you'd told me I'd been spending a few weeks in Jerusalem, I'd have laughed."

"The Old City is haunted by its own ghosts of intolerance. They hurl it like a spear of bias. Their aim is to secure a destiny that is made from deceit and prohibits the holy tenets of most men and women—their belief in hope, faith and love."

Marcus studied Bahir for a few seconds. The late afternoon light flowed from the bay window across the shop and backlit the old man in a golden appearance. Marcus smiled and said, "Spear of bias. I'd bet there have been a few of them hurled around this place over the last three thousand years."

"The sharpest, most revealing, was never hurled. It was simply thrust into the side of Christ and out poured blood and water. Blood symbolized his walk among us, and the water representing his divine status."

"Your coffee is good, Bahir. Your viewpoint is compelling. Sort of mixes with the coffee like sugar. So, tell me, just *who* the hell are you?"

Bahir's eyes beamed. "I am your friend. You are my friend. Friends find a sanctuary in one another's hearts, and they help each other. You saved my life, perhaps a man at my old age might offer some guidance for yours."

"I appreciate the offer, but I'm not looking for guidance in a coffee shop."

"What are you looking for, Paul?"

"At the moment, I'm looking for some answers."

"What are the questions?"

"Why did my wife and daughter have to die? Why did I live? I still see the eyes of the killer. Why did he do it? Most importantly, where can I find him?"

"Sometimes those answers come slowly. Sometimes they never come. Today, we see through a glass darkly, but then we come face to face." Bahir nodded. "Like the puzzles solved by your computer. Now I know in part, but then shall I know even as also I am known."

"What the *hell* are you saying?"

"About your computer?"

"No, that reference about through the dark glass. Where'd you hear that?"

"God."

Marcus shook his head and half grinned. "You spoke to God?"

"Speak. Yes, I do, but I read that reference in first Corinthians 13:12."

"What do you think it means?"

"The passage is said to refer to our limited view and understanding of God when we are alive. The vision will only be clear when we die."

Marcus's cell phoned buzzed once. He picked it up from the table top and read the text sent from Alicia Quincy:

I will call you from a secure line in ten minutes.
Please be available. It's critical.

THIRTY-NINE

Marcus said nothing. He lowered his eyes to the screen and keyed in strokes.

Bahir watched Marcus enter data for half a minute. "What do you see? It is nothing but tea leaves to me. Perhaps you have the eyes of an oracle. Tell me, what do you see?"

"Newton."

"Who?"

"Isaac Newton, at least I see some of his writing."

"Ah, yes, Newton the believer."

"Believer? Most of the world seems to know him only as a scientist."

Bahir grinned. "At one time most of the world thought the earth was flat. Then believers sailed with hope in their sails and faith in their rudders."

"Newton wrote that the prophecies of Daniel and John should not be understood until the time of the end. But then he writes that some should prophesize out of them in an afflicted and mournful state for a long time, but *darkly*. He said *darkly* as to convert only a few people, and in the end, the prophecy should be interpreted to convince many people."

"But to convince many, it must begin with a few…maybe one?"

"If the deaths of my wife and daughter were foretold, that means they were planned. Who would *plan* to kill a child?"

"Is that what you are searching for, a sign God planned your family's deaths?"

"If these things are programmed or prophesied, then what's the use in doing anything if it can be undone by a divine plan?"

"Maybe all is not foretold, all not revealed. There are other forces that tempt the foundation, the hearts in men."

"The last time I was here you mentioned Solomon's Temple. Newton gives his estimates to the size of the building. You said a foundation might exist. If so, it would have to be below the streets. Do you know of any remnants, cornerstones and underground settings that might indicate the size of the temple?"

Bahir stared out the window, light from the setting sun floating in his black eyes. He looked back at Marcus. "You are searching for things perhaps better left in history, tucked away in the Old Testament and buried by centuries of armies, rebuilt and buried again. The temple may exist in God's kingdom, but no one since Christ has seen that. Discovering this information might take you to places no man would wish to journey."

"What are you saying?"

"The road may lead to edges of the world, above and below—to destinations unimaginable in the human mind. What if the glass is dark, like the surface of still, deep water and you only see the reflection of your own face? Or, what if you looked through the glass into the face of God? What would you ask him?"

"The name of the man who killed my wife and daughter."

"And, if it is revealed to you?"

"I'd find him."

"Then what would you do?"

"Kill him."

Bahir said nothing, his eyes filled with gentleness.

"So there are no underground areas, places marking the foundation of the temple, correct?" Marcus asked.

"I did not say that. There are no easy thresholds to cross. Many years ago, two British archeologists, Charles Warren and Charles Wilson explored underground Jerusalem."

"What'd they find?"

"They were looking for some of the original foundations of the Holy Temple. There are said to be many tunnels beneath the Old City. Some think they were looking to discover a secret room known as the Holy of Holies."

"What's that?"

"God's sitting room—a place of seclusion, a room for reflection. It is believed the Ark of the Covenant was, at one time, kept there."

"What happened to the tunnels, access to the underground?"

"Some tunnels have intentionally been blocked. Whether it is by man or God's hand, I do not know. This valley, from here to the Dead Sea, seems to get a major earthquake every eighty to ninety years. The last was in 1927. More than five hundred people died. In 1837, five thousand people perished. We are past due for another earthquake."

"Are there any tunnels, sealed or hidden, that might lead beneath Solomon's Temple?"

"Only someone as wise as Solomon could answer that. However, when the Queen of Sheba asked Solomon what are the most certain things in life, and what are the most uncertain, the king responded by saying, *The most certain thing in the world is death. The most uncertain, is a man or woman's share in the world to come.* For you to discover the answer to the second part, you may have to become a branch of the world to come."

"The world to come—you mean the *future?* No offense, Bahir, but it'd be nice to get a straight answer from you, Isaac Newton, or the Bible."

Bahir lowered his eyes for a moment. He raised them up to meet Marcus's concentrated stare. "Paul, the answers are there. Perhaps you are not asking the right questions."

Marcus's cell rang.

UNKNOWN

"Bahir, can you watch my computer? I need to take this."

"Of course."

Marcus stood and walked to the door as Alicia Quincy came on the line.

FORTY

"Hold on," Marcus said into the phone, waiting for two men on motorcycles to pass. A church tour group walking around him followed in the same direction. "Okay, I can talk," he said, stepping off the street under the shade of a cedar tree a half block down from the coffee shop.

"Thank goodness all went well with the ceremony at the Lincoln Memorial. Bill Gray said if I hear from you to let you know the sky isn't falling."

"What if it had? What would he have said if there had been a double assassination on live television?"

"Paul, Bill is your friend. Let's move on. Since you mentioned assassination, which leads me to the Syrian, Abdul Hannon, he was really an Iranian-born physicist. He'd gone to North Korea, by invitation, ostensibly to tour their nuclear facilities. It's believed he came back with extensive details, and a good working knowledge, to continue the Syrian effort to build a nuclear power plant in the area near the town of Palmyra. It's not publicly known who took him out."

"Who's suspected of doing it?"

"Mossad. They might be the same people trying to hack your work."

"Why, if I'm here on the invitation of the Hebrew University?"

"I can't answer that. But I had a friend at Cyber Command in Fort Mead help me. The hacker appears to be coming from Tel Aviv, deep in the center of the city. It could be the Mossad."

"Or it might be someone making it seem like it's the Mossad."

"If we heard chatter about you, so did others. Some of the computers we have now can cyber sniff twice around the world in the milliseconds it takes a person to blink once. No weapon on earth is that fast, and potentially that destructive if hackers can penetrate military walls or national power grids. Do you think the Kennedy stuff along with the information about the oil spill has somebody worried?"

"I wasn't right about an attempt on the prime minister's life."

"Maybe it had something to do with the assassination in 1995 of Prime Minister Yitzhak Rabin. Maybe you just uncovered it years after it happened. I did some research on that, the killing occurred near city hall in Tel Aviv. I couldn't find a garden or anything representative of a weeping angel near it. Rabin was shot on the fourth of November, not the tenth. Oh, that reminds me…I've uncovered information that indicates Yitzhak Rabin worked under that guy you mentioned, David Marcus. Marcus left Nuremberg after the trials got underway and relocated in what was about to become the State of Israel, but not until he helped them win a war. David Marcus, along with Rabin and others, such as Ben Gurion, were the chief architects of the Arab-Israeli War in 1948."

Marcus blew out a breath. He scanned his immediate area. Tourists strolled through the Old City, an international parade of cultures, stopping to examine the wares of street merchants who could read body language easier than the written word. Marcus felt a headache forming behind his eyes. "You know, Alicia, this stuff that keeps happening? Maybe it's for some kind of reason, and we're just part of the current."

She laughed softly. "Are you saying go with the flow?"

"It's as if the books in the Bible are definitive yet still a mystery of the world, part of the cosmos that's a mix of science and faith. I'm trying to find the edge, maybe the edge of time, to build some kind of clear image. But I can only find little pieces—pieces that alone don't paint a wide swath. It's like trying to look through a stained glass window, too dark at night and too colorful in the day."

Marcus paused, *the Ardon stained glass paintings.* He visualized the large stained glass windows in the Hebrew University library and thought about what Bahir had said, "Now we see through a glass, *darkly,* but then come face to face. Today I know in part, but *then* shall I know even as also I am known."

"What'd you say?"

"I'm just thinking out loud. It was something an old man in a coffee shop mentioned to me. It's from the Bible."

"Paul, I recognize it."

"You do? I didn't know you were a biblical scholar."

"I'm not, but my dad is a scholar of military battles and the generals who led them. He's a big fan of General George Patton."

"What does that have to do with the passage from the Bible?"

"I remember Dad talking about a poem that Patton wrote. It was called 'Through a Glass, Darkly,' and I remember my father reading it at the dinner table one night."

"Patton a poet?"

"Hold on a sec, I'll see if I can pull the poem up online and read some of it."

Marcus looked around the streets of Jerusalem. Women walked by him wearing burkas and dressed in black abayahs, worn from their necklines to their ankles. None looked directly at his face. Tourists crowded around booths and tables of outdoor merchants hawking everything from silk scarves to cheap jewelry and fake designer purses displayed on make-shift folding tables. It was a continuous garage sale on the ancient sidewalks. There was no wind and the air smelled of body odor, goat meat, leather and mixed incenses.

"Okay," Alicia said. "I have it. Part of the poem written by General Patton goes like this: '*I cannot name my battles for the visions are not clear, yet I see the twisted faces and I feel the rending spear. Perhaps I stabbed our savior in his sacred helpless side. Yet, I've called his name in blessing when after times I died.*'"

"Sound like Patton is making reference to Christ on the cross and the Roman soldier who pierced his chest with a spear to see if he was dead."

"If I remember my Catholic upbringing well, water and blood poured from the wound."

"Wait a minute…"

"What?"

"Something's going on."

"What do you mean, Paul?"

"All of this. A poem, written by General George Patton. The reference to first Corinthians. The spear. He said I wasn't asking the *right questions*. Call you back."

"Right questions? Who said that? Paul? Are you there?"

Marcus walked quickly back in the direction of the coffee shop. He saw some men cutting dead palm fronds from a tree. He stopped, his heart hammering, watching the men use curved, serrated blades at the end of long poles to saw off the dried limbs. Marcus wiped a drop of sweat from his left eyebrow, the scar high on his right rib cage tingling. He punched in Jacob Kogen's number. "Jacob, the inscription on the Ardon stained glass window—"

"Yes. What about it? Where are you?"

"In the Old City. The inscription references a spear—do you remember it?"

"It's from Isaiah, and I know the passage well. It reads, '*He shall judge between the nations, and shall decide for many peoples, and they shall beat their swords into ploughshares and their spears into pruning hooks—*'"

"Thanks. I have to go—"

"Paul, why do you want to know this? What have you found?"

"I'm not sure. I'll call you later."

Marcus stood in the heat, his mind racing. He watched older Arabic men, sitting in worn hardback chairs next to their shops. The men studied the approaching tourists, trying to determine their country of origin, and then choosing to greet them in the language of that nation. One man, Marcus noticed, was not watching the tourists. He was younger, muscular body under a stretched T-shirt. He leaned against an ancient stonewall, almost hidden in shadow, and averted his stare when Marcus looked at him.

FORTY-ONE

When Paul Marcus entered Cafez, Bahir was nowhere to be seen. Five customers sipped from small cups and looked up as Marcus walked quickly to the coffee bar. The man behind the counter was young, black hair cut short, wide smile, wearing a T-shirt that read: *World Cup* with an image of a coffee cup under the letters. Marcus recognized him. He'd seen him the night the mugger held a knife to Bahir's throat. He was the grandson who arrived in a car after the attempted mugging.

"Where's Bahir?"

"He wasn't feeling so good. He went home."

"I'm sorry to hear that."

"You were the American who helped Papa when the man pulled the knife. I recognize you. Papa said when you return to give you your laptop. Here, it's behind the counter for safekeeping." He handed the laptop to Marcus. "Would you like some coffee or a pastry?"

"Just water, please. Thanks."

Marcus took the water to the table, sat down and opened his laptop. He keyed in phrases from the Bible and notes from Isaac Newton, and then cross-referenced them with multiple layers of decoding.

... 'this is he that came by water and blood, even Jesus Christ; not by water only, but by water and blood. And it is the spirit that bears witness, because the spirit is truth. The lamb's wound shall yield blood and water...then the beast will breathe out a mountain of fire over the waters of the gulf...the sea will glow and become scarlet, as if the ocean filled with blood – destroying life in its path...

...he makes wars cease to the ends of the earth; he breaks the bow and shatters the spear, he burns the shields with fire...

...through a glass darkly...but then face to face...now I know in part, but then shall I know even as also I am known...

...and they shall beat their swords into ploughshares and their spears into pruning hooks...

Marcus stared at the screen, trying to make sense of the information. "What does it *mean?*" he whispered. He shook his head a moment and looked at his watch. It was after 8:00 p.m. He felt his stomach growling and tried to remember the last time he'd eaten.

Marcus left the coffee shop, his mind on the data revealed and its possible meanings. He walked through the Old City with no destination in mind. Soon he was in the Muslim Quarter. He took a seat at a sidewalk café called Abu Shukri and ordered a plate of kibbe, hummus, pita bread, and a glass of chardonnay. He noticed a security guard standing near the entrance to the restaurant.

As Marcus ate, he heard a shrill yell. An African Grey parrot in a cage near the restaurant door, squawked; and in a perfect Arabic accent said, "Special today baba ghanoush," followed by a laugh and long whistle. None of the other diners seemed to pay attention to the bird whose talents, amusingly, rivaled a carnival barker.

The waiter, an older man with a shine on his dark face, brought Marcus his check. "Was everything good?"

"Yes, very good. Thanks."

The man smiled like he was relieved. "I apologize for the delay in getting your food to you. We were very busy and my waiter didn't show up again tonight. I'm the owner. My wife is the cook. If you know of someone looking for work, tell him to come see me. My name is Radi." He smiled. "You are from the states, right? Which state?"

"Virginia."

He nodded.

"If I come across someone looking for a job, I'll tell them you're hiring," Marcus said, counting out the cash on the table. He got directions back to his hotel and walked down the winding, narrow streets. Soon he found himself on a street that had an occasional archway built over it connecting the buildings and walls on either side of the street. Marcus followed the twisting lane, walking west, hoping to find Jaffe Gate and his hotel.

He walked through the Muslim Quarter following the same tight passageway. He looked up under a streetlight and read the inscription carved into the wall: Via Dolorosa. As Marcus entered the Christian Quarter, he realized there was no one else on the street. He glanced down at his watch: 10:45. He continued to follow Via Dolorosa, the ancient stones underfoot bathed in a warm golden light from the archways. The only sound was the echo of his hard leather shoes against the stone street and walls.

Marcus thought about the data he uncovered from the inscription, especially the last verse, '*and they shall beat their swords into ploughshares and their spears into pruning hooks…*'

"Hey asshole! Remember me?"

Marcus turned around. A man stood in the shadows. Marcus recognized the nervous, high-pitched voice. He could see the glint of a knife in the man's hand.

"Set the laptop on the ground! Toss your wallet! Do it!"

"I remember you. You're the guy who attacked the old man."

"And I'm the guy who told you I'd slit your throat the next time we meet."

Marcus said nothing.

"It's nobody but us, dude. No cameras on this part of the street either. Put the computer down!" The man stepped closer, crouching.

"Do you think you're the first person who's pulled a knife on me?"

"I'll be the last." The man lunged at Marcus. The blade nicked his shirt. Marcus used the back of his computer as a shield countering the man's attack stance. The mugger thrust the knife. The blade hit the steel of the computer. Marcus kicked the man in the chest. The blow was hard, in the center of the solar plexus. The kick sent the knife flying out of the man's hand. He fell to the ground, wheezing and writhing on the street trying to suck air back into his lungs. Marcus set his computer down, picked up the long knife and broke the blade across his knee.

The man caught his breath and scurried backwards on his palms trying to flee. As he attempted to stand, Marcus grabbed him by the shirt and slammed his back against the wall. Marcus held him with one hand and drew back his fist. Then he stopped, the man's eyes wide, frightened and pleading. Marcus slowly released him, the man sliding to the ground, tears spilling from eyes now small and wounded. He sucked in air, chest heaving. "Go on and kill me!"

"What?"

"Just kill me."

Marcus could see the needle tracks on the man's arms. "I'm not going to kill you. You'll do that yourself if you keep sticking junk-filled needles into your body."

"You have no idea what I've seen. You couldn't understand the pain!"

Marcus said nothing for a few seconds. "What's happened to you? Tell me."

The man looked up at Marcus. "Why? I could have cut you."

"But you didn't. What have you seen?"

The man used the back of his trembling hand to wipe a tear from his cheek. "When I was thirteen, my entire family was killed when a suicide bomber walked by the market where my mother, father, brother and sister were shopping. This ring was removed from my father's severed hand. They found it, and other parts of his body, fifty feet from the bomb. You know how many times I almost sold this to buy drugs. That's how sick I have become…my father would be so ashamed of me."

Marcus could see a gold ring with a small ruby inlaid in it.

"How old are you?"

"Twenty."

"What's your name?"

"Mohammed Zaki."

"Mohammed, where'd you go after your family was killed?"

"I was sent to live in a crowded children's home for kids who'd lost families. It was an orphanage, one of the few ever built to handle Arab war refugees. I ran away many times, but always they found me. The people who operated the orphanage were okay, there were just way too many kids there…and they kept coming. Some without arms or legs. I couldn't stand all the crying, the suffering. I had to leave."

"Please, get up."

Mohammed stood, his back pressed to the stone wall.

Marcus said, "You're right, your father probably would be ashamed of you. So the question is what are you going to do about it?"

"I don't know. What do you care?"

"What's your passion? What would you like to do more than anything? "

A gust blew down Via Dolorosa, lifting a piece of soiled newspaper from the street, tire marks across the print. Mohammed watched it for a moment, his eyes shifting back to Marcus. "I'd like to direct movies one day. It sounds crazy, but I love film."

Marcus smiled. "It doesn't sound crazy. It's a goal you can begin moving toward today. You can die on the streets or change your way of thinking. Your choice. It begins by getting a job. Three blocks back there is the Abu Shukri Restaurant. The owner's name is Radi. He's looking for a good waiter. Tell him the man from Virginia sent you. To tie you over, here's some money. Spend it on food, not drugs." Marcus reached in his wallet and pulled out money. He handed it to Mohammed.

"Why are you doing this? I tried to rob you…not once but twice."

Marcus shook his head. "You're not very good as a mugger, and you aren't a killer. Maybe it's time to find your calling. Make some great films."

Mohammed looked at Marcus in disbelief.

Marcus picked up his laptop and turned back to Mohammed. "I do have an idea what you went through. You're not through it yet…I'm not either." He nodded and continued walking down Via Dolorosa.

Mohammed watched him walk away. He glanced down at the money in his hand. He looked up, the clouds parting, revealing a crescent moon hanging over the Old City. For the first time since his family died, Mohammed said a prayer.

Soon Marcus was walking by the Church of the Holy Sepulchre. He paused in front of the church, its ancient walls and facade illuminated in the light. Marcus felt a stab of pain beneath the scar tissue on his chest, the allusion of rain coming from the Hinnom Valley. He started to walk but stopped when he heard a sound.

There were sounds, soft sobbing coming from the church. Marcus stepped a little closer to the old church. The weeping was louder. "Who's there?" Marcus's eyes searched the shadows around the church.

A dark cloud covered the moonlight. The temperature dropped as the wind changed directions, the sounds fading in the cold night air. Marcus turned his collar up and continued his walk alone down Via Dolorosa. The only sounds, again, coming from his leather soles against stones smoothed from ages of those who walked before him.

FORTY-TWO

It was after 11:00 p.m. when Paul Marcus reached his hotel. His mind was on the coding and the revelations beginning to appear. Locals and tourists—mostly people in their twenties, strolled the streets, coming in and out of nightclubs, music and the smell of alcohol, tobacco and burnt marijuana following them. Marcus stepped up to his hotel where a woman was getting out of a taxi, struggling to carry two suitcases, a large purse and two canvas bags. She paid the driver, a razor-thin man with a gold-hooped earring in his right ear. He got back in the taxi.

"Let me help you," Marcus said, reaching for the suitcases.

She turned and smiled, blowing a strand of black hair from eyes that had the power of blue diamonds. Her smile was wide, eyes appreciative, accentuating high cheekbones and flawless skin. She wore a business suit, collar open, and a single strand of white pearls against her olive skin. "Thank you. It looks like the bell captain has the night off."

"Maybe he's on break," Marcus said, opening the door for the woman. He waited for her to walk inside. Even with carrying the other suitcase, bags and purse, she walked like a model, shoulders squared and back straight. Marcus could tell she had the body of a woman who spent time exercising, shapely legs and thin waist.

The bellman came from the elevator, a luggage dolly in hand. He smiled awkwardly. "Madame, please allow me to help." He took the bags while she waited for the desk clerk to finish with a customer.

The woman turned to Marcus and extended her hand. "I'm Layla Koury."

"Paul Marcus."

She smiled. "That's a fine name. Please, let me buy you a glass of wine for your help."

"It was nothing, really. I'm just glad I could—"

"Please, I insist." She looked up, her eyes searching the lobby, and then she smiled. "I'll check in and join you for a nightcap. It's been a long flight. There's a bar off the lobby. Give me ten minutes."

Marcus nodded. "Okay. A nightcap it is." He smiled and turned toward the bar, amazed at how quickly she had persuaded him to have a drink.

— —

They sat at a candlelit corner table, the expansive window overlooking the Old City and the Tower of David. Marcus felt uneasy. The woman was a striking beauty. She wore a trace of perfume, her full lips now with a touch of color, a suggestion she had spent a few minutes freshening up before joining him. He had not sat with a woman at a table like this since Jennifer was killed. A waiter approached. Layla looked at Marcus and asked, "Do you like a full bodied red?"

"Yes, I do."

"Let's not order by the glass. It's what the restaurants and bars want. If I may, I would like to order for us." She looked up at the waiter and said, "Please, bring us a bottle of Cabernet, the Harlan, 2003. Maybe an order of goat cheese, Chabichou du Poitou, if you have it."

The waiter nodded and left. Marcus said, "Your French is excellent. How did you know they had that wine on the menu?"

"Lucky guess."

"You haven't stayed here before tonight?"

"Oh, no. The hotel was recommended to me by a friend."

"What brings you to Jerusalem?"

"My work. I'm finishing my post-doctorate work at Columbia and doing freelance documentary work at the same time. I was in Egypt, Alexandria to be exact, for three months. The turmoil in that country cut my time somewhat shorter than expected. I was there because archeologists found more remains of the ancient city of Rhakotis. I'm wrapping my thesis on the spread of ancient Greek culture to the East, and the impact the Hellenistic period had on Egypt and harbor towns like Rhakotis. Dear ol' Alexander the Great was a fascinating man. He was never defeated in battle."

She smiled, the waiter returning with the wine and cheese. He opened the bottle, poured some into a crystal glass and handed it to Layla. She sniffed, swirled it in the glass and tasted. Her eyes closed for a moment, her mouth wet and sensuous with the trace of red wine on her lips. "Very good."

The waiter smiled and filled two glasses before leaving them alone.

Marcus nodded. "Maybe Alexander was never defeated because he was tutored by Aristotle, although a philosopher, I imagine he would have been a good coach."

Layla raised her glass and smiled. "To the ancient Greeks." They touched glasses and sipped wine. She spread cheese on a cracker.

"You sound American, Mr. Marcus, or may I call you Paul?"

"Paul works well." He half smiled. "Yes, I live in the states. And you?"

"Now I do. New York. I was born in Beirut to a Lebanese sailor and the woman who always waited for his return. But one day, he never came back. I was only thirteen, right at the time a girl really needs her father." She sipped the wine, her eyes suddenly remote, burying concealed thoughts.

"You mentioned documentary work, what kind?"

Her eyes drifted back to his. "I'm freelancing for the Discovery Channel as a producton consultant for a documentary they're doing on the cata-combs of the Mount of Olives. What brings you from the states to Israel? Are you here with your family?"

"No, my wife and daughter died. I'm here by myself."

"I'm so sorry." She paused and deeply inhaled. "What kind of work do you do?"

"I'm sort of a jack of all trades. You mentioned Discovery Channel… in a way I guess you could say, I discover things."

"What kind of things? It sounds fascinating."

"It can be exhaustively boring, but rewarding, too. I'm more of a mathematician, I suppose, than anything else. The Hebrew University of Jerusalem asked me to examine some old papers donated to the library."

"What kind of papers, if I may ask?"

"Some from the scientist, Isaac Newton."

"Really? What are you looking for or perhaps what have you found?"

Marcus smiled. He watched the candlelight flickering in her sapphire eyes. "I have no idea what I'm looking for, and I have no idea what I've found."

She tossed her head, glanced at the Tower of David and touched his hand for a brief second before finishing the wine in her glass. "You sound like a humble person. I like that in a man. Too many people want to tell you how great their work is and often it's not so much about the work as it is about them. I have a feeling you have done some splendid things in your life. You look like the strong, silent type." She laughed and reached for the bottle on the table. "Please, have some cheese. It's so good."

"I just finished eating. Look, thanks for the wine. I'd better be hitting the sack."

She set the bottle back on the table without pouring the wine. "You know, Paul, what I've learned in life, especially after uncovering so many long-dead civilizations?"

"What have you learned?"

"Life's too damn short. What do you say if we, you and me, finish the wine in my room on the balcony overlooking the Tower of David? We can discuss the Hellenistic Period in Jerusalem. Maybe watch the stars above the Citadel, and look toward the east in case a wise traveler forgot his GPS and is lost. What if some exhausted traveler is at the breaking point and seeing mirages in his journey across the Hinnom Valley and the Burma Road?" She smiled and sipped her wine.

Marcus studied her for a moment. "You make it sound like walking through the Valley of Death."

"What's life without pushing one's comfort zone? Let me rephrase, replacing breaking point with a more adventurous tone, like maybe stopping to explore a cave along the journey." She lifted her glass in a toast. "To adventure, Paul!"

They touched glasses, sipped more wine. Layla smiled and turned her head slightly, her eyes sumptuous in the soft light. There was a subtle change in her face, her eyes and even her body, lifting a slender finger to her lips.

She was controlled but still exuding a commanding sensuality that he could feel. He looked down at his wine glass, swirled the wine and met her eyes. "I do appreciate the offer, but I don't know much about the Hellenistic Period in this city. I'd be pretty boring."

"Something tells me you would be the opposite. Maybe it's the anthropologist in me, spending so much time studying dead civilizations...the Alexander the Greats of the world are so far and few between." She smiled and poured more wine into her glass, amiably waving off the approaching waiter.

Marcus finished his wine and stood. "Goodnight, Layla. Thanks for the drink."

She watched him walk out of the bar, reached in her purse for a phone and made a call. "He may be more difficult than first believed."

"He turned you down?" asked a man with a deep, yet whispered voice.

"If I can get this man to succumb, I want half-a-million dollars deposited into my off-shore account."

"Agreed."

"Give me two days."

"Do not fail. Understood?"

"Failure has never been an option."

FORTY-THREE

Marcus worked from early morning through lunch at the university library. Jacob Kogen had a full day of teaching and wasn't expected in the office until later in the afternoon, if then. Marcus keyed in notes on his laptop, shut down and went to Cafez, anxious to speak with Bahir. His grandson said the old man was still not well.

On the way to his hotel, Marcus put in a call to Mama Davis. "How are you?" he asked.

"I'm fit as a fiddle. How are you, Paul? I've been *so* worried about you."

"I'm well, Mama Davis. I miss you."

"I miss you, too. I had a nice visit from your friend, Alicia Quincy. She's such a delightful girl. And she's so thoughtful. She brought me some of that dark Ghirardelli chocolate I like so much."

"You need to remember your blood sugar, okay? Are they checking your sugar levels regularly?"

"Oh Lord, yes. Paul, have you found anything in the Bible you can share with me? I was telling Larry Foster about you. He's a veteran of World War II. He's eighty-seven and has a nice head of silver hair. His wife died seven years ago. Larry was in Germany during the aftermath of the war, too. He told me some fascinating stories about the liberation and the trials that followed. He's looking forward to hearing your Jerusalem stories. Now, my scientist grandson, what have you found?"

"I've found things that I don't really understand. I do believe that science and the teachings in the Bible can co-exist and complement each other. What I'm saying is I've seen things here that have opened my eyes to…"

"To what, Paul?"

"To a universal blueprint that's designed far beyond anything we can understand. We, mankind, seem to be the thing regularly out of balance in the harmony of design; and, yet, we're given so many chances to get it right."

"Remember, it's the journey and willingness to follow a godly path. I pray every night for you, Paul. Is your work done over there?"

"No…not yet. It's just beginning. Well, get some rest, Mama Davis. I love you, and I'll see you as soon as I can."

——

Marcus opened the door to his hotel room. He could sense something was different. The room appeared as he'd left it. He set his laptop on the table and checked the phone for messages. The light wasn't blinking.

"Nice to see you again, Paul."

Marcus turned around at the same instant Layla Koury stepped from the bathroom. She wore a thick, white terry-cloth robe. No shoes, her hair damp. She combed her wet hair. "I hope you don't mind that I used your shower. The hot water in mine was not working well. The hotel staff can't fix it until tomorrow, and they don't have another vacant room. There are few things I hate more than taking a cold shower."

"How'd you get in here?"

She smiled and stepped into the room. "That's not important. What's important is what can happen between lonely travelers." She stepped closer to Marcus, untied the robe and let it drop to the floor. Layla was totally nude.

Marcus said nothing. Her beauty was breathtaking, tanned olive skin, erect breasts and shapely hips. She moistened her full lips and stepped closer. Marcus could smell the scent of lavender soap on her skin. She touched his chest with one hand. He felt the heat from her palm against the scar on his chest. She used the index finger from her other hand to trace across his cheekbone and softly touch his lips. She then pressed a finger to her lips and slid both hands around his waist pulling her body tight against his. She stood on her toes and brought her lips to his mouth. Her sexuality was intoxicating.

"Who sent you?" Marcus asked, breaking from her kiss, the warm taste of her lips and tongue in his mouth.

"I told you. I'm lonely. I find you incredibly attractive. I'm not subtle when I find something I like and think that person will enjoy what I can offer."

"Offerings usually come with strings attached. I like making my own decisions about a relationship—"

"Who's looking for a relationship? Not me. Not you, too. What does mind-blowing sex have to do with a *relationship* anyway?" She smiled and ran her finger across his crotch. "Maybe you should listen to your body. It's speaking volumes right now."

Marcus caught her hand and lifted it. "Put the robe back on and tell me what you really want."

She looked at him in disbelief, her eyes taking in his words as if he spoke a dead language. She bent over to pick up the robe taking her time before turning around to Marcus. She slipped on the robe. "You have no idea what you missed."

"Yes I do, and it's more than an idea. You didn't break into my room for sex. You came here for a less superficial reason. So why don't you tell me what you want?"

She licked her lips and folded her arms across her breasts. "Okay, can we sit down?"

Marcus gestured toward one of the chairs in the room. He sat in another one and waited for her to speak. "Paul, I'm in a position to present you with a great deal of money for your services."

"What services?"

"I represent clients who are prepared to offer someone with your encryption skills a king's ransom if he or she can analyze coding that they believe will be infiltrating some of the state's computers and compromising them."

"What state? What computers?"

"Iran. As you no doubt are aware, Iran has a legitimate right, like any nation to provide clean fuel, electricity to its people. Our country is rapidly moving forward with construction of nuclear *power* plants, but there have been setbacks as other nations seek to disable the systems that control the power networks—the computers."

"Who sent you?"

"My overture to you comes from the highest authority."

"Then you can tell the highest authority to go to hell. I'm not interested."

She smiled, looked down at her long nails and met his eyes. "I'm in a position to offer you ten million dollars. Five million upon the agreement and the balance when you consult and add defense mechanisms to prevent a cyber-worm attack. The money will be in U.S. currency and wired into an account you set up in the Caymans."

"Like I said, you can take my message to the top."

"That's an unfortunate initial decision. Perhaps you need more time to consider the offer. We will be back in touch with you soon. I hope you will reconsider. We're not asking you to build a nuclear bomb. We're simply looking for you to prevent a cyber-attack, an attack that will further delay Iran from having what America and so many other nations have—the option and the *right* to include nuclear power in its grid. I will leave now."

She went into the bathroom and returned wearing a cobalt blue dress. Slinging her purse onto her shoulder, she stepped to the door. As she opened it, Layla turned to Marcus. "What's it worth to you, Paul, to have the two Americans released from Tehran. It would be a shame to have two people so young die in the hands of an executioner, their necks snapped at the end of a very painful rope. Our courts will sentence them to life in prison or to die for crimes of espionage. Maybe that will help you with your decision. Think again. We'll need your answer in the morning. Have a good night, Paul."

FORTY-FOUR

The next morning Marcus stopped at the hotel's front desk before heading to the university. He wrote a note to Layla Koury. Marcus printed her name on an envelope, placed the note inside and got the clerk's attention. "Would you leave this for Miss Koury? Layla Koury."

"Certainly sir. Do you know her room number?"

"No, I don't."

The clerk smiled and tapped his computer keyboard, his eyes on the screen. "No problem, sir. However, that guest, Miss Koury, may have already checked out. Her bill was pre-paid. No receipt requested. She hasn't been by the desk yet. Perhaps she will, if she is still on the property. In the meantime, I will send a message to her room phone and leave your envelope here, should she come to the desk."

"Thank you." Marcus turned and headed for the front door. Walking by a parked taxi, he recognized the gold hoop earring. He recognized the man's face. Marcus leaned toward the open window of the cab where the driver was listening to a soccer game on the radio. "Who's winning?"

The cabbie looked up through bloodshot eyes. "Not my team, that's for sure."

Marcus smiled. "Maybe one day the Americans will have a contender."

The man chewed on a worn toothpick and grinned. "I believe it is not possible."

"Two nights ago you dropped off an attractive woman. She had a lot of suitcases and bags. It was around eleven at night."

"I remember. It's not because of her beauty. I pick up many beautiful women in my taxi. I remember her because she had me sit in the side car park lot with her for one hour. Of course, my meter was running."

"Why'd she have you wait with her?"

"She said she was waiting for someone." The driver grinned. "Maybe that someone was you, eh? When she saw you come up the street, she had me quickly pull to the hotel door and begin to unload her stuff."

Marcus said nothing.

"Crazy woman. Now that she found you, my new football friend, I hope she was worth it."

Marcus nodded, stood straight and walked to his car. Pulling out of the lot, he headed for the Cafez coffee house.

— —

Marcus worked on decoding in the coffee house for more than two hours when Bahir entered. "How are you feeling?" Marcus asked.

Bahir grinned and lifted the palms of his hands in the air. "Much better, thank you. When you get to my age, the common cold is like coming out of surgery. Everything hurts."

"Earlier you said I wasn't asking the right questions."

Bahir smiled with his eyes.

"You mentioned the spear used to stab Jesus at the time of his death. What's more, you quoted a line that's the title from a poem written by General George Patton, *Through a Glass, Darkly*, and it alludes to the damn spear. What's this mean?"

Bahir lowered his body slowly, back straight, into a plastic chair and slid the chair closer to the table. He looked around the coffee shop and dropped his voice. "Some call it the Spear of Destiny or Holy Lance."

"Why?"

"It has been said, prophesied perhaps, that whoever has the spear, if he understands its secrets, its power for good *or* evil, he has the destiny of the world in his or her hands. This would make it one of the most valuable artifacts on the face of earth."

"Does this spear still exist?"

"I am not sure it can be destroyed, no easier than evil can cease to exist. Some of the world's greatest leaders and some of its most ruthless dictators owned the lance. Among these men are Constantine, Charlemagne, Otto, Frederick Barbarossa, and Adolf Hitler. Charlemagne is said to have carried the spear through forty-five victorious battles, but died not long after he, by chance, dropped it from his horse. It is said that whoever has possession of this lance is near unconquerable. However, should the owner lose or sell the spear, he or she will quickly perish."

Marcus leaned closer to Bahir. "If Hitler had possession of it, what happened to the spear after his death?"

"If he lost the spear, possibly it attributed to his death."

"Then who would have it today?"

"I do not know this."

Marcus felt his stomach churn. He looked up from the laptop screen into the old man's thoughtful face. "*Why* is this happening? Why's it happening to *me*?"

"We all have a destiny. Perhaps you are aligned to fulfill a *prophecy*."

"What is that supposed to mean? Aligned by whom? I came here to examine the work of Isaac Newton in reference to his research on the Bible. Now, all of this—the spear, the death of an American president's son, which now looks like he may have been murdered. I dream about the assassination of a guy I never knew existed and then read about it in the news a few days later, so he was alive when I had the dream. Then I see decrypted data that indicates someone is going to assassinate the prime minister. I can find things about other people, but I still don't know who killed my family."

"Perhaps you will in time."

Marcus stared at the laptop. "I've found something else that makes no sense to me."

"What is it?"

"Do you sell wine in this coffee house?"

"No, why do you ask that?"

"Because, after I read this to you, we may want a drink."

FORTY-FIVE

*T*wo Israeli soldiers entered Cafez, stepped to the bar and ordered coffee and scones. Bahir's grandson took their orders. The men waited, eyes scanning the coffee shop. They made small talk, paid their tab and left.

Marcus lowered his voice and looked straight at Bahir. "After deciphering the information or data I entered, the decoded passages read, '*That which has been sealed, the return of the lamb, shall be opened when the pears of the saint using oil returns to a divine heart. A clean force released deliverance from the heart of our Lord and left an open door upon the wounded hearts of man. As the ground shook, the blood fell from above to that which is below…water in the dust, the alpha and omega lies hidden as it is buried in the hearts of man. From the plot of those using oil from pressed olives, from the five crosses, to the head of the garden, one eye weeps for man, one sees revelation in the direction of the temple measured by Solomon. A rose without thorns blooms under a new sun. The truth is found fewer than two hundred shadows of the moon, for the shadow is to the seeker as the seeker is to the shadow.*"

Marcus pushed back in his chair. "My head's spinning. The deciphered information seems more convoluted than the integrated passages. What does it mean? *One eye weeps for man—one sees revelation in the direction of the temple measured by Solomon?* What the hell is this? "

Bahir grunted. "I do not know. I do know you get oil from pressed olives. It is said that five crosses represent the five holy wounds on Christ before he died. The two nails in his hands, one nail in his feet, the crown of thorns on his head, and the wound caused by the spear thrust near his heart."

Marcus touched his T-shirt. He felt the raised scar beneath the cloth. He said nothing. His eyes burned into the screen, his mind rushing. "What is the significance of *'a rose without thorns blooms under a new sun? And the truth is found fewer than two hundred shadows of the moon, for the shadow is to the seeker as the seeker is to the shadow.'* What truth?"

Bahir was quiet for a few seconds. "Some scholars have called the second coming of Christ as a new sun. The shadows of the moon might mean a reference to days and time of measurement. Perhaps you, Paul Marcus, are the seeker. If so, where is the shadow of the moon?"

"It's all riddles. You mentioned heart...the word heart is on the screen... divine heart. Before that it reads pears of the saint using oil...*the* saint using oil, not a saint. Who is *the* saint...a specific person?"

"I do not know."

Marcus continued staring at the words. "And you said one of the five crosses is a wound caused by the spear. The word *pears* on the screen can be formed to s-p-e-a-r."

"Yes," Bahir leaned closer, watching the light from the screen in Marcus's eyes.

"*The* saint using oil..." Marcus paused for a few seconds. "The words *using oil* can spell a name—a name I've never heard. L-o-n-g-i-n-u-s... *Longinus*. Was there a Saint Longinus?"

Bahir's eyebrows arched. "Oh, yes! Longinus was the Roman soldier who prevented Jesus' legs from being broken. To hasten death, the soldiers, men who grew tired waiting for the crucified to die, would break the bones in the legs. That meant those hanging on the cross couldn't use their legs to push up. Longinus thrust the spear into Christ to prove he had already died. This man, Longinus, was an old soldier, half blind. When the blood spilled from the wound in Christ's side, it is said a tiny bit fell into Longinus's eyes. The old man could see well for the first time in years. Not only could he see things more clearly around him, he looked up and saw that even in death, Christ had opened Longinus's eyes to what is and what can be. He devoted the rest of his life to spread that word. He would die rather than renounce his new faith."

Marcus was quiet. He didn't blink listening to Bahir. Then he looked down at the words on the screen again. His voice was just above a whisper.

"...a clean force released deliverance from the heart of our Lord..." His mind quickly rearranged each word. "...a *clean* force...clean can spell l-a-n-c-e. A *lance* force released deliverance from the heart of our Lord..." he paused, his eyes lifting back to Bahir. "How did you know where in this jumble of words to direct me?"

"What do you mean?"

"You *know* damn well what I mean. Every reference you made had something to do with a veiled meaning...a coding within a code. This disorder of text on the screen was what I decoded from interwoven passages out of the Bible against what I uncovered from Newton." Marcus heart hammered. "Corinthians...Isaiah...John...Matthew Daniel...Revelation, seemingly unrelated verses from the Bible, but by using a decryption formula I worked out from Isaac Newton, it reveals this..." Marcus moistened his lips. "And then you point me subtly in a direction to pick up key words. Why?"

"I don't know all the things your computer speaks. Maybe it understands how to sing in harmony with the Song of Songs. Ah, what a lovely song that would be! Music that rocks the cradle of man with a sweetness of verse that is from the heart. It tells us we are not swallowed up in the emptiness of infinity, and in nature our worth is measured and returned by the love we have for others."

Marcus shook his head, pinched the bridge of his nose and pushed back in the chair. "Understanding you is like cracking some damn code. It's frustrating."

Bahir's eyes drifted away.

Marcus said, "Why don't you just go on and spell out the rest? And while you're at it, see if you can find out the name of the man who killed my family."

"I wish I knew that, Paul, but I do not."

"You seem to know a lot...more than you're telling me."

Bahir said nothing.

Marcus used the palms of his hands to rub the fatigue from his eyes. "What does it mean when it reads that *'from the plot of those using oil from pressed olives, from the five crosses, to the head of the garden, one eye weeps for man, one sees revelation in the direction of the temple measured by Solomon...a rose without thorns blooms under a new sun. The truth is found fewer than two hundred shadows of the moon, for the shadow is to the seeker as the seeker is to the shadow."*

"I can only guess."

"What's your guess?"

"Gethsemane."

"What?"

"It could be the garden near the base of the Mount of Olives. The word Gethsemane, in the Syriac language, means oil press or a place olives are pressed for oil. Gethsemane is where Christ was taken prisoner the night before he was crucified."

Marcus concentrated on the words displayed on screen. "It reads…'plot of those *using oil* from pressed olives…' Is it referring to plot of land or a plot as in to conspire?"

"Some refer to a garden as a plot of land."

"The word Longinus…it can spell out *guns n oil*. But what does that mean? It concludes with. *'The truth is found fewer than two hundred shadows of the moon, for the shadow is to the seeker as the seeker is to the shadow…from the five crosses, to the head of the garden.'* "

Marcus closed his eyes for a moment, his thoughts focusing. "Maybe there's something at the head of the Gethsemane garden that's weeping, pointing toward a nonexistent Solomon's Temple."

Bahir nodded. "Perchance it is another temple with the dimensions laid out by Solomon."

"What temple? Where on earth would that exist?"

"I do not know. Something at the head of a garden may point the way."

FORTY-SIX

*B*ill Gray wasn't looking forward to the meeting. The phone call had been abrupt, almost accusatory. How long had it been since he'd seen his former Georgetown classmate? Four, maybe five years? Gray sat on a park bench overlooking the Lincoln Memorial Reflecting Pool and waited for Liam Berenson to arrive. The wind across the water was cold, the surface of the pool rippling like aged skin over the dark pewter water. Gray watched a leaf fall from a cherry tree, one of the few leaves remaining in the tree as nature stripped down for the change of seasons.

"Right on time, as usual."

Gray turned around as Berenson approached. He sat on the bench, glanced at Gray and said, "Good to see you, Bill."

"How's the CIA treating you?"

"Probably not as good as NSA is treating you."

"What's this about, Liam? Neither of us is in the field anymore."

Berenson's narrow face was wind-burned, his cheeks flushed. He looked over the tops of his glasses, his eyes watery, gunmetal grey irises intent. He said, "Paul Marcus has or may be turning."

"What do you mean?"

"We've been following one of Iran's best operatives. She has half a dozen aliases, of course, but her real name is Taheera Khalili. One of her emails, after bouncing from servers all over the world, went to a cell phone we traced to Paul Marcus."

"If Paul received a message from this operative, it's probably because it has something to do with what he's doing, which is the last thing from some kind of breach."

"What's he working on, Bill? Beyond the cry of wolf in the alleged assassination attempt of the prime minister, less than a few hundred yards from where we're sitting right now, what's he really doing there? No one in all the channels of protocol is completely clued in to what our controversial Nobel Prize guy is doing…except you. Why the hell is one of NSA's best former cryptographers contacting an Iranian field agent?"

"She probably solicited him. Paul's no hack. I told you that he's researching some lost papers from Isaac Newton that were donated to the Hebrew University in Jerusalem. He's there by invitation. The Iranians, for that matter, and most covert agencies know who he is and now probably where he is, too. I've asked Paul to keep his ears and eyes open, that's all. It's that simple."

"Not anymore. You reel him in, and do it quickly, or we'll have him shipped back to Langley."

"What's going on, Liam? Who's making this call and why?"

"Do us both a favor and bring Marcus in for a thorough debriefing." Berenson nodded, got up, and left. He walked fast by the reflecting pool, a flock of pigeons scattering beneath his brown wingtip shoes.

FORTY-SEVEN

Marcus walked through the narrow streets of the Old City, the sidewalk merchants sitting by Persian rugs and trays of jewelry. Rainbow colors of scarves and shawls hung at eye-level from walls and clotheslines strung between the aged storefronts. Some of the barkers waved tourists over to them with smiles and body language that suggested they had the lowest prices.

Marcus thought about his last conversation with Bahir. *'It has been said, prophesied perhaps, that whoever has the spear, if he understands its secrets, its power for good or evil, he may have the destiny of the world in his hands. This would make it one of the most valuable artifacts on the face of earth.'* Marcus called Alicia and said, "As a scientist, there was always a clear line between science and religion. One is data driven, the other spiritual. But now I'm seeing how factors of religion—the unseen, can feed the science."

"Sometimes the lines can get blurred," she said.

"But can they corroborate each other? You'd mentioned your father is a military scholar, right? General Patton is his specialty?"

"Yes, Dad's maybe one of the best. Why?"

"If Patton's forces found the spear that was used to stab Christ, if they removed it from Hitler...what became of it? It was called the Spear of Destiny. The legend is that the spear holds some kind of power for whoever possesses it. A dozen of the world's most prominent or dominant rulers are said to have possessed the spear at one time. Hitler may be the last one...

unless General Patton found it. Alicia, I think this spear holds the key to a code I found between Newton and the Bible. If Patton found it, did he return it…or keep it? I know this sounds crazy coming from a guy who has studied science all his life…but the spear allegedly has as much of a curse as it may have power. If its claimed owner loses it…he or she soon dies. Did Patton have it in his possession before his death?"

"I don't know if my dad has *that* information, but I'll ask him. It could take his mind off the cancer. I'll do some research, too. Speaking of research, I found information that points to another odd thing about General Patton after the war."

"What's that?"

"He apparently acquired, maybe stole, documents known as the Nuremberg Laws."

"What are they about?"

"Essentially, they were the dictator's constitution, drawn up by Hitler and his henchmen, that set into motion the process that would lead to the extermination of more than six million people in Europe. The laws consisted of three decrees. One was the law for the safeguard of German blood and what they called German honor. This called for the prohibition of marriage or sex between Aryans and Jews. The next was known as the Reich's Citizen Law, which defined a citizen of the German Reich as one of German blood. The third was called the Reich's Flag Law, and that defined the flag of the Nazi state. Why Patton had these original papers is anyone's guess. They were papers the prosecutors in the Nuremburg Trials needed to use against many of the Nazis criminals. Prosecutors had to resort to using *copies* of the originals."

"What'd Patton do with the originals?"

"He donated them to the Huntington Library in California about a month before he was killed. This same library has the rare Gutenberg Bible. I found out it was printed about 1450 in Mannheim, Germany. The text is in Latin."

Marcus was silent for a moment.

"Paul, are you there?"

"Patton died in Mannheim, Germany. You mentioned that David Marcus played a big role in the Nuremberg Trials, helping to choose who would face charges and the penalties available to the court under war crimes against humanity."

"Yes. What's all that noise in the background?"

"I'm at the Western Wall. People are praying...some are chanting. Alicia, something happened that I want you to know about."

"What?"

Marcus described Layla Koury, the conversations, and said, "She's probably working as an agent out of Tehran. I told her she could deliver a *no thank you* to her director. It was then she mentioned the two Americans being held, and suggested if I cooperated they wouldn't be convicted and risk a death sentence."

"Dear God!"

"The question is this: did Layla Koury *know* of my connection to you, or is it a coincidence that she mentioned the two Americans being held by Iran?"

"I don't know."

"It wouldn't be that hard for that information to be available. Tehran can quickly trace most family and public information connections to your niece Brandi and her boyfriend, Adam. But do the Iranians know you and I have talked...or that I've asked Secretary Hanover to intercede?"

"I wish I knew. What do we do now? How do I tell my sister? Bill Gray has to know. Maybe the president can do something."

"Let's sit on this a little while—"

"Sit on it! Why, Paul? They might *execute* my niece!"

"Not yet, they won't. It's too high profile. And they want something from me."

"Why don't you want me to say something to—?"

"The less we say to anyone right now, the better. Trust me here, Alicia. I have a feeling that the road paved to the capture of your niece was actually planned years ago."

FORTY-EIGHT

Alicia Quincy pulled into the driveway of an English Tudor-style home in Alexandra, Virginia. An indication of her father's illness was in the yard. Leaves. The front yard was covered in autumn leaves. Her father always raked and bagged the leaves before they had time to accumulate. She parked and walked through ankle-deep foliage from the maple and oak trees. The trees surrounded the home, the place where she spent her childhood. She thought about Halloween approaching, how delighted her parents were to hand out candy. *Now only Mom could do it.* Alicia felt it was odd how things like that come to mind when a parent has terminal cancer.

She used her key to unlock the front door and let herself inside. The home smelled different. There was the odor of disinfectant, bleach and medicine. She entered the family room where her dad was sleeping in a large recliner. She looked at his ashen face, heard his raspy breathing. He'd lost so much weight, grey hair thinning, dark circles under eyes that were always so bright, so proud and protective of her. She leaned down and kissed him on the cheek.

"Alicia, I didn't know you were coming. I would have had something prepared for you to eat." Her mother, Helen, came in from the kitchen and gave her a hug. Somehow, to Alicia, her mother looked smaller—almost as if she'd aged in the ten days since Alicia had last seen her. Helen's hazel eyes were red and puffy, shoulders more rounded, the creases deeper in her face.

Alicia said, "That's why I didn't call, I didn't want you to go to the trouble of fixing something. Besides, I already ate breakfast. How's Dad doing?"

Helen looked down at her sleeping husband. "He's a fighter, but the fight is draining him. I can see it in his spirit. Jane from hospice just left. They've been so good. Your father's taking painkillers. He's been sleeping for a couple of hours."

"How *are* you, Mom?"

"I'm okay I suppose. I'm trying to keep on keeping on, and it isn't easy when your father is so sick. We've been married almost forty years now." She blinked back the tears. "With what's happened to Brandi, and with your father's cancer…I guess a person can reach her breaking point. I tried to be strong for your sister, but Dianne and I broke down yesterday, hugged and cried for an hour. Have you heard any news about Brandi and Adam?"

"I hear they're being treated well. We're working hard to get them out. They'll be home soon, Mom."

Her mother nodded and tried to smile. "Let me put on some tea."

Alicia nodded. "That'd be good, thanks."

Helen left the room. Alicia pulled a chair up next to her father's recliner and adjusted the blanket across his chest. His eyelids fluttered and opened. Sam Quincy smiled when he saw his daughter. "Alicia, are you really here?"

"Yes, I'm here Dad. How are you feeling?"

"I've had some better days…and now that you're here, today will make it one of those better days."

Alicia smiled and held her father's hand. "Dad, we'll get Brandi out of Iran soon, okay? I want you to know that."

"I believe you will, I do." He managed to smile.

"I've been doing some research at work, and the subject is something you know well."

"What's that, sweetheart?" He coughed.

"World War II, specifically General Patton."

Her father's eyes opened wider, a sense of vigor now blooming in his face. "What about Patton?"

"I remember that poem you read to me and Dianne when we were kids, the one that Patton wrote."

"You mean, *Through a Glass, Darkly?*"

"Yes, that's the one."

"What about it?"

"Patton makes reference to a spear, maybe the same one that pierced the side of Jesus. Patton supposedly recovered some religious artifacts from Hitler, including what's been referred to as the Spear of Destiny. I wonder what ever happened to it."

"Well, General Patton was in a minor car accident right before he was scheduled to fly home from Germany. He died in an Army hospital a week or so later in Mannheim. There are those who think he kept that spear for a good long time. But who really knows."

"Dad, do you think Patton died from injuries sustained in the accident, or did someone kill him?"

Her father raised his eyebrows. "That's a good question. There are numerous conflicting reports. What we know is he was the only one hurt in the accident. No one else had a scratch. An autopsy wasn't done on the body. It's no secret that Patton and Eisenhower came to despise each other. When Patton accused Eisenhower of caring more about a career in politics than conducting his military job, Ike relieved Patton of his duties and ordered him to come back to the States. The speculation part of all this is who'd want George Patton dead? Ike may have thought Patton was capable of dragging the nation into a war with Russia down the road. Stalin hated his guts, and the feeling was mutual. The Germans were too whipped to retaliate against Patton."

"Did you know Patton removed the original set of the Nuremberg Laws out of Germany right before the tribunals were to begin?"

"Yes, but that wasn't known by many until that library in California, where the papers were stored in a vault for fifty-five years, decided to give 'em to the National Archives in Washington. The document was just four pages, but long enough to set the ground work to create Nazi, Germany, and they were signed by Hitler."

"Do you know anything about the others in the car with Patton at the time of the accident, or the men in the truck that hit Patton's car?"

Sam grinned. "My daughter suddenly sounds like an attorney. I remember reading that the fella who actually hit Patton's car—what the hell was his name?"

"I can find it."

"Okay, anyway, I read that he was flown out of there pretty damn quickly. On whose orders, I don't know. I'm trying to recall something a war veteran told me long ago. These drugs have my mind scattered…but it was something about Stalin and Patton. I just can't remember."

"Don't strain yourself, Dad. Was there anyone else in the truck with the driver?"

"Yes, as a matter of fact, and I do remember his name. James Tower. He was a British officer, one of the Allies who stayed around to help with the clean-up."

"Dad, do you believe Patton wrote that poem, *Through a Glass, Darkly*, because he'd found and kept the spear?"

Sam inhaled and coughed, causing a touch of pink flowering in his cheeks for a second. "Who the hell knows? Ike ordered Patton to return it and all the other religious artifacts the Germans had stolen from the Hofburg Palace and Museum in Vienna. The rumor was that Patton hung on to this spear, and some say he kept it with him at all times…maybe up to his death. Alicia, why this sudden interest?"

She smiled and squeezed his hand again.

Sam said, "I know, you can't tell me. It's all part of your job, right?"

"Right."

Sam coughed.

"Can I get you some water?"

"No, I only use that stuff to bathe in. I could handle a shot of scotch, though."

"I'll ask Mom to make sure it won't be an adverse mix with your medication."

Sam looked toward the pictures of his family on the wall and said, "A mixture like that might kill me."

Alicia smiled at his joke and touched his shoulder. "I love you, Dad."

"I love you, too, sweetheart."

She stood and kissed her father on the forehead.

"I just remembered something else about the British officer, James Tower."

"What's that, Dad?"

"I read that he spoke fluent German, Russian and Italian."

FORTY-NINE

*P*aul Marcus stood near the Western Wall, the sound of people praying in the background. His mind replayed the conversations he'd had with Bahir about Solomon's Temple, its size, and its possible location. He watched Jewish men pray at the face of the wall in a separate area from the women. A fence divided them. Some of the women stood on plastic chairs in order to see over the fence where their husbands and sons prayed. Marcus saw a teenage Jewish boy write on a small slip of paper, whisper a request, and place the paper in a crack between the old stones.

Marcus moved on, strolling through the tide of worshipers, tourists and spiritual pilgrims. They were seeking the touch of a stone wall, the splash of water from an ancient cistern, the scent of anointment oils, the physical cornerstones to harden and set with their internal cathedrals of faith often flawed with hairline cracks.

Marcus glanced up at the Dome of the Rock and the Al-Aqsa Mosque near it. He discreetly observed the Muslims, Christians, and Jews all walking the same streets, together, in a city of contradictions and denial, its borders drawn in the heated sands of conviction. The four quarters of the Old City were communities on the edge, alienated by suspicion and hypothesis. Synagogues, mosques, and churches stood on a two-thousand-year-old stage of non-scripted drama, playing to a world audience where everyone in the house was a critic. Marcus could smell sun block lotion, sweat and cigarette smoke on the clothes of the people he passed. He brushed by a man who stared at him a second too long.

"Paul Marcus."

Marcus turned around. The man was short, balding, early sixties, face heavily lined, dark glasses and wearing a polo shirt outside his khaki Bermuda shorts. He wore sandals. "I'm actually a friend of Jacob Kogen. There's a nice café a few meters to the west. Please, let me buy you a coffee. I'd like to discuss something with you."

"Who are you?"

"I sincerely appreciate the information you delivered about a possible assassination attack on the prime minister. I'm thankful to God that no such attack was made. My name is Nathan Levy. I work for the Israeli government." The director of the Mossad smiled.

"What do you want to talk about?"

"Please, let's sit where it's quiet. As much as I love the old wall, the prayers can become way too loud when many people are here."

Marcus nodded and followed the man to the café. They went inside and took a seat in the far corner, Levy's back to the wall. They ordered coffees and Levy said, "I speak for Jacob and all of Israel, really, when I say we are most appreciative of your efforts to decode the mysteries of the Bible."

"It's not me. It's the vast knowledge Isaac Newton had of the Bible, the people—all the tribes, events and languages. I'm just trying to sort through the cards in the deck."

"It appears that you are making remarkable strides, as you did to receive the Nobel Prize honor, too."

Marcus said nothing, waiting for Levy to tell him what he wanted.

"May I call you Paul?"

"Yes."

"Please, call me Nathan. I imagine that a man of your intellect could do almost anything he engaged his mind to do. You have certainly proven that. In all my years, if there's one thing that I've found to be a constant is that intellect alone is like a boat on top of the water. The engine, the thing that propels a person is the drive—often the entrepreneurial shrewdness required to lessen the drag that can cling to a vessel. Your code breaking effort in medicine is a colossal example of that drive, that quality."

A customer entered the small café and ordered from the counter. Levy sipped his coffee. "Why are we here?" Marcus asked.

"An old friend of mine, Andy Jenkins, was once stationed in Tel Aviv by your government for almost two decades. I was hoping he would eventually retire here. However, his last three years were in Saudi Arabia before retiring in Washington. We often sat in this café, at this very table, and talked about the world in which we live. Andy was injured in a car crash near the West Bank. For years after, he still walked with a limp. He understood the emotional state of the Middle East, and he identified with the *soul* of Israel. Our tiny nation is and always will be a target. For centuries, we were always the moving targets. But not up until now, this very time, have we ever faced possible complete annihilation as a country and potentially as a people."

"Are you suggesting a feasible nuclear threat?"

"The Iranians are dangerously close to having nuclear bomb capabilities. Once they do, they will continue their output until they have an arsenal large enough to rein terror, not just on Israel, but the world. Because, Paul, they are not alone."

"Why are you telling me this?"

"You may be the one person who can stop or greatly delay their nuclear efforts."

"Is this *why* I was really brought over here, to help Israel fight Iran?"

"It's not a fight. It is a chessboard with global consequences. Perhaps you will find a needle in the proverbial haystack with the Bible codes and that Newton matter. In the meantime, Iran, Syria, and the Hamas threats aren't simply going to fade like smoke. What I'm about to tell you is extremely confidential. Only a handful of people know. However, in good faith, we feel that to show you our sincerity, to give you a look at the future, we need to share the past with you. Will you promise me that the information I share with you in this corner spot will go no further than this table? If it does, we will soon know it."

"I'm not sure I want to hear it, but my answer is yes."

"Good." Levy smiled, glanced out the window toward the Western Wall and turned back to Marcus. "You'd questioned Jacob about the killing of the Syrian, Abdul Hannan. He was removed because he was an agent for Iran, and the information he was about to deliver from North Korea's nuclear operation would have greatly advanced the Iranian nuclear bomb effort."

"Look, Nathan, I'm not a covert field operative. I'm a scientist, not—"

"You are the best in the world at encryption. Maybe in your decoding of the Bible you came across the story of Esther. The Old Testament story tells the tale of how the Persians developed a plot to destroy the Jews. Queen Esther prevented it. Her birth name was Hadassah, which means myrtle in Hebrew. The myrtle flower is as much a part of Israel as the Sea of Galilee. The ongoing code name for Israel's defense against a nuclear attack is Myrtus. The worm we are using, Myrtus, is unique to Windows; and we believe it will include the capacity to reprogram the brain, the programmable logic control boards in the computers controlling Iran's nuclear research. We believe Myrtus can be programmed to disguise, hide and bury the changes so they are not found. However, we could greatly use your help with the encoding. You'd be working with some of the very brightest people in the world. It seems the kind of challenge a scientist of your intellect would love to undertake. You would be very well compensated for the rest of your life. We've reached a point, a tipping point, where we need expertise like yours to add features to the worm we know needs to be in place."

"Look, I appreciate the vote of confidence, but no thanks. That's not the reason I'm here."

"Yes it is."

Marcus was silent for a second. "So it's all been a *deception*. You bring me over here under the pretense of decoding Isaac Newton's papers, and all along you really wanted me to code a cyber-attack against your enemy? To hell with that!"

"Look, Paul, Bible codes and all that Isaac Newton material are like the Dead Sea Scrolls—dead. It's ancient history. I'm talking about the immediate and the future, the future of Israel and perhaps many more nations. Your time would be better served if—"

"If what! I may have been deceived in the reason I'm here, maybe you *forged* my name in Newton's papers...but by default I've found something greater than a cyber-attack. By the way, the Book if Esther is the only one not found in the Dead Sea Scrolls. I'm not interested in your proposal."

Levy wrote a number down on a business card that was blank. "Here, take this. It is a private number. I'm the only one who will answer it. Let me know if you change your mind."

"I can't help you." Marcus stood to leave.

"You know, at one time the Persians developed a plot to destroy the Jews. What plot could destroy Israel or perhaps even America? Esther never revealed she was Jewish. Does that sounds like you, Paul? Perhaps you will do as she did and rise up to stop this threat before its deadly consequences are known."

FIFTY

*M*arcus walked north on El Wad HaGai Street through the Old City, heading toward Via Dolorosa. He thought about the conversation he'd had with Nathan Levy. *Why was this happening? Why now and in this place?* The vibration of the phone in his pocket disrupted his thoughts. He reached for the cell and read the incoming text: *We must meet. It is urgent - tonight. Layla.*

Marcus stared at the words across the screen, the sounds of a siren in the distance, the faint *pop-pop-pop* of gunfire like fireworks out of season. *How did she get my number?* His phone buzzed in his hand. It was Alicia. "Okay, Paul, I have some information. Eisenhower had ordered Patton to return the Spear of Destiny, AKA, the Holy Lance, and the other religious artifacts back to from where Hitler had stolen them."

"Where was that?"

"Vienna. The Hofburg Museum."

"When was the spear returned?"

"It says January 7, 1946."

"When was it taken from Hitler?"

"About eight months prior…right before he committed suicide on April thirtieth, 1945. Our Army took possession of it in the name of the U.S. government on that date, around 2:10 p.m. Eighty minutes later, Hitler shot himself in the head."

"So, if it was returned to the museum in January 1946, General Patton had possession of the spear for a few months."

Alicia lowered her voice. "Apparently so…but what's the significance?"

Marcus paused, watching the changes of color on the Western Wall, the setting sun painting the old stone wall in shades of burgundy. "It means Patton could have become very used to carrying that thing around before he was ordered to return it. In that time, Patton could have had a replica made and replaced the real thing with it."

"Maybe he had four replicas made."

"What do you mean?"

"It says in addition to the spear in Vienna, there is one in a museum cathedral near Echmiadzin, Armenia. Another is in Krakow, Poland, and one is in the Vatican. So that's four."

"Could be that they're all imposters."

"And it could be no spear is around after two thousand years, either."

"Alicia, how did General Patton die, and when?"

"Hold a sec."

Marcus strode past the Dome of the Rock, the oldest existing Islamic building on earth, where dozens of people cued up in a long line to enter. Armed security was heavy, uniformed guards watching everyone who approached.

Alicia said, "Some of this I got from my dad, the rest from research. Patton was injured in a car crash near Mannheim, Germany, on December 9, 1945. He was one of three passengers in his car and was in the rear seat with Major General Hobart Gay. His driver was PFC Horace Woodring. An Army supplies truck, driven by Technical Sergeant Robert L. Thompson, turned in the path of Patton's driver, and there was a collision. A passenger in the truck was an Allied soldier, James Tower. The report indicates the wreck was minor. No one but Patton was injured. He was taken to an Army hospital at Mannheim where he died December twenty-first from an apparent heart attack."

"Was an autopsy done?"

"No."

"Mannheim, Germany. I imagine Patton had made a few enemies during the war. Certainly in Germany."

"In Russia, too. Dad says Patton was hated by the Russian military, and even by his own boss, Dwight Eisenhower, for condemning Eisenhower's handling of German POWs."

Marcus was silent a moment, his mind working timelines and prob-abilities. "I wonder if your dad knows the background of the two men in the car with Patton at the time of the accident, the driver of the truck and his passenger."

"I thought you might ask that, so I ran a check on all parties. With the exception of the Brit, James Tower, the rest are long dead. Tower would be in his late eighties. I couldn't track down a last known address."

"What if Patton had the spear-head with him? Maybe on him, in a brief-case, or hidden somewhere in the car, when the accident happened? What if Patton didn't die from his injuries? Maybe he was killed—murdered by someone in the hospital? German, Russian, or someone else—"

"Paul, slow down. What are you saying?"

"What if he was killed so the spear he had wouldn't have to be returned to him?"

"Go on."

"What if this person kept the spear after Patton's death and had a fake made but sold the real thing to someone. Even by 1945, the Spear of Destiny was probably known in many religious and secret power circles as an extremely valuable object. A wealthy person, or someone representing a government—maybe Germany, Russia or even the U.S.—could have bro-kered a deal if it became known on the black market that the spear was on the auction block."

"Whoa, Paul, you need to tell me what you've discovered in those Newton papers? Newton lived a couple centuries before there was a World War II. The place you're standing, Israel, didn't even exist as a nation."

"But Newton found information that predicted the Jews would return here. What if he may have foreseen World War II or even World War III... who the players would be, how it would start, when...and how it would all end?"

"What *have* you found?"

"I'm still finding."

"What do you mean?"

"There is a mention of this spear in Newton's deciphered coding, and he draws references to it in the Bible including this: *'He makes wars cease to the ends of the earth. He breaks the bow and shatters the spear...'* Also, Hitler, the man who possessed the spear, started a war. What would it be worth to someone like him today? Or someone in the background—the power and money brokers behind the next Hitler?"

"What's control of the world's economies and governments' worth? I suppose that is why many of the wars over the last two thousand years began."

"But it's only in the last seventy years we've had nuclear weapons."

"Paul, you mentioned something about shattering the spear…making wars cease to the ends of the earth. What does that mean?"

"I don't know, at least not yet. And I wonder if the original spear still exists."

Marcus looked at the crowd in long, orderly lines at the Dome of the Rock, the golden dome resembling fire smoldering in the sunset. "Shoes must be removed," said a guard waving a metal detection wand down a man's back. The people, Muslims mostly, were quiet, faces vacant. They waited their turns to enter the building and see the ancient rock, a stone that is part of the bedrock of both Islam and Judaism. It is believed that the area was where Abraham was going to sacrifice his son Isaac, near the same vicinity where Muslims believe the Prophet Muhammad ascended into heaven.

"Paul, are you still there?" asked Alicia.

"Yes."

"I forgot one other thing about James Tower, the passenger in the truck that ran into Patton."

"What?"

"My dad had mentioned, which was corroborated in an obscure report I dug up, that Tower was a man who spoke fluent German, Russian and Italian. Maybe he was an undercover agent using the guise of an Allied soldier to gain closer access to Patton."

FIFTY-ONE

Marcus exited the Old City through Lion's Gate. He walked by Golden Gate, which had been sealed closed for twelve centuries, and up to Jericho Road toward the Mount of Olives. Within a few minutes, the sun was turning the clouds in the west into tapestries of mauve and scarlet. Walking east on the ancient road, the Old City was to his left, the air warm, the smell of cedar trees and dust in the breeze. He hiked past the western slope of the Mount of Olives and the Jewish cemetery, thousands of rectangle crypts casting long shadows in the sunset.

Bahir had told him to watch for the golden onion-shaped domes from the Church of Mary Magdalene. Soon, he spotted the iconic Russian architecture of the seven domes, like fairytale castles aflame with reflections of an orange sun dipping below the horizon. Near there he would find the Church of All Nations and the Garden of Gethsemane.

A dozen or so tourists exited from the church with a mosaic of Christ above the arched entrance. The montage was of Christ with his hands open, his eyes looking up, flanked by people bowing their heads. A kneeling woman held a child in her lap. Marcus studied the mural for a moment. As the tourists walked by, a fleshy man, face shining with perspiration, wearing a disheveled Nike golf shirt, looked back at the mural and said, "They told us the wall painting tells the story of the Day of Judgment. Damn inspiring, you know?"

Marcus nodded. A woman next to the man said, "The church is closing. We were the last people in there today. C'mon, Randy, the group is ahead of us, and we gotta catch the bus." They left and Marcus walked toward the side of the old church where a small black-and-white sign, shaped like an arrow, spelled ENTRY. Above the stone entryway were the words HORTVS GETHSEMANI. Over that was a white stone chiseled to resemble a shield. Carved into the shield was a large cross with a smaller cross engraved into each of its four quadrants, for a total of five crosses. Marcus felt his pulse quicken. '...*from the five crosses...to the head of the garden...*'

There was the creak of hinges in need of oil. Marcus looked down when an elderly Russian nun, face pinched from sun and time, shoulders stooped, reached up to shut the iron gates. Through the bars she said, "I'm sorry. We're closing for the day." She nodded and turned to walk away.

"Is this the head of the garden?" Marcus asked.

"The *head?* What do you mean, sir?"

"I'm not sure, really."

She tilted her face and looked up at Marcus, blinking hard a few times, the orange sunset giving her eyes the hue of aged pennies. "I don't think the garden has a head or a tail, for that matter. For the last hundred years or so, people have come though this gate."

Marcus smiled. "By head, I meant an entrance, beginning, and end... or an exit."

She nodded. "I must go now. Good evening, sir."

"Wait, please. Is there a statue somewhere in here? Or is there a painting of someone crying...one eye is weeping and the other is not?"

"The mosaic on the front of the church...it is said our Lord is weeping in the picture. I do not know if He sheds tears from only one eye. I must leave now."

"I know you have rules, but may I look around the garden? I promise to lock the gate on my way out."

The old nun considered the request for a moment. A sudden cool wind blew in from the belly of the Kidron Valley and tumbled over the Mount of Olives, jostling the boughs of a eucalyptus tree near the gate. Then the wind stopped as abruptly as it had arrived. A rooster crowed somewhere in the hills behind the Church of Mary Magdalene. The nun seemed to stand a little straighter, her eyes searching Marcus's face. She touched a silver cross hanging from her neck. "May you find what you seek," she said. "Enter, please. I'm Sister Nemov. I have supper to fix for others up the hill. Just pull the gate shut when you leave. It will lock on its own."

"Thank you. I'm Paul Marcus."

Sister Nemov nodded, eyes closed for a second. She clasped her hands together, knuckles the size of pecans, swollen from arthritis, and stood to one side when Marcus walked through the open gate. She said, "Perhaps you would want to enter the church. It is very beautiful. The Holy Rock of Agony is there, too."

"I appreciate that." Marcus looked around the entryway. There was nothing but old, cut stone and a cobblestone path bordered by white lilies and flowers he'd never seen. "Those flowers smell like junipers."

The old woman smiled. "They are called Myrtus. It's a Hebrew word."

Marcus thought about his conversation with Nathan Levy. *Code named Myrtus.*

Sister Nemov said, "Most people call them myrtle, and it's the leaves which have the pleasant smell, not the blossoms. However, the blossoms always reminded me of stars, maybe the morning star, because they have five petals." She nodded, turned and walked up the hill, limping slightly on her left side moving toward the golden domes of the church of Mary Magdalene.

Marcus stepped into the Church of All Nations, the smell of burning candles, incense, and scented oils wafting from the small sanctuary. The altar, framed by four large marble columns, was made of white stone. Behind it, from floor to ceiling, was a vertical mural depicting Jesus praying on a rock, olive trees to the left and right, an angel hovering high in the sky above him.

Marcus walked slowly, looking at the murals, statues and paintings. He came across a rock, resembling a section of granite, undulated with pits and swells, maybe ten-by-ten in size. It was in the middle of a hall, past a simple altar, where just beyond it, seven candles burned. A few spotlights illuminated a carved image of Jesus hanging from a wooden cross. A small wrought iron barrier surrounded the rock on the floor. It was apparently installed to prevent people from walking across the stone, but diminutive enough to allow them to kneel and touch the rock.

Marcus could see that the creamy white stone was darkened in places near the edges. It was tinged with light browns and mustard yellows, colors a flame could turn a marshmallow. He assumed it was from the multitude of hands that had pressed against the stone supporting people and their prayers. Marcus stepped to the edge of the ancient rock. He looked up above the altar to the image of Jesus nailed to the cross, the light from the flickering candles casting moving shadows over the cross. He felt tightness in his chest, his mouth dry…*to the head of the garden, one eye weeps for man, and one sees revelation in the direction of the temple measured by Solomon, a rose without thorns blooms under a new sun. The truth is found fewer than two hundred shadows of the moon, for the shadow is to the seeker as the seeker is to the shadow.*

FIFTY-TWO

When he stepped outside from the Church of All Nations, it was almost dark. A flushed smudge of the sun's last rays faded far beyond the Old City, the Dome of the Rock now a silhouette. The lights of Jerusalem glowed in a sea of shadows caught between cut granite blocks, adobe, concrete, and glass. Marcus's cell buzzed in his pocket. The screen read: UNKNOWN. Marcus answered and Bill Gray said, "Paul, we need you back here. Something's come up."

"Who are *we*? What's come up?"

Marcus heard Gray sigh into the phone. "The police have arrested a suspect in the deaths of Jen and Tiffany."

Marcus's heart hammered. His palm was damp, fingers gripping the phone. "Are you sure?"

Gray was silent for a moment. "Yes, Paul. A local guy. He's a low life meth head with a long rap sheet."

"I'll catch the first plane out of Tel Aviv."

"I hope this will bring closure to you. Goodnight, Paul."

Marcus disconnected and tried to think. His head ached, scalp tight, muscles knotting in his back. He watched the fog building from the Kidron Valley, diffusing some of the perimeter lights of Jerusalem while a full moon inched above the city. He stepped into a garden near the church. He was alone, exhausted, eyes burning, the sound of traffic far away down the Jericho Road. Stone paths laced through the garden, flowers planted along the paths. Huge olive trees, most with ancient and massive gnarled trunks, stood like aged warriors along the path. Under the moonlight, Marcus could see that the knotted girth of each tree was filled with dark pockets and crevices, many cavernous enough to reach inside the fissures carved into the bark by the knife of time. Some of the trees predated sections of the Old City.

Marcus walked around the gardens, heavy with the scent of hibiscus and olives. *What was the head?* What was he looking for, and would he recognize it if he found it? The moon rose higher above the old trees and a mist snaked through the wrought iron gates surrounding the garden. He could see olives growing from some of the trees. *How many centuries of crops*, he wondered. Who had picked from these trees? Who had found shade under the same branches he now walked beneath where dappled moonlight cast bent and crooked shadows across the paths?

He suddenly felt very tired, heavy fatigue building behind his eyes. He sat on a concrete bench under a majestic old olive tree and thought about his wife and daughter. *Police have arrested a suspect in the deaths of Jen and Tiffany.* Finally. But was it true?

He reminded himself that their deaths were the reason he was here. But what had he done? He felt so disconnected. Alone in a garden.

Soon the fog erased the shadows and Marcus felt a chill in the night air. Something, maybe a bat, flapped wings overhead in the dark, the cool air drifting down his neck. The fog moved, covering the tree trunks and settling beneath limbs that seemed to be floating on top of a white sea. Marcus wondered if he could find his way back to the small exit.

He heard steps. Soft steps. Not the heels of hard sole shoes, but more like steps from sneakers or boat shoes. They stopped. Marcus felt the scar on his chest tingle. He breathed deeply and silently. His mind raced. Did he really hear something? Was someone lost? Was it the man he'd seen watching him? Who and why? He lowered himself to the damp earth and felt around the base of a tree. He found a rock almost the size of his hand. He stood and held his breath. Listening.

"You need not cast a stone." The voice was soft, almost as vaporous as the fog. *Or was it a voice?* A man with an accent that sounded foreign even in a place of multiple nationalities, personalities, customs and creeds.

"Who's there?" Marcus asked. He gripped the rock tighter.

Silence. Only the sounds of crickets. *I'm exhausted. My mind must be playing tricks on me again!*

"I am here." The voice seemed to come from nowhere, yet everywhere.

"Why are you following me?" Show yourself!" Marcus thought he spotted a movement in the fog. His heart pounded. *Fear. When was the last time I was afraid for myself?*

"When you walk through the valley look to the light, as the light will give you a path to seek the truth."

"What truth?" Marcus's heart rate slowed, his breathing easy, tension replaced with a strange sense of peace. He could hear traffic far away on the Jericho Road, the smell of a eucalyptus tree and myrtle leaves swirling in the damp night air. Through the curtain of fog, he couldn't see anyone. "Are you there?"

"Yes." The voice moved, coming from just behind the trunk of the largest olive tree enveloped in mist. "Love is truth. The time of reign grows closer. It is known in hearts and found from that which has been sealed. The blade itself will unseal it. Deliver its message and release the spear into the fire of Etna. Destroy it."

"Where *is* this spear? Etna? Who *are* you? Tell me." The sound of crickets returned. "Show yourself! *Please....* " Nothing. Marcus looked down at the rock he held. He felt foolish and self-conscious, and he dropped the rock at his feet.

"Marcus, it's me, Jennifer."

Jenny's voice. No. Impossible. Just tired. Need sleep. I'm losing it...

"Marcus. It's me, honey. Thank God, you're here! I know how tired you are."

"Jen! Where are you? Is Tiffany with you?"

"No, Marcus. I'm alone."

"Where's the man? I heard another *voice*. Where are you?"

"Over here, sweetheart."

Marcus ran around the trees, olive branches raking his face. "Jen! Where are you? Baby, they have a suspect in custody. Where are you? Where's Tiffany?"

"Right here, babe. Please, come to me."

Marcus felt the barrel of a gun wedge against his head.

"Don't move!" ordered a woman, dropping her American accent.

In the swirling fog, Marcus could see the woman held the pistol with two hands. Through the murkiness, he recognized her face, *Layla Koury*. A face that was once soft and suggestive, now hard, eyes burning through the mist. He said, "It's you…why?"

A dark eyebrow arched over her blue eyes. "You may be the best at decoding, but you can't even tell whether your dead wife's voice is real or not. That's because you're schizophrenic—you hear voices. You're profile said your father and grandfather did, too. A whole family of crazies! This disease, schizophrenia, makes voices sound real in your head. Poor Paul, it's part of your DNA. Maybe it is a sad compromise of your genius." Layla laughed. "You were just talking to yourself like a village idiot. Have you begun hallucinating yet? If not, it's only a matter of time. Usually the strange dreams preface the onset of hallucinations."

"I gave you my answer."

"That's why I'm here. If the Republic…if Iran, cannot buy your talents, you are choosing to aid its adversaries. We suspected it. Now we *know* it. That cannot be tolerated."

"Didn't you get my note?"

"What note?"

"The one I left at the hotel for you. I said I'm willing to play cards, deal."

"You're lying. Regardless, I have my orders." She raised the Beretta higher. "You're not afraid are you? Why?"

"There's nothing to be afraid of."

"Oh, really?" She tilted her head, a smile on her lips, finger curling around the trigger. "Somehow you managed to survive the first assassination attempt. You will have no such luck this time."

"What assassination attempt?"

"The one that killed your wife and daughter. Don't look so surprised. We've known about your talents for quite a while, and we knew it was just a matter of time before Israel recruited you to slow or destroy our nuclear capabilities. That wasn't and isn't about to happen. I won't miss where my colleague failed. You survived a hit carried out by a legendary assassin called the Lion. That never happens, and now your good fortune has ended." She brought her left hand up to steady her aim.

A dozen floodlights illuminated the garden. Layla looked toward the lights.

"Mr. Marcus! Are you still here?" Sister Nemov shouted from the porte cache.

Marcus slammed Layla's arm against the barnacled trunk of an olive tree. She grimaced in pain. He wrestled the gun from her hand. She used her fist, pounding his head and left ear. Marcus drove his elbow into her chin. Layla fell to her knees, spitting blood. He pointed the pistol at her head. "Don't move!"

"Paul Marcus! Is that you out there?" shouted the nun.

"Yes, Sister. Call the police!"

Layla, sprawled on the ground, popped something into her mouth. She bit down hard and swallowed, a peculiar smile coming over her face, blood trickling from the corner of her mouth.

"No!" Marcus shouted. "Spit it out! Don't!"

"You are a foolish man, Paul." She stared at him, the moonlight slicing through a moving cloud and casting shadows over her indignant face. A rooster crowed somewhere behind the Church of Mary Magdalene.

"It's too late for me, Paul. And it's too late for you, too."

"You don't have to waste your life. This is not worth dying for?"

She was quiet, her eyes watching the clouds move across the moon. Then she smiled and met Marcus's eyes. "Yes…yes it is. You don't understand what's at stake for Iran or in the Middle East. The West isn't capable of it. Maybe the next voices you hear will be your wife's or mine. Will you be able to tell the difference?"

She coughed, her chest rising and falling rapidly. Her left arm twitched. Her breathing became labored. A pink froth spilled from her lips as the light in her eyes faded.

Marcus fought back the urge to vomit. He could feel his pulse pound in his neck. *Layla Koury. Who was she?* He reached in her pocket and found a small cell phone. He slipped it in his sock and then he used his phone to take a picture of Layla's face, her lifeless eyes staring directly into the lens. He placed the phone in his pocket, sat on a concrete bench, looked at the lights of the Old City in the distance and waited for the police to arrive.

FIFTY-THREE

sraeli police detained Marcus in the Garden of Gethsemane, combed the grounds with high-powered lights and continued to question him. He repeated his story to three officers who took notes, the air crackling with dispatches from police radios.

The Inspector General moved quickly through the officers, investigators and emergency personnel. The body of the woman was placed in a black bag, zipped and positioned on a gurney to be loaded into an awaiting ambulance. The Inspector General usually didn't respond to crime scenes. He had long since left that to his staff. However, it had come to his attention, while dining at home, that an American, someone doing encryption work for the Hebrew University, had been found with a body in the Garden of Gethsemane.

"Are you Paul Marcus?" he asked.

"Yes."

"I'm Inspector General Aaron Cantor. May I ask what you were doing in this site after hours?" Cantor, in his fifties, wore his salt and pepper hair cut short. His chin bore a small white scar shaped like the letter V. He assessed Marcus through probing calm eyes the shade of light tea.

Marcus said, "I'd asked permission to tour the area. Sister Nemov can attest to that. I was here, in the garden, when I heard a woman's voice. For a moment it sounded like my wife. I called out to her. There was more fog than now. I walked around the olive grove and the next thing I knew was that she had a gun to my head."

"What did she want?"

"To kill me."

"Why?"

Marcus thought about what Layla had said. "I don't know. We didn't spend a lot of time chatting. She was distracted for a second when the lights came on, and I managed to get the gun out of her hand. She swallowed a pill of some kind. It was too late to save her."

"Would you have saved her if you could?"

"Yes." Marcus looked beyond the inspector as the body was loaded into the ambulance.

"When she held the gun to your head, what did she say?"

"She suggested that I was prone to hallucinations."

"Are you?"

"No."

"You said you thought you heard your wife's voice. Isn't your wife dead?"

Marcus looked hard at Cantor. "How'd you know that?"

"It is my business to know these things. One can never be too careful in a place like Jerusalem. It appears you are discovering that phenomenon, yes?"

Marcus said nothing.

Cantor motioned with his hand for Marcus to follow him. "Come with me, Mr. Marcus, please." They walked to the edge of the garden. The fog had finally lifted, the evening cool, the stars over the Old City bright and filled with a sense of antiquity. Cantor pointed toward the walled city. "To keep order and instill a sense of safety beyond those walls is not an easy job. Three days ago a Palestinian man drove a truck into an area where two of my officers were walking. One man was slightly injured. The driver jumped out of the truck and ran. He refused orders to stop. He was shot. Unfortunately, he died at a hospital. Tensions are very tight, more so as we move toward celebrating Chanukah in a few weeks."

"Why are you telling me this?"

"Why?" Cantor turned to face Marcus. "Because, Mr. Marcus, we are sitting on a powder keg. It is one that could erupt at any moment for the slightest misstep. The woman who died here at Gethsemane tonight, she appears perhaps Lebanese or Iranian. She's an agent, no doubt. We may have her identification in Tel Aviv. That's where her body will be taken before disposal."

"Disposal? She has a family."

"Then she chose the wrong profession. I know you *know* her. Why were you meeting her here? What did she want?"

"I wasn't meeting her here. I met her a week ago at the restaurant bar in the hotel where I'm staying. She said her name was Layla Koury. She told me that she was a graduate student. Born in Beirut and educated in the states. She was getting a doctorate in archeology from Columbia University in New York. She'd completed research in Egypt on an ancient city called Rhakotis, near Alexandria, before coming to Israel to consult for the Discovery Channel about the catacomb burials somewhere close to where we are, the Mount of Olives."

Cantor was quiet for a moment. "The importance isn't in what she told you about herself, we assume it's all a lie. The consequence is what you told her about you, and what she really wanted. What is that?"

"I told her I was doing research on some old papers written by Isaac Newton and donated to the Hebrew University and that was that. Nothing more."

Cantor stared at Marcus. "She wanted something. It will be in your best interest to tell us. She could have been working for any agency as a hired gun or a field agent on the fast track up. Why would a trained assassin be sent to kill you? What are you doing inside the university that has caused this reaction?"

"You've spoken with Jacob Kogen, haven't you?"

"I have. However, he did not divulge anything beyond that which we're already informed of—that you are, perhaps, the best in the world at encryption and decryption. You're here to help the State of Israel with something, and that you are well known and respected for breaking some kind of human heart gene code. You're so respected, in fact, that you've been selected to receive the Nobel for your work—should you decide to accept the prize. You do cast a long international shadow, Mr. Marcus."

"It's not my intention, I assure you."

"What else transpired here tonight? Was there anything said that you didn't mention...maybe a word or two she added?"

'Love is truth.' Marcus thought about the voice. Had someone been there? 'You hear voices, Paul Marcus.' He looked at Cantor and shook his head. "It all happened so fast. With a gun pointed at your head, you go numb. Has it ever happened to you, Inspector?"

"Yes." Cantor sighed. "The old Franciscan nun will say nothing of tonight's unfortunate occurrence. May I ask that you do the same?"

"Who would I tell? Let me ask you something. You obviously know how long I've been here and why I'm here. Who else is following me?"

Cantor lit a cigarette, inhaled smoke and blew it out facing the lights of the Old City. "We are. We are following you."

"The Israeli police...why?"

"It's for your own safety."

"I see how well that's working. Then how did she get to me?"

"That's what I inquired. It is being dealt with internally."

"I say nothing about the woman, and you drop the tail. I don't like someone looking over my shoulder, even if, as you say, it's for my safety. It isn't working."

Cantor nodded, tossed his cigarette, smashing it with his shoe. "Okay."

"Why wasn't I told it was the Israeli police following me?"

"Typically, we're never spotted. Perhaps your powers of observation are equal to your skills in mathematics." Cantor smiled and folded his arms across his chest, the moonlight casting dark shadows below his eyes. "How did you arrive here this evening?"

"Walked. But, you should know, shouldn't you?"

"I'll give you a ride back to your hotel. By now, whoever sent the woman probably knows something happened to her. I have a feeling she was just the beginning."

"I have one last thing. I was raised around guns. Let me have her Beretta."

Cantor exhaled with a grunt and shook his head. "Routinely, that would never happen. However, after tonight—after our misstep and the apparent danger you obviously are in, I will look the other way while you pocket her gun. If it ever comes up, this conversation never happened. But, you take her pistol at your own risk."

"Thank you."

"If you find you have to use it, Mr. Marcus, I hope your aim will be true."

FIFTY-FOUR

Back at his hotel, Marcus looked at the phone log on Layla's cell. He memorized the number that she'd last called, a number that appeared on the log five hours earlier. He hid her phone behind a potted plant in his room and went in the bathroom to shower. He turned the water as hot as he could stand it, letting the torrent beat down on his neck and shoulders. He closed his eyes, the steam rising around him, like the mist in the Garden of Gethsemane. He heard the man's voice. *'The blade itself will unseal it. Deliver its message and then release the spear into the fire of Etna. Destroy it.'* Marcus shook his head under the water and opened his eyes wide.

Images of the woman's face popped in his mind like rapid-fire pictures. Layla getting out of the taxi at the hotel. Her wide smile. Turning to him at the front desk. Sipping wine at a corner table, the Tower of David in the background. Her body when she dropped the robe. Her kiss. Her face at death. That image melted into the macabre face of the man who killed his family. That heinous expression liquefied and was replaced by the iconic figure of Christ on the cross from the Church of All Nations. Marcus held both his hands to the side of his spinning head, Layla's final words echoing through his skull. *"The one that killed your wife and daughter. Don't look so surprised. We've known about your talents for quite a while, and we knew it was just a matter of time before Israel recruited you to slow or destroy our nuclear capabilities. That wasn't and isn't about to happen. I won't miss where my colleague failed."*

After a few seconds, he opened his eyes, turned the water off, towel-dried, slipped on shorts and a loose shirt. He started to walk out on the

217

balcony and stopped. He shut off the light in his room and slowly opened
the sliding glass door. The breeze teased the curtains. He could see the
moon rising over the Old City. He was mentally and physically exhausted.
Yet, he felt alive, believed in a sense of purpose for the first time since the
deaths of his family. He thought about the sunset view of the valley when
he'd climbed a hill off the Burma Road and sat on the outcropping of rock.
Tonight he wanted to step out on the balcony and howl at the damn moon.
But something stopped him.

Was someone out there with a night scope on a rifle?

He closed and locked the doors, then sat at the table in his room
and turned on his laptop. His fingers flew through the Newton data, centuries of Biblical statistics and correlating passages weaving in the story
of Esther and the Hebrew spelling of her name and the myrtle flower.
Marcus whispered, "Esther…Myrtus…Revelation…John…" *A hero vehe-
mently tints juror s…*

*…the blade itself shall open that which was sealed…and not to be revealed to the
wicked, who meet secretly, conspire, become the rule behind the throne…and covet the
forged supremacy of evil in which domination of my people is their purpose…'*

Marcus pushed back from the desk, his eyes burning into the screen,
thoughts racing. He paced the room for a moment, his lips dry, blood,
charged with adrenaline, surging through his veins. He listened to the night
sounds, the rhythm of the Old City in harmony. He walked into the bathroom, ran cold water and splashed it on his face, dried off and stood back
over his computer.

Marcus looked at the mobile phone he'd taken from Layla's body. He
picked up his phone, emailed the photo of Layla to Alicia and wrote:

This woman tried to put a bullet in my head tonight. Alias - Layla
Koury. The one I mentioned to you. Run a face scan for an ID.
Thanks –

Marcus picked up the pistol and placed it under his pillow. He stretched
out on the bed. "No dreams tonight," he mumbled. "No damn nightmares
tonight." Marcus closed his eyes and felt the subconscious ebb of sleep just
as his phone buzzed.

UNKNOWN. He pressed the button.

"Paul, it's Alicia. Are you okay? Were you hurt?"

"I'm okay."

"What happened?"

Marcus told her and added. "She said the murders of Jennifer and Tiffany, the killer leaving me for dead, was a planned assassination. It was carried out by Iran to prevent me from being recruited by Israel to impact Iran's nuclear effort."

"Dear God, Paul…I'm so very, very sorry."

"Listen to me, Alicia. Bill Gray told me they arrested a local suspect. He wants me back immediately. He's lying. Why?"

"I don't know."

"Are you sure?"

"Yes, Paul. Please, believe me. I'm telling you the truth."

Marcus was silent for a long moment. He said, "Try to find out what's going on there? Be careful."

"I will."

Marcus blew air out of his cheeks and looked at the drapes across his balcony window. "Layla said it was her colleague who killed Jen and Tiff. I want to find him. I'm assuming she killed herself because she would have been questioned—questioned damn hard, maybe tortured by the Mossad."

"You go to the Holy Land to decipher Newton and biblical passages and you get caught in an international cyber war and learn your wife and daughter were murdered in an attempt on *your* life to prevent you from going exactly where you are today. That must have been really tough to hear. Are you all right, Paul?" she asked softly.

Marcus sat farther up in his bed, pillows bracing his back, the moonlight spilling into his room, and the smell of gun oil from the pistol under the pillow next to him. "No, not really. I'm a bundle of emotions—angry, confused, sad…too damn many feelings to explain and not sure what to believe. But, Alicia, something else happened to me tonight. Something that I can't explain in any rational terms, so I won't even try. But it's affected me. I thought I might have hallucinated in the olive grove, but I heard a voice. No, I *spoke* with a voice. It was real. Do you understand me? "

"What voice?"

"A man. He told me to find the spear—to destroy it. It's the key to—"

"To what, Paul?"

"To the destiny of a perfect home that's been given to us, maybe the *fate* of planet earth."

"You're serious, aren't you?"

"Yes."

"What are you going to do?"

"Find it…destroy it. I have no other option unless I'm really suffering from some horrible psychosis. But I feel, at least I think, all of this is very real."

"Let me help you."

"Alicia, do some research. Go back to the time John Kennedy Junior was killed. Who had the most to lose or win in the event of his death? Clinton was president, and his wife was warming up for the New York Senate seat, the same race where Kennedy Junior could have run for the same office had he decided to so—"

"Paul, what does this have to do with the—"

"Look at who was running for president in 2000. Could Kennedy have been in the mix? As it was, George W. Bush and Al Gore became locked in the most contentious presidential race in U.S. history. It was the only election decided by a majority vote in the Supreme Court. If Kennedy had run for the Senate in New York, beat Hillary Clinton, he may have decided to face Bush in 2004, assuming Kennedy wanted the office. Would he have even wanted the office? We'll never know."

"Paul, I've looked under plenty of rocks before, but this one might be a boulder."

"Dig for anything classified under the accident investigation. Any witnesses? Can you find military or rescue personnel who worked the scene when Kennedy's plane went down? On a larger scope, look for the money trail or trails. See where they intersect. Find the bits and pieces that make investments, mergers and buyouts more than a twist of fate. Look for subtle things that eventually become more than coincidental, the people on the director's boards, their political alliances. Start to see if a pattern emerges from Wall Street firms, defense contractors, global banks, hedge funds, and private equity investments. Look at multinational corporations tied to lobby groups financed by government vendors who've managed to fly under the general radar with non-compete contracts. And the most important thing—"

"What, Paul?"

"See if any of it has a history or even a remote political or financial connection back to World War II, General Patton, or maybe the Nuremburg Trials."

"This is a big job—it could take some time."

"Alicia, you're the best I've ever seen at research, hacking, gathering and correlating cyber data. There may not be any connections—no smoking guns. But dirty money has a way of staining the fingers of those who spend it. Find the fingerprints."

"You know *something* don't you, Paul?"

"I know the best chance we have of getting your niece, Brandi, out of that hell hole is finding information we can control if we have to… and maybe dealing a hand the Iranians can't resist. Call me soon as you get something."

"Goodnight, Paul."

"Be very careful in your digging and watch your steps."

Marcus disconnected and got out of bed. He knew that it was just a matter of time before whomever was on Layla's phone log would know she'd died. After that, they'd know that a call coming from her phone was a trap. Marcus retrieved the dead woman's phone from behind the potted plant, scrolled to the last entry and pressed the button.

FIFTY-FIVE

*T*he voice was that of a man, deep, slight Persian accent. "Taheera. Is the job done? Was the target eliminated?"

"So her name was Taheera," Marcus said. "I liked Layla better. And no, that target's still here. You're talking to it."

"Who is this?" The voice was flat, anger subdued, but there.

"The target at your service—Paul Marcus, and before you hang up and remove all trace of this line, I made the call to let you know I've reconsidered the offer by your government."

"What offer?"

"Cut the act. I don't have the time or the stomach for it. It's not a matter of if it will happen, it's *when* a cyber attack will happen on your nuke operation. You want me to decode a cyber-worm…then you release Brandi Hirsh and Adam Spencer."

"You sound like a man with delusions. Our nuclear operation is purely as an alternate power source. Regardless, there is no threat or attack—"

"Bullshit! Its code name is Myrtus."

"How did you *know* that?"

"If your centrifuge hasn't been eaten by it…it's just a matter of time. You want it stopped, you set those kids free."

"What assurance do we have that you will comply if these two are released?"

"We'll make a trade. The worm was probably delivered when someone stuck a flash drive in one of your computers and set it in motion. You've got

Russians, Germans and who knows how many consultants working in your nuclear program. Any of them could have delivered the cyber hit. You load your operating system onto a portable drive. Meet me in a public place. Give me the drive and give me a week to deliver the cure for your worm. You schedule a press conference where your president or supreme leader says he's reconsidered the plight of the two Americans and is going to release them on humanitarian grounds in a good faith movement."

"I do not have the authority to—"

"Then get it! Or you find somebody who has it!"

"How can I contact you?"

"I'll hang on to Layla's—no, Taheera's phone. You have the number."

"Mr. Marcus, I will speak with my superiors. This, of course, will be decided at the highest level. However, remember one thing: should you try to deceive us, your head will be removed with a dull knife."

— —

Alicia Quincy needed hours of undistracted time to run extensive research and analytics. She took a comp day and worked from her apartment, a second fresh pot of coffee was brewing, giving off a final hiss when the last cup of water percolated through the dark Colombian grounds. She sat at the bar in her kitchen, hair pinned up, dressed in a sweatshirt and jeans, leaning toward the computer screen. She pulled records for every federal defense contract issued in the past decade. She profiled members of the board of directors from companies with global footprints in telecommunications, media, aerospace, banking/finance, private equity, healthcare, energy/power and biochemical. She analyzed which asset management companies have been given large public pension funds, how the contracts were awarded and which members of Congress or the U.S. Senate had a possible role in the procurements.

She finished the second pot of coffee and could feel palpitations in her heart when she began to see patterns emerge. She looked away from the screen for a moment. Her mind racing, the implications building as the layers of complicity revealed a buried trail that intersected with America's past, present and maybe crossing its future.

Alicia looked at her watch, picked up her phone and made a call. "Brad, hi, it's Alicia. How's the Justice Department treating you these days?"

"Can't complain. White-collar crime is bad for most businesses, but it alone is enough to keep us in business for the next century. Anything new with your niece?"

"We're told negotiations continue. But that's *all* we're told."

"I wish I had some overseas experience, maybe there'd be something I could do."

"You're sweet, thanks. Brad, I remember you telling me about your younger brother. The one who worked at a bar in Boston—"

"That's my brother Mark. He worked at Foleys"

"Right. You said Mark served a man at the bar one night, not too long ago, who said he was a diver on the wreck site when John Kennedy Junior's plane went down off Martha's Vineyard."

"Yeah, Mark said the guy told him he was a former Navy Seal diver. He'd pounded back a few too many drinks that night and Mark cut him off. My brother was studying journalism at the time, until that profession went into the shit can. The guy said, for one last drink, he'd give my brother the story of a lifetime. Something about Kennedy's plane."

"What happened?"

"The customer threw up on the bar. Mark called the guy a cab and quit his job the next day. He's been working in PR since graduation."

"How can I contact Mark?"

"I can text you his number. He's here in DC. What are you working on, Alicia?"

"Nothing yet. Just looking at bits and pieces. Thanks, Brad."

— ▪ —

Alicia met Mark Rockford for coffee at the Starbucks on the corner of 16th and K streets in downtown Washington. Mark, early twenties, gelled hair combed straight back, looked at Alicia through inquisitive, sea green eyes and said, "My brother told me about your niece. I hope there's a positive advance soon." "Thank you." Alicia sipped her coffee.

"So you're interested in the dude with the Kennedy Junior story?"

"Yes. Brad told me some of what happened that night. What'd the man tell you?"

"Not a lot. He was the last customer still sitting at the bar on a Tuesday night near closing. I remember there was a couple at a table, but this guy was the only one at the bar. We'd been chatting for a while as I'd served drinks. He told me his girlfriend had recently left him, and the kick between the legs is that he had a bout with lymphoma. The guy was in his early forties, tops. He asked me if I was going to be a bartender all my life, and I told him I was interested in journalism. His eyes got wide and said he could give me the story of a lifetime."

"What was that?"

"That's what I asked. He told me he was one of the Navy divers that found John Kennedy Junior's plane off the coast of Martha's Vineyard. He said the crash wasn't an accident. I fluffed this dude's comments off to the booze. But then he said that he saw a hole blown through the tail of the plane and the hole looked like it blew out from the inside of the plane."

"Did he say he had anything else?"

"Yeah, right before he vomited sausage pizza all over the bar. He said he and a Navy diving buddy were the first divers to see the plane, and he snapped an underwater picture of the wreckage. I told him to bring it to me and I might write a freelance story for the Boston Globe."

"What happened?"

"Never saw the guy again." Mark reached in his wallet and pulled out a receipt. "The fella left his credit card receipt on the bar. I kept it in case he ever came back or...well, here it is." He handed the receipt to Alicia.

"May I have this?"

"Sure. You think you can track him down?"

"Maybe." Alicia looked at the receipt. "His name's Greg Owen."

"Yeah. I know you're with NSA. Why does the agency want to find this guy?"

"I can't say much...you know...national security."

"I remembered one of the things this guy, Owen, said. He told me that, for more than a year after the Kennedy accident, he felt like he was being followed. He said sometimes he still does."

FIFTY-SIX

Marcus arrived at the Hebrew University early. He had confined his work to a brand new computer with no outside access, no Internet connection. A few minutes after 10:00 a.m., the phone next to him buzzed. "Mr. Marcus, this is Shirley at the front desk."

"Yes, Shirley."

"Dr. Kogen is off campus in meetings this morning. I have a woman on line three who wanted to speak with him. Her name is Gisele Fournier. She is the person who donated the remaining Newton papers to the library. She's the granddaughter of the gentlemen who bought them in England. She's asking if we have any news or developments to share with her. Since you are doing so much work with these papers, I thought you might want to take the call for Dr. Kogen."

"Okay." Marcus pressed the button for the blinking line. "This is Paul Marcus."

"Hello, my name is Gisele Fournier. The receptionist told me Professor Kogen is out and that you are researching the Newton papers I donated to the library."

"That's correct."

"May I ask you, have you found anything?"

"There are many notes that Newton made. His research is the most exhaustive I've ever seen. It's going to take a while to penetrate furthermost areas. The majority, I believe, will never be understood. I'm still not sure how much Newton himself understood during the last years of his life."

"I see. I just thought that, because my grandfather used to...never mind. Thank you, Mr. Marcus. I'm sorry if I bothered you."

"Wait, please, Miss Fournier. You haven't bothered me. I appreciate your donation to the library. What did you start to say about your grandfather?"

"My grandfather was a collector."

"A collector?"

"Yes, he was an antiquities dealer by trade. He spoke four languages, and he knew history, especially biblical history quite well. He traveled, buying and selling religious artifacts around the world, often working with biblical archeologists."

"Is that why he had interest in the Newton papers?"

"Yes. My grandfather was going to resell the Newton papers. However, once he began reading and studying them, he thought they belonged in a place like the Hebrew University Library in Jerusalem, and he wanted them donated after his death."

"Why, if I can ask, why did he want them donated after his death since he bought them back in 1936? He'd kept them for decades."

"I believe it's because he found something in them that frightened him. That's the reason I am calling you."

"How was he frightened?"

"He was convinced that prophesies Newton found foretold of a vast nuclear war. And he thought the key to preventing the war was to keep a biblical relic from the hands of madmen, men who would have no qualms about using nuclear weapons."

"What biblical relic?"

"I'm not certain. I do remember, as a little girl, my grandfather taking me to a park in Paris that had a special place in his heart. It's a Japanese garden near the UNESCO building. There is the figure of a winged angel. The small statue was given to UNESCO by the city of Nagasaki, Japan. The little angel is disfigured, blind in one eye, the result of the nuclear bomb dropped over Nagasaki. The angel, with her wound, was found in the rubble from a large church that was leveled by the bomb. Everything else was destroyed. My grandfather used to say that it was a sign, a prophetic symbol, of man's inhumanity to man and how it affected God. The angel looks like she's crying."

Marcus closed his eyes for a moment, his mind racing over the decrypted verses. '...*to the head of the garden, one eye weeps for man, one sees revelation in the direction of the temple measured by Solomon...*'

"Mr. Marcus, are you still there?"

"I thought of something I read. Do you know which direction the statue faces?"

"Direction?"

"You said it's in an outside garden, right?"

"Yes."

"Can you recall which direction in Paris it's facing—from the statue, the angel's point-of-view?"

"Let me think. In the direction of the Seine River, I believe. I haven't been there in quite a few years. The last time I was there they were installing a memorial and planting an olive tree in memory of the Israeli Prime minister who was assassinated, Yitzhak Rabin."

"When did they install the memorial?"

"Umm...almost ten years ago. Why?"

"Just curious. Do you know if a ceremony is scheduled to mark the tenth anniversary?"

"Yes, I read about it."

"When does it occur?"

"Soon, a week or so, I think."

"Miss Fournier—"

"Please, it's Gisele."

"I'm Paul. Gisele, was your grandfather involved during World War II?"

"How do you mean, involved?"

"Was he in the military?"

"No, but he was part of the French Resistance."

"Did he ever enter Germany after the war?"

"I'm not sure. My grandmother, his wife, is here and she's fifteen years younger than my grandfather was when he was alive. If you hold a minute, I can ask her."

"Okay." Marcus could hear Gisele explaining in French and then the slow answer coming back from an older woman.

"Paul, my grandmother said he went to Mannheim, Germany, after the war."

"Ask her if she knows why he went there."

Gisele asked the question of her grandmother. "She told me he went there to meet someone, a man."

"After all these years, can she possibly recall his name?"

"I'll ask her." Half a minute later, Gisele returned. "She said it was an easy name to remember because the man came to their home one night for dinner. Also, he had a similar name to the Tower of London. His name was James Tower."

FIFTY-SEVEN

WASHINGTON, DC

A credit card receipt with an address was all that Alicia needed to follow electronic tracks made by Greg Owen. Most of his purchases were within ten miles of greater Boston. She pulled up a satellite map and zoomed down onto his townhouse in Bay Village. She used the street view camera and found a 2014 black Hyundai Sonata with a license plate registered in his name.

Alicia located his private cell phone number in a secure database and uploaded his phone's GPS tracking grid onto her phone. She looked at the screen on her phone and could tell that if Greg Owen had his cell phone with him, he was at home.

She pulled up the roundtrip flights from Washington, D.C., to Boston, locked her apartment and drove to Reagan International Airport. She parked in the short-term lot and paid cash for a roundtrip flight to Boston. At 8:30 a.m., she boarded United's flight number 860. At 9:59, the plane landed at Logan International Airport. Within minutes, Alicia rented a car and followed its GPS to 12 Church Street in Bay Village, Mike & Patty's Sandwich Shop.

Alicia found the black Sonata parked on the street. She entered the deli filled with the scent of espresso coffee, bacon and eggs. Less than ten people were in the shop. She walked up to a man sitting alone in the rear of the restaurant. He had close-cropped blond hair, thick arms and shoulders. He studied his tablet screen and looked up at Alicia. "Do I know you?"

Alicia smiled. "Greg Owen?"

"Who wants to know?"

"My name's Alicia Quincy. May I sit here?"

Owen glanced around the shop. There were more than a dozen tables. Diners occupied only about half of them. He shrugged. "Sure, why not?"

"Can I buy you breakfast."

"I just finished eating. I don't want to come off rude, but what do you want?"

Alicia lowered her voice. "May I call you Greg?"

"Sure."

"Greg, I spoke with a friend of mine. His name is Mark Rockford, and he used to work as a bartender at Foleys. He said you were his last customer one night a couple of years ago, and you told him an interesting story about John Kennedy Junior's plane accident."

Owen stared hard at her. He looked around the deli and lowered his voice. "Who the hell are you, and how'd you find me?"

"Look, I'm a friend. Please, you can trust me. I'm not wearing a wire. I'm simply acquiring information. After I walk out that door, you never existed. I can promise you that."

"What's this about? Who do you work for?"

"NSA."

"Why are they interested after all this time?"

"Because, until I heard about some of what you saw—what you told my friend, Mark, we had no idea that the crash of Kennedy's plane was anything but an accident."

Owen watched traffic outside for a moment. "What'd you say your name was?"

"Alicia."

"Alicia, that sounds like bullshit to me. I reported what I saw. But my superiors informed me that I didn't see part of the plane's tail blown up. Travis and I were debriefed on what we saw. We were told that we were mistaken and all of the data was classified."

"Who's Travis?"

"A buddy of mine from the Navy."

"Where's he today?"

"Dead."

"May I ask how he died?"

"A .22 bullet through his brain. They said he committed suicide. But anyone who knew Travis would know he didn't have a suicidal bone in his body. I remember one time we were in Iraq and the talk came around to some of the guys in the service, those who were pulling three and four tours of duty, those who'd lost wives and families to divorce, a few were eating their own bullets. Travis said we didn't have permission, the right, to commit suicide any more than we have to commit murder."

"Do you think Kennedy, his wife and sister-in-law, were murdered in that plane?"

"That was the smoking gun. The impact of the ocean probably killed them."

"Did you see signs of a bomb inside the fuselage?"

"I was in 110 feet of water. It was the hole in the tail that I saw—about the size of a basketball. I did a little outside research right after Travis was killed. I spoke with a mercenary soldier I know, an expert on explosives, and he said that a charge can be exploded in a small plane with a spark generated by a barometric switch that's triggered by the altitude of the plane. This means that the killer could have picked the altitude for the explosion of Kennedy's plane. Makes it look like an accident, but it works better over land cause the damage from the crash usually wipes out most everything. Not so much in water."

"Did you find the bodies?"

Owen deeply inhaled, licked his lower lip and stared out the window. "Yeah. Damn shame." His eyes met Alicia. "I'd heard the plane had a black box, which is rare for a plane that size. The NTSB said its battery had been removed. Travis said one of the Navy investigators told him the plane's Emergency Locater Transmitter was shut off and so was the fuel valve, two things that don't happen by accident."

"Anything else that you can remember?"

"This whole thing had a bad smell to it. There was a witness to the plane's explosion, a guy fishing off the beach that night. Try to find him. Gone. Kennedy made a radio call to the flight tower on Martha's Vineyard on his approach. Try to find that record or the air traffic controller he spoke to. You can't. So now, all these years later, is the government really going to reopen the investigation, a *real* investigation? What prompted it?"

"A change in events. Do you have a photograph of the plane wreck?"

Owen smiled. "I must have been pretty drunk that night in the bar. Don't remember even telling the bartender that. Yes, it was 1999, so I used an underwater film camera. I made one print."

"May I have it or the negative?"

Owen pursed his lips for a second. "This one will be for Travis. Sure, I have it in a safe deposit box. Today, I'm selling my dive shop. I've been battling cancer. I'm told it's in remission. Where do you live? I can meet you tomorrow."

"I live in Washington."

"I guess that makes sense. I have to be in DC this Friday. Maybe we could meet for lunch or dinner, and I'll bring the picture."

Alicia smiled. "Lunch sounds good. Meet me at Tabard Inn Restaurant on N Street in DC. Noon."

"Maybe I should have asked for your ID, but those can be faked. I don't think the sincerity in your face can be, at least I hope not. Maybe now, after all this time, something will finally happen. The victims deserve it. Too bad Travis won't be around to see it."

FIFTY-EIGHT

*J*acob Kogen entered the room where Marcus was working and said, "How is the new computer performing?"

"Fine. As long as it stays off the Internet and no one else has access to it, we should be okay."

"Good."

"I had a visit from a friend of yours."

"Oh, who is that?"

"He said his name is Nathan Levy. I assume he's Mossad."

"What did he want?"

"He wanted me to help the Mossad cryptographers elevate their cyber offense to a level that would essentially take apart or greatly slow down Iran's nuclear efforts."

Jacob sat down and blew out a raspy breath. "What do you mean? Would this set off explosions in Iran?"

"These bombs are silent. They don't blow up anything. They're designed to lie dormant, like a hidden cancer inside the operation system of high-end computers. When certain things happen, such as a system engaging a new workflow, the worm comes out of its cocoon and begins a systematic attack. It could destroy motors and gears, making centrifuge production impossible, in essence rendering the entire operation down to cyber shreds."

"Is there technology to do that?"

"Don't look so damn surprised. You baited me! You or the Mossad probably forged my name on the Newton papers, when the real reason you brought me over here was to aid Israel by encoding a cyber attack against Iran."

Jacob shook his head. "No! Never would I do such a thing. Paul, I didn't know this technology even existed. And if I had known, I would never have portrayed a ruse to bring you here."

"Bullshit!"

Jacob stood. "Please! I'm a man of mathematics, science and religion. I, just like Newton, firmly believe in the Bible and what it reveals to us. I also believe that it can show us other things if we can dig deeper, learn more, translate and decipher the old text. I had nothing to do with Nathan Levy's contacting you."

"But you do *know* him."

"Yes, of course I know him."

"Was he the contact you spoke with when I told you I thought the prime minister was going to be assassinated at the Lincoln Memorial?"

"Yes."

Marcus stared out the university window for a few seconds. He leveled his eyes back to Kogen. "Can you really trust him?"

"Of course. Why?"

"He, or someone in your intelligence, needs to bring out all the troops again."

"What do you mean, Paul?"

"I mean to prevent a new assassination attempt."

"Oh God...what do you know now?"

"I read the prime minister is going to be at a UNESCO park, a memorial in Paris. He is scheduled to speak at the memorial that was erected to commemorate the life and death of former Primer Minister Yitzhak Rabin. The event is planned for the tenth anniversary of Rabin's death. That's in four days."

Jacob sat down, his face filled with deliberation, his eyes probing the unseen for a sense of direction. "Tell me, Paul. You have cracked it, haven't you? I can *feel* it. You have discovered something in Newton's notes—the Bible, that's opening these visions, these doors into the future. Newton didn't just write your name in his notes. He took *dictation*, and he received it from the word of God."

"I spoke with Gisele Fournier, the woman who donated the remaining Newton papers to the library."

"Yes…and?"

"I have reason to believe that a reference to a weeping angel in the Bible is somewhere in the same UNESCO park where the prime minister will speak. I'm going there."

Alicia sat alone in the patio garden of the Tabard Inn Restaurant and looked at her watch for the third time: 12:45. She located Greg Owens' number in her cell and hit the dial button. The call made an abrupt, sharp sound and then went to silence. No rings. No voice-mail. Alicia keyed in the GPS mode grid from Owens' phone. She could make out a faint signal coming from the northwest side of the district. Alicia stared at her phone. "Oh, no," she whispered. "The river."

She stood and walked quickly inside the inn and entered the stylish bar, an old episode of Law and Order was playing above the bar on a wide plasma screen. Alicia caught the attention of the bartender. "Excuse me. Would you turn on the news?"

"Sure." He reached for a remote control and flipped through the channels. "Any preference on the channel?"

An image caught her eye. "Stop! Please turn up the sound."

There were images of a car being pulled from the Potomac River. The graphic in the lower part of the screen read: *Live Video from Chain Bridge*. A news reporter, off screen said, "A witness told us he saw the car plummet off the Chain Bridge about ninety minutes ago. Rescue divers found one person in the submerged car. The car was in about twelve feet of water on the bottom of the Potomac River. They report the body, which is that of a man, was found on the driver's side of the car. The vehicle is a late model Hyundai Sonata. We don't have a positive identification of the victim. Why the car veered off the bridge is not yet known. The investigation will continue when the car is hauled and inspected. Ron Brooke, News Three."

Alicia felt tightness in her chest. She remembered the words Greg Owen had said, *"Too bad Travis won't be around to see it."*

FIFTY-NINE

Sam Quincy could feel the prop blast from the choppers descending into the Mekong Delta of Vietnam. He lay on his back, his blood mixing with the rich mud from the swamps, a single round from an AK-47 through one leg, shattering his femur. Dead and dying men scattered all around him. They were boys mostly—some young as eighteen, talking to God, others crying for their mothers.

Sam opened his eyes, the delta of South Vietnam dissolved into the still grey of a dawn filling his family room. He looked at the oaks and pines through the bay window. He tried to sit from the near prone position in his recliner, blankets up to his chest. Sam could taste the morphine in his mouth, smell it in his pores along with the stench of rotting organs inside his body. He managed to adjust the chair to a sitting position.

He thought about his granddaughter held captive in Iran, his conversation with Alicia; and through the haze of drugs, he remembered an obscure detail of World War II that he'd discovered in his research years ago. It was mentioned to him by a veteran who had been a chief assistant to one of the U.S. lawyers who prosecuted members of the Third Reich in the Nuremberg Tribunals. The man had spent a few days in the liberated Dachau concentration camp in Germany, saw the bodies stacked like cordwood, the adult survivors resembling human skeletons, unable to stand or speak, eyes wide and welling with tears like warehoused, abused and abandoned children.

Sam closed his eyes for a moment, and then he looked across the family room where Helen slept in the fetal position under a quilt, her face traced with worry even under the illusion of rest. Sam wanted to get out of the damned chair and walk to her, to lie down with Helen and simply hold her. Just one more time. One more morning to wake up by her side in their bed. But he could no longer stand on his own.

He closed his eyes and concentrated. *The WWII veteran, what the hell was his name? Better write it down for Alicia.* He struggled to reach the pad of paper and pen on the table-lamp. "C'mon body…move again," he mumbled, unable to get close enough. Sam found his cell phone on a small stand next to his chair. He called Alicia.

"Hi, Daddy," came her voice through a vapor of awakened slumber. He knew she tried to sound alert.

"Hey, sweetheart…I know it's early, but I remembered some information, something that might help, since you were asking about that spear."

"Are you okay?"

"I'm whispering because I don't want to wake up your mom. Also, I wanted to share a sunrise with you."

"That's so sweet."

"Alicia, a vet from the big war, Lawrence J. Foster—met him at a VFW in Charlottesville. Anyway, he worked as a prosecutor's assistant in the Nuremberg Tribunals and later took a job with the OSS, the predecessor to the CIA. He told me a soldier by the name of Marcus…don't know if that's his first or last name…and another man had foiled an attempt by Stalin to find that spear you mentioned. Stalin wanted to bring it to Russia, and he'd handpicked his top assassin to bring it back. The story goes that this Marcus knew somebody even better than the man Stalin chose. The man was a spy in the French Resistance…last name of Fournier. Probably long since dead. I heard he was very good as an operative and a pain in the ass to Germany and Russia. He could have sold the Spear of Destiny to anyone with a big bank account."

"If it's true, this sounds like the accident involving Patton was anything but an accident. Maybe someone wanted him hurt or killed in order to find and steal the spear."

"That's a possibility. Most of the theories in this direction say if Patton was taken out, and that's a big *if*, it was because someone wanted him silenced since a few people feared he was going to eventually drag the nation into a war with the Soviets."

"Dad, the man named Marcus, was his first name David?"

"David, I think. Yes, that was his name."

"Maybe Stalin never took possession of the spear. What happened to Foster, the man who shared his story with you?"

"That's been at least twenty years ago. I haven't seen him since." Sam coughed, felt his heart flutter.

"Are you okay, Dad?"

There was long pause as Sam tried to regulate his breathing, his pulse erratic, blood pressure dropping. "Sweetheart…"

"Yes, Daddy."

"Look out that bedroom window of yours, Alicia. See this gorgeous new day greeting you?"

"Yes, Daddy, I see it."

Sam stared though the bay window into his back yard, many of the trees now without leaves, a powdering of frost on the ground. He smiled when a chipmunk stood on the wooden deck banister, rocking back on its hindquarters and rotating a small acorn in its paws, nibbling through the shell.

"It's a fine world, sweetheart. A world we should be proud of and protect."

"It is a fine world, Dad, and it's a splendid sunrise."

The light from the dawn filled Sam's face with a radiance he'd never seen in his life. He was young again, running through the fields and vineyards near his boyhood home in Northern California. Sam eased back in his chair and looked at his sleeping wife. "Tell your mother, sister and my granddaughter how much I love them," he whispered, his eyes meeting the rising sun. "I love you, Alicia."

"I love you too, Daddy." Her eyes filled with tears.

"I'm home, in the vineyards of Napa Valley, and it's a grand morning… as you said…it's splendid…"

"Daddy…are you okay? Dad…please…don't…"

"It's a beautiful sunrise…you see it, Alicia?"

"Yes, Dad...it is...please, don't go." Tears streamed down Alicia's cheeks.

Sam was smiling and walking through vineyards in the spring, the vines exploding with tiny blossoms, the herbal fragrance sweet. He inhaled the baby's breath of a new season, his weak heart beating for a final moment, a moment he shared with his daughter.

"Daddy...we love you, too. We love you so much." Alicia stared at the sunrise, tears streaming down her cheeks.

SIXTY

Marcus took a seat at a sidewalk café in the northern side of Jerusalem, ordered bottled water and removed Taheera's cell phone from his pocket. He thought about calling the number, speaking with the man who is "consulting with his superiors." *Should you try to deceive us, your head will be removed with a dull knife.*

Marcus sipped the water. He wore dark glasses, watching the incoming tide of humanity walk down the street toward Damascus Gate. There was a caravan of departing tourists' buses—the throaty sounds of diesels protesting, bus drivers downshifting to maneuver through the streets.

He set both mobile phones on the table just as his phone buzzed. It was Alicia. "Paul…" There was a long pause.

"What do you have?"

"My father died two days ago."

Marcus felt his chest tighten, his scar pulsate. "Alicia, I'm so very sorry to hear that. I wish I was there."

"I do, too. The only positive things about his death are that Dad is no longer suffering, and we had time to prepare for his passing. Brandi, in Iran, has no idea her grandfather just died. They were really close. She won't be here for his funeral."

"Maybe she'll be home for Christmas."

"I pray."

"How are *you* doing, Alicia?"

"I'm a little numb. Not at his death, because he's no longer in pain, but what hurts is the reality of him not being here, ever again. I can't just pick up the phone and call him. It's beginning to creep up around me. Dad called me the morning right before he died. He wanted to watch a sunrise with me. I was looking out my apartment window when the dawn broke, and Dad was watching the sunrise from our backyard. Paul, I felt so connected to my father…even though I wasn't physically there. I felt we were in the *same* room with a window to the universe…the same instant he was experiencing a daybreak that took him back to his boyhood home." She paused, speaking just above a whisper. "I miss him so much. It hurts." Her voice trapped in sinew, mucus and memories.

"I wish I could have met him."

"A few weeks ago, Dad asked me if he'd been there…you know, been a father when a girl needs one."

Marcus was silent, letting Alicia reach deep inside the well of her soul.

"Dad said he hoped, if nothing else, he'd given me some fond memo-ries…good memories to draw upon because he said those were the picture postcards we mail to ourselves on Sunday mornings."

"It sounds like he was a remarkable man."

"He was." Alicia pulled a strand of her dark hair behind one ear. "I have almost a month's vacation time stored. If I don't take some of it, I'm gonna lose it. After the funeral I want to—no, Paul, I *have* to get away. You need my help. I can be just as effective in Israel as I can in Washington, maybe more so. Would you mind if I came there?" Alicia bit her lower lip.

"It'd be good to work together in the same time zone. I could use your help. Tell me when you're arriving, and I'll be at the airport to pick you up."

"Thanks. I'm going to go back to my parent's house to wrap my arms around my sister Dianne and Mom. Dianne hasn't heard from Brandi in three months. We don't know if the Iranians are providing her with insulin. This, on top of Dad's death…"

"Alicia, don't lose faith. We'll find a way to get Brandi and Adam out of Iran."

"I haven't lost personal faith, but I've come damn close to losing what little faith I have for a big slice of the human race." Alicia told Marcus about her conservation with Greg Owen and his death by drowning in the

Potomac River. "The reports say he blew out a tire and the car careened off the bridge. His car was three months old. I checked the records. Owen bought it new, and it couldn't have had much wear on the tires. Paul, he said the picture he took underwater showed a hole in the tail of Kennedy's plane. He was bringing it to me before he was killed. Police say they didn't find anything in the car except his registration and a few personal effects. Someone wiped it clean."

"Did you find anything Kennedy was doing before his death that may have prompted this reaction and cover-up?"

"Try this one on for size. In 1997, his Magazine, *George*, published an article by the mother of the man convicted of killing Prime Minister Yitzhak Rabin. She alleged that her son, Yigal Amir, was provoked to do the assassination because Rabin had signed the Oslo Peace Accords, essentially opening deeper negotiations with the Palestinians over the occupied land."

"Does your research indicate who supposedly provoked Amir?"

"His mother said it came from inside the Shin Bet, the agency charged with Rabin's security. There is, of course, nothing to substantiate those accusations. Rabin's widow was not too happy that Kennedy gave the mother of her husband's killer a public platform in the magazine. There's also evidence that John was going to reopen the story of the assassination of his father while tracking down leads on the assassination of Yitzhak Rabin."

"Alicia, when you peel back the layers, the worms retreat."

"Speaking of worms, I uncovered a few rocks which show some dark, slimy things living, breeding and cutting covert deals under the cover of darkness."

"I'm listening."

"There's a company here in Washington, headquarters off Pennsylvania Avenue, conveniently not far from the Capital, White House and the Pentagon. It's called the Kinsley Group. They have an office in New York, too. Paul, for all practical purposes, this company is America's ninth largest defense contractor. The reason that's odd is because they are, essentially, a private equity investment company. But the board of directors is like a *who's who* of former politicians and heads of state. And these are the ones I could find by doing some easy digging. The rest took heavy lifting. I have a call in to a close friend of mine who works for the Justice Department. He may be in a position to shed some light on this."

"Meet him somewhere like a crowded restaurant."

Alicia looked out her kitchen window toward the front street. A cable installation van sat in front of her neighbor's home. "Paul, what are you saying?"

"Just be very aware of your surroundings. Anything else?"

"I'm still digging in that dark area. On another front, I've found something."

"What?"

"When I was talking with Dad he remembered a couple of names from the General Patton accident or incident. One was a guy who was an assistant to the U.S. prosecutor in the Nuremberg Trials and later worked with the OSS. His name was Lawrence J. Foster. The other man was someone thought to have been a member of the French Resistance, a shadowy figure who was a thorn in the side to Germany, and apparently Russia, too. Dad heard that it was this guy who was believed to have been involved with David Marcus in stopping the Russian hit man. The Frenchman had the last name of Fournier."

Marcus said nothing.

"Paul, are you there?"

"Yes. Alicia, before you fly here, go back to visit the Mayflower Assisted Living home. Spend a little time with Mama Davis. One of the residents there is a man by the name of Larry Foster. It's a long shot—but find out if he's the same Lawrence J. Foster who worked with David Marcus during the Nuremberg Trials. If he is, ask him where we can find James Tower."

SIXTY-ONE

PARIS, FRANCE

A chilly November wind blew through the heart of Paris. Paul Marcus got out of the taxi and zipped his windbreaker. He paid the fare and walked half a block to the UNESCO World Headquarters on Place de Fontenoy. Gisele Fournier had said she would meet him at the entrance to the Garden of Peace near the rear of the massive Y-shaped building. Marcus found directions and exited the building, heading toward the garden.

A woman sat alone on a park bench, tossing breadcrumbs to a flock of sparrows. She looked up when Marcus approached, shielding the vivid morning sun from her eyes.

"Gisele?"

"Yes, how are you, Paul?" She stood and smiled.

"Thank you for coming." Gisele had a warm smile, slender neck, shoulder-length auburn hair, and hazel eyes that returned the morning light.

"I hope there is information here that can help you."

Marcus looked at the expanse of manicured trees, shrubs, and flowers tucked in deep pockets of shade. He could hear the flow of water running over stones somewhere in the garden, the scent of damp moss in the air. Gisele said, "The Garden of Peace was designed by Isamu Noguchi. He was a Japanese sculptor rather than a gardener. Growing up in Paris, this garden has always been one of my favorite places to go, or to *hide* in the heart of the city of light. At first, I came here with my grandfather. After his death, I came alone—although I never felt alone. The first thing we'll see is the Fountain of Peace."

Marcus followed her, walking by a flowing fountain, stepping across rocks with water moving around them. A stone path curled its way through pines, cherry, plum, magnolia, willow and lotus trees. Boulders were interspersed with the appearance of natural statues standing upright in the garden. She touched one of the rocks, then looked at Marcus and smiled. "Noguchi said his installation of rocks were the bones of the garden. Plants come and go, but he felt the rocks gave it an everlasting foundation and spirit."

They crossed a stone bridge, the breeze whipping through the willows, causing the bamboo stalks to rub together emitting cries like cats howling in the wind. Gisele said, "The ancient Japanese Shintoist believed that *divine forces* are part of nature, a spirit found in plants, mountains and waterfalls. This garden, like earth, is a branch of the universe in which we're supposed to be its caregivers—it's providers, not dominators or takers. My grandfather used to come here and say that the more we care for the environment, the lungs of the earth, then the easier it will be for us to draw the 'breath of life.' Before I take you to the weeping angel of Nagasaki, I'll show you where the memorial to Yitzhak Rabin is located."

"Gisele, what was your grandfather's name?"

"Philippe…Philippe Fournier."

Marcus walked with her to the north side of the garden. There was a single olive tree planted in the midst of a sculpted arrangement of steel. Gisele pointed. "There is the memorial."

"It's separate from the Garden of Peace."

"Yes, but close neighbors."

Marcus looked at the surroundings, the roofs of buildings, nearby roads, high rise hotels—anywhere an assassin could get off a concealed shot. There were many places. A single leaf fell from the olive tree and tumbled across the fresh-cut grass toward the massive UNESCO headquarters.

"What are you thinking?" she asked.

"I'm thinking how difficult it would be to protect the current Israeli prime minister in this area."

"Do you believe someone will make an attempt on his life here?"

"At this point, that's a very good possibility."

Gisele glanced away for a moment. "After those Al-Qaeda terrorists stormed the Charlie Hebdo magazine offices and killed all those people... seventeen died in the shootouts, including the grocery store. Paris isn't the same. France isn't the same. It never will be." She looked at Marcus. "If someone is trying to kill the prime minister, why don't you go to the police?"

"That's the first start, and then I go higher than the police."

"I'm sure there will be high security for the ceremonies. Come, I will take you to the weeping angel."

They returned to the garden's entrance. Marcus inhaled the cool air, the scent of evergreen shrubs lingering in the breeze. He said, "It's beautiful here. I can see why you are drawn back to it. Where's the statue of the *weeping angel?*"

"We passed by it. I wanted you to see, maybe to *feel* the garden and have a better understanding of the little angel's place in it. It's directly behind the Fountain of Peace. Right there." She pointed to a stone wall. "There she is."

Marcus stepped closer to the statue, which was no larger than the size of a honeydew melon. The angelic face was that of a young girl with shoulder-length hair and wings lifted upright from her shoulders. The left eye looked fractured, closed with a dark smudge under the eye, giving the appearance of the statue weeping. Marcus touched the face, his finger tracing the fissure that was, at one time, an eye carved into stone.

Gisele said, "The little angel was the only thing recognizable in the rubble from what was the Urakami Catholic Church in Nagasaki after the atomic bomb was dropped on the city. My grandfather used to say her face spoke volumes, and her scars were a sign, a poignant reminder of the hell that nuclear weapons can unleash on earth."

Marcus looked in the direction the statue faced. Gisele said, "Grandfather once told me the statue of the angel reminded him of one he'd seen during a trip to Rome after the war."

"That seems like an odd time to visit Rome. I imagine there are a few thousand statues in Rome."

"Perhaps only one resembles the weeping angel. My grandfather told me he saw it when he visited the Castel Sant'Angelo. He said it was one of the ten sculptures on the bridge across the River Tiber leading to the castle.

He said the angel had the face of a young woman, but she carried a lance in her arms."

Marcus looked back at the statue, the ashen stone face staring off to the southwest. He turned his head in the direction and pointed. "Gisele, if I were to start walking from here, in a straight line, what is the first large cathedral I would come to?"

She gazed to the southwest, eyes searching for Parisian landmarks. "There is the Pantheon Monument in the Luxemburg Gardens. The Pantheon was originally built as a church or a cathedral. But now it is more like a crypt for the famous. Some of the bodies in there include Marie Curie, Voltaire, Alexandre Dumas, and many others."

"How large a building is the Pantheon?"

"Oh, I don't know. It is very big."

"Is there a cathedral beyond the Pantheon, still following the direction the angel is looking?"

Gisele stood on her toes for a moment. Then she closed her eyes. "Yes, but it is not Notre Dame. That is more toward the northwest. In the same direction, as you Americans say, the way the crow flies…the crow would fly into the Cathedral of Chartres." The chilly breeze tossed her hair. She looked toward the southwest, her eyes slowly meeting Marcus.

"Where is that?" he asked.

"It is in the village of Chartres, about fifty kilometers from Paris. The cathedral is unlike any in Paris, maybe the world."

"What do you mean?"

"It's mystical, really…and it is difficult to explain. Chartres Cathedral is said to have the finest and oldest stained glass in the world. There is an ancient labyrinth in the sanctuary. I remember going there as a little girl and counting the steps to the center of the labyrinth. I recall it was two hundred and seventy steps to the center. Most cathedrals in France have tombs, either in their crypts or somewhere on the grounds. But this is not the case at Chartres. The cathedral, which is very large, is a testament to the living. It was built as a holy shrine to the Virgin Mary. In Chartres is the tunic Mary wore when she gave birth to Jesus."

"Gisele, listen to me. This may sound strange, but I need to ask a big favor of you."

"What favor?"

"My French is fair, but not good enough. Use a pay phone to call the Paris police department. Demand to speak with whoever's in charge of security at the Rabin Memorial dedication. They need a large police presence tomorrow."

"Why do I call from a pay phone? What do I tell the police?"

"You don't have to identify yourself. When you make the call, pull a scarf over your head, wear dark glasses, and then go home. Forget we ever spoke. Tell the police that tomorrow someone will try to kill the Israeli prime minister."

SIXTY-TWO

The Parisian sky swirled with slate colored clouds chasing each other, the hint of sun squeezing through the grey and resembling a dying white ember on charcoal. It was late in the afternoon when Marcus walked inside the Cafe Le Flore, a small restaurant facing the Seine. The river reflected the grey mood of the clouds, the city soaking in a bath of pewter twilight.

Marcus's phone buzzed in his pocket. He answered and Gisele Fournier said, "Paul, I'm home. I wanted to let you know that I called the police and spoke with Inspector Victor Roux. He asked me where I got my information, and I wasn't sure what to tell him."

"What did you say?"

"I told him that an extremely reliable source told me, and I felt a duty to call the police. When he asked to meet with me...I just disconnected the phone."

"Thank you for making the call."

"It is no problem. Do you *really* think the prime minister is in danger?"

"Yes."

"This must come from my grandfather's papers, the Isaac Newton papers and the Bible. Maybe this is some of what my grandfather *saw*. What brought real terror to his eyes was the divination of nuclear war. What do you do next?"

"I don't know. I've never done anything like this in my life. Gisele, the Chartres Cathedral...can you remember anything more about it?"

250

"Yes, years ago. It was summer, the longest day of the summer. I remember it well because of something my grandfather showed me."

"What was that?"

"He took my brother and me to the old cathedral during the Summer Solstice. I remember that the sun was in a unique position in the sky to shine though the dark of the stained glass window called Saint Apollonaire. The sun made the window really stand out, and it was so beautiful. There is one tiny portion through the dark glass where the sunray came in at a perfect angle to strike a stone in the floor. The light hit a nail in the center of the only rectangle stone on the floor. Grandfather said he heard the nail was one that entered the hand of Jesus. Paul, I have to go now. I'm joining my aunt and brother at our small cottage between Boulogne and Calais. Please let me know if you need anything more."

Marcus ordered French espresso coffee and a croissant. He looked across the Seine at Notre Dame. His thoughts bounced from the Rabin Memorial ceremonies to be held near the Garden of Peace to the information Gisele told him about the Chartres Cathedral. *I remember going there as a little girl and counting the steps to the center of the labyrinth. I recall it was two hundred and seventy steps to the center.*

He opened his laptop, scanning information about the Chartres Cathedral. Marcus quickly learned that many people considered the cathedral itself as a holy shrine, a tribute to the Virgin Mary. *What could a reference to two hundred seventy steps mean, if anything? It's the number of days the average baby is in the womb. Is the cathedral a stone and glass womb on earth? What's inside it? What's to be released...to be born? Maybe nothing.* He looked at the pictures of the ancient church, the twin spires, one was 365 feet high, and the second was shorter at 349 feet. He found the elevation and dimensions of the church. Then he emailed the information to Jacob Kogen and added: *see how close in size Chartres Cathedral is to what we think Solomon's Temple was....*

Marcus thought about the lone olive tree centered in the steel sculpture near the Garden of Peace. He quickly found a front-page story in the Parisian newspaper, *Le Figero*, about the Israeli prime minister's visit to Paris. There was a picture of the prime minister and the French president. Marcus converted the story to English and read the details of the visit and ceremonies at the Rabin Memorial. The event, expected to last thirty minutes, would open with remarks by the mayor of Paris before his introduction of the prime minister. The story indicated that American Secretary of State, Merriam Hanover, would be attending the ceremonies, too. She was staying at the Hotel de Crillon and flying to Egypt after her stop in Paris.

Marcus made a call to her mobile phone. The Secretary's assistant answered. Marcus said, "Secretary Hanover asked me to stay in touch with her. I know she's here in Paris. Something has come up that she should know about. I need to meet with her today."

"Mr. Marcus, we just got in from de Gaulle. Secretary Hanover's afternoon is fully booked with meetings through dinner. She can't meet with you—"

"Please, put her on the line."

"I'm sorry. But that's not possible." The woman ended the call.

Marcus set his phone on the table. He looked through his computer bag and found Taheera's phone. He held it for a moment, his eyes focused on the last number dialed. His cell rang. He set the dead woman's phone down and picked up his mobile. "Paul Marcus, this is Nathan Levy. Jacob Kogen said that you were concerned there will be an attempt on the prime minister's life in Paris."

"I think it's going to happen during the tenth anniversary ceremonies at the Yitzhak Rabin Memorial adjacent to the Garden of Peace at the UNESCO headquarters."

"Is this information drawn from the same source that indicated the prime minister's life was in danger when he made an appearance with your president at the Lincoln Memorial in Washington?"

"Yes."

"That wasn't a credible source. What makes you think anything has changed?"

"The information better fits. The time and location of the Lincoln Memorial best matched the given parameters at that instance. Now, with the tenth anniversary of the Rabin Memorial to be commemorated in Paris, the other clues, such as the weeping angel, are more obvious. The Nagasaki Angel, the only piece of a church that wasn't vaporized during the bombing of Nagasaki, is in the park."

"We will have more than adequate security. Paul, your decryption talents are, no doubt, without equal. Let us hope, however, the information you are receiving from your sources, the Bible and writings of Isaac Newton, are inaccurate. The time you are placing in decrypting ancient codes and writings could be, in my opinion, better served with the challenges of the present and future. Have you reconsidered my offer?"

"That's not what I came to the Middle East to do."

"But yet you have become the prophet of doom, the early warning of impending assassinations that do not materialize. You are wasting your time. Jacob Kogen is a man looking for signs from God when, in fact, evil is constantly rearing its ugly head. These ancient texts are hieroglyphics that have no bearing whatsoever on today's complex issues. I trust you can understand that."

"A lot of today's complex issues are really pretty simple and have been the same for two thousand years. All that's changed is the choice of weapons."

"How long will you be in Paris?"

"I didn't say I was in Paris."

"I assumed as much because you told me about the statue of the angel. I was aware of the Rabin Memorial. Paul, please don't take advantage of our hospitality and stray into other pastures. Our team is very good—so good, in fact, I'm told we can look for cyber fingerprints, or coding techniques unique to the author. Since you are only one of a handful of authors capable of such coding, I trust you have no illusions about what I'm saying."

"Before you threaten me again, you'd better take seriously the information I just delivered to you. Levy, you want me working for you, right?"

"I am listening."

"You find the bastard who killed my wife and daughter. He's an Iranian agent."

"How do you know this?"

"Because the other agent sent to kill me, Taheera, had no reason to lie when she was about to shoot me in the head. She told me an agent killed my wife and daughter, and then left me for dead because they didn't want me recruited by Israel. Now, if you want me to damage the Iranian nuke operation, you kill the son-of-bitch that destroyed my life."

SIXTY-THREE

Marcus left the café, caught a taxi and arrived at the Hotel de Crillon on Place de la Concorde. He entered the lobby and walked across the imported, honey-colored marble floor, which reflected light and glass from the opulent chandeliers. Before approaching the concierge's desk, he glanced at the plasma monitor listing hotel events. An attractive young woman, whose nametag read Dominique, sat at the desk. "Dominique, I'm running late for Secretary of State Hanover's dinner. Is it in the Batailles Room?"

She smiled, her eyes dazzling, bouncing light from the chandelier above her station. "No sir. That dinner is being held in the Marie-Antoinette Room on the second floor."

"Thank you."

Marcus took an elevator to the second floor. When the elevator doors opened, he could feel the hushed, efficient orchestration of a restricted, invitation-only dinner party. Guests, holding cocktail glasses, chatted in semi-circles while waiters in tuxedos delivered champagne and hors d'oeuvres. There was the smell of garlic, steamed crab and money in the air. Men in dark suits and short haircuts roamed the halls. Hotel security manned a metal detector leading to the Marie-Antoinette Room. Security agents checked ID's while the crowd filed into the dining room. Marcus weaved his way through the guests and then stopped beneath a massive crystal chandelier to the far right of the entryway. He stood away from the throng, watched and waited.

When the last few late arrivals were ushered into the room, Secretary of State Hanover's entourage arrived, and she was in the center flanked by assistants and bodyguards.

"Secretary Hanover!" shouted Marcus, lifting his arm. Two members of her security team were quickly in front of Marcus.

Secretary Hanover stopped and turned toward him. She smiled and walked over to Marcus. "It's okay, gentlemen. This is Paul Marcus, the Nobel Laureate in medicine. It's good to see you, Paul. Last we spoke you were in Jerusalem. What brings you to Paris?"

"Secretary Hanover, may I speak to you in private?"

"I'm sorry, but Secretary Hanover is already late for the dinner," interrupted her assistant, Jennifer Greene. She was tall, thin lips, and a sharp nose that supported black-framed glasses. She held an iPhone and an iPad like weapons.

"It's okay, Jennifer. Paul, I have a couple of minutes. Let's step over there." They walked a few feet away from the group. "I'm hoping you have good news and you've decided to attend the Nobel proceedings with the president."

"Secretary Hanover—"

"Paul, I told you to call me Merriam."

"Merriam, I have reason to believe that there will be an assassination attempt on the prime minister during Thursday's ceremonies at the Yitzhak Rabin Memorial."

Her eyes opened a little more and she tilted her head. "What have you heard and where'd you hear it?"

"I haven't heard anything. I found something. I found it buried in biblical texts, information that indicates a possible plot to kill the prime minister."

"Paul, I don't want to seem like you're shouting wolf, but this is the second time you've approached me about a potential threat to the prime minister's life. Our intelligence found no indication, not the slightest evidence that anything was there during the Lincoln Memorial ceremony. I assure you, security will be heavy at the Rabin Memorial, too."

"I'm not shouting wolf. Maybe I'm wrong again. But if something happened and I made no effort to warn anyone, I'd have a hard time with that."

"I understand. It's not unlike security in the world's airports—better safe than sorry. I need to go make a speech. I hope to see you in Stockholm." She turned to leave.

"Has any progress been made on getting Iran to release Brandi Hirsh and Adam Spencer?"

"We haven't forgotten them. However, I'll be frank with you, Paul. The talks have stalled. We've done all we can. I'm hopeful there will be more international pressure for their release, but the Iranians have waged a nasty campaign to convince people that the two Americans are spies. Those allegations are so farfetched it's incredulous. Iran wants to play hard ball."

"Maybe we can throw a perfect game."

"What do you mean?"

Jennifer Greene, iPad wedged beneath one arm, thumbs punching the keys on her phone, approached. "Excuse me, Secretary Hanover, Ambassador Bertrand is waiting to introduce you to his guests."

She nodded and said to Marcus, "I'm sorry, but duty calls."

"Can you get a security clearance for me at the Rabin ceremony?"

"Of course. I'll make sure of it."

She turned to walk to the regal dining room. Marcus said, "Tell the president I'll be in Stockholm with him."

Secretary Hanover looked back over her shoulder and smiled. "Thank you, Paul."

"At the Rabin Memorial—be careful and be very aware of your surroundings."

— —

Marcus registered at the Paris Eiffel Cambronne Hotel. He unlocked the door to his room, and then set his laptop and small suitcase on the bed just as his phone rang. Jacob Kogen said, "Paul, out of hundreds of European cathedrals, you have found the one that is the closest match possible in size, scope and engineering to what we know of Solomon's Temple."

"In what way?"

"It was built with the same measurement, the same sacred geometry used in the building of Solomon's Temple. The Chartres Cathedral is without a doubt one of the most amazing structures on earth, and it looks like it is probably near the exact size as Solomon's Temple. The interior layout of Chartres is the shape of a large cross, and the massive roof is built like a horizontal cross. The cathedral is equivalent to a stone and glass book of the Bible. Much of the entire Bible, from creation to the final days, is told within the cathedral's portals, and found on the most remarkable stained glass images ever created by man. Not only is their beauty world renowned, but also the colors have never been duplicated. The glass is said to have qualities that transmute or change sunlight, removing ultra violet and allowing the interior of the church to glow from a warmer spectrum of light. The Blue Virgin window is believed to be the best example of stained glass art in any cathedral. Here's something very interesting, Paul. Pilgrims entering the church often say they feel as if the combination of light, images in the glass, the biblical icons of Creation and the Last Judgment, give them an experience never found in any other building on earth."

"What do you mean?"

"They say it's like some form of spiritual baptism, and many are profoundly changed just by entering the building and staying a while."

"I read that it houses a tunic worn by Mary, mother of Jesus."

"That article of clothing was actually given to Chartres Cathedral by Charles the Bald, the grandson of Charlemagne who had the tunic in his possession."

Marcus closed his eyes for a moment, the words of Bahir ricocheting in his mind. *'Charlemagne is said to have carried the spear through forty-five victorious battles, but died not long after he, by chance, dropped it from his horse. It is said that whoever has possession of this lance is near unconquerable.'*

"Paul, are you there?"

"Yes. Did you find out anything about light from the summer solstice entering the cathedral?"

"Yes, during two minutes of the equinox, a long, narrow sunbeam strikes an iron nail in the only rectangle stone laid within the thousands of other stones in the floor. No one alive knows the significance of it. An architect, whose identity was kept secret, designed the cathedral. It's believed that the Knights Templar had it built."

"What can you find out about the labyrinth in the sanctuary?"

"It's a big mystery, too. The number of steps to the center is 270. The center looks like a flower with six petals. Something else I believe you will find very intriguing."

"What's that?"

"Chartres Cathedral was the site of the School of Chartres. It was like none other in Europe."

"How?"

"It attracted the brightest students from the four corners of Europe who wanted to study the spiritual sciences. The short of it is that the teachers combined a Platonic philosophy within scriptures found in the Bible. They applied reason to faith to find a ground between the simple acceptance of what God had revealed and…well…"

"What are you saying, Jacob?"

"Let's put it this way, the School of Chartres, was probably the closest place on earth during the Middle Ages where the goal—the curriculum, was to learn, understand and possibly attain *absolute* knowledge. Is this the thread Isaac Newton was searching for? Can it be found hidden in the mortar of Chartres Cathedral?

SIXTY-FOUR

At six a.m., the digital alarm chirped from Marcus' phone on his bedside table. He got up and looked out the hotel window. The Paris cityscape was in silhouette. Dawn broke as if a smoldering match was burning beyond the horizon, the sky looked aged—a sulfurous chemical grey. The Eiffel Tower resembled a lighthouse rising above a sea of taxis and commuters moving in elliptical orbits below the hotel.

Marcus made coffee and was walking to the shower when his phone rang. It was Alicia Quincy. "I spoke earlier with Larry Foster at the Mayflower Assisted Living center."

"Is he the same guy from the Nuremberg Trials?"

"Yes. He's eighty-eight and in fairly good health. No signs of dementia."

"What'd he say?"

"He says he knew James Tower. Said Tower was thought to have been British, but in reality he was an American who worked for the OSS at the end of World War II. After the war, he relocated to England. Foster said Tower was one of an elite group who carried out daring missions over Germany during the latter part of the war. After the war ended, he was in Mannheim, Germany, the same time General Patton was there. That's all Foster could remember."

"That's all we need. So James Tower is still alive?"

"Yes. I found his address."

"You could find a needle in a haystack."

"Only if it left a cyber-trace somewhere. I'll text his address to you. He lives in Wallingford, a village about ninety minutes west of London."

"How are you Alicia?"

"Okay." She sighed. The funeral was hard. "Because Dad was in such pain, Mom's at peace with his death, but she still misses him terribly when the silence sets in. It took the cancer two years to kill Dad. I'm ready to come to Israel."

"I'm in Paris."

"Paris! What are you doing there?"

"I have reason to believe that the hit on the prime minister was never meant to happen at the Lincoln Memorial."

"What do you mean?"

"The weeping angel wasn't the Lincoln statue. I believe it's a statue of an angel resurrected from the rubble of a nuclear bomb over Nagasaki. The statue was placed in the UNESCO Garden of Peace in the heart of Paris."

"Secretary of State Hanover is there for the ceremonies."

"Yes. I met with her. She and everyone I've talked with seem to look at me with a cynical eye after the Lincoln Memorial. But something in my gut...my heart is telling me this is the place it's going to happen."

"Dear God...I hope you're wrong."

"I do too."

"I've busied myself researching the Kinsley Group."

"Have you found anything more?"

"Yes." She lowered her voice on the phone. "The Kinsley Group has people on their payroll that are from the White House on down. They include a former presidential chief of staff, secretaries of defense, state, treasury and ex-chairman of the Securities and Exchange Commission. The roster of former and current advisers and directors on their payroll includes a mixture of some of the most powerful people in the nation and even around the world."

"So we have a private equity company morphing into a defense contractor."

"Yes. The Kinsley Group conducts business within what's known as the iron-triangle of industry, government and the military. So what you have, for example, is a past secretary of defense setting policy while in that position.

When he leaves the cabinet level post, the policies he set in place help funnel in huge government contracts, most of them worth billions, and our new Kinsley Group consultant and his friends reap the rewards he planted."

"I'd call that a slight conflict of interest."

"They're so big, like BP and the oil spill disaster—the Kinsley Group pays fines as part of the cost of doing business. They even consider bribes as part of their business model. They were fined fifty million dollars for making payments to middlemen in exchange for investments into the California Retirement System and Florida's Education Retirement System. The middlemen are multimillionaire pimps who get huge kickbacks for setting up these deals."

"Who are they?"

"Jonathon Carlson, one in particular, owns a ten-thousand acre Texas ranch where he flies in board members from Kinsley and the state retirement system directors to hunt exotic animals by day and frolic with exotic dancers in hot tubs by night. So far I know of two banks that received taxpayer's bailout dollars and are complicit in some of these investments. The Kinsley Group retains some of the nation's top PR and law firms to caulk the cracks and paint the walls when needed."

Marcus was silent for a few seconds, and then he said, "Would there have been reasons for any members of this group, its board, advisors or people they do business with, to take out John Kennedy Junior? If Kennedy had become a senator, or president, could they have feared that one or some of their billion-dollar deals might be at risk of not happening? And if so, what were these risks and the transactions underway that fit that timeframe? How long before they were completed would they have been planned? What events happened around the world to influence these multi-billion dollar deals?"

"Those are all good questions. I think some of the answers are related to the death of Israeli Prime Minister Yitzhak Rabin. Something else, Paul, I found names of two former members of the Kinsley board who are believed to be or have been members of an ultra-secretive faction. I don't know the name of this club, but I do have two names."

"Who are they?"

"I'd rather not say over the phone. I'll tell you when I arrive in Paris?"

"Paris?"

"I'm changing my flight as we speak. Bonjour."

Marcus sipped his coffee and set his cell phone on the dresser just as Alicia's text arrived: James Tower – 1281 Canterbury Road, Wallingford – England.

— —

Alicia opened the door to her family home. Her mother sat quietly by herself in the living room. She looked up from the photo album she held in her lap. She closed the album when Alicia entered the room.

"Hi, Mom. Are you okay?"

Her mother blinked her eyes then looked out the bay window into the backyard. She watched a cardinal land on the edge of the birdfeeder and peck at the seed. She looked back at her daughter. "The cardinal was your father's favorite bird."

Alicia smiled. "He loved to hear them sing in the spring."

"Once a week, for forty-one years, he filled the birdfeeders. The birds relied on him. I saw a blue jay land on your father's shoulder one time. It was a bird that had fallen from its nest as a baby, sort of fluttered down from the big oak out back. Dad put it in his shirt pocket while he climbed the oak tree and placed the little bird back in its nest." She looked up at Alicia through watering eyes. "Oh, honey, what am I going to do without your father? I miss him so much."

Alicia embraced her mother and simply held her. After a minute she said, "Mom, I'm going overseas."

"What?"

"I'm going to do everything I can to help Brandi. I can't stand to see Dianne like this. I'm going to do my best to bring Brandi home."

"How will you do it?"

"I don't know. I just feel compelled to go there." Alicia lifted the small golden cross from the chain on her neck. "Mom, if I get in some kind of a situation where I can't speak with you, somehow I'll find a way to get this necklace to you. When you receive it, you will know I'm fine. Okay?"

She looked at her daughter, eyes swollen and sad. "Okay, baby. Alicia, you were always so different from your sister and brother. You're a risk taker, just like your dad. If he were here, I'm sure he'd tell you to do what you feel you need to do. As your mother, I say do it with care. Just return to me, please? "

"I will, Mom."

SIXTY-FIVE

CALAIS, FRANCE

Marcus rented a Peugeot, pulled onto the A16 and drove to the coastal French town of Calais. He paid the fee at the terminal entrance and steered the Peugeot inside the train-car of the Chunnel. Thirty-five minutes later he arrived in Folkestone, England. After clearing customs, he punched the coordinates into the GPS and followed the vocal directions through the outskirts of London toward the village of Wallingford.

A winding road led him through farm fields that had been plowed under after a recent harvest. Sheep and cattle dotted the pastures, and smoke from farmhouse chimneys meandered in the still, crisp morning sky.

"Your destination is ahead on the right," came the last direction from the GPS. Marcus stopped the car in front of a small, white cobblestone home with a faded picket fence around most of the yard. He got out of the car and quietly closed the door. The sound of a cow mooing came from somewhere behind the home. A song thrush warbled from a pine thicket in an adjacent pasture. Marcus stepped to the front door and knocked. A dog barked inside, and he could hear someone shuffling around.

The door opened slightly, the face of an old man peering from behind the tarnished brass chain. His snow-white hair was uncombed, faced deeply lined with a slight drooping of his left eyelid. Near the floor, a small dog poked its nose out of the opening and sniffed. Marcus smiled, looked at the old man and said, "Hello, Mr. Tower."

"Who are you?" His accent had a slight British tone.

"My name's Paul Marcus. I'm from Virginia. My grandmother lives in an assisted living center, and it's the same place where an old colleague of yours now lives. Larry Foster sends his regards."

Tower snorted and cocked his head. "I don't know anybody named Foster."

"It's been a long time. But some things people don't forget. Things like tragedies in the war, the loss of friends, the loss of innocence…and the killing of General Patton."

Tower stared through the opening in the door, his sea blue eyes dimming for a moment in the past and then igniting as they focused on the present. "Who the hell *are* you and what do you want?"

"I'm doing some research. I won't be long. May I come in?"

The old man started to close the door. Marcus shoved his foot in the opening. "Please, Mr. Tower. I have to speak with you."

"What if I have a pistol in my hand? I could shoot you where you stand."

"I have no doubt that you could. But from what I understand, your killings were justified. We were at war. You had a code of honor, and I'm willing to bet after all these years…you still do."

The old man said nothing for a few seconds. "Give me a second." He eased the door shut. Marcus could hear him coughing, the coughs long and deep. A half minute later he removed the chain from the lock and opened the door. "I expected one day somebody like you'd come knocking. Decades went by and no one ever did. Finally, I figured I'd die and take the wounds to my grave. Now here you are. Come in, I have nothing to lose. Not now. Hell no, not anymore."

The little dog, a terrier, sniffed Marcus's shoes and followed him to a leather couch. Tower said, "I was just pouring a cup of tea. Would you like to join me?"

"Thank you."

"Please, have a seat. I'll bring the cups."

Marcus sat on the couch and looked around the living room. The home smelled of old newspapers and brewed tea. There was only one photograph. It was of a woman, a brunette. She was standing near some cliffs overlooking the sea, her wavy hair windblown. She had a strong resemblance to a young Elizabeth Taylor.

"That was Annie," Tower said, shuffling back to the living room, a cup of steaming tea in either hand. "She was my wife." He handed Marcus the tea and then sat down in a worn, brown leather chair across from him.

Marcus reached for the cup. "Where was the picture taken?"

"Ireland. The Cliffs of Moher. Annie loved it there. She loved the hills and the sea. She was a big city girl, New York, who fell in love with the country. Ireland became her favorite place. We went there a lot until she died. That's been fifteen years ago." The old man stopped, his mouth turned down, and he looked away from her photograph.

Marcus lifted his cup of tea and held it a moment. Tower said, "I didn't put poison in it."

"I don't believe you would have." Marcus sipped the hot tea.

"Why are you here?" Tower coughed, a raspy sound rattling in his lungs.

"The truth."

"I often wondered what that ever really meant."

"Why?"

"Maybe it was from war wounds…wounds to my head. My psyche, I guess." He grunted. "What truth are you looking for?"

"General Patton. I have reason to believe his death was planned."

"Are you writing a book or something?"

"No."

"Then why do you want to unearth old ghosts? Tell me *why* you're here."

"I've been researching the Bible, plugging in ancient text and looking for syntax, patterns of language correlated with dates and geometric measurements of space and time. These things show a relationship to the design of a long ago destroyed building, to a theory of mathematics and to knowledge that began in a time that only a few people could recognize and appreciate."

The old man looked straight at Marcus, holding his gaze for a few seconds. A grandfather clock in the corner of the room chimed. "What's that have to do with me?"

"Because, in other forms—in other manifestations, I believe the reason Patton died still exists today, and it may be part of the sum, or part of the reason others died and may die. I want to find a way to prevent that."

Tower stared at Marcus, his senses looking for the slightest hint of deception. He sipped his tea, placed the cup and saucer on the table in front of him and leaned back in his chair, his eyes shifting to a picture window overlooking a pasture. "At first I thought it was something that the very top down said had to be done for the security of the nation. They called it a justified pulling of a bad weed in the garden of evil. I don't buy it anymore. He was killed because, as I was told, Patton had lost his mind and was a great danger to America."

"Who told you that?"

There was a knock at the door. Tower looked at his watch. "Come in, Liz."

A woman in her late twenties, dressed as a nurse, entered and smiled. Her crimson hair was pulled back in a ponytail. She carried a canvas bag and a notebook. "Liz, this is Paul Marcus. He's visiting me from Virginia."

"Pleased to meet you," she said.

Marcus smiled. "It's good to meet you. Am I interrupting anything?"

The woman turned her head to Tower, deferring the answer to him. He chuckled. "Elizabeth and her colleagues have become my best and only friends these last few weeks. You see, Mr. Marcus, I'm dying. Maybe you're interrupting death. That's okay, though. If I make it until the end of next month, I'll have outlived the doctor's prediction by a year. But right now, speaking with you, I feel that at this moment, I'm more alive than I've been in a long time."

SIXTY-SIX

The hospice nurse counted pills on the kitchen counter while Tower led Marcus into the backyard. Tower pointed to a sycamore tree. "I planted that tree the year Annie and I and moved from the states. It'll outlive me, and that's fine. I've become rather fond of my friend, the sycamore. I won't even pick flowers now. Life, in any form, especially the beauty of flowers, seems like an utter gift to me. I see and appreciate things, the wondrous things, which I never even thought about during the war." His thoughts drifted, eyes filled with secret memories.

"Why was Patton killed?"

Tower slowly turned his head toward Marcus. "I don't think anybody alive really knows. I'm probably the last one alive who could, perhaps, most accurately speculate, and I'm not sure. I have my theories. The top guys in the OSS wanted Patton out of his job, wanted to quiet him. He was ranting about the way Eisenhower handled the war and its aftermath. It pissed off some big players. I even met with the OSS head, William Donovan. We called him Wild Bill, and he sure as hell was. I was recruited by the OSS, and I spent a lot of time behind enemy lines, Germany, where I did what was expected. I never liked it, not one damn bit. But, you know, it had to be done. When I was told that Patton, the great general I always believed he was...when I was told he'd crossed the line, I found it hard to believe. But they said Patton was about to drag us into a war with Stalin. They told me Patton was insane, the war had finally broken him, and he had to be stopped from shooting his mouth off."

"How was it planned?"

"The car accident was set up. The idea was to get Patton in the hospital and take him out there."

"Is that where you killed him?"

"I *didn't* kill him. I actually couldn't get inside the hospital because it was heavily guarded. Rumor was that the killer used a drug, administered from a needle, which simulated a heart attack."

Marcus sipped his tea. "Do you believe that's what happened?"

"They didn't do an autopsy."

"You said you thought it was justified, but not now...why?"

"That's why I'm here in England. One thing I was told I'd have to steal during the accident scene was a small black attaché case that Patton always carried since shortly after Hitler died. Patton had a spear that Hitler had looted from some Austrian museum. It was believed that the General carried it with him always in that briefcase. The OSS wanted the spear."

"Why?"

"They didn't say, but I'd heard the spear was some kind of powerful weapon."

"Did you get it?"

"Yes, but in all the confusion, as Patton was taken to the hospital, I hid it in my Jeep and took it back to my hotel that night."

"Did you give it to Donovan or anyone with the OSS later?"

"I almost did. But I got to thinking about why the little head of a spear was so important to the OSS. And if it was so damn important and powerful, was it the real reason the general was killed? Did his death have nothing to do with Patton's politics or the fact he said what he thought...even if it pissed off Eisenhower?"

"What happened to the spear?"

"After Patton died, I met Donovan and another OSS operative, Claude Bremen, at the Connaught Hotel bar in London. We were sitting at a corner table, and Bremen asked if I found the spear. I told him it wasn't in Patton's Cadillac; at least I couldn't find it in all of the confusion. He hit the table with his fist and said I was incompetent and maybe the Russians had found it in the hospital. They ordered a bottle of Irish whiskey and started knocking them back. After a while, Bremen told me how the OSS originally began in a private room at the Rockefeller Building in 1933. At that point, he grinned one of the most chilling grins I'd ever seen on a man. He laughed and said that a group of very wealthy and powerful men, and their heirs, would always control the government because they could manipulate the intelligence that they *chose* to share with congress or the president."

"What do you mean?"

"They had a long range plan, a 'hundred-year plan,' he called it, a plan to direct the balance of power. I was damn naïve, and thought he meant balance of power in our own government. He smiled and corrected me…said it was to run the balance of power around the *world*. But it would begin in our own country. So I started thinking hard about that. If congress and the president are stage-managed by powerful shadow groups, then who's really running the nation…or the damn world, for that matter? Having done what I did in the war, I felt dirty. I was really nothing more than a hit man, and that picture didn't sit too well with me. I told them that. I told them I'd have no more of the lethal charades."

"What happened?"

"A strange look came over their faces. They seemed to sober up pretty damn fast. They left the bar, and I never saw either one again. But I did see others. I moved back to Albany, New York. I knew they were watching me. A stalker left his tracks in my tomato garden one night. Our dog was a barker and must have scared him away. When he came back a few nights later, I was waiting for him. Before I snapped his neck, he told me his superiors—the top of the food chain, said I'd been seen meeting with known Russian spies. I was set up and all in the name of national security. I dumped his body in the Hudson. I knew they'd keep coming, so Annie and I left—left the country I'd fought for and almost died for many times. We lived all over Europe, even Cairo, never staying too long in one place. Years past and they started dying off, and then we settled in England."

"This one-hundred-year plan you mentioned. Have there been any events since your meeting with Donovan and Bremen that you think might connect to that plan?"

Tower's unkempt white eyebrows rose. He nodded his head. "Hell yes. The financial crisis is one of the most recent. What these people have done is criminal. But it's America's middleclass taxpayers who are the casualties of an undeclared war between them and the men who would be kings."

"How far do you think this secretive group would go to set and achieve their agenda and goals?"

"If someone could rise to be potentially a big thorn in their side, nothing is off the table. They're ruthless. I've tried to follow their mongrel pedigree line from the people I knew to their associates that came into office or great financial power."

"If John Kennedy Junior had not died in that plane accident, if Kennedy had become president, would he have been a thorn in their side?"

Tower coughed, his eyes watering. "I don't think a Kennedy would fit well into this group."

"What do you mean?"

"In the last twenty years, look at the number of U.S. Senators and members of congress who died in plane crashes a few weeks before the elections. Senator Paul Wellstone is one example. When Kennedy Junior's plane went down...I had my doubts as to it being an accident. Look, his father and uncle were both taken out. If he had plans to seek the office his father once had, I'm sure he would have interfered with some of the goals in a one-hundred-year plan. If they'll kill John Junior, they'll kill anyone who gets in their way, just like they did to a war hero like Patton."

"What happened to the spear Patton carried?"

Tower pursed his lips and grunted. "Lawrence Foster, the man you first mentioned, was working as an assistant prosecutor in the Nuremberg Trials. He'd introduced me to David Marcus, a man I came to know and really respect. Over drinks one night, I told him I'd hidden the spear in a bank deposit box in London. David said he knew an antiquities dealer, a gent who bought and sold religious art, someone who would have a huge interest in the spear. Also, he told me that he heard Stalin had a standing offer of a hundred grand to any of his men who could find the spear. David had access to the Russian and German POWs, so I didn't doubt him for one second. I was hurting for money. David set up a meeting between me and a Frenchman...can't recall his first name but his last name was Fournier."

Tower coughed and sipped his tea.

"Did you meet with Fournier?"

"Yes, twice. He said he wanted to get to know me, and for me to know him, as friends. Fournier was cut from a different tree. I remember him as a deeply religious man. He told me he'd bought some papers from a Sotheby's auction in London in 1936. The papers had to do with something Isaac Newton had left—notes on how science and religion were both part of what and who God is and always was. Fournier was a scholar, philosopher, theologian, and now I believe he was spy, a damn good one, too. He said he was authorized to offer me money for the spear."

"Authorized by whom?"

"He wouldn't say. It didn't make much difference to me. We met at a public park, the Jardin du Luxemborg in Paris. He was waiting for me at the Fountain de l'Observatoire. The fountain is a work of art. The world, like a globe, is held up high by statues of four women. Fournier said the women represented the four quarters of the earth. We made the exchange, shook hands, and that was the last time I ever saw him."

"Do you remember if there was anything engraved on the blade of the spear?"

"My memory isn't *that* good. There was something, though...numbers or letters...I can't recall. It looked like Latin or maybe Roman numerals."

"Do you speak Italian?"

"Used to, but not much anymore."

"Did Fournier speak Italian?"

"As I recall, he was fluent."

"Did Fournier tell you what he planned to do with the spear?"

Tower inhaled deeply, his lungs wheezing. "He told me that he was returning it to the Temple of David. I told him I thought the Temple was destroyed a lot of centuries ago. He said the cornerstone exists. And he said something else."

"What's that?"

"I've thought about that often through the years. I can close my eyes and hear his voice when he was standing next to the fountain in the park. He said that cornerstone could be seen through a dark glass with the purest of white light. And in this place a rose without thorns blooms under a new sun." Tower slowly turned his head toward Marcus. "I never knew what that meant. Don't suppose I ever will."

"Did Fournier tell you anything else?"

Tower looked down as his hands, fingers knotty from arthritis. He slowly raised his head and met Marcus's eyes. "Yes, he did. He said in August 1944, a secret meeting was held at the Maison Rouge Hotel in Strasbourg. I believe he was there, in what capacity I have no clue. Anyway, a Nazi official, who had close ties to Heinrich Himmler, presented a document titled the Red House Report. They knew the war couldn't be won. So they wanted to set up a Fourth German Reich, but this one was to be an economic force, not an army. And to pull it off, they planned to funnel hundreds of millions of dollars in looted gold and money out of Germany. They wanted a secret escape route through Rome and Switzerland to transfer some of their Nazi brethren out of the country. It was called the 'ratline,' because rats board boats by crawling down the rope lines. It became better known as the Odessa Plan."

"Did that route lead to Argentina?"

"Yes."

"Who was in this meeting?"

"They were industrialists, men representing some of the largest companies in Germany. I. G. Farben, Thyssen Steel, to name two. Later, during the Nuremberg trials, a half dozen of I.G. Farben's executives were tried and convicted for using slave labor in their plants, the same plants that manufactured Zyklon B, the poison used at Auschwitz and Dachau. Farben manufactured pharmaceuticals, too. They *bought* Jewish women, prisoners, from the Nazis and used these women in horrific experiments, mostly involving new drugs they would bring to market after they worked out dosages that wouldn't kill or disfigure a person."

"How did the prosecutors know which men from Farben to put on trial?"

"It wasn't hard to discover that. They all turned on each other as the shit hit the fan. David Marcus culled it down to the worst of the worst for prosecution." Tower stopped and raised one white eyebrow. "Is that why you're here?"

"What do you mean?"

"You said your name's Paul Marcus? Is this about David Marcus, are you a relative?"

"No. But I know he was killed. Do you know who was behind it?"

"I've often suspected one of the Farben guys had it done. This Red House Plan, the economic recovery of Germany, eventually became the European Union. After the war, there was rebuilding money available, and it came from some of the same places as the money to finance the war did."

"Where was that?"

"Thyssen Steel for one. Thyssen was a huge German conglomerate. It and some other German companies with connections to American banks and investment companies were a part of the financial supply chain. Fritz Thyssen, using some of John D. Rockefeller's Standard Oil money, helped finance the Nazi buildup. A lot of Thyssen Steel money was deposited in the Union Bank Corp in New York. Prescot Bush, the father and grandfather of two former presidents, and George Herbert Walker were members of the Union Bank's Board of Directors. They may not have known anything about all this stuff. I haven't a clue. But I do know the U.S. government seized and shut down that bank in 1942 under the Trading with the Enemy Act."

The nurse entered the room and gave Tower his second morphine pill of the day. He looked at Marcus through weary eyes. "I just remembered something else connected to that spear, something I've often thought about."

"What?"

"Fournier told me that one of the reasons he was hiding it was to keep it out of the hands of someone who could become the next Hitler."

"Who was that?"

"I can't recall his first name. He was a historian and an industrialist, someone who had controlling interests in a number of American companies. This included an investment company with connections to Thyssen Steel and the Farben Company. Man's name was Chaloner. I think the emphasis was on the *loner* part of the name."

"This group you mentioned—of the powerful and wealthy—do *they* have a name?"

"Through the lips of a drunken man, I heard they were called the Circle of 13."

Marcus stood to leave. "Thank you for your time."

"What do you plan to do?"

"I don't know."

"There are rats in the ship. Somebody would have to sink the ship at sea to drown them. I'm not certain that's possible. I'm keenly aware of one thing, Mr. Marcus. You're treading in dangerous waters. You'll have to be smarter than them; I just hope you are. Hellfire, I wish I were young enough to join you."

The old man gazed out his bedroom window, the ghost of memories as obvious as the cataracts in his eyes.

SIXTY-SEVEN

CALAIS, FRANCE

As Marcus drove from the port in Calais, he called Gisele Fournier. "Gisele, what is the name of the person you spoke with at the Paris police department?"

"Inspector Victor Roux, why?"

"Because I hope he is taking your warning seriously. I have even more reason to believe the threat on the prime minister's life is very real."

"Paul, what is happening?"

"Layers of complicity maybe connected to events around World War II."

"What do you mean?"

"I'm trying to figure that out. I need to ask you something else."

"Of course, what is it?"

"Your grandfather...did he ever mention Solomon's Temple to you?"

"Yes. He told me he wished he could have seen it because he *saw* it in a dream."

"Did he say what it looked like?"

"He only told me that there was perhaps one cathedral on earth that was built with something my grandfather called sacred geometry. And he believed it was very close to the size of the Temple Solomon built."

"Where is that cathedral?"

"It is the same one we talked about earlier—the Chartres Cathedral. Chartres is believed to have been built in secret by those who refused public recognition because they wanted the Virgin Mary, in her home on earth, to receive respect and acknowledgment."

"Do you remember if your grandfather ever mentioned to anyone in your family about a spear he might have found?"

"Spear? What kind of spear?"

"The ancient kind, like something a Roman soldier might have carried."

"No, but remember, I told you my grandfather was in Rome, after the war, when he saw a statue of an angel on the bridge over the River Tiber leading up to the Castel Sant'Angelo. The statue held a lance in her hands, and Grandfather said the face reminded him of the weeping angel in the Garden of Peace."

"Do you know if he ever returned to Rome or the Vatican in later years?"

"Not that I know of, no. Paul, I am at our cottage north of Bordeaux Saint Clair. My grandfather kept some of his things here. He wrote poetry and letters to friends when he was by the sea. He tended a small garden here before he died."

"Did he ever write anything about a spear or a lance?"

"I'm at his old desk in our cottage. Grandmother never tossed out his poems, letters and things. Let me look around—hold on a minute."

Marcus drove through the French countryside toward Paris. He could hear her opening and closing desk drawers. Gisele said, "Here's a sealed envelope, and it's addressed to a woman…looks like a nun named Mother Pascalina Lehnert. The address is the Vatican in Rome."

"Can you open and read it?"

"I feel strange, like I'm violating a trust with my grandfather."

"Did he ever ask you not to open it?"

"No."

Marcus could hear her ripping through the envelope. There were a few seconds of silence. "This looks like a copy of a letter. The beginning is written in French. The ending paragraph seems to be in something that looks like a cross between Hebrew, Latin and Arabic. I can't read that, but the French says, *'Dear Mother Pascalina, please inform the Pope that we are praying for a swift recovery in France and the rest of Europe from the aftermath of such a terrible war. It is my hope and sincere prayers that never in the future of mankind will such inhuman activity be resurrected. We must remember that soon a rose without thorns blooms under a new sun. Like the flower beneath a spring snow, it will rise. The cornerstone left from the Temple will stand tall in the shadows and support a future built on faith and love. I close in leaving the Pope with the assurance of spiritual delivery and the words found below that were written by John and left with Longinus.'* Paul, that's all I can make out."

"Can I get a copy of that?"

"No problem. Where are you?"

"Halfway between Calais and Paris."

"I can meet you in a couple of days back in Paris."

"Thank you, Gisele."

"Paul, I found something else in my grandfather's desk."

"What is it?"

"It looks like a badge or a medallion. It's gold and there is an image of an angel standing on a rock. The angel, a male figure, is holding a spear and he's stabbing a snake. I have never seen this before now…but now it makes sense." Her voice dropped to a whisper.

"Gisele, what make's sense?"

"It wasn't talked about much in the family. My grandfather was believed to have been one of the few remaining members of a secret group of Frenchmen who belonged to a faction that went all the way back to the fifteenth century. They were called the Order of Saint Michael."

"Who are they, or who were they?"

"I don't know. Paul, I must go. Someone's coming."

They disconnected and Marcus thought about what she told him. He thought about the words in the letter. *Was it a code? Why address it to a nun at the Vatican to be given to the Pope?* Marcus picked his phone back up and punched in a text message to Alicia: See what you can find on Mother Pascalina Lehnert. Probably dead. Worked at the Vatican – WWII period. Who was she?

SIXTY-EIGHT

Near the outer edge of Paris, Marcus's phone rang. Alicia said, "Mother Pascalina Lehnert was about as close as anyone to Pope Pius XII. She began as his housekeeper and worked her way up to his executive secretary. She was the first woman in the Vatican with an influential role. Many in the Catholic Church gave her the nickname of Virgo Potens, the powerful virgin. She served the Pope for forty-one years. She was his chief confidant, and she was a woman personally responsible for providing assistance to thousands of Jewish war refugees who came through the Vatican. Why the sudden interest in this nun, Mother Pascalina?"

Marcus filled Alicia in on his conversation with Gisele Fournier, and then he told her about his discussion with James Tower. "He's dying, and with little time left, Tower seemed relieved to tell me about the plot to assassinate Patton. He said this secret group laid out a one-hundred-year plan to gain control of world governments, banking, commerce, media…you name it. And he believed that JFK Junior, had he announced interest in a senatorial office or even a run for the presidency, wouldn't have been part of this plan."

"A shadow regime hidden within our government. Who are they?" she asked.

"The Circle of 13."

"Never heard of them."

"Not surprising. Maybe you can dig deep enough to find a thread."

"Okay. Anything else?"

"See if there's a remote connection to a Nazi smuggling ring in, near or around the Vatican after World War II."

"The Vatican? Is this related to Mother Pascalina or the Pope?"

"Maybe."

— —

Marcus and more than two hundred invited guests made their way to the Yitzhak Rabin Memorial on the rich green lawn of the UNESCO headquarters in the heart of Paris. The skies were blue, a breeze from the west. The scent of pine, moss, and running water met the people clearing security and taking seats in bone-white foldout chairs set at a 180-degree angle around the stage near the memorial.

Marcus stood closer to the Garden of Peace under a pine tree and watched the late arrivals clear security. Coffee, tea, hot chocolate, and finger pastries were served from five white linen tables manned by waiters in crisp jackets and black ties.

Marcus could see Parisian police and security agents staked out all around the perimeter, men with binoculars scanning the rooftops, men in dark glasses scrutinizing each guest, watching the Avenue de Segur, the roof of the UNESCO building, and studying the catering staff. Guests passed under a metal detector and two bomb-sniffing German Shepherds were held at bay on leashes. As the last of the crowd found its seats, Marcus felt a sense of relief with the unconcealed security presence.

Secretary of State Hanover entered the area from the UNESCO building and walked with the Israeli prime minister and his delegation toward the stage. The Mayor of Paris greeted his guests warmly, shaking their hands and escorting them to the stage and podium. He opened the ceremonies speaking French and then continued in English.

— —

Heydar Kazim locked his office door. He ran his hands through his dark hair and then did five push-ups. His lips were thin, a serrated white scar under the left eye. His hawk-like eyes were dark, calculating and yet emotionless.

He removed the modified case under his desk containing a French-made Giat FR F2 rifle, opened the case and began assembling the rifle. Within ninety seconds, the sniper rifle was in one piece. Kazim moved to the window. Like all windows on the east side of the building, it had horizontal louver slats to minimize the direct morning sunlight. For Kazim, it was like shooting through a portal with the ultimate elevation and concealment.

He pushed a bookcase near the window, extended the bipod supports for the rifle on the surface of the bookcase, and began to sight through the scope at the target less than 150 meters on the east lawn of the property.

— —

Secretary of State Hanover spoke, thanking the city of Paris for its hospitality. She said, "On this, the tenth anniversary of the installation of the Yitzhak Rabin Memorial, it is good to know that the people of Israel and America have an ally in the great nation and people of France. We have stood in alliance with one another when countries, led by dictators with a singular vision of world or regional dominance, would rise up and seek to conquer and tyrannize the people of other nations. When Prime Minister Yitzhak Rabin was alive, he was instrumental in bridging the gap between Palestinians and Israelis by working to create the Oslo Accords, which was the keystone to building a future of peaceful co-existence."

— —

Kazim centered the crosshairs in the riflescope across the face of the American Secretary of State. He held his breath for a few seconds, could feel his steady heartbeat in his finger resting on the trigger. He disengaged the safety and watched. A police helicopter hovered between the UNESCO building and the Seine River. Kazim found a cigarette lighter in his pocket and then moistened an unlit cigar with his tongue. He lit the cigar and waited for the American woman to finish her bullshit at the podium.

— —

The morning sun went behind a cloud when Marcus looked up at the UNESCO building. Something caught his eye—a tiny flicker, like a spark. The flicker of yellow came from the center window. Marcus stared at it. Something was slightly different than the surrounding office windows. Most of the other windows either had the blinds closed or open. This was one of three windows that had just one slat of a blind open, and behind that slat was the tiny spark he'd seen.

Marcus looked at the stage where Secretary Hanover was stepping aside while the prime minister shook her hand and took his place behind the dais. "Good morning, everyone," he said. "It is indeed an honor to be standing here, a special place where the Garden of Peace offers a respite to people everywhere who come to this great city and visit the UNESCO headquarters." His voice was strong and yet filled with humility. "Also, it is an honor to stand next to the memorial of one of Israel's finest diplomats, Yitzhak Rabin."

Marcus looked back at the building, his eyes focusing on an office with the open slant in the blinds. There was movement. He could see the silhouette of a man. The man was holding something. Maybe it was a camera with a long lens. *A rifle.*

Marcus turned toward the stage. He ran hard. The Israeli Prime Minister gestured toward the Rabin Memorial. The crowd looked in that direction. "Get down!" shouted Marcus. The prime minister looked across the audience to where Marcus was running and shouting. "Get down! Sniper!"

The sun came out from behind a cloud, and the prime minister narrowed his eyes. Two security men chased Marcus, running toward the stage. A red flower instantly blossomed from the prime minister's white shirt. A second bullet hit him in the temple. Blood, skull fragments and brain pieces splattered across the laps and faces of the dignitaries sitting in the seats behind him. He fell dead to the stage.

Marcus was tackled to the ground in front of the podium. Guests screamed and ran. Some pointed to the UNESCO building. Security agents bolted to the building, speaking into their sleeves, nine-millimeter pistols drawn. Marcus was lifted to his feet, his eyes meeting the ashen face of Secretary Hanover. She stared at him, her mouth opening, words drowned out by the noise. She stood in the chaos and wiped drops of the prime minister's blood off her face and hands.

— —

Heydar Kazim ran down the fire escape stairs, landing at the final step before police and government agents could get a bearing on where the shots had originated. He opened the back door of an awaiting taxi and said, "To the Champs Elysees."

"No problem," said the driver, pulling away from the UNESCO building. "Do you have a particular place on the Champs Elysees that you wish to go?"

"No, just the avenue is fine."

"Yes sir."

Kazim sent a text message: It is done. He placed the phone inside his coat pocket and closed his eyes. He would enjoy a nice dinner, beginning with escargot and wild mushrooms, shrimp and cognac, followed by wine-poached salmon with black truffles. A chilled bottle of chardonnay would complement the food. Kazim thought about the name Champs Elysees, the French name for Elysian Fields. He half smiled remembering that in Greek mythology, Elysian Fields meant...*the place of the blessed dead.*

SIXTY-NINE

Marcus looked at his reflection from the one-way glass on the far wall of the interrogation room. He sat at a small table, alone. For more than two hours police detectives and members of the French DGSE came and went, each asking the same questions in a different way.

The door opened and a man walked in the room. "Good afternoon, Mr. Marcus. My name is Andre Juneau." He smiled, took a seat across the table from Marcus, leaned back and crossed his legs as if he were getting ready to watch a football game. He wore wire-framed glasses, his greying hair parted. Trimmed mustache. His body telegraphed a candidness that Marcus felt was an open trap, manufactured and hard as steel.

"Mr. Marcus, I'm aware that you have been asked many of the same questions more than once. Some of my colleagues believe you are lying." Juneau didn't blink—his light brown eyes unreadable.

"I was trying to save a life! Why the hell would I lie?"

"You also are a man of many talents—a winner of the Nobel Prize… and most interesting to me is your background as a cryptographer. NSA wouldn't even tell us you work there."

"I don't work there."

"Then for whom do you work?"

"No one."

"Is that a fact? Regardless, France has a reciprocal arrangement with the NSA. So their absolute silence about you is more than curious to me."

"Look, Mr. Juneau, I told the rest of your entourage that I've been researching biblical codes and prophecies. Up until today, I had no idea if any of it was real. I had suspicions that there might be an attempt on the prime minister's life. But I didn't know how real it would be until it happened."

"What were you doing at the ceremonies?"

"Trying to prevent an assassination."

"I see. Mr. Marcus, have you been contacted by anyone...perhaps someone who had information about this horrible event."

"No."

"So you saw it foretold in passages from the Bible, correct?"

"No, I decoded information from ancient texts and information from..."

"From where?"

"Biblical studies conducted by Isaac Newton."

"So, am I to understand that you have a crystal ball into the future?"

"No, I have a glimpse into probabilities of some future events...ones that I think can be changed with intervention."

Juneau tilted his head, his eyes changing from a passive gaze to amusement and then impatience. "Intervention? Then why did you not intervene to prevent the killing?"

"I tried. I contacted authorities in Israel, America and called *your* police department right here in Paris."

"Who did you speak with here?"

"Inspector Victor Roux."

Juneau nodded. "Are you certain?"

"Yes, why?"

"Because the Paris police department does not employ an Inspector Roux."

Marcus stared at Juneau for a few seconds. "I don't believe you."

Juneau shrugged, his shoulders raised, hands turned palms up. "There is no Inspector Roux here. Mr. Marcus, did you speak with Roux?"

"No."

"Then who did?"

"A woman I met."

"What is her name?"

"Look, she has nothing to do with anything. Her grandfather had possession of the remaining Newton papers. She'd donated them to the Hebrew University Library in Jerusalem. I'd found a reference to a weeping angel. She knew of a statue like it in the UNESCO Garden of Peace. After she showed me the statue and the Rabin Memorial near it, I asked her to alert the Paris police."

"What is her name?"

"Gisele Fournier, and she'll tell you the same story."

"How long will you be in Paris?"

"I don't know."

Juneau smiled. "Unlike you, Mr. Marcus, I cannot read the future. But I can promise you that your future will be quite dark if we find you are complicit in the murder of the prime minister. As a courtesy, please stay in Paris for forty-eight hours."

— —

Marcus took a seat at an outdoor café table across the Seine from the Cathedral of Notre Dame. He turned his collar up in the slight chill. A waiter with gelled hair and stubble on his face approached. "Bonjour, monsieur. Déjeuner?"

"Bonjour. No lunch. Parlez-vous l'anglais?"

"Yes."

"Grey Goose, ice and a slice of lime."

"Very good, sir." Marcus called Gisele. The phone rang and went to her voice-mail. "Gisele, the police are going to contact you. They're saying the guy you spoke with, Inspector Roux, doesn't work there. Something's wrong. Be careful. Don't let anyone see the letter your grandfather wrote. Call me and I'll tell you where we can meet that's safe." He disconnected, called Jacob Kogen and said, "I'm done with the research on the Newton papers and the Bible—"

"Thank God you're okay, Paul. This is so tragic. I can't put it into words."

"I will! *Preventable!* How does that sound, Jacob? Your government brings me here to help its cyber terrorism, you toss me a bone called the

Newton papers, and I chew on it and find real terrorists. But what the hell does Nathan Levy do about it? Nothing! And your prime minister has his head blown off. I find information that indicates a possible assassination, and no one does anything to stop it."

"What could we have done?"

"Cancelled the prime minister's appearance!"

"Paul, listen to me. He was informed, warned again about your prediction, and *he* decided he would not hide from threats."

"Well, now you have your damn proof-of-concept. This experiment you had with me the last few weeks put the camel's nose under the tent and now he's coming inside."

"What do you mean?"

"What I mean is this could be the beginning."

"The beginning of what, Paul."

"The beginning of the end."

"Dear God, what do you mean—"

"I don't know. I have to go." Marcus disconnected. The waiter brought the drink to the table. "Merci."

"Avec plaisir."

Marcus squeezed a lime over the ice while, on the screen of his phone, he read updated details of the assassination. The news story said the assassin had taken two shots from the third floor of the UNESCO building. The shots came from an office used by a consultant who'd only been there for three days. The suspect or suspects were still at large.

A text message arrived from Alicia: Paul, I just caught the news. This is so frightening. My flight lands in the morning at 9:36. Can you meet me at de Gaulle Airport? I have some important information for you.

Marcus sipped the vodka. He looked at Notre Dame across the Seine while the bells tolled for five o'clock mass. A mist drifted from the river and met the horizon of tarnished silver, settling a grey overcoat on the back of the city of light. The cathedral bells sounded far away, as if the ringing were soft echoes in a dream. He closed his eyes and tried to remember the last time he prayed hard.

SEVENTY

Brandi Hirsch sat on the cot in her prison cell and looked down at her trembling hands. She extended her fingers. The shaking was worse today. *Getting worse every day,* she thought. *Dear God…please help me.*

Brandi pulled the dirty bed sheet over her shoulders and hugged her upper arms. The sheet smelled of dried sweat, vomit, and diarrhea. When she tried to stand, the small cell began spinning. She licked her parched and cracked lips, which were encrusted with dried blood. Brandi was glad there was no mirror in her cell because she was afraid to look at her own face. She knew her face was emaciated—could feel its sunken features. Her dark hair was filthy and matted. Her eyes were dead with dark circles underneath.

Brandi stared through the bars, through the two-inch glass in her cell, to the prison yard one story below her. She watched a guard smoke a cigarette, his eyes hooded beneath a billed hat. He crushed the cigarette under his black boot, scratched his crotch, and walked toward a guard tower.

Brandi closed her eyes, a single tear spilling down one cheek. *I don't want to die here. Is Adam okay? Miss him so much…miss Mom. Don't even know how Granddad's doing with his cancer…just want to hug him again. I miss Aunt Alicia's smiling face…and Grandma…her chicken pot pie. I can smell it. I can taste it.*

She wiped the tear from her cheek and sat down on the cot and pulled her knees beneath her chin.

—▬—

Paul Marcus took a taxi to Terminal One at Charles de Gaulle International Airport. Hundreds of people moved about, pulling luggage behind them. The airport announcements were being made in French and English. Marcus stood near the *Arrival* section and waited. His phone buzzed: UNKNOWN.

"Paul, this is Merriam Hanover. We…no…I *personally* owe you a huge apology for not taking serious enough the information you brought to us. It's just that, after the first non-incident at the Lincoln Memorial, we didn't know how much stock to put into the data. Working with the French and Israelis, we now have every available resource pulled in to find the assassin. I'm trying to understand how your research is giving you a prophetic glimpse into the future. What else have you seen? What can you *tell* me?"

"I can't explain it beyond what I've told you. I've simply taken old biblical notes from Isaac Newton and used a computer to search for possible codes in the Bible that can reveal more."

"What portions of his notes? Specifically what were you searching for?"

"At first, it was to find out who killed my family."

"Have you found that?"

"No. It doesn't work that way…I can't press a button like an app on a phone or tablet and download answers. The information is a process, a slow reveal, that's never the same thing I'm looking for when I start. It's like I'm being dealt a hand of cards, and it's not always about the future. Sometimes it's about the past."

"What do you mean?"

Marcus paused, scanning the sea of people for Alicia's face. "Has anyone or any group taken credit for the assassination?"

"Not yet. No one has come forward from any Palestinian faction— nothing from Hezbollah, Hamus, al-Qaeda, Muslim Brotherhood, or other groups."

"I have reason to believe that the assassin who killed the prime minister was a hired hand that pulled a trigger. The head—the corporate brains, ordered it. Find that."

"Any thoughts on where we'd look?"

"Try starting with the same place that's holding Brandi and Adam. Iran."

"Corporate brains and Iran in the same breath—are you aware of something we aren't?"

"I don't know what you know. It's a good bet that the prime minister had sanctioned the cyber war that is racing between Israel and Iran. Possibly he was taken out to retaliate or slow it down. Maybe that's finding the bargaining ground. Merriam, find a way to leverage some of our expertise in cyber warfare. Use it as a poker chip. Give the Iranians something they want in exchange for the release of Brandi and Adam." Marcus heard her sigh into the phone.

"Paul, if we did that, Brandi and Adam would be the poster children for a constant procession of American hostages held ransom for intelligence. And, when it comes to nuclear intel, there's absolutely *no* way. The president simply won't go there. I'm sorry. I have to take a call from—"

"Merriam!"

"I have to take a call from the vice president. I'll call you back in a few minutes. I want to ask you something." She disconnected.

Marcus spotted Alicia pulling a flight bag. Her hair was swept back, and she was dressed in black jeans, low heels and a jacket. He watched her for a moment, waiting for her eyes to find his. Alicia seemed to peel away from the crowd, or stand out from the pack of people. She saw Marcus and smiled—a wide radiant smile that beamed down the long corridor.

"Welcome to Paris," Marcus said, stepping up to her.

She stopped pulling her suitcase, stood there for a moment and then reached up to embrace Marcus. "It's so good to see you." They hugged. He could feel her hands clutch his back.

"How was the flight? More importantly, how are you, Alicia?"

"Better now. I was numb during the funeral. I cried all I could cry. Mom has a sense of peace in her face I haven't seen in three years. Dad suffered much too long. The last time I was in Paris I was a teenager."

"Well, then welcome back. Are you hungry?"

"Starving."

They began walking through the airport.

"Paul, I need to tell you something that I couldn't tell you electronically."

"What?"

"Bill Gray is under a lot of pressure by the CIA? They think you've turned, working for Iran."

"Why?"

"I don't know all the details. It may have been in an intercepted email from the Iranian operative before she died?"

"Taheera? She killed herself. The Israeli police know it. The Mossad knows it, and I'm sure the CIA is aware of it."

"But they don't know everything that transpired between you and Taheera before she took her life, and why."

"Bill Gray said a suspect was arrested for murdering Jen and Tiffany. That's not true, right?"

"There hasn't been anything in the news media about that. Bill's under a lot of pressure—"

"Gray lied to me! He lied to get me back so Langley could interrogate me—"

"Halt!" shouted a man from the crowd. Within seconds four men surrounded Marcus and Alicia. All four leveled pistols at them. Inspector Andre Juneau stepped forward. "Mr. Marcus, turn and face the wall. Place the palms of your hands on the wall. Spread your legs. Miss, you do the same thing."

"I don't think so!" Alicia fired back. "Who are you? I don't see any ID—"

"Paris police! And you will be searched for a weapon whether you like it or not."

SEVENTY-ONE

Another half dozen members of the de Gaulle Airport security formed a semi-circle as backup behind the Paris police.

Marcus looked at Alicia and said, "This is Inspector Juneau and his colleagues. I'm a person of interest in the assassination of the prime minister. Alicia has a solid alibi, Inspector. She was in the U.S. at her father's funeral."

"Search them," Juneau said, his lips barely moving.

Dozens of spectators watched the police pat down Marcus and Alicia. She said, "I just got off a plane. How could I have a weapon?"

They ignored her and continued the search, one man opening her luggage. The man doing the body searches finished and nodded. Juneau said, "Ranger vos armes." The men holstered their guns. "Mr. Marcus," Juneau continued, folding his arms, "you and your companion need to come with us."

"Where and why?" Marcus asked.

"We have some questions that only you can answer. We have a room here at de Gaulle for this sort of thing."

—●—

The room was bright white. No windows. A small conference table and four chairs were in the center. A telephone sat on a stand near a green plastic eucalyptus plant in the corner. Marcus assumed the room was wired.

Inspector Juneau and one other man sat across from Marcus and Alicia. "Mr. Marcus, Juneau began, leaning back in this chair. "You have become a curiosity to me. You were instructed not to leave Paris for at least forty-eight hours."

"I'm in Paris."

"You and your companion are here at the airport, only a short distance to the rest of the world."

"My *name* is Alicia."

Juneau smiled. "We know who you are, Miss Quincy. What we don't know is what you are doing here. A former NSA employee meets a current one after an assassination." He shifted his eyes to Marcus. "So you two are here in the airport, heading in the direction of the departures, walking quickly I might add, when we stopped you."

Marcus shook his head. "We were heading in the direction of the taxis."

"Miss Quincy, why are you here? Perhaps to deliver or pick up something from Mr. Marcus, yes?"

"No, and that can be understood as a *hell* no. We're old friends, as you suggested, former colleagues. I'm here to take in Paris. Any suggestions on what to see and do in the City of Light?"

Juneau ignored her and altered his stare at Marcus. "We managed to locate Miss Gisele Fournier."

"Good, did you find the guy on your staff she talked to?"

"No, and we would have asked her about that, but there was a slight problem."

"What's the problem?"

"She's dead."

Marcus felt his stomach catch, the adrenaline flowing into his bloodstream. "How'd she die?"

"From the surface, it looks like she was the unfortunate victim of a traffic accident. However, there were no other cars involved. Her car was found at the bottom of a cliff about fifty kilometers south of Calais. No witnesses. No skid marks, and our investigation reveals the brakes were in proper working order. We did find her mobile, and the last call she made was to your number."

Marcus said nothing.

"What was the nature of your discussion?"

"She told me more about her deceased grandfather, the same grandfather who showed her the weeping angel in the same Garden of Peace where the prime minister was shot."

"Why the interest in her grandfather, a man who is dead?"

"He led a fascinating life, and one that somehow pointed me to the garden and the tragic event that happened. The only thing sadder is that it didn't have to happen. Your department was aware of the possible assassination attempt. So were the Israeli and the U.S. governments."

Inspector Juneau lowered his head for a moment and rested his arms on the table, his eyes moving from Marcus to Alicia and back. "Miss Fournier's mobile pinged from a cellular tower near Calais. It's the same tower where your mobile signal pinged. We checked the surveillance tapes from cameras at the Chunnel Port. The video shows you, in your car, driving onto the Chunnel and driving off the Chunnel in England. What were you doing in Britain, especially after our office asked you to stay in Paris briefly while we investigated the murder of the prime minister?"

"First of all, I'm not complicit in the assassination. Secondly, if you were checking surveillance tapes, you already know I was at the port before the assassination."

"What were you doing in England?"

"On a quick day trip. Sightseeing."

Inspector Juneau smiled and nodded. "Miss Fournier's car was found at the bottom of a cliff not too far from where you caught the Chunnel to Britain. Why was it important to kill her? What did you take from her... besides her life?"

"I haven't seen Gisele since I met her in the Garden of Peace."

"Why would she have been near Calais the same time you were returning from England?"

"Her family has a seaside cottage near there."

"Where do you think she was going before her car plunged off the cliff?"

"I don't know."

"I think you do."

"Not knowing when the accident happened, I don't know for sure. But she was planning to leave her grandparents cottage to return to Paris and bring something to me."

"What was that, Mr. Marcus?"

"A letter her grandfather wrote. You found her mobile phone, did you find the letter?"

"No, as a matter of fact, there was nothing more on her person than a few cosmetics in her purse and a small overnight bag. We recovered no letter."

"Then maybe someone else did."

"What are you suggesting?"

"I'm saying she was killed trying to deliver an important document to me. Now it's gone. Somebody has it. That's who you need to find, because whoever has that letter is most likely connected to the assassination of the prime minister."

Inspector Juneau smiled, his dark eyes shifting from his lieutenant back down to Marcus. "I think you have quite an imagination."

"Think what you want. Either charge me with murder or leave me the hell alone. Let's get out of here, Alicia."

"Not so fast, Mr. Marcus." Juneau stood. He nodded to his lieutenant, a heavyset man, jowls wobbling as he stepped quickly in front of the door. "Turn around, both of you, place your hands behind your back."

Marcus phone rang. "You mind if I take this call? It's the American Secretary of State." Before Juneau could answer, Marcus said, "Madame Secretary did you speak with the vice president?" Marcus smiled, both eyebrows rising. "Secretary Hanover, we seem to have a little problem here, specifically at de Gaulle Airport."

"What is that?"

"I'm about to be arrested for suspicion."

"Suspicion?"

"Yes, Inspector Juneau with the Paris police department thinks I may have had something to do with the assassination of the prime minister. But, as you know, I tried to prevent that from happening."

"Let me speak with the Inspector."

Marcus handed his phone to Juneau. "She wants a word with you."

Juneau looked at the phone and then at Marcus before talking it. "This is Inspector Andre Juneau."

"Good morning, Inspector. This is Secretary of State Merriam Hanover. I just wrapped up a successful meeting with President Sarkozy. I, too, will be at de Gaulle shortly. I hope security is equally as good for me as it is for my friend, Paul Marcus. I assure you, Inspector, Paul Marcus travels with the highest security credentials, and he is in no way connected to the assassination of the prime minister except by default. He was trying to warn us, a prophetic and a most altruistic gesture. Unfortunately, security at the UNSECO property wasn't as efficient as it is at de Gaulle. I will vouch for Paul Marcus. Please release him immediately from custody and into my recognizance, if need be."

SEVENTY-TWO

An hour later, Marcus and Alicia ordered breakfast at the Café Beaubourg on Rue Saint Martin. Alicia sipped her coffee. "Paul, the assassination, it was like you predicted. Not in the Lincoln Memorial, but here in Paris in the shadow of the UNESCO building, an organization that is the very foundation for world peace. And now, the death of Gisele Fournier. Who's *behind* this?"

"I don't know. Gisele was going to bring me the letter or a copy of the letter her grandfather had written to Mother Pascalina, Pope Pius's assistant. I believe the letter was coded, and I don't know what was said in the last paragraph. Gisele said it was written in a language that wasn't familiar to her." Marcus stirred his coffee. "Before the prime minister's assassination, security at the UNESCO headquarters was heavy. Metal detectors, bomb-sniffing dogs, helicopters, dozens of cops and agents, and those were the ones you could see. Still, the assassin got off two shots, and he did it from an office on the third floor of the building. Inspector Juneau and the French DGSE interrogated me for three hours."

"You're the one person who tried to warn people that this may happen."

A waiter brought two plates of omelets, sliced tomatoes, croissants with butter and fruit, and refilled their coffee cups before exiting.

Marcus said, "I'm only the messenger. But whoever heard of a whistle-blower blowing a whistle *before* the event has happened? That's what the authorities—police can't grasp—reporting or predicting a murder before it happens. Even Secretary Hanover can't get her head around it. By the way, she did tell me the talks to free Brandi and Adam are at a standstill. I feel bad telling you that."

Alicia held her coffee cup in two hands and looked at the steam for a moment, her eyes filled with reflection. "I'm so fearful for them, Paul, and I feel helpless. My sister is holding news conferences, doing whatever she can to keep Brandi and Adam's faces in the news and on the minds of people."

"We'll find something, Alicia, which will get Iran's attention to release them. I'm not sure what, yet, but we will. Let's go back to the Vatican for a moment. Did you find anything about a connection to the Roman Catholic Church during the underground flight of Nazi war criminals?"

"Yes, but it wasn't the Vatican. It was a Catholic bishop tossed out of the Vatican. Pope Pius XII had a very difficult time with an Austrian bishop who was a Nazi sympathizer and a devout follower of Hitler. This man's name was Alois Hudal. He apparently had been extraordinary as a member of the Roman Catholic Church. He was known as a master communicator and an excellent writer, too. He's believed to have helped engineer the escape of some of the most notorious Nazis, including Josef Mengele—the Angel of Death, and Klaus Barbie. Paul, it's almost like Hudal had a Faustian pact with the devil. Klaus Barbie was directly responsible for the deaths of 14,000 people. One of those deaths included a member of the French Resistance, a man named Jean Moulin. Barbie is believed to have personally beaten Moulin to death while he was strapped in a chair nailed to the floor."

"French Resistance…Philippe Fournier was a *member* of the Resistance, too."

"Maybe there's our connection. Before Pope Pius tossed Hudal out of the Vatican, the Pope had been dealing with the plight of eight million Russian Catholics under the Stalin regime. If he'd come down publicly against Stalin, many of these Russian Catholics would have been sent to the gulags. The Pope had seen first-hand what Nazi Germany had done. What if, after Hitler's fall and Patton's death, Pope Pius had tried to keep the Spear of Destiny from getting into the hands of Stalin?"

"James Tower told me Fournier was *authorized* by someone to buy the spear. Gisele said her grandfather, Philippe, had been in Rome shortly after the war…and she mentioned that he saw a statue on the bridge leading to the Castel Sant'Angelo. The statue resembled the face of the weeping angel in the Garden of Peace at the UNESCO headquarters. But the statue on the bridge in Rome was carrying a lance...a spear."

Alicia raised an eyebrow. "Could the real spear be there, in Rome, today?"

"Did you do a search to find the gothic cathedral closest to the mission of the Catholic Church?"

"That took some digging and vetting because most of it is subjective, a popularity vote in the twenty-first century might give Notre Dame the number one spot. But during the eleventh century that wasn't the case. The old cathedral in Chartres, an hour south of Paris, aligned well with the Roman Catholic Church because Chartres was called the Virgin Mary's seat on earth. Aside from Christ himself, Mary is iconic with the Catholic Church."

Marcus said nothing for a few seconds.

"Paul, what are you thinking?"

"I'm trying to put myself in the shoes of Philippe Fournier after he bought the spear from James Tower. Did he originally go to Rome to deliver the spear to the Pope, or did he receive payment from the Pope to buy the spear and hide it somewhere else?"

"Remember, I found four locations for the spear, or alleged Spears of Destiny, and one was in the Vatican."

"Yes, but those are publicly known. With four out there, it would be difficult to steal all four. What a brilliant plan!"

"What?"

"What if they, the Catholic Church, made replicas of the original spear, scattering them in guarded museums and in the Vatican, and, all the while, they had the original hidden somewhere?"

"Where?"

Marcus shook his head. "I don't know. Did you find any more information about the Circle of 13?"

Alicia blew a strand of hair from over her eye. "I've had to hack my way into information. At one time, I only needed a name and social security number to pull up every document ever written about someone from birth to obit. These guys or their watchers are like phantoms. Officially, of course, the Circle of 13 doesn't exist. But in reality, they're a members-only, billionaire's club that's far beyond anything or any person connected to secret societies, like the Bilderberger Council, Skull and Bones, Freemasons, Illuminati, Council of Nine or some of the others. From what I've been able to piece together, the Circle of 13, undoubtedly, represents the most powerful people on the face of the earth. There are only thirteen members at any given time. It's believed they can create or decide things that affect, directly or indirectly, every person in the world. They make the decisions as to when wars will start, how long they'll last, and what nations will be involved. Part of all this is the supply chain, the financial infrastructure of wars, which means who will lend money to support the war efforts and rebuild the countries involved after the last poor nineteen-year-old soldier is buried."

"Who *are* they?"

"I've cross-referenced everything at my immediate disposal. Through a lot of sifting, following rumors and innuendos that sometimes lead to more sturdy bridges, I'm getting a short profile only because they can't completely hide the money trails since the money moves electronically. Those trails, of course, leave fingerprints. This secret group is believed to run the central banks of Europe, our biggest banks and even our own Federal Reserve System. Paul, this gives them the leverage to choose discount rates, money-inventory amounts, control derivative and hedge funds, even the price of gold and the countries granted access to loans. Since they have controlling ownership in major banks, they have the power to set interest rates, creating billions of dollars for themselves."

Marcus stirred his coffee and sat quiet for a moment. "If you run commerce, the banking systems, and have all of the power over mortgages and credit cards, you control the very core—the lifeline of people desperate to hang onto a job, a home, and a way of life. Any group, such as the rising middle class, could be wiped out or knocked down several notches if they became too financially powerful."

"That leads to people reaching breaking points. Ready to accept whatever rations the gatekeepers hand them in exchange for their services and civil obedience."

"That was one of the reasons we cut the umbilical cord to the king of England. We declared that the creator had given us certain unalienable rights, such as liberty and the pursuit of happiness and a good dose of self-governance."

Alicia lowered her voice. "These secretive billionaires decide who will run for the heads of state offices around the world. They own huge industrial and high tech companies, providing them the power to set wages. They ignore or bend governance regulatory laws because they have politicians who write the soft laws in favor of the polluting and often abusing business paradigms these companies create. To spin a public relations campaign for their hidden agendas, they have majority stakes in global news media companies. Meaning they can twist politics, economic news and events to sway the public to follow their way of thinking."

"If you own the media, you can create artificial events that stoke fear in the hearts of the people…essentially wearing them down like a fighter trapped in a corner and getting hit repeatedly in the head. Do you have leads—names of people suspected to belong to this group?"

"Jonathon Carlson and Alexander Van Airedale are two suspected to belong to the group or have ties to it. Carlson is CEO of Integrated Security Corporation. Van Airedale heads UDT, a multinational company that does contract work around the globe, anything from roads, bridges, pipelines to power plants. His company is believed to have been associated with the German giant, Siemens, when they were caught and fined a record one-point-two-billion dollars for bribery schemes."

"That's quite a toll to pay for violation of international securities laws."

Alicia shook her head. "They didn't think they'd get caught. It's the same mindset that fueled the greed on Wall Street with the banks. With billions to be won or lost, these ruthless people plan ahead for years, setting strategy and people in place."

"Maybe John Kennedy Junior would not have fit in their plans."

"Maybe."

"If General Patton was assassinated and, if JFK Junior, his wife and sister-in-law were all murdered…are the incidents related? We know a lot of this began with the Nazi buildup through the end of the war and into the Nuremberg Trials. James Tower believes David Marcus's death could have been in retaliation to his involvement in the trials. Industry tycoons like Fritz Thyssen played a role in financing Hitler's rise. They had ties to American investment firms and banks that could launder Nazi money. The European Union evolved from the economic rebirth of Germany. Philippe Fournier learned of the players at that meeting in Strasbourg, Germany, when the Red House proposal was revealed. James Tower called it a one-hundred-year plan. If it began in 1933, it won't be too long before they may achieve their goals."

"How can they be stopped?" Alicia pushed her plate away.

"If someone can find a way to expose them, these thirteen might fall like the Berlin Wall fell years ago…brought down by the people. But it won't be easy."

"What do we do next?"

"We go to an ancient cathedral in France."

"If you're suggesting Chartres, what exactly are we searching for?"

"Maybe the tunic worn by Mary, Jesus' mother at the time of his birth, and possibly the spear that entered his body at the time of his death."

SEVENTY-THREE

*T*he dead woman's phone came to life in Marcus's pocket with a soft buzzing. He stopped eating, his eyes meeting Alicia. He reached in his pocket, retrieving Taheera's phone. "Alicia, I have to take this call." He pressed the receive button. "This is Paul Marcus."

"Mr. Marcus, I have spoken with my superiors. We are in a position to negotiate with you." The man's voice was even, unruffled. "What we don't know is whether the Myrtus worm has infected our operating systems. If it hasn't infiltrated our structures, how can we prevent it from happening? If someone has managed to penetrate security, is the worm in a sleeping stage? If it is, what can we do to prevent it from attacking?"

"Are all your enrichment plants on the same mainframe system?"

"No."

"Which plant do you feel may be the most vulnerable?"

"Let me answer that question by simply saying that our facility at Natanz is where our top priority lies at the moment."

"I'll need defense firewall schematics of the plant's operating systems. Deliver it to me on a hard drive. I'll look under the hood for you. If I see something suspect, I'll try to find out what it can or might do…and if possible, I'll kill the worm."

"How do we know that we can trust you?"

"You don't, not any more than I can trust you. But at this point, two American lives—innocent lives are in the balance. A dead worm is a good trade for two lives."

303

"Meet me tonight at the Le Square Trousseau Café at one Rue Antoine Vollon. Be there at seven o'clock. One thing, Mr. Marcus, I will be watched just like we're watching you and the woman at the café where you two sit."

Marcus moved his eyes without turning his head. The man continued. "If we feel there is a hint of surveillance, there is *no* deal…except you will then meet a fate that is very much worse than death. The woman will watch your death before it is her time, and we will kill the two you want released."

"Listen to me. If there's surveillance, I won't know it; and it'll be because the French government thinks I'm a suspect in the assassination of the Israeli prime minister. So your people can just deal with that since you probably caused this shit."

"At this point, Mr. Marcus, I will ignore your condescending remarks."

"I'll be at the restaurant, and tomorrow I want to see your president call a news conference to announce the release of Brandi and Adam. Are we clear?"

"We will release one person first. The other shall be freed after you deliver your part of the contract." The connection ended. Marcus looked at his watch: six hours remained before 7:00 p.m.

Alicia leaned closer to Marcus and lowered her voice. "Paul, who was that? What did he say to you?"

"I don't know his real name. He's Iranian. I'm meeting him tonight."

"Why?"

"To do some work."

"What *kind* of work?"

"To see if I can spot and kill something called Myrtus. It's a covert malware worm that may be eating a hole into the operating system of Iran's nuclear program. Israel, or maybe, we planted it there. I don't know."

"Paul, you're *not* a field operative! If you're caught and convicted of spying, you'll spend the rest of your life in prison. You can't risk that. The CIA suspects you're working for Iran. This is all they need."

"I'm not spying! I'm not compromising any U.S. interests or secrets—"

"You'd be helping Iran develop its nuclear program and that's—"

"That's what? I'm not going to help them develop their nuclear capacities. Look, Washington has stopped negotiating with Iran to free Brandi and Adam. It's a damn international draw. The Iranian Revolutionary Guard will convict them of spying and sentence them to life or worse. You asked me to help *you*, to help *them*. Secretary Hanover's efforts have died on the vine, and now Brandi and Adam will face an Iranian tribunal."

Alicia's eyes welled. "What *can* you do?"

"Run a diagnostics coding on the system that operates the Iranian nuclear facility at their Natanz plant. The Myrtus worm, if it's in their system, should be able to digitally fingerprint any computer that it can infiltrate. By fingerprint, I mean it can differentiate the machines it weaves through, looking for the machine it will eventually destroy. When it finds that specific computer, the worm will lie dormant until a pre-programmed series of events occur within the computer. Then it will attack it with such strength it can destroy entire centrifuges."

"How?"

"By causing the systems to implode, or eat itself, like an extreme cancer."

"How does the worm know to attack?"

"Probably…it would recognize when a system is going into its final check stages or online operations."

Alicia was silent for a half minute, her eyes watching the traffic outside the restaurant. Then she turned back to Marcus. "Does this mean Brandi and Adam will be coming home immediately?"

"The Iranians will announce the imminent release of either Brandi or Adam tomorrow. The person remaining will be freed when I find and destroy the worm."

"Dear God! What if you *can't* find it? What if you can't *destroy* it?"

"I'll do the best I can to infiltrate their system and locate the worm."

"How do they know there's even a worm in their system?"

"They suspect it. They know about Myrtus, a code name for the worm. Apparently their intel indicates one or some have been planted by subcontractors, maybe Russian, Chinese, German or Indian engineers hired to build the plants. Probably someone easily bought and paid for by the Mossad—the people who most likely did the work to develop the worm."

"How do you *know* this?"

"That's not important. What's important is freeing Brandi and Adam."

"When and where are you meeting this man?"

"Tonight, 7:00. The Le Square Trousseau Café."

"I want to be there."

"No! If they know you can't identify them, you'll be okay."

"Listen to me! They don't know who I am. My niece has a different name. I haven't been listed in any news media as a relative. I *need* to be there. I'm coming."

SEVENTY-FOUR

Marcus and Alicia arrived at the Le Square Trousseau Café fifteen minutes early. They entered the café and took a table in a corner, walking by portraits of nineteenth century Parisians hanging on the wall. Most of the light fixtures were tulip shaped, and a massive La Victoria brass coffee machine hissed behind the bar while a paunchy, red-faced bartender made espresso after espresso.

Alicia glanced around the café, which was filling with locals and tourists. "Do you know what he looks like?"

"No. Only the sound of his voice."

A waiter, wearing a black vest, bowtie, white apron and black pants, approached the table. "Bonsoir, vous en train de dîner?"

Marcus said, " Non, un espresso et un cappuccino, s'il vous plaît. Parlez-vous anglais?"

"I speak English, okay." He smiled and poured two glasses of water.

"I would like sugar, also," Alicia said.

The server looked out the window for a moment, his mind retrieving something. Then, looking at Paul, he said, "Are you Mr. Marcus?"

"Yes."

The server nodded and reached inside his vest, pulling out a white envelope. "I was asked to give this to you. I will bring your coffee drinks." He turned and started to leave.

"What did he look like?" Marcus asked.

The waiter shrugged. "Umm, like no one and like everyone."

Marcus handed the man a twenty Euro note. "Does this jog your memory?"

"He had very short hair, like he shaves his scalp weekly. Dark eyes. Over six feet tall, and he was wearing a jacket with a black high-neck sweater under it." The server turned and exited. Marcus opened the sealed envelope to bold type.

> **You are being watched. Do not use your mobile phone. Turn it off now. Walk to the hotel at Rue 9 Rue d'Aligre. Second floor. Room 229. You have 12 minutes to get here or the deal is off, and the Americans will be sentenced and executed within one week.**

"What does it say?" Alicia asked.

Marcus said nothing, his heart pounding.

"Paul, what does it say?"

"He's changed locations on us."

"Where?"

"A hotel at Rue 9 Rue d'Aligre. Let's walk. Turn off your phone!"

"That means they're watching us, right?"

"Yes." Marcus stood. "You should stay here, or catch a taxi to my hotel. It's—"

"I'm coming!"

"No! Alicia, this will be very dangerous."

"I don't care! Brandi's in a hell of a lot more danger."

Marcus said nothing for a moment, his eyes searching hers.

They asked for directions to the location, left the café, and started walking toward Rue d'Aligre. Across the street was a park with swing sets and picnic tables. Beyond the wrought iron gate, the trees were stripped of leaves in the late autumn, crooked limbs motionless against the golden glow of streetlights. The breeze pushed a single swing, making a creaking sound. Marcus turned his collar up on his leather coat and looked at Alicia. "Are you cold?"

"A little."

"Here, take my coat."

"No thanks. I'm more nervous than cold, really." She tried to smile.

They walked the remaining way in silence. Motorcycles and cars sped down the street, the smell of coffee and wine flowing from a bistro. A little farther down, they could see the neon from a hotel sign. "Looks like the place," Marcus said. "Remember, assume that their room is bugged, they may be wired for sound and video, too. Any communications between us will have to be marginal and undetected."

They entered. The lobby was bathed in a bluish color, illuminated by two sputtering florescent lights that were within days of burning out. The elderly desk clerk sat behind the counter in the small lobby and watched a soccer game on television. He didn't look up when Marcus and Alicia entered an elevator that reeked of sweat, sour perfume and cigarette smoke. Marcus pressed the button to the second floor.

They walked down the hall and found room 229. Marcus knocked. Nothing. There was only the hum from an exit sign, *sortie*, at the end of the hall. He knocked again. The door opened, and a man with a shaved head, wearing a black leather jacket and a turtleneck, said, "You had thirty seconds left, Mr. Marcus. Do you always cut things so close?"

"You didn't give us much time to find this place."

The man gestured for them to enter. "Come in and sit at the table." They walked to a small wooden table. The man stared at Marcus a moment. "Why did you bring the woman?"

"Because I wanted to come," Alicia fired back.

He turned his head to her, his black eyes apathetic. "Why would you choose to be in a position that could lead to serious consequences?"

"Because I worked with Paul, and I'm here to assist him."

"What do you mean…worked?"

"When he was with NSA."

"I don't believe you."

"Frankly, I don't give a shit *what* you believe."

The man's nostrils opened wider, as if he was sniffing for fear from her pores. His jaw line was hard. His rigid eyes took in her whole body. "I am Rahim. You are?"

"Alicia."

"What is your surname?"

"Quincy."

"Alicia Quincy, if you ever swear at me again, I will cut out your tongue. Do you understand?"

Alicia stared at him.

Marcus said, "No one's here to threaten anyone. Where's the drive?"

A second man came out from an adjacent room, closing the door behind him. Rahim said, "Search them, Narsi."

Narsi took on an air of importance, puffing his strapping chest and arms to emphasize his physique in the tight, black T-shirt he wore. A week's worth of stubble grew from his olive face, and his dark hair resembled steel wool double-stitched across his head. "Arms straight out," he ordered. Marcus complied and the man padded him down from chest to ankles. He took Marcus's phone and the phone that had belonged to the dead woman, Taheera. He did the same thing to Alicia and said, "Arms out and give me your purse." She lifted her arms, and he quickly searched the purse, removing her phone. Narsi took the batteries from all three phones and set everything on the table.

"Where's the hard drive?" Marcus asked.

Rahim cut his eyes to Marcus without turning his head. "Do you think we were going to let you walk out of here with a hard drive containing our nuclear operating system on it?"

"We agreed that I would—"

"We agreed on the terms, Mr. Marcus. We never said how you would conduct the job." He gestured to the adjacent room. "We have computers set up in there and a secure satellite link on the rooftop connected to Iran and the motherboard."

Rahim stepped to the door, opened it and motioned for them to follow him. A widescreen monitor was wired to three computer towers. Cables from a satellite dish snaked through the windowsill. He said, "*There* is your hard drive, Mr. Marcus. That one stays with us. Our team in Nantaz will monitor everything you do. How long will it take?"

Marcus stepped to the computer, opened the system and said, "That depends on how complex the worm is, and I won't be able to tell until I look inside the grid and run some tests. Myrtus can operate only within the Windows platform. Your programmable logic controller won't differ that much from any that Siemens or any vendor of nuclear centrifuges sells its product to. What will be different is the nearly indecipherable coding that manages it, especially as your system comes closer to going online. I'll raise the hood and run a complex diagnostics. But I won't do a damn thing until your president goes on international television and releases the first hostage."

Rahim's mouth turned down like a horseshoe between his nose and chin. He said, "Narsi, do you have the funnel?"

Narsi opened a drawer and held up a glass funnel, like something found in a high school chemistry lab. He lifted a glass bottle and held it so Marcus could see the label: sulfuric acid. Rahim smiled. "Mr. Marcus, I never cared for American metaphors—raise the hood. But since that is what you people comprehend the easiest, let me be clear. You will begin now or Narsi will shoot the woman through her right knee. If you corrupt or tamper with our system, beyond finding and destroying the worm, you will watch us pour sulfuric acid through that funnel and into her vagina and then over her breasts. She will beg us to kill her, which we will do…but very slowly."

He turned to Alicia. "Miss Quincy, we will release the first infidel tomorrow. And it will not be your niece."

SEVENTY-FIVE

After more than eight hours tracing codes on the Iranian system, Marcus felt the muscles between his shoulder blades tighten. As he worked, Narsi and Rahim came in and out of the room, speaking heated Farsi into satellite phones. Alicia sat on a cot near the wall behind Marcus and tried not to think of Brandi. She stepped over to Marcus and whispered. "I have a very low profile. I'm not on anyone's grid. How'd they know I'm Brandi's aunt?"

He leaned back in the wooden chair. "I don't know."

"How are you coming? Have you found something?"

"Yes, it's in there. The worm's ability to reprogram external program logic controllers could toss a wrench into it. I can see software that's been installed to try to eradicate the worm, or worms. But I can't tell if it's been effective. The programmers could have built in a mechanism that will cause even more damage if someone attempts to remove it."

"I wonder who is responsible for embedding it there."

"Could be any contractor with a flash drive. It's so sophisticated that whoever created it had help. It may have been Israel's baby, but someone else probably fathered it."

Rahim and Narsi entered the room. Rahim said, "Our chief prosecutor appeared on television one hour ago to announce the release of Adam Spencer." He glanced at Alicia and added, "The *fiancé* of your niece."

Alicia looked at Marcus and said nothing.

Rahim said, "Reporters were there and the BBC is filing its story now. We can watch the feed." He pressed a hand-held remote control device and images filled a small plasma screen to the left of the computer screen. Iran's chief prosecutor stood on the steps in front of the judicial building and spoke to reporters in Farsi. The news story cut to scenes of Adam Spencer as he was escorted from the front of Evin Prison and whisked away in a waiting car. The next video images showed Adam at the Tehran International Airport.

In English, the reporter said, "Chief prosecutor Oshnar Abbasi said an indictment has been handed down by Iran's judiciary bringing charges against the two young Americans. However, he said the government decided to release Adam Spencer on humanitarian grounds. He added that Brandi Hirsh will be held and court proceedings are underway. If she is found guilty on charges of espionage, the verdict could lead to the death penalty. The two Americans were arrested in northern Iran when they allegedly walked across the Turkey – Iran border when they were picking berries. U.S. Secretary of State, Merriam Hanover, said efforts to free Brandi Hirsh will continue, and she is hopeful the twenty-two-year old woman, who is said to be diabetic, will be released soon. John Cunningham, BBC, Tehran."

Rahim half smiled. "The girl will be released when your job is finished."

"Who guarantees that? How do we know that?" asked Alicia, her voice now raspy.

"Because, when a Muslim man tells you something, when he offers his word, it is his bond. This is something almost unheard of in the West." He looked at Marcus. "That is why the girl will not be released until we have been convinced, Mr. Marcus, that you have removed the worm and created software patches that prevent its return."

"Look, I found evidence of an infiltration. I'll track the worm to where it's embedded, and then I will kill it. But, before I do that, I want you to promise me that Brandi will be released as soon as the Myrtus worm is destroyed."

Rahim crossed his arms, looked at Narsi and said, "Get Jalil on the satellite phone." Narsi nodded, left the room and began connecting the call. Rahim stared at Marcus and gestured to the computer screen. Then he turned on the camera above the screen. "Our engineers are watching you, Mr. Marcus. Show us where the invader lies in our system."

Marcus could see an engineer's image in the corner of the screen, knowing the high definition camera was beaming his face and voice to a secure room deep in one of Iran's nuclear plants. He used the mouse to highlight lines of code. "This is the coding that works directly with the frequency converter drives that are part of the Siemens S7-300 system and the associated modules. It looks like the worm is designed to only attack those program logic controllers with the variable-frequency drives."

"How does it do this?" a voice off screen asked from the computer speakers.

Marcus avoided looking directly in the camera. "I've been able to determine that it is specifically engineered to monitor the frequency of the centrifuge motors. It will only attack systems that operate, or spin, between eighty and twelve hundred hertz. I am writing a software patch that should diffuse the binary code, the file, and render it useless in its present state."

In a thick Persian accent, another question came from the speakers, this time from the person in the corner of the screen. "We need you to send a copy of that patch to us. Can it be used to shield against future attacks?"

"Yes, until your adversaries figure out you've got a wall up. Then they'll try something else."

The same voice said, "Indeed, but by then we will have accomplished our immediate goal."

In Farsi, a new, fast-paced voice came over the speaker. Both Rahim and Narsi immediately stood erect, their eyes fixed on the screen. Marcus listened closely, trying to make out the few words he could remember from the language. When the voice stopped, Rahim responded back in Farsi.

When they finished, Marcus glanced up at Rahim then looked directly into the camera. "Rahim, make sure your president understands this. Tell him if Iran continues this path, no one wins. There is no way that a mutually assured annihilation in a nuclear weapons race will ever be won by your country or any nation. It's genocide. The entire Middle East will be destroyed. Your decisions here will directly involve China, Russia, North Korea, Turkey, Britain, Pakistan, the U.S. and the rest of the card-carrying nuke club. There will be nothing left to fight for."

Rahim repeated the words in Farsi. There was a long silence and the voice responded in a slower, deliberate tone. When it stopped, Rahim moistened his lips and cleared his throat. "I am to tell you that America and its president are the worst form of hypocrites. He said he will have no further discussion with you about this subject."

Marcus glanced at Alicia. A vein pulsed in the side of her neck, her eyes red-rimmed. She leaned toward the camera and said, "Paul has done what you wanted. Let Brandi go! Damn you bastards to hell!"

Something was said quickly in Persian. Narsi grabbed Alicia by the hair and pulled her head back. He held a long knife to her throat. Rahim glared at Alicia and shouted, "Enough! Sit on that cot! Do not open your mouth again." He stared down at Marcus. "Finish the job!"

— —

Marcus worked all night and through the next day, only leaving the chair to use the bathroom. Rahim and Narsi rotated turns sitting at the console next to Marcus while he worked. His eyes burned and his head began pounding. Dusk drifted over Paris and the hotel room again grew darker. Alicia slept periodically, Rahim silencing her each time she spoke. A few minutes after 7:00 p.m., Marcus made his final keystroke, turned to Rahim and said, "It's finished." He pointed to the screen. "Here's the file where I built the software patch before I encoded it and fused it in your operating system."

Rahim stared at him a moment and sipped cold coffee. "Are you sure the invading worm is no more?"

"I found the worm and stopped it, like I said I would. Your centrifuge motors aren't in danger now."

Narsi entered the room and Rahim turned his head toward Alicia for a second. "Take the woman, Mr. Marcus, and leave." He glanced at the glass funnel on the console. "Remember what I told you we would do to her and her niece if you are not truthful with us."

"Everything I told you is the truth."

Narsi reached down to grip Alicia by the forearm. She pulled away and stood. "Don't touch me!"

Marcus rose slowly from the wooden chair. His back was in knots. "I finished your job at seven p.m. Monday. We expect that Brandi will be released on or before seven p.m. Wednesday."

"I spoke with our president. He agrees the girl will be released, but not for seven days. He wishes to make certain the job is done. Leave now."

"That's bullshit!" Alicia said. "That's not our agreement. You—"

"Silence woman!" Narsi's fists clenched at his side, a muscle squirmed like a moth fluttering under the skin below his right eye. His breath reeked of onion and decay.

Rahim's eyes were hooded and unreadable. Narsi motioned for Marcus and Alicia to follow him to the door.

Marcus said, "We want our phones back, all three. I want to stay in contact with you. Your end of the bargain is not done yet."

Narsi looked hard at them, his eyes furious. Rahim handed them the cell phones. "Keep Taheera's phone in the event we need to speak with you."

Narsi said nothing. He opened the door and gestured for Marcus and Alicia to leave. They walked out into the hall, and he closed the door behind them.

Once in the elevator, Alicia leaned her head back against the wall. She released a pent up breath. "Paul, thank you so much for everything you did."

"Let's hope Brandi is freed."

They walked out into the Paris night. It was clear. The moon, almost full, illuminated the streets. They walked for a block in silence and then Alicia looked over at Marcus. "I'm happy and yet sad. I pray that Brandi will walk free, but somehow I feel we signed a pact with the devil. If removing that worm causes Iran to develop the atomic bomb…what have we done if it leads to a holocaust?"

Marcus was quiet for a moment. "Maybe it won't come to that."

"What if those bastards don't let Brandi go when the deadline's reached? We can't even tell anyone. This is so damn weird."

Marcus said nothing. He watched a car drive slowly by, the driver hidden in the cloak of night, the tap of brakes when the car slowed and then resumed speed. "Alicia, your stuff is still in the trunk of my car."

"I almost forgot about that."

"I don't trust Rahim any farther than I could toss him. And Narsi looks like he loves to play with chemicals. They're hired psychopaths. I'm sure we're being watched. My room has two beds, maybe you should bunk there."

She stopped walking and looked up at him, the radiance of moonlight in her eyes. "Thank you."

"We'll get some food back at the hotel."

"Sounds good. I'm starving."

Marcus smiled, and they continued walking. He glanced up when a small cloud eased its way in front of the moon. Marcus had no idea that between the cloud and the moon, a satellite camera followed his every move.

SEVENTY-SIX

Marcus sat in a chair in his room, rested his head and listened to the sound of water running while Alicia showered. He thought about what he'd done by finding and neutralizing the Myrtus worm buried deep in the Iranian nuclear operating system.

Exhaustion in his body filled his mind and his thoughts began drifting, the resonance of the shower water fading, and the drone of traffic on the streets retreating like distant drums beyond the strata of the city buildings.

Darkness flooded his conscious mind and images filled his subconscious. Two sparrows flew from a date tree and perched on the cliff near where Marcus sat overlooking the Mediterranean Sea. He watched the sun dissolve into the sea, the breeze cool, and the valley filled with emerald shadows. He felt a strange peace wash over him.

A wind across the valley carried the scent of lavender and almonds floating amidst the remote softness of a flute and a woman's voice layered beneath the rustle of the date palm fronds. *"Marcus, we are fine…live, my love…live…"*

"Jen…Jenny, is that you?"

The sun vanished beneath the Mediterranean, and dark settled upon the valley. A moonbeam broke through the boughs of a cedar tree, a shaft of light falling on the granite cliff next to him. Marcus stared at the spot for a few seconds, then he reached for the aged stone. Suddenly, his hand was bathed in creamy white light. He felt a sharp pain in the center of his hand, followed by a throbbing that was soothed in a soft whisper, as if the concealed voice came from ancient sea currents found in the depths of a seashell. *'The blade itself will unseal it. Bring it forth...deliver its message...then release the spear into the fire of Etna."*

"The fire...where? What fire...?"

"Paul? Paul, are you okay?"

He opened his eyes, blinked away double vision and fatigue. Alicia stood next to his chair. She wore a white terry cloth bathrobe, courtesy of the hotel, and a towel wrapped around her damp hair.

She touched his arm. "I didn't want to wake you. But you were talking in your sleep and perspiring. I thought you might want to lie down in the bed since you haven't slept in two days."

Marcus said nothing, his eyes meeting hers. Alicia adjusted the robe and felt a drop of water run down the center of her back. "Paul, why are you staring at me? I feel self-conscious."

He shook his head, closing his eyes for a moment. "No...I'm sorry. It's just that the last time I saw a woman in a white bathrobe was before she tried to kill me. Give me a second to shake the dreams out of my skull."

Alicia nodded, her eyes soft, compassionate. "Were they nightmares? You were saying odd things in your sleep."

"Sometimes I can't differentiate the nightmares from...." He blew out a breath. "What'd I say?"

"I only heard a little. You mentioned Jenny's name, and then you said something about a fire...where's the fire, you asked. What were you dreaming?"

"Same thing I've been seeing—dreaming for the last few days. I see an explosion, like a huge bomb, white-hot fire and gases. Then I'm standing in a cold, dark place...maybe a field. There are no trees. It has the look and feel of twilight all over the world, and dark ash is falling like black snow."

Alicia hugged her arms. She gently touched his shoulder. "You need sleep."

Marcus stood and smiled. "Maybe there was something in that dinner... something I'm allergic to. A shower might rinse away the weird dreams."

— ▬

Marcus showered and changed into fresh jeans and a black T-shirt. As he entered the room, Alicia looked up from her laptop. "Feel better?"

"Cleaner."

"That's a start."

"What are you working on?"

Alicia smiled, glancing down at the computer screen. "I was watching the news coverage of Adam leaving. I'm so happy for him, and so sad that Brandi's still in an Iranian prison."

"We have a few days left before she's released."

"Do you think they'll keep their end of the deal?"

"I don't know. But if they don't..."

"What, Paul? What happens if they don't?"

"Maybe the White House will grow some balls and intercede."

Alicia sighed and looked at the notes she had written by her laptop. "I moved from watching the international news on my laptop to digging for information. You always call it *research*, but the truth of the matter is I'm a hacker on cyber steroids. I'm trying to get my mind off Brandi and the last forty-eight hours. This is a sort of bizarre therapy for me. Like a high-end video game. I have to focus and block everything else out. I'm hacking deeper into the inner realm of the Circle of 13."

"What have you found?"

"Most of the people in this club don't use digital communications, or they have assistants do it for them and speak only in generalities. That's a lot of what I'm getting—meeting locations, times, logistics, food and even liquor preferences. They all seem to like expensive single malt scotches. I did find where Senator Wyatt Dirkson took an impromptu trip, or an undocumented trip to Texas where he stayed three days and nights at the ranch of billionaire Jonathon Carlson. The good senior senator is pushing hard in congress to get a majority behind his bill, the proposed National Security Act. This bill, if enacted into law, would provide more than thirty billion dollars to fund massive satellite surveillance technology. It would mandate GPS monitoring and registration in all cell phones sold in the U.S. Also, it would authorize the government to obtain access to the browsing history of people using Google and other Internet search sites, social pages and apps."

"Sounds like the Patriot Act on speed."

"You got it. In Senator Dirkson's case, a direct benefit, if this bill is passed, is Jonathon Carlson and one of the companies in which he has controlling interests, Integrated Security Corp, or ISC for short, would stand to make a lot of money, and the senator would get a huge financial kickback. Both men attended the same Ivy League schools, and both have colleagues and deep connections within the Kinsley Group. And look at this… Carlson's grandfather, on his mother's side, Andrew Chaloner, operated the private investment firm of Chaloner and Shipley, which had financial ties to Thyssen Steel before World War II. The investment made them money. Here's the flip side, by investing in the infrastructure that financed the Nazi party, the investments eventually contributed to the deaths of ten million people."

Marcus was quiet a moment. Then he said, "James Tower mentioned the name Chaloner, but he couldn't recall the first name. All of these revelations, the puzzle pieces, it's as if they've been opened to take us into the lair of spiders who've been weaving a web of deceit for almost a century."

"Maybe longer. Chaloner and some of the other families in the circle go back three centuries. It's a conga line of DNA that takes them…" Alicia paused. "Paul, it's traceable all the way back to the seventeenth century."

"How are you spelling the name, Chaloner?"

"C-h-a-l-o-n-e-r. Why?"

"Because I remember something Isaac Newton wrote about a court trial, and now we have the connection with Andrew Chaloner during World War II. James Tower said this guy, Chaloner, was in the market for the Spear of Destiny. Maybe Philippe Fournier knew it, too, and somehow managed to use the Vatican's money to buy it from Tower because Tower had told Bill Donovan that he never found the spear on General Patton."

Alicia said nothing for a moment. "What did Newton write?"

"It was buried in some of his biblical notes. Newton said the genesis of evil, the seed first spawned in the Garden of Eden, can be handed down, father to son, mother to daughter, or any combination of a family tree because our roots come from the tree of the knowledge of good and evil. He wrote this while summing up in court his prosecution of a convict, a man by the name of William Chaloner."

"Newton the scientist became Newton the prosecutor?"

"One and the same."

"So who was Chaloner?"

"I don't know much more about him. Chaloner apparently crossed paths with him after Newton accepted a position from the King of England to become Warden of the Royal Mint. See what, if anything, you can find on William Chaloner."

"Give me a minute." Alicia cross-referenced names and dates, keyed in data, and watched her screen fill with information. "Listen to this. This guy, Chaloner, wasn't just your average run-of-the-mill, seventeenth century rascal—he was to crime what Newton was to science."

"How?"

"Give me a sec." She paused and read. "This indicates Chaloner became Newton's nemesis. Counterfeiting was epidemic in London around 1690, when Newton took the job at the Royal Mint. Newton streamlined the Royal Mint, and introduced paper currency. Before that, all coins were hand-struck from the Royal Mint. England was going through a banking and economic crisis, not unlike what we've experienced. Chaloner was a mastermind in the underworld of counterfeiting, fraud, and high concept crimes, truly a brilliant criminal. Newton used his scientific prowess, his mind and incredible attention to detail to trap Chaloner in his own fraudulent game. This information says it took Newton a year to do it, but he caught what many consider the smartest criminal in England during the seventeenth century. He *personally* prosecuted Chaloner on charges of defrauding the Bank of England, counterfeiting, and high treason."

"So the greatest scientific mind, Isaac Newton, laid a trap for a man of immense intellectual capacity, and he won. What happened to Chaloner?"

"Let me see…." She read silently a few seconds. "He was executed. Says he died by hanging. Not the kind where the condemned prisoner drops and his fall results in a broken neck. This is the type where the executioner kicks the apple box out from under the guy at the end of the rope and the victim dies slowly."

"You said that Jonathon Carlson's grandfather was Andrew Chaloner whose firm invested in Thyssen Steel before World War II. Can you find any connection between Carlson and the William Chaloner in Newton's time?"

Alicia looked from Marcus to her computer screen. "Give me a minute." She pulled strands of hair behind her ears and began punching the keyboard. Her eyes were transfixed on the screen, plowing deeper into her analysis. She paused briefly to write something on a notepad then continued tapping the keys. In less than a minute, Alicia looked up. "I have news for you."

"What?"

"Jonathon Carlson, on his mother's side, is a direct blood descendant to William Chaloner, the criminal mastermind who, as we discussed, fought Sir Isaac Newton 300 years ago…and lost."

SEVENTY-SEVEN

arcus's phone rang. Alicia looked at him. Marcus glanced down at his watch. 1:07 a.m. He stood and walked to the chest-of-drawers where the phone sat, its tiny, red light flashing with each ring. Marcus looked at the caller ID. UNKNOWN. He answered, and Bill Gray said, "Paul, intel tells us Taheera Khalili is dead."

"I could have told you that if you'd asked."

"Did you kill her?"

"Your same intel should have told you she committed suicide. Before that, she had a pistol pointed at my head. She told me Jennifer and Tiffany were killed by an Iranian operative. Why'd you lie to me, Bill? Local suspect! Bullshit!"

"We, rather the CIA, had reason to believe you'd been recruited by Iran."

"Do you really believe that?"

"No, but I'm a cog in the wheel. Come home, Paul. If you don't, they'll find you."

"Listen to me! Tell them to try finding the assassin who killed Jennifer and Tiffany. One of his aliases is the Lion. Find this guy."

"The Lion. If it were the same assassin, you wouldn't have survived the hit either. He doesn't miss."

"But he did. What do you know about the Lion...do you know his name?"

"Tell Alicia to report back to work. You continue as you are and you'll put her in the cross-hairs, too. You don't want her blood on your hands."

"What do you know about the Lion you're not telling me?" He looked up at Alicia, the light from a lamp falling softy on one side of her face.

"Look, Paul, I hate to be the one to tell you this, but I have some bad news. It's your grandmother...she had a brain hemorrhage—a massive stroke and she has slipped into a coma. I'm sorry."

Marcus said nothing. His heart pounded. A sharp pain flowed through his stomach and guts as if he's swallowed broken glass. "How do I know you're not lying?"

"I would never stoop that low."

"You stooped lower when you told me police made an arrest for the murders."

"I hope one day you'll forgive me. I thought it was the best, safest, and easiest way to get you back home."

"Home? What does that mean anymore, Paul? The killer of my wife and little girl is out there. Obviously, you know something about the Lion that you won't tell me. Well, let me tell you something, if the CIA won't make an effort to find him, I will." Marcus disconnected, his heart hammering in his chest.

Alicia waited a moment, then asked, "What is it, Paul? What happened?"

"If Bill's honest, my grandmother is in a coma. She had a stroke."

"I'm so sorry." She touched his arm, her eyes searching his face.

"She's all I have left."

"It's obvious how much she loves you—her eyes lit up each time your name was mentioned. I feel fortunate that I had a chance to sit and talk with her."

Marcus looked at Alicia and nodded. "I'm glad you did, too." He walked over to the window and looked to the street below at the falling rain and the blurred movement of the taxis strolling through the neon lights reflecting off the wet streets.

Alicia closed her laptop and walked over to Marcus, but said nothing. She looked up into his eyes, which were filled with pain. She touched his cheek and hugged him. They stood there, holding each other, the rain rolling down the outside windowpane, rainbows of light reflecting from pools of water across the streets of Paris.

Alicia reached for Marcus's hand, looked up into his eyes and kissed the inside of his hand. "Come to bed. Let's get some rest."

He nodded. She glanced at the two queen-sized beds. "Which one do you want, the bed closer to the TV or closer to the wall?"

Marcus smiled. "It doesn't matter."

"Okay, I'll take the one closest to the TV." She climbed in the bed and crawled underneath the sheet and blanket.

Marcus shut off the light and got in the other bed. He rested his head on the pillows and closed his burning eyes, his grandmother in his thoughts.

Alicia said, "Do you mind if I watch a little TV? Maybe I'll find a movie to lull me into sleep."

"I don't mind."

Alicia turned on the plasma screen and flipped through the channels, stopping to watch a French talk show. Through an interpreter, the host was interviewing actress Angelina Jolie on the set of the movie she was filming in the south of France. Alicia changed channels and stopped as images of Adam Spencer came on the screen. The video showed him being greeted at Reagan International Airport in Washington. He was met by a mob of reporters. A CNN reporter said, "Adam Spencer will be taken to Georgetown University Hospital for observation and a checkup. He appears thin but in good health. He wouldn't comment on specific questions pertaining to what he's been through the last six months at the hands of the Iranians. However, he said the release of his fiancée, Brandi Hirsh, is all he's thinking about."

The image was a close-up of Adam, his face pained, hair unkempt, and clothes that looked like he'd slept in them for weeks. He said, "We've been treated humanely. I'm convinced that they'll soon discover the detainment of Brandi and I was a simple mistake. The borders between that stretch of Turkey and Iran are not visible. My concern is making sure that Brandi will be home soon, and it's my prayer that she'll be reunited with her family before Christmas."

The screen filled with a picture of Brandi smiling and sitting on the Santa Monica Pier, blue water visible in the background. The image faded to her after she'd been in prison for a few weeks, her face empty, eyes dark. The reporter said, "The Iranians aren't saying exactly why they only released Adam Spencer. His fiancée, Brandi Hirsh, who has had diabetes since she was thirteen, sits in a cell at Evin Prison north of Tehran at the base of the Alborz Mountains. Secretary of State, Merriam Hanover, wouldn't comment as to whether negotiations are underway to secure the release of the young American. Robert Simpson, CNN News, Washington."

Alicia sat on the edge of the bed, legs drawn up, staring at the screen. "I took that picture of Brandi on the Santa Monica Pier last year. I don't even know how the news media got it. Brandi was so full of life there. Look at the photo of her in that prison. She has dark circles under her eyes." Alicia turned to Marcus. "Paul, I'm so cold all of a sudden. Can I lie next to you for a moment? I am so frightened for her."

Marcus nodded. "Sure."

Alicia climbed in bed and turned her back to Marcus. She said, "If you'd hold me a minute, maybe I'll stop shaking. Just seeing Brandi on television, the sad and helpless look in her eyes, is tearing my heart apart."

Marcus wrapped his right arm around Alicia's shoulders. She adjusted her body to meet his, the warmth immediate. He could smell the scent of lilac soap on her neck, the heat from her back warm against him. Then there was the first soft sob, the deep inhalation and erratic shudder of muscles as she tried to hide her crying.

"I rarely cry. Believe me. I miss my dad so much...and I'm so afraid for Brandi. I don't want her to die in that hellhole, Paul."

Marcus held her closer and said nothing. She gently sobbed, her body radiating heat, her fists clutching the sheets. Within a few minutes her breathing became regular, her trembling gone. She turned to face Marcus. "I'm sorry. You learned your grandmother had a stroke, and I'm the one crying."

"It's okay."

She reached out and touched his cheek with the tips of her fingers, tracing the structure of his face. "Paul, all of these revelations you've uncovered...the same group that killed Patton probably killed Kennedy Junior, maybe his father. Do they really have roots going back to the Nazis? Is Jonathon Carlson part of it? What else have they done? Who else have they killed? What do you know from Newton and those Bible codes? What have you found that you *aren't* telling me?"

"I'm still trying to understand them. I think finding the Spear of Destiny will be key. Maybe I'll never understand this stuff. Maybe Newton never did."

"But you *know* something. I can feel it somehow. You knew the prime minister was going to be assassinated. You've uncovered this connection with the Circle of 13 back to 1933. You peeled back the information from the Nuremberg trials to David Marcus and Philippe Fournier. Isaac Newton fought William Chaloner three centuries ago. Now we have a great, great, great grandson, Jonathon Carlson, connected by his grandfather to the atrocities of World War II; and Carlson's company is one of America's biggest defense contractors today. Where is it all heading?"

"I don't know. All I know is that more than six million people died as slaves and prisoners under the Nazi Germany regime. What if some American companies and the people who ran them were complicit in that? They may not have turned on the gas in those death chambers, but they financed the people who did. After the horror of it all, what if they helped them escape and with the money they looted from the afflicted people and nations?"

Alicia used two fingers to gently press against Marcus's lips. She touched her fingers to her lips. The flicker of bluish light from the silent television screen danced in her eyes. She inched her body closer to Marcus, reached for his hand and leaned in to kiss him. Her lips were soft, searching. Marcus could feel the pulse rise in her hand.

She kissed him again, her lips hot, searching. He returned her kiss, the taste of her mouth, sensual like honey on his tongue. They kissed slowly, probing. Alicia moaned softly. Marcus used his thumb to push a strand of her dark hair away from her eyes. "I'm not sure if this is the right thing at this time..."

Alicia sat up quickly, and walked to the window, her back to Marcus as she stared at the traffic below. She turned to him and said, "You're right. I don't want to make love with you just because I'm feeling vulnerable. I want it to be for the right reasons."

Marcus stood and kissed her softly. "Would you like some water?" he asked.

Alicia sat back on the bed, stacking the pillows behind her. "That'd be good, thanks."

— —

A few hours later, Marcus sat up in bed. He reached for the lamp in the semi-dark room, the only light in the room coming from a small opening in the curtains. He felt for the switch under the lampshade, his fingers touching something that seemed out of place. Marcus found the lamp chain and pulled it. Light filled the room, waking up Alicia. He leaned down and looked under the lampshade. His eyes narrowed, staring at the object, no larger than a thimble, stuck at the base of the brass socket.

Marcus straightened and held a finger to his lips. Alicia's eyes opened wide. She got out of bed and stepped up to the lamp table. Marcus pointed to the bug and then took Alicia's hand. He picked up the TV remote and turned on the volume and then led her toward the bathroom. He whispered in her ear. "I don't know who planted it or what they've heard. When we talk now, speak at a normal level. Keep any sign of stress or awareness of the bug out of your voice."

"I am so glad we didn't make love, it—"

"It's okay. I'm going to check the entire room for additional bugs. We have to get out of here." Marcus walked back to the lamp and turned off the light. He stepped to the curtains and looked through the slight opening to the street below the hotel. A lone taxi lumbered by, its exhaust puffing smoke on the chilly and damp night. Marcus scanned the line of cars parked across the street. All looked unoccupied. All but one.

He spotted the tiny glow of a cigarette on the driver's side of a parked Peugeot.

SEVENTY-EIGHT

At 5:00 a.m., Marcus placed a call to the Mayflower Assisted Living center in Virginia, apologizing for calling so late. The night nurse on duty was empathic and said, "Your grandmother had a severe stroke. We did all we could before transporting her to Georgetown University Hospital for further treatment."

"What's the prognosis?"

"I'm not a doctor, but her age, it doesn't look good. I'm so sorry. She is one of the most delightful residents we have, a real pleasure." Marcus thanked the woman, disconnected, and called the hospital. He was told his grandmother was resting but unresponsive. He was asked if she had a living will. "No," Marcus answered. "At least she never spoke of one."

"Do you have power-of-attorney over her affairs?"

"Yes."

"Mr. Marcus, I hope I don't sound callous when I suggest that we need to have you make arrangements in the event of your grandmother's death. If you choose to remove her from life support, please transmit a signed authorization form to us. You can download one from our website. I'm sorry you're faced with this. Please let us know your decision as soon as possible."

Marcus held the phone in his hand for a moment, not sure what to do. He glanced over at Alicia and used a hand signal to indicate they were leaving the room. They turned up the television volume and quietly left.

Ten minutes later, they were exiting the hotel building from a side entrance. Marcus flagged down a taxi, and the two of them climbed into the back seat. "Bonjour, parlez-vous anglais?" Marcus asked.

The taxi driver looked in his rearview mirror at them. His eyes were puffy, a long, thin face, mid-fifties. "Of course, I drive a taxi. Where can I take you?"

"Chartres. Do you go there?"

"Yes, but not often. It is about a one hour drive." He pulled away from the curb.

Marcus glanced out the back window. A car was following in the distance. "At the second traffic light take a right."

"No problem, however, that is not the way to Chartres."

"It doesn't matter."

The driver signaled and turned right entering the intersection. After a block, Marcus looked out the window again. The car made the turn. "I'll add a two hundred dollar tip if you can lose that car behind us."

The driver glanced in his rearview mirror. "There are two men in the car."

"Can you lose them?"

"It is no problem. I was one of the drivers with Team Porsche at Le Mans in 1977. But that was another time. Before two divorces, a broken leg…Mais c'était il ya une éternité—a life time ago, yes. Hold on." He floored the accelerator, raced down Rue Poliveau, made a sharp left turn and sped down an alley. He cut to the right and went up a second alley, knocking over a garbage can and accelerating. Alicia squeezed Marcus's arm. After a block, the driver pulled onto Rue de Tolbiac. He sped into the commuter traffic, pulling in and out of the cars and trucks, heading south on A10. "We have lost the car you didn't care to have following us."

Marcus looked out the back window. The car was nowhere to be seen. "Did you win at Le Mans?"

"I was in the lead at the twenty-fourth hour, and then I crashed at sunrise. A morning like today."

Marcus glanced out the window. The pink of dawn shimmered over the Seine River. He inhaled deeply, exhaling slowly. Alicia watched the traffic, her face secluded in thought. The driver looked at Alicia in the rearview mirror, and then lowered his eyes to the road. "Many go to Chartres looking for something. Are you two pilgrims?"

"Not in the traditional sense," Marcus said, his eyes burning.

The driver nodded. "Some people believe the old cathedral is the most holy in the world. My mother took my brother and me there when we were teenagers. She said the cathedral is Mary's *womb* on earth. Our time in the womb is the safest. Then we are born. I don't know why that car was following you, but I hope you will find safety in the womb of Chartres."

In less than an hour, the taxi driver turned off the main road and drove the back roads toward the town of Chartres. The taxi wound through a small hamlet, the rural road leading across the wheat fields. Marcus looked out the window. Ahead, in the distance, Chartres Cathedral, with its massive spires, seemed to float above the wheat fields like an optical illusion. He touched Alicia and pointed. Her eyes bright, focused.

"Paul, it looks surreal from here—almost like the Emerald City in the land of Oz. I can see a huge church and nothing else around in any direction. I don't know why, but I feel an unusual connection with it…like it's somehow calling me."

SEVENTY-NINE

CHARTRES, FRANCE

*M*arcus and Alicia drank dark coffee and ate warm beignets with apple fillings in a small café near the narrow Eure River. The spires of Chartres Cathedral rose high above the town of Chartres, which was trimmed in landmarks from the Middle Ages. They finished eating and walked across an ancient stone bridge over the Eure. The river flowed quietly through limestone medieval arches that vanished beneath the dark water.

They walked through the town, the scent of baking bread in the air when they passed through an alley by a bakery. Chartres Cathedral stood before them. Alicia stopped and simply stared at the enormous cathedral. "What a breathtaking church! I've never seen anything like it."

"The word spectacular doesn't seem to convey what we're seeing. Let's walk around the exterior before we go inside."

As they came closer to Chartres Cathedral, two tourists' buses pulled into the cobblestone parking lot, doors swinging open and pilgrims from all over the world descending, similar to sports teams anxious to play on a new court. Marcus and Alicia passed by the chattering hordes. Nearby, street vendors hocked religious trinkets.

The cathedral wore a coat of ancient history over the massive spires, flying buttresses and portals carved by hands of master sculptors. The statues and stone effigies inset at the entrances spoke with a universal body language that needed no interpreter: biblical icons carved in stone. The closer Marcus came to the cathedral, the more his heart raced. He looked at how the morning sun fell across the building, poking light into dark crevices, warming granite faces of angels and biblical figures that had witnessed a thousand years of mornings and sunsets clinging to the mortar of the cathedral.

Marcus used the GPS feature on his phone while he studied the engraved history. "Each portal, each entrance, tells a story."

"What stories?" Alicia asked.

"From Adam and Eve to the great flood, through the time of Christ and the Book of Revelation."

"It's the Bible set in stone." She smiled and touched his arm.

"Apparently, a lot of it's here, either on the exterior or inside. The stained-glass windows are said to be some of the best remaining on earth. We're looking at the eastern portals. Let's move around and see the southern and western entrances."

Alicia followed Marcus. He walked beneath a weeping willow tree, its leaves pumpkin orange. He stopped and wrote numbers on a pad of paper. "When are you going to tell me what we're looking for?" she asked.

"I told you that already."

"I understand—it's the Spear of Destiny. But this cathedral is the size of Mt. Rushmore. We don't even have a clue where to begin looking."

"Maybe we do. If we can figure out a few things, possibly the clues will be more visible...and if the spear is hidden inside, we might have a chance of finding it."

Marcus wandered slowly around the exterior. He watched a worker using a high-pressure water hose to clean mildew from an exterior wall. The worker stepped down from a painter's ladder, leaned it against a portico and returned to the pressure washer rattling on the lawn. He shut it off and wound up the hose.

"My apologies for the noise."

Startled, Marcus and Alicia turned around to face a man who stood on the paved walk with a dozen fresh-cut roses in his hands. He grinned and said, "The upkeep of Chartres is constant. But she wears her years well. I'm Father Davon."

Marcus guessed that the priest, who spoke with a slight British accent, was in his late sixties. He had a dark beard streaked with white hair, the pattern and contrast looked amusingly as if ice cream had dripped through his whiskers. His blue eyes sparkled in the light. "You're from America, I assume."

"How can you tell?" Marcus asked.

"After working as a guide here for thirty years, I can usually tell. Most pilgrims enter through the western portal. I was trimming the late-bloomers in the garden and saw you and the lovely lady wandering about like two lost sheep." He extended a rose to Alicia. "The bouquet is for the altar. However, this one's for the lady."

She reached for the rose. "Thank you! That's very sweet." She sniffed the bud. "It smells lovely, and there are no thorns on the stem."

"It happens, rarely, but it happens."

Marcus studied the priest for a second. "I suppose a rose without thorns blooms under a new sun...even this late in the season."

Father Davon nodded, his beard parting in a grin. "Yes, indeed. I've heard that. May I ask your names?"

"I'm Paul Marcus. This is my friend, Alicia Quincy."

"I am pleased to make your acquaintances. My old British bones tell me that you two aren't typical tourists making a religious pilgrimage to Chartres. A million people come here each year. Very few would know the significance of what you just said: *a rose without thorns blooms under a new sun*. The rose is a metaphor for Mary, and the new sun is Christ. I'm curious. What is it you are seeking?"

"We're seeking some answers. We're hoping they might be found at Chartres."

Father Davon smiled, the breeze tickling his beard, birdsong coming from the trees. "What are the questions?"

"What sacred artifacts are here?"

Father Davenport grinned. "*All* of Chartres is a sacred artifact. The cathedral was built on high ground, land believed to have magnetic connections with the heavens. I would be honored to show you around Chartres and answer your questions."

Marcus looked at Alicia for a moment. She smiled and nodded. "Okay," Marcus said. "A place this large requires a compass or a good guide."

Father Davon motioned for them to follow him. "Indeed, this is the place that will stay with you long after you return to your homes. No one knows who the architect was—the person who actually drew the plans for Chartres. In the days when Chartres was built, it wasn't about making a name, a personal statement, as is often the case with builders. It was about making an earthly home for the spirit—the mother of Jesus, Mary. That was reason enough for the sweat equity and ingenuity that went into this magnificent cathedral. Many believe the Knights Templar was the driving force behind the construction." The priest pointed to the western portal where hundreds of stone carvings above the entrance told stories. "Up there is the story of The Last Judgment. You can see Christ's ascension into heaven. There is no indication of the wound on his side, the gash he received from the spear of the Roman soldier, Longinus. Perhaps this indicates a second coming and ascension."

Marcus touched his chest, feeling for the scar beneath his shirt. "What is that?" he asked, pointing to a carved image of an old man hunched over a portable desk on his lap, his hands writing across a stone ledger.

Father Davon chuckled. "That statue is a depiction of the Philosopher's Stone, a man seeking pure enlightenment. Such was the School of Chartres, which existed in this cathedral for almost two centuries."

Marcus scanned the wall of statues, faces, figurines, gargoyles, full-length depictions of saints, kings and queens. The sheer number of images in stone was blurring. His eyes stopped on one group of four statues, each standing on elongated pedestals. One statue was of a longhaired man with a spear in his hands.

"Who is that?" Marcus pointed toward the statue.

"It's believed to be Saint Theodore. No one knows for sure."

"What are you thinking, Paul?" asked Alicia.

"I'm not sure what to think."

Father Davon smiled. "You asked about sacred artifacts here. Let's walk to the north portal, and I'll show you something that may keep you up at nights."

As they walked around the cathedral, Marcus snapped pictures with his phone and punched in equations. "I'm betting this cathedral is about as close to any building on earth to matching the size of Solomon's Temple."

Father Davon stopped for a moment. He seemed to search for the right words. "Both were built using the sacred geometry, the cubits measured by the dimension of the human body and the spirit of God. Sort of like Da Vinci's *Vitruvian Man*, a blend of art, architecture, science, nature and spirit all in a proportion that can be replicated and manifested into stone."

"How does that translate to this cathedral?" Alicia asked.

"Here at Chartres, the builders used measurements and design codes derived from the circle, square and the triangle. I believe the same system was used in the building of Solomon's Temple, a mix of the sacred cubit and the golden ratio. Not unlike some Greek or Egyptian architecture." The priest pointed to engravings on the north portal. "Speaking of Solomon's Temple, that image depicts the Ark of the Covenant being transported from Jerusalem to right here at Chartres."

Marcus looked closely at the carving into the pillars of the north portal of the church. The images portrayed the Ark of the Covenant pulled by an ox cart.

Father Davon said, "The story links the cathedral as a commemoration of the transportation of the Ark. Many believe the Ark was stored here in the crypt for two centuries until it was taken away."

"Taken where?" Marcus asked. "Who took it?"

"No one alive knows. Perhaps removed from Jerusalem by the Knights Templar, and maybe returned there by the same group. Or taken someplace else."

Marcus touched the inscription at the base of the pillars. 'Hic Amititur Archa Cederis," he said. "It's Latin and means…through the Ark thou shall work."

"Impressive," mused Father Davon.

"What does it really *mean*?" Alicia asked. "Through the Ark thou shall work."

Father Davon shrugged. "I suppose it's up to one's personal interpretation. Perhaps not unlike much of what John left behind in the Book of Revelation. The words often are more than words—they are symbols and metaphors that can keep our inner compass pointed in the right direction. Gravity grips the human body. Chartes grips the soul."

Marcus said, "When you pointed to the ascension of Christ on the other side of the cathedral, you mentioned the spear that Longinus had used to prove Christ had died. Is that spear *here*…is it here at Chartres?"

Alicia held her breath for a moment, looking from Marcus to the priest. Father Davon stared at the Ark carved in stone, his thoughts as mysterious as the inscription on the pillar. "Perhaps you and Alicia can return to Chartres at night. This is a remarkable structure anytime, but at night it transforms itself. If the Spear of Destiny is here…I've never *seen* it. However, a thousand years ago, in their curriculum, the teachers at the School of Chartres spoke of the spear. Rather than tell you about it…come back tomorrow night, the night of a full moon, and I will *show* you something."

EIGHTY

*U*sing assumed names, Marcus and Alicia checked into the Mercure Hotel at 3 Rue du General Koenig. Marcus asked for a third floor room.

"I have one with a very nice view of the cathedral," said the balding front desk manager. "How many nights will you be with us?"

"Just one," Marcus said, paying in cash. They got directions to the room and took the elevator to the third floor. Once in the room, Marcus said, "Don't turn the lights on yet."

"Okay," Alicia stepped inside and stood just beyond the threshold.

Marcus closed the curtains to the three windows overlooking the lighted cathedral. He noticed that the moon was almost full rising above the spires. "The moon's rising between the steeples on the cathedral. Tomorrow night at this time I guess we will see whatever it is that Father Davon wants to show us."

"What happens if it's cloudy?"

"I don't know."

"Can I turn on the lights?"

"Yes."

"Do you think they, whoever they are, do you think they're out there searching for us?"

"Yeah, I do."

"Why, Paul? Was it something they overheard in the room they bugged?"

339

"Well, whoever it was, heard a lot more than we wanted them to—we just don't know who or why."

"Was it the damn Iranians…the French DGSE, Israelis, the CIA or maybe someone within the Circle of 13? Jonathon Carlson?" Alicia's anxious laugh got caught in her throat. "Maybe they're all looking for us."

"We didn't ask for the posse."

"No, we didn't. Paul, let's turn the tables even more and look for them."

"Who do you have in mind?"

"We start with William Chaloner, blood relative to Jonathon Carlson, and we work our way down." Alicia smiled, opened her laptop, logged on, and began hacking though layers of coding.

"I'll pick up dinners-to-go and gallons of French roast coffee." Marcus stepped out of the room and walked to the end of the hallway. He stood in an alcove and used Taheera's phone to call the Iranians. Rahim answered on the second ring. Marcus said, "Your tech people now know that what I did has effectively stopped the Myrtus threat."

"Why are you calling, Mr. Marcus?"

"I want to see Brandi Hirsch on a damn airplane like we agreed. I have a flash drive that is the key, the lock and key, which must be inserted in your system to extend the Myrtus shutdown indefinitely."

"No! I don't like what I am hearing from you."

"I don't give a rat's ass what you *like*. This is the way it goes down, Rahim. I'll hand the drive—the key—to you after Brandi's on the plane home."

"I will speak to those higher than me, and we shall do the exchange—the final exchange. I assure you, our president hates games."

"You want your nuclear reactors to melt down? If Brandi's not released, your end game will be hell on earth."

"Expect my call very soon."

— • —

Six hours later, long after they'd eaten food in their room, Alicia looked up from her laptop. "Carlson may be a smart businessman, but he's not the most tech savvy."

"How so?"

"I've accessed his iPhone and iPad. His password is Circle M Ranch. That's the name of his Texas property. The M is significant because it's the thirteenth letter in the alphabet, as in Circle of 13."

"Now that you're inside, you can monitor everything he sends and receives."

"Carlson has very little in the way of email, at least on the hard-drive I'm camped on at the moment." She read silently. "But, what he does have speaks volumes."

"What do you mean?"

"Look at this."

Marcus leaned in to view the screen. Alicia said, "Carlson received an email from someone called watchdog@senate.org. It reads: *Looks like 51-49 will go. Took a lot of arm-twisting. House should be no problem. WD.*" Alicia looked up at Marcus. "I'm betting ol' WD, AKA Watch Dog, is the illustrious senator, Wyatt Dirkson."

"Carlson responded, he said: *Good news. The bad news is the target has more info than we thought on k junior. Don't know his intentions. He's digging up skeletons. And he's seeking the object – still valuable in that regard. We can file treason charges – or quietly resolve the issue. Members to convene – DC location. Tuesday, 9 a.m.*"

Alicia said, "He's talking about you—or us. Treason charges. That asshole! Quietly *resolve*, as in put a bullet through our heads. I'm used to hacking and finding out these kind of threats and complicity about other people… but now we're in the crosshairs."

"K junior no doubt is John Kennedy Junior. Object is probably the spear. Carlson *wants* it like his grandfather wanted it."

"The last person to have touched it, we think, was Philippe Fournier. He may have taken it to Rome."

Marcus shut out the lights and stepped over to one of the windows. He opened the curtains. From the top floor of the hotel, the view of Chartres Cathedral was breathtaking. The moon overhead was plump and oozing radiance, pale light settling over the back of the ancient cathedral like a pastel shawl. Marcus said, "Or maybe it's in there. I'm hoping that whatever Father Davon wants to show us will help point the way."

EIGHTY-ONE

*I*t was dark when Marcus and Alicia returned to Chartres Cathedral. Fog climbed up from the Eure River, swirling at the tops of weeping willows and silver maple trees, their yellow leaves wet and falling like golden confetti in the haze. A full moon rose from the east, casting the twin spires into silhouettes. The moonlight illuminated the cathedral in soft white, creating pockets of deep shadows. Mist caressed the stone faces and floated toward the massive wooden doors as if silent spirits waited to be invited inside.

Marcus and Alicia approached the north portal. She hugged her upper arms and said, "This is like we're in some kind of dream. I almost want to pinch myself. It feels as if time doesn't have a twenty-four hour cycle here. I know that *sounds* really weird. Father Davon seems to know more than he's telling us about the spear."

"I think he knows *something*. Maybe he was simply picking and pruning those roses, but it felt like he was waiting for us to arrive. Almost like the rose without thorn information was some kind of very old code."

"He said the north door would be left unlocked for us." Alicia turned the antique wrought iron handle. The ancient wooden door opened, its hinges moaning, the sound traveling deep into the heart of the cathedral. They stepped inside and closed the door behind them. "Oh…my…God," Alicia mumbled, her head slowly turning, eyes trying to take in the light and the stone architecture. Hundreds of candles burned in candleholders on walls and tables around the cathedral. Chandeliers and soft lights illuminated statues and ornate biblical scenes carved in iron and stone, the light reflecting off polished brass and dancing through dark arched passageways that seemed to lead far away.

The moonlight, which filtered through the vast stain-glass windows, filled the cathedral with an interior rainbow, soft hues of blue and pink, as if the atoms in the light now could be seen with the human eye. They walked toward the altar. It was in the center of polished marble, seven steps leading up to the altar. A dozen roses sat in the middle of the marble table. Alicia whispered, "Those are the roses Father Davon picked. Look at that." She pointed down the long corridor to where a perfect circle of candles surrounded a stone labyrinth. "Let's check it out."

"I wonder where Father Davon is. Maybe something came up that caused him to be delayed."

"That would mean we'd have the run of this incredible church for a while." She smiled and walked to the labyrinth, stopping at the entrance, her eyes searching the stones and following the maze to the center stone. "It looks so old. Let's see where it leads us," she whispered. Alicia entered the labyrinth, following its web, stepping carefully on each stone. Marcus followed behind her, glancing up at the stained glass from the different perspectives achieved by walking the circles within the labyrinth.

When Alicia got to the center, she knelt down and touched her palm to the stone. The centerpiece was cool, shaped like a flower, six petals. "Paul, there is a power in this place, a power I've never felt in any church. I can't describe it. Can you *feel* it? I could sense it in the taxi, looking across the wheat field at Chartres."

"Yes. Something's here."

"The question now, is the Spear of Destiny here?" asked Father Davon, stepping out of the shadows, the light from the circle shimmering in his wide eyes.

"Do you always do that?" asked Alicia.

"And what is that?"

"Pop up like a ghost. You're so quiet. We didn't hear you come in."

"I was already here. I wanted to give you and Paul a little time to sense the uniqueness of Chartres. It looks as though it's working."

Alicia pushed a strand of hair behind her right ear. "What's the significance of the flower in the center of the labyrinth?"

"It's a destination of the heart, the soul. A journey Socrates may have found before his death. Some people have called this ancient labyrinth the road to Jerusalem. I believe it's meant to take you on a higher journey. The labyrinth, like Chartres, is part of the sacred geometry, which, in its purest levels, is designed to open your mind and spirit to become closer with God. It lifts the consciousness to wider, and perhaps, *wiser* aspects. Walking it, you see and feel different parts of Chartres, the various views of the stained-glass, the solitude of a journey that is more of a destination of the heart than a physical place."

Marcus looked at the circle of candles, their flames dancing without the feel of air circulating. "You said you didn't know if the Spear of Destiny is here, but you were going to show us something?"

"Ah, yes…indeed, the spear." Follow me. Father Davon led them through the long corridors of the cathedral. He stopped at one immense stained-glass window and pointed to it. "That's the Blue Virgin. It's considered the most pure of colors found in stained glass anywhere on earth. Look at the blues, it's like the sun was shining from the depths of a deep blue sea. And that is just from the light of the moon. No one is sure how the old masters achieved it. It simply cannot be duplicated today."

He led them through a winding maze, and they entered a room lit by a few candles and reduced lights. Two golden winged angels were on either side of an elaborate, ornamented gold display box, the top portion forming a triangle. A bone white cloth lay wrapped over a bar in the center—a long shawl on an intricate, bejeweled rack.

"This is what many on their spiritual pilgrimages come to Chartres to see, the Sancta Camisa. It is said to be the tunic of Mary, mother of Jesus, the actual shawl she wore the night she gave birth to Jesus Christ our Lord."

Marcus stared at the tunic without saying anything, his mind drawing references from the Bible passages he'd researched. Words from Luke 2:34 coalesced in his thoughts as if someone whispered in his ear, the hushed echoes traveling down the arched passageways filling the cathedral with a chorus of soft voices. '*This Child is destined for the fall and rising of many in Israel, and for a sign which will be spoken against…a spear will pierce through your own soul so that the thoughts of many hearts may be revealed.*' Marcus pinched the bridge of his nose, the room suddenly warmer, closer. His eyes met the priest, neither man speaking.

Alicia moistened her lips and said, "It's beautiful. Do you really think it's the one Mary wore when Christ was born?"

Father Davon smiled. "No one can say with complete authenticity. Perhaps, like the Spear of Destiny carried by Charlemagne, it is the true tunic. Possibly it is not. What *is* important is the symbolism, the visual imagery something tangible can deliver to so many who will never achieve what was taught at the School of Chartres, only because it requires a mindset that many will not allow themselves to achieve."

"What mindset?" Marcus asked.

Father Davon nodded and smiled. "Please, allow me to continue our tour." He led them through a series of archways and corridors lit with soft light that painted a tawny glow up into the porticos and staircases leading toward the ceiling. They walked to the sculptures of a mother and child, both fully clothed, wearing crowns and each with darker skin. "Some call her the Black Madonna. No one knows how the statues arrived at Chartres. Some pilgrims don't notice the color of her face. Others do. It's not so much observation as it is perception. That's what the School of Chartres was all about, *perception*."

"How do you mean?" Alicia asked.

"More than a thousand years ago, in this cathedral, the School of Chartres was, in essence, a seminary—a seminary that looked at the Platonic approach to philosophy, natural science, the arts and the universal mind of a loving God. For almost two centuries, the greatest minds, intellectuals, gifted students all over Europe came here to learn. Most could not achieve the highest standards of admission for acceptance into the school. But for those who could, the enlightenment—the education was nothing short of a life-altering experience."

"How was that?" Marcus asked.

Father Davon laced his fingers together and closed his eyes for a second. "The teachers, men like Bishop Flubertus, brought in the lessons from knowledge honed by the ancient Greeks and combined them with parables from the Bible, keeping alive the virtues of the Virgin Mary to understand complete faith that is usually beyond our initial power to grasp. The teachers taught the students, the new theologians who would leave here, how to realize the signs John wrote in Revelation, looking beyond, much deeper than the apparent and literal meaning."

"Are you suggesting an *absolute knowledge or wisdom*, something that people, such as Isaac Newton, sought to understand?" asked Marcus.

"I think a better term would be a distillation of the soul that aligns as close as humanly possible to God. It's like stripping away the manmade harnesses, the prejudices, allowing the soul to gain a greater perception, without fear, as it's fed with the nutrients found in the universality of God's complete love. That is the arduous path to absolute knowledge, or at least the new discernment that is realized when we learn to love unconditionally—to put our brothers before us. In Revelation, John writes from a higher dimension in which time becomes a *visible* medium. The past, present, and future are displayed in a non-linear vista."

Alicia let out a breath. "This is all very good stuff. But in the real world of good and evil, my niece is being held hostage in Iran. Egypt, Tunisia, England, Libya, Syria and other parts of the planet are erupting in civil chaos. How does an ancient school, its teachings, have anything to do with the Spear of Destiny?"

"Because we're talking about *your* destiny, the fate of Paul, me and the rest of the world we share with our fellow humans. The Spear of Destiny has been desired and sometimes acquired by those with a keen insight into the *times* in which they lived. Evil travels a crooked path, but a path nonetheless." Father Davon looked up at a stained-glass window high in the cathedral. "Come, the time is near, and it is brief. I told you I would show you something. What it *means* is something no one knows."

EIGHTY-TWO

After walking for more than a minute in silence, Father Davon stopped. He looked up at a grand stained-glass window and pointed to it. "If you look to the right of the window, about half way up from the bottom, you might make out a small, clear spot. It's no larger than a nickel. But it's all that's needed."

"Needed for what?" asked Alicia.

"For the light." Father Davon smiled.

Marcus looked at the window, the reds and blues lustrous from the rising full moon. Then he lowered his eyes to the floor where he spotted a nail protruding from a rectangular stone, the only one of its shape in the entire floor. The stone was the color of pewter, and looked much older than those around it.

Father Davon said, "Some people believe that whoever designed the Saint Appolnaire window did so with the summer solstice in mind." He stepped toward the rectangular stone. "During the summer, June, at the Summer Solstice, there is a period, less than thirty seconds when the sun's light comes through a clear spot in the window and strikes the nail in that unique stone. No one alive is sure of the significance."

"But this isn't June," said Alicia.

"Indeed. I believe there is more meaning in what happens only one other time a year, and that time is tonight. Each November, when the full moon rises and aligns with the portal, that tiny spot in the window, something happens. Very few people know of it. And no one knows what it means." Father Davon pointed to the window. "Look."

The moon inched higher in the sky and a milky light poured through the window in a single shaft, striking the nail.

"Wow," Alicia whispered. "How'd they ever…?"

Marcus stepped closer, kneeling down. He studied the long shadow cast by the nail. He looked up, the milky light streaming through the small opening, and then he looked in the direction the shadow fell. "It's indicating due west."

Marcus measured the length of the shadow using his forearm as a gauge. It went from the tip of his finger to his elbow. He looked back in the direction the shadow pointed, and then he touched the head of the nail with the tip of his right index finger. Warmth, a sense of energy, ran up his arm, transmitting to every part of his body. He looked at the priest, then at Alicia. They seemed distant, as if he was looking at them through opaque water. Marcus heard a whisper. *'The truth is found fewer than two hundred shadows of the moon.'* His heart hammered in his chest, vision blurring. He stared at his finger on the nail, his hand heavy, his hearing so acute he thought he could hear the photochemistry of the light pouring through the window. The light striking his finger seemed to be encircling the entire room. Marcus couldn't blink. Eyes wide. He lifted his finger and his vision returned.

"Paul, are you okay?" Alicia asked.

He stood slowly, sweat beading on his forehead, heart pounding. He looked to the west in the cathedral, and then he stared at the nail, the moonbeam fading at his feet. He whispered, *"For now we see through a glass, darkly…"*

Alicia held her hand to her lips. "The *poem*…General Patton."

"It's originally from Corinthians," Father Davon said, his voice subdued.

Marcus looked back to where the shadow had pointed. *"The truth is found fewer than two hundred shadows of the moon, for the shadow is to the seeker as the seeker is to the shadow."* He looked at Alicia, his eyes on fire. "Now, I *know* what it means."

Marcus began walking west, counting his steps. The direction led him across the heart of the cathedral to the western portico exit. He stopped at the door and whispered, "One hundred eighty nine." He tried to open the door. It was locked. "Father, can you open it?"

"Yes, of course. What is it you've found?" He pulled a key ring from his pocket and flipped through the keys, inserting a large, bronze key in the discolored lock, turning it.

"I don't know just yet." The doors swung opened. Marcus walked outside, counting under his breath.

Alicia followed right behind him, the priest behind her.

Marcus stopped in front of the far right side of the entranceway and said, "One ninety nine." He looked up. The statue of the ancient philosopher, hunched over his writing table, staring down at him, stone eyes animated in the moonlight.

"Paul, what is it?" Alicia asked. "What have you found?"

Marcus looked from the statue to the stone faces in the portico, his eyes searching for clues. *"The truth is found fewer than two hundred shadows of the moon, for the shadow is to the seeker as the seeker is to the shadow.* That shadow cast by the moon on that nail is a cubit long, the sacred geometry. Following the direction the shadow fell, west, by one hundred ninety nine cubits, led me to this spot—directly to the image of the philosopher's stone. Some refer to him as the truth seeker. *The truth is found fewer than two hundred shadows of the moon….* So you see, the shadow cast by the nail to this point is one hundred ninety nine lengths, just under two hundred. *For the shadow is to the seeker as the seeker is to the shadow."*

"What do you think that means?" asked Father Davon.

Marcus scanned the faces of the statues. "It's called the Golden Section, a reference to the Golden Ratio, the measurements of the sacred geometry that built Solomon's Temple…and this cathedral. It's defined by the number pi." Marcus pulled out a small notepad and used a pen to figure the measurements. He made quick, bold strokes. "It can be found by using a geometric shape, such as a triangle, circle, square or rectangle. That nail was in the center of a stone carved as a rectangle. So if I use a rectangle as a base, divide a line segment at a unique point where the ratio of the whole line, line A, for example, to the large segment, B…the ratio to the larger segment…B…to the small segment…C…."

"You've lost me," Alicia said.

"In other words, A is to B as B is to C. *The shadow is to the seeker as the seeker is to the shadow."* Marcus's eyes followed an invisible line from the figure of the philosopher to the statue holding the spear. He looked at Father Davon. "You said the figure up there…the man with the spear, his name was Saint Theodore."

"Yes, as far as we know."

"I think his identity has been mistaken. I believe he's really Saint Longinus."

"You mean the soldier turned saint after he pierced the side of Jesus Christ?"

"Yes!" Marcus looked around the area and saw the painter's ladder propped up where the worker had left it. He ran to the ladder and brought it back.

"Paul, what are you doing?" Alicia asked.

"Searching." Marcus set the ladder in front of the sculpture and climbed the ladder. He used the tiny flashlight on his phone to search around the statue. He slowly moved the light over the sword, scabbard, across the statue's face, up the spear shaft to the head of the spear. He looked in the fissures and gaps between the sculpture and the wall. Nothing. Then a large white moth emerged from a crack in the cathedral behind the figure's head and flew into the night. Marcus pointed the light at the opening.

An object.

Marcus held the flashlight with one hand and reached into the crack, pulling out the head of a spear.

Alicia hugged her arms. "Oh…my…God!"

With a trembling hand, Marcus examined the spearhead, slowly turning it over. There was an inscription on one side, text very small and precise: השולש םירשע דחא םירשע הספילקופא

Marcus stepped down from the ladder, his legs weaker. He turned to Alicia. "Paul, you found it! You're holding the Spear of Destiny in your hands. Is there an inscription on it?"

"Yes." He handed the spear to her and she examined it.

"So this was the actual spear, the point, that pierced the side of Jesus Christ…I can't believe I'm holding it." She turned over the spear and studied the text for a few seconds. "What's it say?"

"May I see?" asked Father Davon.

Alicia angled the inscription toward him. He ran his finger across it. "If this is truly the spear that entered the side of our Lord, it is priceless." He made the sign of the cross. "Chartres is where the clothing worn by his mother, Mary, is to be viewed by those seeking a greater connection to a physical union with Christ. And, now this...I am speechless. May I borrow your light to read the inscription on the blade?"

Alicia looked at Marcus a moment. Neither one spoke. Marcus held the phone above the spear, pressing the button that engaged the flashlight. Father Davon read silently for a moment. "I'm astonished. It's Hebrew and makes a reference to apocalypse, maybe a chapter and verse in the Book of Revelation. I think it says—"

Father Davon's head jerked backward. A bloody hole opened in the center of his forehead. The back of his head exploded, the bullet splattering blood over the stone eyes of the statue that held the spear. A second bullet slammed into the old wooden door of the cathedral. A third shattered a piece of limestone from the image of an angel.

Alicia stumbled and fell, dropping the spear.

"Go, Alicia! Now!" Marcus scooped up the spear, grabbing Alicia by the arm. "Run!" She stared in horror at the dead priest. "Run!" Marcus pulled her down the worn marble steps. "Move!" he shouted, pulling her off the cathedral steps while bullets slammed into the thousand-year-old marble and granite.

They bolted down the ancient streets of the town. A cloud covered the full moon, the cathedral a silent witness to their escape into darkness.

They ran for blocks, darting down alleys, finally stopping to listen for someone following them. "I have to catch my breath!" Alicia said, looking over her shoulder. Clouds passed and the radiance of a full moon drenched the sleepy town of Chartres in an illusion of sanctuary. "Father Davon—he's...he's...."

"He's dead. They were, no doubt, trying to kill us all."

"Who's trying to kill us?"

"I don't know."

"The Circle of 13?"

Marcus, sweat dripping down his face, said nothing.

Alicia shook her head. "Maybe it's the Iranians. Maybe Brandi's been—"

"Why the Iranians? They have no reason—"

"Paul, they don't need one!"

Marcus looked at the head of the spear in his right hand. "Maybe this is the reason. Maybe they want this. What's it worth to the powerbrokers in

Tehran? Cairo? Russia? China? Or how valuable would it be to the Circle of 13?"

"But none of them *know* we've found it? I wonder what the inscription on the spear means."

"They might be aware we were searching for it. Before we found the bug in our room, we were talking about it."

"And, we were talking about Jonathon Carlson. What if he knows? What if he sent the killers?"

"Someone knows—we can speculate all day about who? The real question is why? How much do they know, and how have they been following us? But, right now, we have to figure out how to lose them."

Alicia blew out a long breath. "You're right, they could have heard us making plans to come here."

"We need to get out of Chartres undetected and soon. Maybe there's a train leaving for Paris."

"Paris? Why should we go back to Paris?"

"It's the quickest way to get to Jerusalem. That's the direction this spear is pointing us. But we have to send this spear on its own Fed-Ex flight."

"*Where* can we send it?"

"To Jerusalem, the place its journey started. It'll arrive at a little coffee shop in the heart of the Old City."

EIGHTY-THREE

At an altitude of 30,000 feet, Alicia turned to Marcus, whispering under the drone of the jet engines. "The spear may arrive before we do."

"Bahir will hold it for me."

"If you know what that inscription means, why haven't you told me?"

"Because I'm not sure what it *really* means. The text is in ancient Hebrew. It seems to make a reference to the Apocalypse or the Book of Revelation, the twenty-first chapter, verse twenty-three. When we packaged and shipped the spear, I looked up that part of Revelation on my cell to be sure. It reads: *'And the city had no need of the sun, neither the moon to shine in it…for the glory of God did lighten it, and the Lamb is the light that will be there.'*"

"What do you think it *means?*"

"I believe it's referring to the future of an eternal day—a future that may be found where the sun and moon won't literally shine because God will illuminate it."

"Where do you think that is?"

"Maybe Jerusalem. Let's try to get some sleep."

———

They landed in Tel Aviv. The sun was rising over the air traffic control tower. Paul Marcus wore dark glasses walking through the Ben Gurion International Airport. He looked away from the security cameras mounted on walls and support beams and away from the faces of those he knew were watching him. He and Alicia had checked no luggage. They cleared customs and caught a shuttle to the long-term parking garage where he found the Toyota as he'd left it.

Marcus dropped to the concrete floor of the garage, searching under the car. Alicia watched him for a moment, and then she casually looked around the garage for security cameras. Marcus popped the hood, probing for any sign of a bomb or tampering of the engine. "Looks okay," he said, opening the car doors.

Alicia got inside. She held her breath when Marcus turned the ignition. The car started with no problem. "How far is Jerusalem from the airport?" she asked.

"Depending on the traffic, about an hour."

"I wish I were seeing this with you under different circumstances."

Marcus cell buzzed. It was Bill Gray. "Paul, look, the shit is hitting the damn fan at Langley. I've done all I can to keep them at bay. They say they have reason to believe you're using this so-called intel about the Lion as a smokescreen. In spite of what I've told them, they believe you're now working directly for Tehran."

"I'm doing the exact opposite! You know that. I didn't just take a vacation to the Middle East."

"I know that, Paul, but things here are escalating. They want you back in the U.S."

"Who does? Look, Alicia and I have uncovered some dark secrets, some of which reach to the people who've appointed or been appointed to CIA positions."

"What do you have?"

Marcus quickly summed up his findings. Gray said, "No one could have predicted you'd step into a lair of rattlesnakes. I don't even know what to—"

"All I need is a little more time, Bill. As long as you and Secretary Hanover have my back, maybe I can get through this, not for me, but for what it's about to reveal. These people have to be stopped."

"As much as I want to watch your back, I can't. No one can now. You need to tell Alicia I'm ordering her home. The risks are far too dangerous."

"You tell her." He handed the phone to Alicia.

"Hello, Bill."

"Alicia, I know you're there on vacation days, but it's over. This is out of control. Paul's risking his life, and he can't put yours on the line, too. Pack it up and return to Washington."

"I can't do that."

"You have no choice."

"You're wrong, Bill. As long as my niece is sitting in that Iranian shit-hole, it means I have a choice. Therefore, I'm going to do whatever I can because not a damn soul in Washington, or Langley, is doing shit. Goodbye, Bill." She disconnected and folded her arms across her breasts. "Let's get out of this parking garage."

Marcus nodded, put the car in gear, and placed a call to the *Cafez Coffee Shop*. Bahir told him that nothing had arrived from Fed EX. "Okay," Marcus said, "we'll be over this evening, maybe it'll be there by then."

He drove out of the garage, paid the parking fee, and started to pull onto the road. A woman talking on a mobile phone stepped in front of his car. Marcus slammed on the brakes. He came within two feet of hitting her. The woman glared at Marcus.

Something slid from under the seat and tapped Alicia's left foot on the floorboard. She reached down and lifted up the object. "It's a cigarette lighter, and it's an old one."

Marcus stared at the lighter in her hand. Alicia said, "There's an inscription on it. It reads: *To "M" with love. Your adoring wife.*"

Marcus said nothing for a few seconds, his mind replaying the rainy night he gave a ride to the army colonel he met near Abu Ghosh. He drove from the terminal parking lot onto the highway. "It came from the guy I picked up that night in the rain. He said he was David Marcus."

Alicia turned her head toward him, and then she looked at the Zippo in the palm of her hand. "It can't be the same David Marcus, a.k.a. Mickey Stone or David "Mickey" Marcus, from the Nuremberg Trials, unless he was in his late eighties or early nineties."

"He was no more than about forty. He must have left it in the car that night I picked him up."

Alicia set the lighter on the console. She glanced out the window and looked at the traffic, then at the hills of the Israeli countryside resting to

the east. "All of this, you know, the spear, these connections to World War
II, the deaths of General Patton, Kennedy Junior, the Nuremburg Trials,
the formation of the Circle of 13, the assassination of the prime ministers, the murders of Father Davon, Gisele, your family, even the Iranians
holding Brandi as a spy…it's just too much to wrap one's head around—all
of it seems, now, like some ominous picture puzzle morphing into a huge
disaster."

"Maybe it's a picture of hope."

Alicia looked at Marcus driving toward Jerusalem. "Brandi's supposed
to be released in two days. If she isn't, there's not a soul we can go to. No
one we can tell, or we'd risk espionage charges filed against you."

"Maybe we won't have to go to anybody. Who the hell could we really
trust? The Kinsley Group, with its roster of former politicians on the payroll, is so embedded in the Middle East that we'd have to use a lug wrench to
twist them off the oil rigs. Jonathon Carlson's grandfather had ties to Nazi
Germany, and much of Carlson's wealth today was built on those investments. His grandfather ostensibly wanted the spearhead that Patton took
from Hitler's vault. When we get to the hotel, let's see what we can find out
about the remaining members of the Circle of 13." Marcus changed lanes
and accelerated around a car.

There was a buzz from one of the phones in his pockets, and he knew
it wasn't his mobile. Marcus pulled out Taheera's phone and answered it.

"Mr. Marcus." The voice flat as the first call, yet it had the same intimi-
dating tone Rahim used when he spoke during the forty-eight hours Marcus
spent coding the Myrtus worm hidden in the belly of the Iranian nuclear
operation. "The time is growing closer, Mr. Marcus. We need to set up a
meeting."

"If Brandi isn't released in two days, there will be no meeting."

"You are in no position to offer a veiled threat."

"Okay, I'll lift the veil. The only way that coding is going to continue
is when you get the updated coding I installed on a flash drive. It's the key
you need to keep in the ignition. We have an agreement. Your engineers can
see the centrifuge problems you experienced have now ended, and it was
because of what I did. If you want it to continue, the girl must be released as

we agreed, and then you get the flash drive with the coding that will be your lifeline for that plant."

"The girl will be released. I shall call you right before she boards the plane and tell you where to meet me. Bring the Quincy woman. I have something to tell her."

EIGHTY-FOUR

Alicia spent four straight hours on her computer at the small desk in the hotel room. Marcus picked up orders of hummus, grape leaves, lentils, flat bread and baba ghanoush and brought them back to the room where they ate. He called Bahir and asked about the package.

"It arrived a half hour ago. Are you coming, Paul?"

"Yes. Until we get there, what is the most secure place in your shop?"

"You mean a place where no one would ever find this?"

"Yes."

"I have such a place. As a matter of fact, it hasn't been used since 1935. I will keep it in there until your return."

"Thank you." He disconnected and turned to Alicia. "The spear's arrived."

"Great...and so has some new information."

"What do you have?"

"Carlson received an email from someone named Thomas Andrew Jenkins. In it, Jenkins tells him the *acquisition* will be made soon...the *birds* have landed. He says the acquisition will be ready for the next meeting."

"*Acquisition...birds have landed.* Maybe the acquisition is the spear. Birds could mean us...our flight landing. Who is Thomas Jenkins?"

"I dug through every clearance I could. Jenkins is now a consultant with the Kinsley Group. His background listed him as working in sales for the Coca Cola Company in Tel Aviv and then he went to work for one other company, Regions Oil Limited. I suspect that was his cover. It gave him a license and credentials to travel across the Middle East."

"You're saying CIA, right?"

"Yeah."

"What'd you say is his full name?"

"Thomas Andrew Jenkins."

Marcus thought back to his first meeting with Nathan Levy. *An old friend of mine, Andy Jenkins, was once stationed in Tel Aviv by your government for almost two decades.'*

"What's wrong, Paul? What are you thinking?"

"How long was he with Regions Oil, and who are they?"

"Let me see." Her fingers raced across the keyboard. After half a minute, she looked up at Marcus. "He worked twelve years in sales for Regions Oil, an international company with operations in Israel and the U.S. Net profits last year were 27 billion. Regions Oil was established in 1988 as an outgrowth of agricultural organizations from the Kibbutz Movement. And, today, three companies own Regions. Controlling ownership, at fifty-five percent, is the PetChem Consolidated Group. Its chairman is none other than Jonathon Carlson. Regions purchased the operations of Genesis Petroleum, including the refineries, terminals, pipelines, and retail assets in the U.S. and continued the expansion of its business in the Middle East."

Marcus was silent.

Alicia added, "Here's another thing. Senator Wyatt Dirkson, at one time, was on the Board of Directors for Genesis. The man who's now the interim prime minister of Israel was formerly on the Board for Regions. As the ride at Disneyland serenades us, it's a small world after all."

"So it seems."

Marcus's phone buzzed on the counter. The caller ID displayed: *Hebrew University.* Marcus answered and Jacob Kogen said, "Paul, I have only slept a few hours a night since you left on your journey. I know you've found something. We must talk."

"I'm listening, Jacob."

"No, in person, please. I want to review what you have found. But even more than that, I wanted to tell you to be very careful. The Mossad is following you."

"How do you know?"

"They've questioned me about your whereabouts, what you may have said the weeks you were doing research here."

"What do you mean, *may* have said?"

"I don't know for sure. By the line of their questioning, I'd surmise it has something to do with the enemies of Israel. Most likely, Iran."

"Jacob, listen to me. I haven't done anything that will compromise the safety and security of Israel. If anything, what I have done and will do is something that will further protect it. You're going to *have* to trust me here."

"I do. I trust you with all my heart and soul. This is providence. It *must* be. I have no doubt in my mind. But it is very dangerous because evil is fighting you. Dark forces will keep coming at you with savage repetition."

Marcus said nothing

"Paul, we must meet."

"I'll call you."

"Please, be very careful."

—•—

They entered the *Cafez* coffee shop in the late afternoon. Half a dozen customers sat at the tables, some reading Arabic newspapers, others reading from tablets, iPads and laptops. Marcus led Alicia to a table in the far corner just as Bahir came in from the back room with a bag of coffee beans in his arms. He grinned when he saw Marcus, set the bag down, went behind the curtain to a rear room and came out with a small FedEx box. He brought it to their table with a cup of coffee in his other hand for Marcus.

"Paul, I have missed you my friend. I hid this well, under an old trapdoor. Even my grandson doesn't know the trapdoor exists."

"Why is it there?"

"Perhaps I will show you." Bahir's face bloomed.

"Bahir, I want you to meet Alicia Quincy."

Bahir grinned, his eyes suddenly luminous. "Paul leaves to return with the most wonderful gift in the world, the company of a beautiful woman. It is my honor to meet you, Alicia."

She smiled and reached to shake his hand. "Paul told me how much he appreciates your friendship. I'm delighted to finally meet you, too."

Bahir nodded and set the box on the table next to the coffee cup. "It is rare a man sends a present for himself and arrives the same day to find it waiting for him. You did not tell me what is in the box. If it is a secret, I shall go grind twenty pounds of Ethiopian beans. Only first I find out what coffee your friend would prefer. Alicia, what may I bring you?"

"The Ethiopian sounds exotic."

Bahir bowed slightly, walked to the counter and filled another cup. He returned.

"Bahir," Marcus said, glancing around the coffee shop. "Please, sit down. I want to show you something. First, I need to tell you what Alicia and I have been through the last few days."

The old man waived to his nephew to bring him a coffee, took a sip, and then listened without interruption. When Marcus finished, Bahir said, "I'm fearful that your journey is only *beginning*. Please, let me see the spear. I have waited all my life for this."

Surprised by his last comment, Marcus looked at Bahir quizzically for a moment then discreetly opened the box. He lifted out the thick newspaper wrappings that encased the spear to protect it, and carefully uncovered the spiritual artifact. Lying on the seafood cooking section of the *Ouest-France* newspaper was the Spear of Destiny.

Bahir simply stared at it for a half minute in total silence, his dark eyes unblinking. A fly landed on his coarse hand, crawling to the tip of his thumbnail. Bahir finally waved the fly away. He lifted his eyes to Marcus, tears welling above his lower eyelids. "It is astounding. Here in my little coffee shop, in a corner table, lies the blade that pierced the body of Christ. The event turned a Roman soldier into a believer who achieved sainthood. And the spear, with its inherent power, was left for whoever had the means and presence of mind to *acquire* it." He wiped his eyes with the back of his hand, revealing the brown-dotted age spots. Looking at Alicia before shifting his glance back to Marcus, he said, "Billions of people call our earth home. You are the only one who found this…the only one who understood and figured out where to seek it."

"I don't know if I had a *choice*. What do you think the inscription means?"

The old man took a pair of reading glasses from his shirt pocket, held the spear low, using his body to block it from anyone. He turned the spear over and slowly read the language, his lips moving, but with no words coming out of his mouth. Then he cleared his throat. *"The city had no need of the sun, neither the moon to shine in it…for the glory of God did lighten it, and the Lamb is the light that will be there."*

Marcus looked around the coffee shop. All patrons seem oblivious to what was going on at the back table. "Bahir, what does it *mean?*"

"What do you think it might mean?"

"The passage is from Revelation. I'm not sure what it's referring to, but I *feel* the reference to the city is right here—the Old City of Jerusalem."

"Is it a riddle?" Alicia asked.

"No." Bahir's unkempt eyebrows arched. "It is not a riddle. It is an answer."

"What do you mean?" asked Marcus. "An answer to what question?"

"To the one you've carried for a long time, Paul. As the whole universe was brought forth from one by the power of one God…so all things are born perpetually from this one force according to the character of nature… of God. We do not come into the world at birth. We come *from*—from the source of life, like an apple comes from a tree. The miracle of that which is above is moveable to that which is below. It is *one*. We, all of us, every atom and every cell, are *one* with God. He is perfection, all above, below and beyond, comes from a single whole, a strength that is the ultimate influence because it is the ultimate love. As invisible as gravity, yet it is the might, the power and mind that placed the entire universe into motion and breathes life into its center…mankind. Your wife and daughter are part of that, loved and well. They are in a dimension that may be not visible to all, yet, but it is not anonymous."

Marcus said nothing, his chest filling with weight. Alicia looked down at the spear and then into the old man's face. Bahir touched the spear with his index finger. "You are partially correct in your reasoning of the city as referred to on the spear. But, the city is the *new* Jerusalem, not the old one, where we are an eternal *community* made from one designer. That which is above is also below through all, and the universe."

There was a soft jingle of glassware behind the counter. "What's that?" asked Alicia. Bahir stared at the coffee in his cup, his aged face reflecting from the dark surface. The reflection broke when the coffee began quivering.

Bahir stood. His customers looked around, some unplugging their laptops, others glancing nervously out the windows. Five seconds later, the buildings of Jerusalem began to tremble and break apart.

EIGHTY-FIVE

"**O**utside!" shouted Marcus. "Earthquake! Keep away from the buildings."

"Oh shit!" Alicia said, watching the cups and plates crash from behind the bar. The coffee shop emptied in seconds. People struggled to keep their balance, the earth shaking violently under their feet. Marcus, with the spear secure in his pocket, held Bahir by the back of the old man's shirt and helped him find the door. Dust billowed from the streets, blowing through the shop like hot ash.

They made it outside, the force of the earthquake knocking Alicia down. Marcus lifted her up. "Get to the center of the street!"

Hundreds of tourists, shop owners, and business people scattered across the streets of the Old City, the earth moving and shaking beneath them. Marcus looked to the west and saw a construction crane topple into a nearby high-rise building, shattering windows and sending a stream of glass and debris to the streets below. Ancient stones rained down from structures and archways that have stood on the same ground for a thousand years.

Large cracks erupted in dozens of spots on the wall that encircled the Old City. Stones dropped from the Western Wall, sending worshipers fleeing. There was nowhere to run as the Old City swayed and bucked, the earth rose and pitched, stretching and shaking its shoulders as if it was coming out of a long slumber. The Dome of the Rock shook and groaned. Lions Gate crumbled, creating an open passageway.

Then it stopped. In less than forty-five seconds, the earthquake ended as abruptly as it had started. Immense dust clouds rose above the city. Marcus looked up and saw the sun turn blood red through the dust. Air-raid sirens and alarms rang out. People cried. Some stumbled around, dazed, going into shock, bleeding, weeping, and calling out names of loved ones.

Marcus turned to Alicia. "Are you hurt?"

"Just bruised. Maybe it's over."

"There may be aftershocks. Bahir, are you hurt?"

The old man said nothing. He stood in the center of the street and prayed silently. He glanced up at the red sun, turned to Marcus and said, "It is time."

"What do you mean, it is time?"

"It is the sign. Come." He walked toward his coffee shop.

"Don't!" Marcus shouted. "There may be an aftershock."

"It is over. Come! Now, Paul!"

"Don't let him go in there alone!" Alicia yelled.

Marcus ran to the door and put his hand on Bahir's shoulder. "Let's stay outside."

"The earthquake is finished. I have something to show you." He walked inside his shop. Marcus followed. Alicia hesitated a few seconds, looked at the debris around her, smoke and dust boiling over the city, the blare of air-raid sirens and the cries of injured people. She ran inside the coffee shop. Bahir led them behind the counter, stepping over broken cups, dishes and pots of spilled coffee. He found a large flashlight and walked into the back room.

"What are you doing?" Marcus asked.

"I want to show you something." He opened a locked cabinet, pulled out a large rolled paper, removed a rubber band and unfolded the paper on his desk. It was a map.

"This is the map of excavations done when the British explorers, Charles Wilson and Charles Warren were here. At that time, of course, this building was not a coffee shop. It was a supply center for their tools. Only a few people alive know it was the last opening they dug into a series of tunnels that unearthed beneath Jerusalem." Bahir slowly traced the light across the map, a drawing that was more than a century old. It illustrated a series of tunnels under Jerusalem. Alicia looked at Marcus and then at Bahir.

"Why are you showing us that?" she asked.

"Because it was prophesied that which was sealed up, below, would be opened by the force above." He looked at Marcus. "The hand of God may have opened the door. If so, will you enter?"

"Enter where?"

Bahir knelt down and rolled away a rich Persian rug across the floor. He unlocked a wooden trapdoor and lifted it. Then he pointed the light into the dark. There was an old ladder propped near the entrance. Marcus could see it led to a tunnel. "Bahir, what am I searching for?"

"If the earthquake has removed the barrier, a place even Wilson and Warren never found, you might find that which was left behind by Daniel. It's been sealed for centuries, but perhaps the time for the unveiling is now among us."

Marcus looked at the old map. "Which way would I go?"

Bahir pointed with the tip of his bent index finger, tracing the series of excavations that went in seven directions, one forming a loop, one stopping in a dead-end. "There is an area beneath the Jaffee Gate, here is the Temple Mount, and over there is the Church of the Holy Sepulchre. This last tunnel…it is believed to lead to the Holy Place and an inner room called the Holy of Holies. It splits in sections." He used a pencil to mark the continuation of the tunnel. "This is the way you should go."

"What is the Holy of Holies?" Alicia asked.

"It is said to be God's sanctuary, for atonement and renewal of spirit— the Most Holy Place."

"Why do you think Marcus should go there?" she asked.

Bahir shifted his eyes from the map to Alicia. "The Holy Place is a sacred altar room before God's earthly sanctuary, and it may hold clues to…," Bahir stopped talking for a second, then continued, "he may realize more than he finds."

Marcus looked at Alicia, tiny particles of dust moving through the beam of light. "Will you go with me?" he asked.

She nodded. "Yes."

EIGHTY-SIX

They waited a few minutes for the dust to settle, and then Bahir handed Marcus the flashlight and extra batteries in a Ziploc bag. He gave Alicia the map.

Marcus turned and stepped onto the top rung of the old ladder. He slowly climbed down, knocking spider webs off the rungs as he went, sending particles of dust drifting through the beam of light. "I'm at the bottom, Alicia. I'll shine the light on the ladder so you can see."

"Okay." She stepped onto the first rung. As she lowered her foot, she looked up into the compassionate eyes of Bahir. He said nothing, only offering a reassuring nod while he softly closed the trapdoor. Alicia listened to him walk away and then turned to her attention to Marcus. "I wish we had a second flashlight."

When she reached the bottom on the ladder, Marcus slowly moved the light across the small grotto. There were entrances to three tunnels, one to the left, one to the right, and one in the center. The opening to each was a little more than six feet high by about four feet wide. Alicia unfolded the map and said, "Looks like we go to the right. There's no scale, so I'm guessing we have about a three hundred meter trek, maybe more. The tunnel splits in at least four sections. We just need to follow the line Bahir drew."

"Let's go." Marcus entered the mouth of the tunnel on the right; the smell of dust, mold, water, and damp earth met them just a few feet inside the dark passageway. "Stay close behind me. This place is filled with spiders and some damn big webs." He shone the light far down the tunnel and began walking.

The air was cool, heavy—the farther they entered, the scent became ancient, mixed with tannins, as if the air had been held hostage in the guts of the tunnel for centuries. An icy drop of water fell from the ceiling, striking Alicia on the back of her neck and running down her spine. "Glad I'm not claustrophobic," she said, nostrils flaring, wiping the dust from her eyes. "This is like weaving our way through the catacombs of a place time forgot."

"In about another fifty feet, the tunnel makes a Y and veers to the left and right. Let's have a look at the map." Marcus held the light on the map for half a minute, getting his bearings. He continued walking. "Check it out." He pointed the light to an old torch handle stuck in a crude wooden holder fastened to the curved wall of the tunnel.

"When they excavated, flashlights weren't invented."

"I don't think the light bulb had been around long, if at all." She followed Marcus another fifty feet.

The earth moved. Alicia was tossed against the side of the tunnel. "Paul!"

"Aftershocks! Cover your head."

Alicia felt sand trickle out from between the old stones over her head. Then nothing moved, the aftershocks stopping after a few seconds. "I'd be lying if I didn't admit I'm scared out of my freakin' mind. Here we are crawling around in old tunnels under Jerusalem after an earthquake."

"We can turn back."

She looked at Marcus' face. "Tell me *you're* not scared." She straightened, knocking the sand from her shirt. "Let's go."

They walked farther, coming to the turn. Marcus stopped, his foot stepping on something. He aimed the light down at his boot. A human skull, eye sockets hollow and dark as the tunnel, stared up at them from the muck and wet sand. A brown spider crawled from one vacant eyehole.

Alicia inhaled deeply and bit her lower lip. They continued walking, finding another cold and smothered torch mounted on the side of the tunnel wall. Marcus said, "This place is full of those old torches. Can you imagine using one of these to see around down here?"

"No, I can't."

Marcus nodded and continued following the tunnel, snaking its way under the heart of the Old City. After another thirty yards, the tunnel narrowed in height and width. Marcus had to lower his head to keep moving. They stepped over fallen rocks and loose sand. Then they came to an area in the tunnel that seemed to stop. Rocks were piled up to his chest. He aimed the flashlight into the center of the pile. "It looks like there's earth behind it. Hold the light."

Alicia gripped the flashlight while Marcus inspected the obstacle. He picked up a few large stones and threw them aside. "Maybe this is the end of the road," she said. "Or maybe we took the wrong tunnel."

"Bahir said it would be this one."

"It feels like we've come a half mile."

The ground moved—violently. The aftershock tossed Alicia and Marcus to the floor of the tunnel. The flashlight slammed against a rock and went out. Rocks showered down around them, the tunnel filling with dust and the instant odor of sulfur.

"Paul! Are you hurt?"

"No. Are you okay?"

"Just a few more bruises, but I'm all right. I've never been in dark this dark. I have no sense of direction." Feeling along the base of the wall, she found part of the flashlight. "The flashlight's broken! Oh shit…we can't see an inch in front of our faces." She coughed. "How will we find out way out?"

"Only Bahir knows we're down here."

She heard him moving, scraping for something. "What are you doing? Paul, where are you?"

"Here." A flame flickered from his hand. "I don't know why I put that old Zippo lighter in my pocket, but I'm glad I did."

Alicia exhaled deeply, eyes wide, watching the flame dance. "Let's try the torch on the wall. Maybe it'll light."

Marcus stood, stepped over rocks to the torch mounted on the wall and removed it. He sniffed the head of the torch. "I can smell oil and something like tar. Maybe, even after a century, they're preserved because this place is naturally climate-controlled and has no sunlight." He touched the lighter to the top of the torch and a flame rose, slowly, and then it grew brighter.

Alicia smiled. "Let there be light...." She pointed to the end of the tunnel. "Look, that last aftershock created a small opening."

Marcus stepped up to the opening, which was barely the width of his shoulders. He reached through the gap with the torch. "Hold this. Looks like a door to a room. I'll crawl in, and you can come after me."

Alicia held the torch while Marcus wormed his way though the cavity. "Give me the light," he said, reaching back though the hole. He took the torch so that Alicia could follow him. Inside the room, they both stood, astonished, the light from the flames bouncing shadows across ancient religious artifacts.

"I'm speechless," Alicia said, her eyes taking in the stateliness.

"I think we're arrived in the place they called the Holy of Holies."

The room was finished in white marble, inlaid with gold. A table, carved from snow-white marble, was positioned in the center of the room. The table held three gold candelabras, gold goblets and a single place setting with a gold plate. Vases sculpted from white onyx and mother-of-pearl stood on each side of the table. The rear section of the room was hidden behind a ripped veil draped from ceiling to floor.

Alicia said, "That curtain must be at least sixty feet high. Look at the cherubim embroidered on it. It's beautiful. What's behind it? Let's take off our shoes."

He held the torch and used one hand to pull back the heavy covering. In their stocking feet, Marcus and Alicia stepped through the veil.

Marcus moved the torch, looking from corner to corner. "It appears to be a perfect cube...ten cubits by ten cubits."

"That is spectacular.

Alicia touched her hand to her mouth. "Oh my God," she whispered. "Paul, is it what I think it is?"

"It's the Ark of the Covenant." Marcus felt his heart pounding, his eyes moistening.

The Ark, elevated on a slab of pure white onyx, was the size of a foot-locker, finished in ornate gold. Two golden angels were perched on either side of the crest. They were kneeling, facing each other, the tips of the wings almost touching. A gold ring was fastened to each of the four corners at the top of the Ark.

"Hold this a second." Marcus handed the torch to Alicia. He used his right arm, the tip of his finger to his elbow, to measure the Ark. "It's one and a half cubits wide and high, and two and a half cubits long. It conforms perfectly to the golden ratio."

"Paul, look at that." She pointed to a vase, less than two feet in length, positioned to the right side of the Ark.

He knelt down beside it. "Give me a little more light."

"What is it?"

"I'm not sure. The top is sealed to the vase in something like candle wax." Marcus pulled the head of the spear from his pocket. He positioned the tip of the blade at the edge of the wax on the perimeter of the sealed opening.

"What are you going to do?"

"I'm opening it."

"Maybe we shouldn't."

"Maybe we should. Maybe that's *why* we're here." Marcus carefully worked the blade into the old wax, moving around the entire edge. He set the spear on the floor and used both hands to work the cover from the body of the vase. "Bring the light a little closer." Marcus looked in the aged vase, reached inside and pulled out a rolled up paper scroll. He unrolled it on the floor of the room and used the light from the Zippo to read the words. He said nothing for half a minute, the torch casting shadows across the white room. Then he used his mobile phone to snap a picture.

"Marcus, what is it. What's on that old paper?"

"It's written in Hebrew." With care, Marcus placed the scroll back into the vase. He used his lighter to reseal the wax.

"Marcus, can you read it? What is it…and who wrote it?"

"It may have been written by Daniel…but I think it was *dictated* by…by someone else. It's the events of the end of days."

The room began to quiver, the gold goblets rattling on the table. The tips of the angel's wings trembled. Marcus grabbed the torch and picked up the spear. "C'mon! Let's get out of here!" They ran to the opening, Marcus holding the torch while Alicia slipped through the hole. He followed.

The earth shuddered. Sand, pebbles, and larger stones fell like a hard hailstorm on top of them. Marcus grabbed Alicia by the hand and ran through the dark tunnel. A wall of rock and earth crashed down behind them resealing the opening to the Holy Place.

EIGHTY-SEVEN

A half hour later, they made it back to the grotto, the ladder still where they'd left it. Marcus climbed the ladder, knocking on the trapdoor. He waited a few seconds and knocked again.

"Maybe you can push it up," Alicia said.

Marcus braced the palms of both hands under the trapdoor and started to push just as it opened, the smiling face of Bahir looking down at him. "Thank God you two made it safely." Marcus stepped back down the ladder, took the torch from Alicia and let her exit. He extinguished the torch on the floor and climbed up the ladder. Bahir closed and locked the trapdoor, pulling the rug back over it. "I believe the aftershocks are gone. Did you make it to your destination?"

Alicia said nothing, looking at Marcus. He said, "Yes."

"And, was what you hoped...was it there?"

"Bahir, you had the map. You *knew* which tunnel to take. Did you ever go there? Did you ever make it to that sacred room?"

"I went as far as I could go. It was not meant to be for the British explorers a century ago. And it was not meant to be for me. But for you two, the time is now. What did you find?"

"What Newton tried to find. Is my laptop under the counter?"

"Yes." Bahir led them back out to the coffee shop. He reached below the counter and retrieved the computer.

Marcus turned it on and uploaded the picture he'd taken of the old document. He pulled the last coding he'd broken from Newton's papers, his fingers jabbing the keys, his eyes staring hard at the coding. A few seconds later, Marcus read the Hebrew words that materialized across his screen. His hand was trembling as he stuck a flash drive in the side of the computer and transferred the information. Then he deleted it from his computer.

"What is it, Paul?" Alicia asked.

"I think Bahir knows." He looked at the old man.

Bahir closed his eyes for a moment. "It is not what you now know, Paul. It is what you choose to do about it. I believe, at this point, you no longer look at life in a linear fashion."

"What the hell *can* I do?"

"Whatever you believe you can do."

"Where is He?"

"Where is who, Paul?"

"Is all this, the second coming? Is this when the world ends! Tell me, Bahir. You know, don't you?"

"It is not where the physical likeness of God may be at this moment. The significance is what we, mankind, are going to do. That's where you, Paul, and now you Alicia—man and woman, can or cannot become who and what you were chosen to be…messengers."

Alicia hugged her upper arms. "What *is* the message?"

Bahir smiled. "The message is what Paul figured out. God is walking among us, but is not ready to fulfill the destiny, because part of that fulfillment is forgiveness."

"What do you mean?" asked Alicia.

"Fulfilling what he left behind, the *capacity* of human love for one another. It is the word of God. The example was displayed in the deeds of Christ. The *Angel of Death* will pass over those who are or will become believers. The rest shall perish. Like the webs you had to break through in the tunnel, you will knock down webs of evil spun by wicked people… those who will try to stop you. It is a warning…the last warning. You had to begin a journey to find its consequence, a passage that has not reached its final destination. Paul, you need to finish it. Transport the result of your discovery to the world and unveil those who will stand in your way."

Marcus shook his head. "How?"

Bahir looked at the empty computer screen, and then his eyes met Marcus. "I hear Sweden is charming this time of year. Go, Paul! Do not squander time, because there may be precious little time left to throw away." Bahir reached up and touched Marcus's shoulder. Then he turned and did the same to Alicia. "It is time."

Marcus shut his laptop and Bahir stood up, stepping to the open door of his coffee shop. Marcus and Alicia followed. "You must go now," Bahir said.

Marcus looked at the old man a moment. "Thank you...thank you for all you did. I'm going to miss you."

Bahir smiled. "I shall see you again." He glanced at the smoke and dust outside over the Old City, his eyes meeting Marcus. "Your journey, my friend, is not over, Paul. The rest will be much more difficult. Follow the compass within you. It will lead you." He used both of his hands to grasp Marcus's right hand and said, "I feel, perhaps see, that the man who killed your wife and child, his time grows short."

"What do you mean, 'grows short'? Where is he?"

"He comes from a den of evil. Be ready. Follow the instructions given to you."

Bahir turned to Alicia. "Look at me, let me see your eyes."

"Okay, but what are you looking for—"

Bahir touched her wrist, his eyes searching then connecting, pulling her quickly into a place where the wail of the sirens in the distance faded. Bahir's voice was slow, above a whisper, purposeful. "The man who hurt you when you were a little girl...you will *never* fear that memory again—he perished in a house fire after your eighteenth birthday."

Alicia stared at Bahir for a few seconds in silence, the air-raid wail slowly returning, and the staccato chop of helicopters arriving. Her eyes watered. "Thank you," she whispered.

Bahir hugged her and then embraced Marcus before leaving the shop. He stepped out into the swirling smoke and steam that oozed up from the crevices and rubble of a smoldering Jerusalem. Within seconds, he was gone, lost in the clouds of dust that drifted above and down across the Old City.

EIGHTY-EIGHT

*M*arcus and Alicia walked through the destruction scattered across Jerusalem. Most of the ancient buildings remained intact. Some of the newer high-rise hotels were tumbled as if they'd been standing in front of a firing squad. There were sounds of people sobbing, human misery layered in with air-raid sirens, the blaring of car horns, and the ratcheting blast of helicopters circling the city. Hundreds of rescue workers and paramedics attended the injured, searching through the rubble.

"This is unbelievable," Alicia said, her voice raspy. "We've got to help—"

"Continue walking! Evacuate the area immediately!" a police officer shouted to Alicia. He pointed toward the clearest path. "Leave!"

They followed his direction, caught in the river of people running down Via Dolorosa and heading left on Beit HaBad, stepping over twisted steel and ancient stones.

A helicopter flew close overhead, the prop wash blowing dust and dirt into the air, the noise drowning out the howling of air-raid sirens. Alicia shielded her eyes. Marcus held her shoulders, pulling her closer to him. "Let's get out of here!" he shouted.

They found the Toyota, its hood crushed and almost buried under rubble. "Maybe our hotel is still standing," Marcus said. They walked through streets littered with fallen trees, downed utility poles, rocks, glass, building debris, stalled cars and hundreds of people walking, most outwardly lost.

One man wasn't lost.

Marcus noticed him when he and Alicia walked through Damascus Gate, a man wearing a baseball cap, carrying a shopping bag. There was no sense of a tragedy around him. Nothing that would indicate he was walking through piles of rubble and human suffering caused three hours earlier by an earthquake. He casually strolled around the ruins like a detached tourist on holiday, stopping to snap a picture with his cell phone and then to resume his hike through a daytime nightmare.

— —

Marcus carried his laptop in one hand, the flash drive in his shirt pocket and the spearhead in the back pocket of his jeans.

Alicia stopped him after they made it out of Damascus Gate. "Paul…" She looked around the city, her eyes wide, penetrating, filled with force. Sweeping an arm broadly in front of her. "All of *this* hell on earth…it's starting, isn't it? What's on that flash drive? What's the damn *meaning* or message? Is God walking around down here in all this shit? Is he somewhere in what's left of Jerusalem? And, how did Bahir know I was raped as a girl?"

Marcus held her by the shoulders. "Alicia, listen to me! I don't know all the answers to the things you're asking. He said the bastard that killed my family—said his time grows short. Does that mean he's about to die or be arrested? All of this is happening in layers, timed in increments."

"What exactly did you find on the scroll in the vase?"

"It's the continuation of Daniel's prophecy of seventy weeks. I believe it's got a dotted line to Revelation thirteen, twenty-one and twenty-two."

"What does that *mean*?"

"I believe a New Jerusalem will rise out of this destruction, physically and spiritually. Before it does, China, Russia, America, Israel, Turkey and most of the Middle East, including Israel, Iran and Syria, might engage in confrontation. It has the potential to become a nuclear holocaust."

"When? Now? What's the date?"

Marcus said nothing, fatigue weighing behind his eyes. He looked all around them at the destruction to the Old City and then at Alicia's face. "Soon…I think." A helicopter approached, flying over the Temple Mount.

Alicia watched it for a moment. "And we've helped Iran by destroying the worm that gives them the green light to nuclear weapons. Brandi is still in that shithole. You've got the fate of the *world* on a damn flash drive, and we have—"

"We have each other. But we must move. Now!" Marcus looked over his shoulder. Evacuees streamed out of the Old City. He reached for Alicia's hand, glancing over Alicia's shoulder. He saw a man in the distance, unmoved by the chaos, coming closer.

EIGHTY-NINE

*T*he electrical power was still on at the hotel. They were told it had suffered minor damage. Marcus approached the desk clerk. "I've had a package in storage for me, Paul Marcus, room 719."

"Yes, Mr. Marcus. I'll check for you." The clerk left the reception area. Two other clerks manned the front desk and checked guests in and out, the conversations anxious, all talking about the earthquake. Marcus scanned the lobby to see if the man had followed them inside. The clerk returned with a FedEx box. "Is this the package you're referring to, Mr. Marcus? It has your name on the label, but there is no shipping address."

Marcus smiled. "That's it. Thanks." He took the box and walked quickly with Alicia to the elevator. Marcus punched the button to the fourth floor.

"Paul, are we being followed?"

"I think so."

"Maybe it's the same people who killed the priest."

"I don't know." Marcus tore the package open, reaching inside for the pistol.

Alicia looked at the pistol for a few seconds, and then her eyes met Marcus. The elevator stopped on the fourth floor. Marcus stood in front of Alicia, the pistol in his right hand, both hands behind his back. His heart hammered.

The elevator door opened. A maid entered, eyes red and wet, on her way out of the hotel, carrying a stack of white towels. Marcus said, "May I have a towel?"

"Yes." She handed Marcus a towel and turned back to watch the numbers on the control panel, the elevator rising and then stopping on the seventh floor.

Marcus wrapped the towel around the gun and stepped out into the corridor. He nodded to Alicia and she followed. They entered the room, locked the door, and Marcus lifted a finger to his lips. He held the pistol and searched the room, the closets, under the beds, behind the curtains. He then searched for listening devices, turned on the television and said, "Maybe we're safe for a while."

Alicia looked up at the television, the images of emergency crews helping evacuate the injured from the wreckage of the Old City. She stepped to the window and watched the smoke and ash rise over Jerusalem, the flashing lights from police cars and ambulances, the helicopters circling, air-raid sirens wailing in the distance. "It's surreal. Like some kind of Armageddon. Look, Marcus, there's something else on the news."

The video cut to a volcano, fire and lava belching from its top. The voice-over journalist said, "Officials don't know if it will be a major eruption, but one of the most infamous volcanoes in the world, Mount Etna in Sicily, is erupting. Authorities say thus far the eruptions are minor. However, they caution that the eruptions could become catastrophic because thousands of people live in the shadow of the volcano."

Marcus inserted the flash drive in the side of his laptop and read the words in Hebrew on the screen. "*At that time Michael, the great prince who protects your people, will arise. There will be a time of great distress among nations. At that time your people—everyone whose name is found written in the book—will be delivered. Michael returns as he did five decades and one year after the third horn was plucked away. Behold and seek the angel whose lance guards the passage to Michael. Know that the day of Michael's return marks the season of the beast and the slaying by the prince. From the date of the holy order, from the time the third horn was plucked, ends with the 1260 days and the passage to Michael. The season of his return draws near, for he is the alpha and the omega. In this horn were eyes like the eyes of man and a voice speaking great things… for the things which are seen are sequential, but the things which are not seen are eternal.*"

Marcus pulled the spearhead from his pocket and held it in the palm of his hand, lifting his eyes to the television and fiery plumes belching out of the ancient volcano. His mind cut to the evening in the Garden of

Gethsemane. "Deliver its message and release the spear into the fire of Etna. Destroy it."
Marcus pinched the bridge of his nose, his scalp tightening. He remembered
Taheera's words before she committed suicide. *"The disease, schizophrenia,
makes voices sound very real in your head. It's part of your DNA, Paul. Maybe it is a
sad compromise of your genius."*

Alicia watched the television for a minute then looked at Marcus. "You
know, all my life I've heard some people say, even when things got rough,
that everything happens for a reason. I never really believed that until now."

"I didn't either."

"But now I know that all of this is for a reason. Paul, how'd Bahir
know what happened to me when I was a girl? I never told anyone, not my
parents, not my sister—I told no one about being sexually molested by a
close family friend. It's an internal wound that often I thought was healed,
but then something happens—a scent, an article of clothing that was like
his…and the wound opens again. That buried rawness has kept me vulnerable at unexpected times in my life, catching me off guard. Now I know he's
dead." Her eyes watered, she licked her lower lip and inhaled deeply. "And
now, Paul, for the first time, I really believe the dark shadow from the fear,
shame and hurt the rape instilled—has lifted. I feel free. When I was being
raped, a weird thing happened. I was just a little girl, but I remember the
pain was unbearable and the smell of alcohol on his breath was nauseating.
All of a sudden, I felt as if I broke away from my body. My conscious mind
went someplace beyond the physical pain. It was as if it was happening to
someone else, and I was being held in a cocoon far away until it ended. But
later, during dark times, the damage to my soul would open and consume
me, and it has been a struggle for me to fully trust and heal."

She walked over to Marcus. He reached out and held her, warm tears
dampening his shoulder. He caressed her hair and kissed her closed eyes.
Neither said anything for a minute. Alicia smiled, her face filled with buried
thought. She stepped back and lowered herself to the edge of the bed and
sat, her cheeks flushed. She looked back at Marcus. "I am free…and I'm
grateful for Bahir's kindness and happy to be here with you. What are you
thinking?"

"Just how small, how insignificant we are in the whole of things, and
yet, how much we're really cared for in this narrow world." He glanced out

the window, the chaos palpable in the Old City. "For years, I felt like the only way to quantify, to calculate the worth of something was to measure it in terms of some subjective scale, or a linear focus, as Bahir said. Never stopping long enough to view and feel the whole painting—the bigger picture. Now I understand the real link is below the surface. It's the human fountainhead of *being*—being connected in the passage of good and bad times together—the bridges of life we walk across as one. Alicia, we didn't choose this…didn't ask for it, but somehow we're here. We have to finish it…wherever it takes us."

Alicia smiled. "My father always used to say he'd cross that bridge when he came to it. We have to do the same…and we have to do it together."

Marcus looked from the window, his eyes meeting Alicia. "We are back in Jerusalem…where it began. Something…or someone is coming. We'll be able to share it when we learn it—a passage, a link, something that we haven't found…but I think we will…and very soon."

Alicia stood, used two hands to wipe her face. She looked steadfast, and walked to the small desk in the corner of the room. She opened her laptop and began culling in deep and far-reaching layers within the hidden empire of Jonathon Carlson.

"What are you doing?" Marcus asked. He opened the clip to the Beretta, counted the bullets and slapped the magazine back in the pistol.

"I'm boring farther into Jonathon Carlson's world. For a man who's supposed to be smart, he's careless on his computer and his correspondence. After I spend hours in these sewers, I get the feel for how the rats really live. It's easy to follow their shit."

Marcus smiled and sat in a chair near the mini refrigerator. He closed his eyes and felt sleep creeping up around him.

— —

Six hours later, Alicia was still staring at the laptop screen. She began to sense the Carlson kingdom was an amorphous, seething creature that could alter its shape in order to prevent detection. She peeled though the layers of bonds, partnerships, income interest, bank accounts, payment transfers and hundreds of other small moves on his global chessboard. She calculated his assets to be in the neighborhood of fifty billion dollars. She found land and building acquisitions and leases held all over the world tied to thousands of bank accounts and holdings listed under hundreds of names, most fictitious. She traced the electronic money trails from Paris to Gibraltar to Athens to Kenya, Libya and Egypt…and finally Syria. Carlson's Consolidated Energy Services was a clearinghouse for money laundering and illegal weapons trade. Alicia's eyes were like heat-seeking missiles, examining every detail, focusing on each nuance of each complex relationship, looking for correlations and blemishes.

Another two hours and she worked in a near self-induced, hypnotic trance-like state of mind. She understood the inner working of Carlson's cyber world from the perspective of inside his computers. It was as if she were part of the electrons moving through Carlson's empire—balance sheets—emails—money transfers from Luxembourg to a Cayman Islands' bank. Percentages of almost every transaction funneled into the island through non-existent, post-office-box companies.

Something caught her eye. An email *arriving* while she moved with ease inside his computer, she read the encryption:

Marcus may be in a position to implicate us on the K jr situation. Increase reward by 10-mil. Leverage and maneuver Tel Aviv into capture if possible. Retrieve spear and flash-drive immediately!

"Screw you, asshole," Alicia whispered. *Click…click…click…* "See if you can trace that."

She stood from the small table where she'd sat for twelve straight hours. After going to the bathroom, she touched Marcus on the shoulder. He opened his eyes, and she said, "It'll be morning soon. We can't stay here. I have what we need to sink Jonathon Carlson."

NINETY

*T*he morning light brought the extent of damages from the earthquake. Israeli authorities estimated that the destruction would cost more than three billion dollars to repair. At least seventy-nine people were dead and dozens more missing and feared dead. Aftershocks were felt as far west as Cairo, Egypt, and they spread into the western section of Iraq.

Alicia said, "I spent most of the night in Jonathon Carlson's sewer. I need a very hot shower. I've uncovered further connections…links that substantiate a pattern, a legacy of involvement in the Middle East and much of Europe for a long time." She handed Marcus a notepad. "I jotted down a bullet-point summation."

Marcus took the notepad and read silently. After a minute, he looked up at Alicia. It all makes sense…*oil n guns*…all comes together. Israel is in the crosshairs, and they don't know it or won't recognize it. Maybe they will now."

"There's civil unrest, protests going on in most of the countries in the Middle East, all but Iran. The Internet and social sites have opened younger faces and minds to what's outside the insular bubble that the kings and dictators have erected since World War II. Autocratic rulers are toppling from Egypt to Oman. The unknown is who will gain control and what will their relationship be with the West—with Israel?"

Marcus nodded. "Especially Israel." He reached for his phone and punched in numbers. "I wonder if cell towers are still standing."

"I'm getting strong Internet reception."

After a half dozen rings, Jacob Kogen answered. "Are you okay, Jacob?"

"Yes, Paul. We're safe. Where *are* you?"

"Here in Jerusalem. I'm at a hotel, but I'll be leaving soon, if taxis or shuttles are running. The rental car was destroyed."

"The library and university have very little damage."

Marcus looked at the television screen, the channel on BBC International, to see reporters scattered all over Jerusalem doing live broadcasts, most via satellite phones.

"Paul, the university is on your way to the airport. Can you stop in a for few minutes? I have something I need to share with you."

"Okay, I'd like to brief you on something, too. It's the reason, I hope, that I was brought over here." Marcus disconnected, walked across the room, and wedged the Beretta in the small of his back, under his belt.

Alicia looked up. "What's going on, Paul?"

"We're leaving, but before we go, we have to make an impromptu stop."

— —

Inside the library at the Hebrew University, in the lobby near the Ardon stained-glass windows, Marcus introduced Alicia to Jacob Kogen. Jacob said, "I'm saddened that the Old City has been taken to its knees in the aftermath of the earthquake. We shall rebuild. I hope your next journey here meets you with calm and the damage done to Jerusalem is no longer visible."

"Thank you, Jacob," Alicia said. "My prayers are with the victims of the disaster and their families. Those windows…the stained glass is so beautiful. It reminds me of Chartres."

Jacob smiled. "The panel on the right is from Isaiah 2:3-4. Jacob shifted his eyes to Marcus. "Paul, you must leave Israel. Let's talk in the research room. Nathan Levy is convinced you are working for Iran. He believes that you had something to do with the stepped-up operations of their nuclear program."

Marcus said nothing, looking at the white board beyond the desk piled with Jacob's paperwork. The mathematical problem Marcus solved was still visible in the dry erasable ink. "Jacob, you're going to have to trust me here, okay?"

"Of course."

"I did nothing to compromise the security of Israel. But, for your own safety, the less you know the less that can hurt you. Alicia's niece, Brandi, and her fiancé were being held by Iran. Adam was released. Brandi is still there. I'm doing everything I can to free her and still not do anything to create a nuclear buildup. Do you *believe* me?"

"Yes, Paul. I believe this is part of a larger plan."

Marcus reached in his pocket and pulled out the head of the spear. "I know this belongs to the bigger plan. We discovered it at Chartres Cathedral. It was hidden behind a marble statue, maybe the sculpture of Saint Longinus. Using the measurements of the sacred cubit, combined with the information I decoded from Newton and the Bible, '...*for the shadow is to the seeker as the seeker is to the shadow...*' we found it."

"Astounding...prophetic...may I see it?"

Marcus handed the spear to Jacob and said, "Someone knows we have that. And they want it enough to kill for it."

"What do you mean?"

Marcus told him and added, "The real value in the spear isn't the alleged power it has, but rather the direction it points."

"What do you mean?"

"The future. It's written on the other side of the blade."

Jacob held the spear under his desk light. He turned the blade over, his eyes narrowing as he read. "It's in Hebrew. '*The city had no need of the sun, neither the moon to shine in it...for the glory of God did lighten it, and the Lamb is the light that will be there.*' Paul, what do you think it means?"

"It pointed us to passageways under the Old City, right after the quake. Look, Jacob, we found...the Ark of the Covenant."

Jacob's mouth parted. He set the spearhead on the desk and slowly sat down, knees weak, his eyes looking up to meet Marcus. "Hidden beneath Jerusalem?"

"Yes."

"Words fail me."

"We also found something else"

"What?"

"A vase, sealed. I opened it. Why? Because in spite of Nathan Levy's deception, I believe that's what I was drawn here to do. I think the words were from Daniel…or at least what God told Daniel and had him seal in a vase."

"What did it read? What did the words say?"

Marcus took the flash drive from his pocket. He held it in his out-stretched hand. "It's on this. I snapped a picture of what we discovered and loaded to this drive. We've found words sealed from thousands of years ago that resonate today, right *now*. And they've pointed Alicia and me to a cancer that's been festering since before Newton, now about to rise to the surface."

"What *is* it, Paul?"

"A few weeks ago, I showed you how Newton used the Bible to predict the return of the Jews to a homeland, and Newton figured the date. What he didn't know is that the Arab-Israeli War of '48 wasn't as much motivated by the acquisition of land as it was the possession of oil. Business interests, many of the same that supported a war that cre-ated the holocaust, supported the stability of what would become the new Middle East. The seeds of OPEC were planted then. The govern-ments of the U.S. and England became the underwriters of the region's stability…and eventually the leading force in the oil industry. For some companies, those ostensibly with ties to the German oil and chemical giant, I.G. Farben, the goal was the solidarity of Arab states. Why? It would be more lucrative than the establishment of an Israeli state and the likely polarization of oil-rich Arab territories. A new oil cartel was rising from the Suez Canal to Iran. I believe those sitting on trial as Nazi war criminals in Nuremberg, those former Farben executives, looked to their corporate partners in Britain and the U.S. to align the new Middle East to ensure all oil wells flowed to the West. Guys like David Marcus—tough, smart military men, could prolong the fighting against the Palestinians, and men like him were killed."

Jacob's eyes lowered. "*Who* was behind it?"

"A select few people whose families have a centuries old creed and business interests that they think gives them a license to cross international laws and borders to undermine humanitarian efforts that may interfere with them making money. These people will gut a nation if it can add to their coffers and power, usually by building infrastructures that often lead to wars and the funding of wars."

Alicia added, "And they'll do business in the charade of development and production to *prevent* wars, as oxymoronic as that might sound."

"What do you mean?" Jacob asked.

Marcus said, "Specifically, the National Security Act that's being proposed in the U.S. Congress, the same one that was discussed in the G8 Summit this summer. If the bill is passed, a firm called Integrated Security Corporation may do a lion's share of the global satellite communications development."

Alicia nodded. "It's the fox watching the hen house scenario. That company is controlled by a man named Jonathon Carlson."

"Who's he?" asked Jacob.

"A multibillionaire who not only controls Integrated Security Corporation, but PetChem Consolidated Group that's believed to have connections to the Russian oil conglomerate, Rosneft, the largest oil company in the world. Carlson may have engineered a deal to extract oil and gas from Syria under an exchange for arms agreement. Carlson didn't just happen to become a savvy, cutthroat businessman. His dowry goes back a few centuries directly to Isaac Newton."

Jacob's eyebrows arched. "*Newton*...what do you mean?"

Marcus slid the flash drive back into his pocket. "Alicia is one of the best researchers in the world. What she found is a tie, a historical and biological link, to a man named William Chaloner, a brilliant criminal that Newton had to trap in order to prosecute for crimes against England. Jonathon Carlson is a direct descendent to William Chaloner. And to put it in closer viewpoint, Carlson is the grandson of Andrew Chaloner, the man whose firm, Chaloner Industries, backed and financed the companies that built the Third Reich in Germany."

"Dear God," whispered Jacob.

"Some of these executives at one company, Farben, were charged with crimes against humanity and tried in Nuremberg after the war. David Marcus helped prosecutors bring the charges against these men. I believe it was Andrew Chaloner who wanted this spear after General Patton was killed. And I think it's his grandson who wants it today." Marcus lifted the spearhead from the desk.

Jacob's eyes opened wide behind his thick glasses. "From Newton's time, three hundred years ago, to events of today...all related...and all foretold by prophets like Isaiah, following the word of God."

"Alicia found information that reveals David Marcus and Yitzhak Rabin worked closely together during the Arab-Israeli War in 1948. They'd negotiated a cease-fire. Marcus was killed the next day. Decades later, Rabin was assassinated. I think David Marcus may have been, too. And now Prime Minister Meltzer was assassinated. The new interim prime minister, Eilam Cohen, is a man who was educated in the U.S. at Yale, and was a classmate of Senator Wyatt Dirkson—the same man pushing the International Security Act. He's also the same man who spent a luxury weekend at Jonathon Carlson's Texas ranch. Dirkson is priming the pump for a run at the presidency. Most likely it's Carlson and his political cronies who had something to do with the deadly final flight of John Kennedy Junior when his plane went down in the water near Martha's Vineyard. Kennedy, in his magazine *George*, published a story written by Guela Amir, the mother of the man found guilty of Rabin's assassination. His name is Yigal Amir. His mother contended, at the time, that Amir was goaded into the killing by someone with the Shin Bet."

Jacob shook his head slowly. "When I saw your name in the Newton papers, never would I have known all of this would unfold. It is God's plan...and now as his messenger..." Jacob glanced at Alicia. "You both are his messengers, perhaps. What will you do? What *can* you do?"

Marcus looked at the spearhead in his hand. "Get rid of this...for good, literally, and deliver a memorandum. We have names and faces. Jacob, if there is a true axis of evil, I think we've been guided to uncover it. It could lead to all hell breaking out on earth to stop it. But this little blue-green planet is all we have. I believe it's worth fighting for."

Alicia looked at her mobile phone. "It's a few minutes before three. Jacob, do you have a TV here?"

"Yes, why?"

"In a few minutes, the Iranians are supposed to free my niece, Brandi."

NINETY-ONE

*J*acob led Marcus and Alicia to a vacant teacher's lounge. He switched on the television and handed the remote to Alicia. She scanned the channels, stopping when she came to a *Breaking News BBC – Ahmadabad* graphic on the screen. She said, "I'm connecting to the Islamic Republic of Iran News Network on my laptop, too."

On the television screen, the image cut from a news anchorwoman at her desk in London to live video of a jet on the tarmac at Tehran International Airport. The video then cut to shots of Brandi being escorted under guard from a black Mercedes through the airport. Part of her face was covered by a dark blue khim .

A TV news anchorwoman said, "Iranian television is providing this live feed of American citizen Brandi Hirsh being escorted through Tehran International Airport near Ahmadabad. The Iranians have held the twenty-three-year old woman for more than seven months awaiting a ruling on charges of espionage after her and her boyfriend, Adam Spencer, allegedly walked across the border between Iran and Turkey. Spencer was released earlier. They said the border was poorly marked and they'd been picking berries and taking pictures of wildflowers."

"She looks so young," Jacob said, his eyes filling with compassion.

The anchorwoman continued. "Iran's president said Hirsh was being released as a humanitarian effort and to reach out to the West in a gesture of good will. U.S. Secretary of State, Merriam Hanover, in a statement released by her office, said that she's cautiously optimistic that Hirsh will be released and would have more to offer when and if the young American boards the plane and leaves Iran."

Alicia hugged her arms watching Brandi walk up the steps leading into the jetliner. When Brandi entered the plane and the portable ladder was rolled away, Alicia held her breath while the plane taxied down the runway and lifted off in the air over Iran. She turned to Marcus, tears rolling down her cheeks. "You did it, Paul. Brandi's coming home." She stepped to Marcus and hugged him. Jacob beamed.

Taheera's cell phone buzzed in his left pocket.

He pulled it out and held it for a second. Alicia stared at the phone. "Don't go. You don't *have* to go now. Brandi's gone from that damn hellhole of a country. Screw them! Don't answer it."

"I have to."

"No you don't!"

"Trust me, Alicia." He answered the phone and touched the speaker-phone button.

Rahim said, "Mr. Marcus, we assume you saw the girl board the plane. What you didn't see was the package that boarded with her. It's a bomb. We call it insurance. If you do not make our appointment, the plane will explode. You will be responsible for her death and the deaths of the other two hundred people aboard. Meet me in one hour at Emek HaMatsheva Park. It is called the Valley of the Cross, and the place is located off Lilyan Road near the Israel Museum. Bring the drive that will continue the protection of our operating systems. One hour or the plane will explode over the Mediterranean Sea, and your girlfriend will never find the smallest pieces of her niece's body."

NINETY-TWO

They entered the lobby, the large room drenched in a rainbow of colors filtered from sunlight through the Ardon Window. Alicia said, "We've got to reach Secretary Hanover!"

"And tell her what?" Marcus asked. "That the Iranians planted a bomb aboard a U.S. plane bound for London—"

"We have to do something!"

"We have to get that plane safely on the ground. They only way to do that is to meet the Iranians. Alicia, stay with Jacob."

Jacob nodded. "Please, I will take you to my home—"

"I can't! I have to go!"

Jacob turned his head to Alicia. "I wish you would come with me, but I do understand your need to go. I pray that your niece and the others on the plane will be safe." Turning back to Marcus, he said, "Paul, where can you reveal your discoveries to a world that desperately needs to hear it? The information on that flash drive is God's handwriting on earth's wall…sealed by Daniel. The spear you carry in your pocket has been and now continues to be sought after by those who believe it delivers power to whoever possesses it. You must pass through the Iranian den of hate to continue this journey. Others will no doubt, hunt you, too. Where will you go?"

"I'm not sure yet, Jacob, but keep me in your prayers. The taxi we called should be here by now."

Marcus and Alicia started toward the front door just as Jacob spotted a black Mercedes pulling into the lot.

Jacob held up his hand. "Wait!"

"What is it?" asked Alicia.

"I recognize one of them getting out of that car. He's Nathan Levy's associate. He's Mossad! You must leave through the back way! Follow that corridor around to the exit where you will see my car—a black Honda. I will stall them in my office." Jacob handed Marcus the key and pointed to a hallway. "Go!"

Marcus nodded, grabbed a roll of duct tape from a maintenance cart near the vacant reception desk, and ran with Alicia toward the exit.

"May God be with you," whispered Jacob, watching the men in dark suits approach.

NINETY-THREE

*M*arcus drove east out of Jerusalem, surveying the earthquake damage, maneuvering the Honda down crowded streets. Alicia looked out the car window, her heart in her throat. "This is horrific. I think we—" Her phone buzzed. She looked at the ID and recognized the code. She glanced over to Marcus. "It's Bill Gray."

"Answer it."

She inhaled deeply. "Hello, Bill."

"Alicia, are you okay?"

"Yes."

"Is Paul with you?"

"Yes."

"Look, all hell is breaking lose over the channels. Something has happened to motivate the Iranians to deal—something, we believe coming out of Natanz. Brandi is on a plane. The Secretary of State's office is out of the loop, other diplomatic channels are scratching their heads. What's going on, Alicia. I need to know now!"

"Bill, no one in the State Department, NSA or the CIA could do shit. It's that simple."

"You're not a damn field agent! Come in."

"Until Brandi's safe, that's not going to happen."

"Put Paul on the line."

She handed the phone to Marcus. Gray said, "Paul, I need to know what you know about a Russian physicist named Abromov defecting to Israel."

"What makes you think I know anything?"

"Your encryption is the best, but there's always an Achilles heel, always a link. You know that."

"Listen to me, Bill. Whoever gave you that information belongs to a very complex web of deceit. Who told you?"

Bill Gray was silent for a few seconds. "What can *you* tell me?"

Weighing his odds before answering, Marcus gave Gray a quick summary and added, "We don't know how far the web stretches, and who the players are. I can tell you that there's a bomb on Brandi's plane. Courtesy, Tehran."

"What!"

"Don't rush the plane. Just watch it in London. I don't know whom you can trust. I know whoever gave you that intel is someone you cannot trust."

Gray said nothing for a moment. "Thank you, Paul."

Marcus was quiet, driving through the traffic, a cloud passing over the midday sun causing a dark shadow to descend over Jerusalem. "Bill, has anyone made an effort to locate this assassin, the Lion? I could use some help here."

"I wish I had better news. Too much is classified, and no one really knows who or where the Lion is because no one alive has seen him."

"I'm alive. I've seen him. And I'll see him again." Marcus disconnected and punched numbers into his cell phone to call the personal line of Nathan Levy. Levy answered with an indistinct response. "Where are you, Paul?"

"I suspect you know where I am."

"My men were ordered to find you so we can simply talk."

"We can use a telephone for that. Where's the Lion?"

"You made a foolish mistake meeting earlier with the Iranians. We know that because of the changes *you* made to their operating systems. You extricated or compromised the Myrtus device. The Iranians are resuming the operations of their centrifuges. Why did you succumb to them?"

"Listen to me, Levy. I did nothing to compromise the security of Israel, or the rest of the Middle East, for that matter."

"How are we to believe you?"

"Because what I'm telling you is the damn *truth*. You may not recognize it in your line of work, but that's what it's supposed to look like."

"Paul, I am holding a piece of paper in my hand, a note that you wrote to a woman with the alias of Layla Koury. Her real name was Taheera Khalili. She was an operative for Iran, one of the best. In this little message, you told her how much you enjoyed your dinner and evening with her, and that you wanted to meet to discuss her proposition. In other words, Paul, you were looking to cut a deal. How *much* did they offer you?"

"You forgot the part where she tried to put a bullet in my head."

"That's what you tell us. How do we know the deal simply went bad and you killed her?"

"I guess this is another time where you're going to have to learn to recognize the truth when you hear it. What I did was what I had to do to gain the freedom of Brandi Hirsh, who's sick and needs immediate medical care, and Adam Spencer, both of whom were being used by Iran as political pawns."

"You'll never get out of Israel. We'll find you."

"Call off the dogs, Levy. I'm not your enemy. Your enemy is the one who engineered Rabin's killing. They're the same people who just shot Prime Minister Meltzer. Who is the Lion?"

"I don't believe you."

"You brought me here under the pretense of the Newton project, and you *used* Jacob Kogen and his passion for Bible prophecies to do it. But what you didn't factor in was Isaac Newton, his deep research of the Bible and mathematical genius for identifying patterns and creating code, and what that information might reveal. It's already revealed the meaning of ancient scripture, faith and evil, the latter including warring schemes from Babylonia to the Middle Ages to Isaac Newton's time, and through World War II...all the way up until today—this very moment in time, Levy. Would you like to know what else it's revealed?"

"Paul, you're delusional. You're *sick* and you need help."

"On the contrary, Levy. I have no illusions. I have facts. The prophetic handwriting on the wall is anything but covert, as was your contact, Andy Jenkins, who is a consultant today with the Kinsley Group. I know that Jenkins helped put into place the events that led to Rabin's assassination, which created the vacancy for interim Prime Minister Cohen to slip into office. Back in 1997, John Kennedy Junior opened a crack into the dark when he ran the story in his magazine *George* that suggested Yigal Amir, the assassin, didn't act alone. Two years later, Kennedy was considering a run for the U.S. Senate, and his plane was taken out of the sky. Those same people, who don't have the best interest of Israel in mind—those who murdered Rabin, Kennedy and Meltzer for their own interests—are the driving force behind what has happened and what is going to happen."

"You're wrong. I would trust Andy Jenkins with my life."

"I hope that's not a mistake you're willing to make."

"Am I to believe you received all of this from some obscure Bible prophecy?"

"That's up to you. I need to share something else with you about the prophecy."

"Don't waste any more of my time. We're coming for you."

"Listen to me, Levy. The information I have indicates a perfect storm is building across the Middle East, and Israel can either do its part to diffuse it, or it will become swept up in it. Everything you've thought for the last few decades, since the 1948 war is no longer *relevant*."

"What are you talking about?"

"Look what's happening all around Israel right now. Egypt, as you knew it, no longer exists. There's unrest in Jordan. These are the only two Arab nations clinging to a peace treaty with Israel. You can see what's unfolding in Libya, Lebanon and especially Syria. Saudi Arabia may not be that far away."

"There are no surprises here. Israel is used to defending itself."

"Levy, it's not unlike the dove that Noah released, it returned with a sign of hope—a twig of faith that *our* journey means something to the *world*—"

"Enough with your psycho-babble! You don't know what you're talking about regarding the Middle East. But the real point here is that you've met with our sworn enemy—and worse, you have raised the threat of nuclear war."

"I've lowered it! You'll see. I've found information that paints a gloomy picture for the entire planet if we don't stop the insanity. There are powerful, secret global syndicates drawing lines in the sand that have enormous stakes in terms of power and money."

"Your thinking is mired in conspiracy, hypothesis, and rhetoric, all with no sound reasoning."

"Israel is surrounded by an enormous population of Muslims who have been living on the perimeter of the past, insulated by oil and dictatorships. But the curtain is falling on that era due to the rise of social media. If Israel convinces itself that the political unrest and changes in Egypt, Jordan, Syria and Lebanon prove they cannot co-exist with the Arab States, then the threat to Israel is even greater."

Levy said nothing for a few seconds. "Your rhetoric is just politics, nothing more, Paul. You attribute these revelations to biblical prophecy. It's nonsense—an interpretation gone awry."

"There is no interpretation here. Who is the Lion? Who does he work for?"

"Pull the car over in the car park past the next intersection. I will meet you, and we'll tell you."

Marcus looked at his cell for a moment. He disconnected and turned to Alicia. "Give me your phone!"

"What?"

"Your mobile! They're tracking us. It might be yours, mine or both." She handed her phone to him. Marcus pulled over to the side of the road, removed the SIM cards to the phones and slipped them into his pocket. He got out of the car and opened the back door to a parked taxi.

"Where to?" asked the driver.

"The airport." Marcus hid the phones under the back seat. "Wait a second! I forgot something. Look, here's fifty dollars. Just drive around the block a few times. If I'm not back here in ten minutes, keep the money, okay."

"My pleasure."

Marcus got out of the taxi and the driver pulled away from the curb, submerging into the flow of traffic.

NINETY-FOUR

Marcus drove on BenZivi service road as he entered into the Emek HaMatsheva Park. The Monastery of the Cross appeared beyond the verdant green terrain, ancient olive trees and exposed boulders. The monastery's high fortress-like walls still stood after the earthquake. The round dome was barely visible above the timeworn sandstone exterior of the wall.

He pulled the car onto the grass, shut off the engine and said to Alicia, "Listen to me. You don't have to go in there."

"Yes, I do."

"Rahim said he'd meet me in the courtyard." Marcus wedged the Berretta under his belt in the small of his back.

"When Brandi is home, in the arms of Dianne and my mother, I'll finally breathe easier." She took in the expanse of the monastery with a sweeping glance. "Paul, look at the wall around that place. The monastery appears older than any building I've seen, and that's saying a lot for Jerusalem. It looks even older than the Chartres Cathedral."

"Somewhere right around here is believed to be the spot where the tree was cut that would be made into the cross they used to crucify Christ."

Marcus and Alicia got out of the car and walked through knee-high grass acutely aware of the contrast between the beauty of their surroundings and the reason they were there. Wild Persian buttercups grew in patches near the rock outcroppings, its sweet fragrance drifting in the breeze. The sound of Jerusalem traffic seemed far away, overpowered by the birdsong orchestrating from the olive and cedar trees. Alicia said, "It's hard to believe that the tree carved into the cross to hang Christ on was from right here," she paused and inhaled the gentle wind, "and now we're approaching this area two-thousand years later, finishing a deal with the devil. This feels so damn weird." Alicia looked across the dark portals built into the fort-like walls. "Do you think they're watching us?"

"Probably."

"There are no cars near the monastery. No tourists. Maybe no one's here because of the earthquake. I wonder what they use this place for today."

"I heard that a few monks still maintain it, but not many people ever see them."

They came to a closed wrought iron gate, which sat across an arched entryway built from massive stones. Marcus pulled the gate open, the hinges screeching from lack of oil. They walked into the old courtyard. It was laced in aged wrought iron banisters tiered along cobblestone paths, and dotted throughout with cedar trees, stone benches and tables. They stepped around a wall and into a garden area.

"Halt! Both stop where you are."

Marcus and Alicia stopped walking. Rahim said, "Now, turn around, slowly."

They turned to face Narsi and Rahim. Narsi gripped a pistol and pointed it in the center of Marcus's chest. "Where is the flash drive?" Rahim asked.

Marcus reached into his shirt pocket. "Right here."

"Hand it to me."

"I have no problem with that. I do have a problem with a pistol pointed at me."

Rahim gestured and Narsi lowered the gun. Rahim smiled. "Let me have the drive."

"As far as I know, Brandi's plane hasn't landed safely."

"Now that you have brought the drive, it will."

"What assurance does Alicia have that her niece will not be harmed and that her plane will touch down without incident?"

"We are here, aren't we?"

Alicia said, "That's not good enough. Brandi still has two hours before landing."

Rahim grinned and stepped closer to Alicia. "I follow the Koran. It does not permit me to lie if I am to follow it in every respect. And I do. Now, give me that drive."

Marcus tossed the flash drive to Rahim. "That's part A."

Rahim looked at the drive in his hand. His eyebrows arched. "Part A?"

"Part B is in the safe inside my room at the Mount Zion Hotel." Marcus pulled a business card from his shirt pocket and handed it to Rahim. "On the back of the card is the combination to the room safe. The room is rented for another three days. Here's the key to the room. You can go get the other drive and you will have all you need. The drive you have, the red one, is to be inserted in the operation system first. It's the key to unlocking the Myrtus worm. The second drive has the final dose of coding needed to kill it for good."

"This wasn't part of the deal."

"Neither was a bomb! Your people made the *decision* to plant a bomb on a plane that's carrying her niece and two hundred other innocent people. That's a game changer."

Rahim grinned and glanced at Alicia. "The woman comes with us." Narsi pointed his gun at Marcus.

A man suddenly appeared.

In the courtyard, a monk stood near the base of a tall cedar tree, his face hidden by the hood, his body covered by a long, white cloak. Narsi looked at the monk.

It was all the time Marcus needed. He drew the Beretta from his back and leveled the gun at Rahim. "Tell him to drop the gun! If he doesn't, I guarantee I'll put a bullet in your heart before he can point that barrel my way."

Rahim's lips tightened. A vein wriggled above his right eyebrow. "Put your gun down, Narsi."

"I can take him!"

"Do you want to chance that?" Marcus asked.

"Put the gun down!" shouted Rahim. Narsi did as ordered.

"You've got the drive," Marcus said, motioning for them to leave. "You know where the other one's located. You have the combination to the safe. Now go! I don't want to ever see you two again."

The men turned to leave. Rahim paused and said, "If these flash drives fail, part A and part B, part three is C, *see* us come for you. And we'll start with the woman and the internal acid bath first. Payback is hell on earth."

Marcus said nothing for a few seconds. "Hey, Rahim!"

The men turned around.

Marcus said, "Here." He reached in his pocket, pulled out Taheera's cell phone and tossed it to Rahim. "It's Taheera's mobile. I don't want to ever see it again, either."

Rahim dropped the phone into his coat pocket and the men walked out of the courtyard.

Alicia glanced back toward the monk. "Paul, where'd he go? The monk…he vanished."

NINETY-FIVE

*M*arcus drove south on Highway 6, keeping to the speed limits. He took Highway 35 into the town of Kiryat Gat. "Let's see if Brandi's plane landed safely," he said, pulling into the parking lot of the train station.

Alicia found an Internet connection on her laptop. "Give me a sec." She punched the keyboard. "Yes! Brandi's plane is fine. She's at Heathrow. There's coverage on the BBC." Alicia's eyes watered. She wiped a single tear from her cheek. "Look—there's video of my sister Dianne and her husband, Sam, meeting Brandi."

Marcus glanced at the screen and smiled.

Alicia said, "Thank you, Paul. You risked so much for this moment."

"So did you. The risks haven't gone away. When the Iranians insert the two flash drives, it will be a matter of minutes before the combination shuts down and destroys their entire nuclear facility at Natnaz."

"What did you do?"

"I created a personality into the Myrtus worm. The programming gave the Iranians the illusion that the worm was disabled, but in reality I programmed it to destroy the centrifuges at a specific time. And this will happen even if Rahim doesn't insert the flash drives into their system. It's been preprogrammed."

"Paul, you should get some kind of medal. But, yet the Mossad, CIA, and madman Jonathon Carlson are all hunting you."

"Unfortunately, they're hunting both of us. And that's because you're with me. Alicia, get off here. Catch a train. Get out of Israel. Contact Bill

Gray. He'll get you back to the states. It's me they want. They'll come for me."

"No! I can't leave you!"

"Brandi's safe. It's too dangerous! You *have* to leave."

"I won't abandon you."

"They want the information on the other drive I have, and they want the spear. For madmen like Carlson, it's the illusion of absolute power if they can own something like the Spear of Destiny, the spear being the ultimate power trophy. Go on, you can leave now. Just disappear until this ends."

"Will it end, Paul? The information on the drive might help it end. It might help start a fresh tomorrow. But, we don't know that. I do know that I can't catch some train bound for nowhere after what we've gone through together. I'm not leaving you alone. Not now. Not ever." She leaned over and kissed him tenderly on the lips.

Marcus searched her eyes. He glanced at a train pulling into the station, and then reached under the front seat for the spearhead and flash drive, which he deposited back into his pockets. "Okay, let's go. First, we need to find a disposable phone and make a call."

— —

Ten minutes later, Marcus paid cash to buy a disposable mobile phone from a store in the heart of Kiryat Gat. He returned to the car, got in the front seat with Alicia and said, "Key in the GPS locator data for the mobile phone I tossed to Rahim."

Alicia nodded and tapped the keys. A few seconds later, the screen filled with a satellite map grid of Israel. She pointed to the moving dot on the screen. "Looks like they're going toward Tel Aviv."

"Maybe they're heading to the airport." Marcus used the mobile phone to dial Nathan Levy's number. "I have some information that you can use."

"The taxi driver wasn't happy when my men surrounded his car. You know we'll find you, Paul."

"Two high-level operatives, most likely from Iran's MOIS, are going to be leaving Israel soon. Would you like to see what interesting stories they might share with you?"

"What are you talking about?"

"One says his name is Rahim. The other goes by Narsi. Probably aliases. But I do know one truth—they are carrying two flash drives they believe will completely disengage the Myrtus worm and make their Natnaz plant all well again."

"What do you mean, *believe*?"

"I can text the satellite tracking numbers to you for Rahim and Narsi. Then you can do whatever it is that you do."

"What do you want?

"Three things. You let us board a plane from Ben Gurion. Secondly, I want you to get in touch with your old pal, Andy Jenkins. You find a reason to call him. What I want is access to his cell number. I want the ID of the Lion."

"I don't know his ID. Come in, Paul. We'll discuss the other things."

"I, quite frankly, don't have time to stop in your office for a chat." Marcus looked at his watch. "Got to go now. Call me back quickly or your two MOIS operatives are going to be out of the country." Marcus disconnected. He felt his muscles tighten across his back.

Alicia looked at him. "What'd he say?"

"He'll call back. And he'll text Andrew Jenkins cell number to me. We need to hack it to see if we can get to Carlson and his posse."

"Are we going to the airport?"

"Yes, but not Ben Gurion. They'd never let us board a plane. I'm just trying to buy us time to cross the border."

"What border?"

"Egypt. We'll fly out of Cairo."

NINETY-SIX

*M*arcus tore off a piece of duct tape to secure the spearhead to the underside of the car's dashboard. Then he used a small screwdriver to remove the door panel from the driver's side. He taped the Beretta inside the open cavity and replaced the panel. As he tightened the last screw, a text arrived on his phone with the number to Andrew Jenkins mobile phone.

Nathan Levy called immediately. "I just sent Jenkins number to you. I have made arrangements for you and the woman to have safe passage out of Ben Gurion. Now, where are the operatives?"

Marcus glanced down at the laptop screen. "I'd say they're about thirty miles east of the airport. I'm sending the coordinates to you as we speak."

"You said these men *believe* the drives they carry contain coding to disengage the Myrtus worm. What do you mean?"

"The worm has already been programmed to eat itself alive, rendering the Natnaz centrifuges harmless. It doesn't require a key. I used that tactic for leverage, a bargaining chip to ensure Brandi Hirsh's safe exit from Iran."

Alicia turned her head to Marcus. He continued. "That has happened."

"How do we know what you say about sabotage on the worm is true?"

"Because it's programmed to happen in three days. Again, Levy, this is where you'll need to have a little faith. I'm sure your boys will know when it happens. I'm sending the GPS coordinates to you now. Happy hunting." Marcus disconnected.

Alicia said, "You actually preprogrammed that worm when we were holed up in the hotel working under the scrutiny of the Iranians—was *that* when you created the self-destruct coding?"

"Yeah."

"How did you know when to encode the shutdown to three days after Brandi was released?"

"I didn't know for sure. I felt it, and I tried to make Brandi's release happen."

"Paul, you guessed! What if you were wrong and Brandi had—"

"Had what? She'd still be sitting in the damn prison!" He exhaled and touched her hand. "I'm sorry. I didn't mean to shout."

Alicia said nothing.

Marcus glanced out the front windshield. "The border's a long drive. The air conditioner in this car isn't working. Maybe you can get some rest in spite of the heat."

Five hours later, Marcus and Alicia arrived at the Rafah border crossing south of the Gaza Strip. Dozens of buses, old vans and cars lined up to cross into Egypt. Some people camped in small lean-tos made of discarded aluminum and attached to palm trees. The anxiety in the air was as visible as the heat inside the Honda. Marcus lowered all four windows, trying to catch a breeze. The hot, dry air across the Sinai Peninsula seemed to crawl inside the small car.

Alicia watched the crowds, a few people holding up signs written in Arabic. "Wonder what they're protesting?"

"It looks like it has something to do with not getting across the border." Marcus inched the car closer, the smell of diesel fumes heavy, buses idling and belching dark smoke in the heat of the afternoon. He watched Egyptian border guards approach the cars, vans, and buses. The guards were dressed in black. They wore black berets, and some carried clipboards. All carried guns. Two men stood to either side of the entranceway, rifles slung over their shoulders, dark glasses on their faces. Eye movement undetected.

Alicia said, "God help us if they find that gun. If they find the spearhead, it might wind up in the hands of the Muslim Brotherhood and whoever is leading Egypt."

"Give me your passport." Marcus licked his parched lips, his shirt damp from sweat. He eased the Honda up to the crossing. A stoic guard approached, leaned down closer to Marcus's open window.

"Passports."

"No problem," Marcus said, handing the man two passports.

Alicia smiled. After a half minute, the guard returned the passports. "What is the nature of your visit to Egypt?"

"Sightseeing. My girlfriend and I have always wanted to see the Great Pyramids. Maybe take in a camel ride, too." Marcus saw him gesture to another guard who approached the car.

"Open the trunk and step out of the vehicle." He leaned further in the open window. "You, too, miss."

Marcus thought about the Beretta behind the door panel. The Spear of Destiny taped under the dash—the flash drive in his *pocket.*

Too late.

"Get out of the vehicle," ordered the guard a second time.

"No problem," Marcus said, opening the door and standing next to the car. Alicia did the same. Another guard used a metal pole with a round mirror on the end to look under the car. He walked around it, slowly, stopping and then continuing. The guard next to Marcus used a hand-held metal detector wand.

"Spread your legs and raise your arms."

Marcus did as ordered. The guard moved the wand across Marcus's pant legs, along his arms and across his chest.

Beep – beep – beep.

He stopped the wand, moved back over Marcus's shirt pocket.

Beep – beep – beep.

"What's in the pocket?"

"It's just a flash drive. Harmless."

"Let me see it."

Alicia glanced at Marcus while the second guard patted her down and then looked in the trunk of the car.

"Sir, let me see what is in your pocket."

Marcus nodded. "Sure." He lifted the flash drive from his shirt pocket. The guard took it and studied the small drive for a few seconds. Marcus felt a drop of sweat inch down his right side over his rib cage, the scar on his chest tightening.

"What is on this?"

"It's just a back-up for my computer. Never know when a computer will crash and all your work goes down the tubes with it." Marcus smiled. The guard held the drive in his fingers.

"No! Nooooo…" came a wail from the bus behind them. The men turned to see a woman being dragged from the bus by another guard. A large man and a frightened boy were behind her. "Please!" She shouted. "Our son needs medicine! He's sick, diabetic. We must go to Cairo!"

The guard next to Marcus handed him the flash drive. "Enter! Move on!" he ordered. The men hustled back to assist the guard with the screaming woman and her family.

Marcus got in the car and pulled away, glancing in the rearview mirror, his mouth dry, back muscles knotted. Alicia let out a chest full of pent up air. "Paul! What the hell were you thinking? That flash drive tucked away in your freakin' pocket. Imagine if he'd taken it."

"But he didn't."

"You couldn't have known that. A twenty-something Egyptian border guard was patting me down while the other held the future of the world in the palm of his hands for a few seconds."

"If he knew what it was…what would he do?"

"What could he do?"

"The right thing."

Alicia said nothing for a minute. She looked out the window. "How long do you think it'll take us to cross the Sinai Peninsula?"

"I'm hoping that when the sun comes up in the morning, we'll be across the Suez Canal."

An hour later, Marcus drove west into the heart of the Sinai Peninsula. The sun crept low over the horizon and highlighted the weathered, treeless hills with a reddish glow. Marcus gazed at the vast land, bleak—life long since herded from its deserts and bare mountains. The land seemed tired, as if it harbored an old soul. It had the odd feel of something foreign, similar to the abstract desolation of the moon. It was romantic from afar, but up close it had the harsh and craggy face of a landscape plowed from thousands of years of painful history.

"Look at that," Alicia said, pointing toward a camp less than fifty feet off the road.

"They're Bedouins. Dinner time, maybe."

There were tents scattered in the midst of small clapboard homes of plywood and corrugated steel. Three camels knelt and ate grass piled beside them. Bedouin men, women, and small children sat around a fire. They ate, drank tea and talked, wood smoke curling into a dark, cherry-colored sky.

Marcus looked at the smoke and thought about the history of the region, the burning bush, wandering tribes of Israel, the plagues of Egypt, a divine covenant of a promised land, and an Exodus led by Moses. Now the old earth, the miles of rocks and sand, was a place gone astray in a fracture of time, covered by rust left over from the Iron Age. The sand was saturated in the soft glow of embers renewed in twilight from the fading burgundy sun.

Alicia looked at the immensity of the desert, the terrain now the reddish color of a robin's breast. She glanced over at Marcus. "You've been very quiet. Are you okay?"

"Yeah, I'm okay."

"Thanks, again, for what you did for Brandi. Paul, what we're going through…it's mysterious and it's powerful. I'm not sure how and why I'm with you at this moment, but I just want you to know how honored I am to be with you."

Marcus looked at her for a second. "I'm glad you're here, too. I just want to keep you safe, and that seems harder and harder to do."

"I imagine we're driving through some of the area where Moses led his people to the Promised Land."

"Probably. Maybe it's that covenant, that promissory inference that has led to the lines drawn in the sand."

"What do you mean?"

"The other message we're carrying on the flash drive is from what Daniel wrote. The information gleaned by Newton, it's the exact opposite of so much today. Its message is opposite from a divided Jerusalem. It's contrary to the gluttony and greed in much of the world—the evil built through the centuries by the heirs of those who call themselves the Circle of 13."

"Yeah, but for people like Jonathon Carlson, he can pretend to hear, speak and see *no* evil. But if you're doing all three, you can't play a shell game when electrons move your money and messages. Give me a few hours of quiet time, and I can turn the tables on more than one of Carlson's offshore accounts."

"Maybe Robin Hood had it right."

"After we get to Stockholm...what then, Paul? We're seeing a seismic movement in world events, ones that seem to be prophesies...but we don't know...I'll just say it. We don't know when the final days will occur."

Marcus said nothing. He glanced at his rearview mirror.

Alicia said, "Do you know something, have you seen...something you aren't telling me?"

"There's a missing link. If we get lucky, and if I'm right, we might find it."

NINETY-SEVEN

Marcus first saw the lights at 4:03 a.m. He'd driven that last eighty miles through the Sinai Desert with no sign of cars, people, towns or life. Nothing. Nothing but a cloudless, inky black sky filled with the shimmer of stars. Alicia slept in her seat, knees pulled up, and her head resting on a small pillow she'd bought six hours earlier.

The road was long and straight. Marcus looked in the rearview mirror and saw the headlights far away, on the edge of the flat topography. *Must be at least ten to twelve miles back.*

But the car was gaining on him—gaining with each minute. Marcus accelerated, moving the speed from sixty kilometers-per-hour to more than eighty. *Maybe just someone in a hurry to get across the peninsula.* Marcus pinched the bridge of his nose and shook away fatigue. He looked at the curved moon over the desert. The moon resembled a lopsided smile hanging in the sky just over the tops of sand dunes.

Within minutes, the car was less than a kilometer behind him. He pushed the speedometer needle to ninety. The headlights grew closer. "All right," he whispered. "I'll slow down and you can pass me." He lifted his foot from the accelerator pedal and gradually let the speed drift back down to eighty.

The headlights came nearer, and the high beams flashed on, light filling the rearview mirror. "Go on and pass me, pal," Marcus muttered.

Alicia opened her eyes. "Is everything okay?"

"Someone in a hell of a hurry is riding our tail. They won't pass."

Alicia glanced in the side-view mirror the second it was shattered by a bullet. "They're shooting!" She ducked down in her seat.

"Hold on!" Marcus cut the wheel to the left and spun around in the road. The pursuing car passed. A man in the passenger side fired another shot. A bullet went through Marcus's back windshield. He drove onto a rough side road. Unpaved. He gunned the engine, dirt and rocks scattering in the night air. He steered toward massive sand dunes and rocky hills.

Alicia turned. "They're coming back!"

Marcus said nothing, gripping the wheel. The Honda bounced hard through deep potholes the width of trashcan lids. "We can't outrun them! Maybe there's someplace to hide in those hills. Keep your head down!"

Alicia braced herself, both hands against the dashboard, head lowered. Marcus crisscrossed around old growth trees and huge boulders. He drove behind a large outcropping of rocks that led up to cliffs. He shut off the headlights and stopped the car. "Get out!"

"Where can we go?"

"Into those hills."

"I see their headlights! They're getting closer."

Marcus reached for the Beretta he had slipped back between the seats. He ripped the tape and spear from under the dash. "Come on!" They ran up a sand dune and over to rocky cliffs laced with dark crevices.

Their pursuers were less than one hundred meters away. The car's high beams raked across the cliffs. A rifle bullet shattered rocks a few inches above Marcus's head. He lowered to the ground, pulling Alicia with him to hide behind a ledge of rock. Marcus watched the two men get out of their car. "One's carrying a rifle," he whispered, looking around them. "Over there. There's some old steps carved into this hill. Let's go for it!" They bolted toward the pathway. A bullet shattered rock above their heads.

Marcus used the ridge to steady his aim. He fired. The shot hit one man in the chest. "Run, Alicia!"

She followed him. The path twisted, leading in and out of fissures. The old stone was cool to the touch in the chilly desert air. "Over there! Paul, it's a cave."

"It's our best hope."

"We don't even know who's chasing us."

"They're chasing us because they're tracking us."

"Tracking! How? Maybe it's the car—something hidden in Jacob's car."

"I don't think so because that was his wife's car. He rarely drove it." They ran for the cave. Another high-powered rifle bullet slammed into the cliffs. The round ricocheted. A bullet fragment hit Alicia in her right arm.

"Marcus! I've been shot! My arm…"

"Hold on!" He led her into the cave. It was absolute darkness. Alicia tripped on a rock and fell. Marcus helped her up and fished for the Zippo lighter in his pants pocket. He lit the wick, the flame casting a yellow glow a few feet into the cave, shadows dancing on the wall. A bat flew from the ceiling, its wings brushing against Alicia's hair as the animal darted out the mouth of the cave.

"Let me see your arm." Marcus ripped Alicia's sleeve away from her bloody right arm. Blood flowed, dripping onto the floor of the cave. "I don't see where the bullet made an exit wound. I have to stop the bleeding." He tore the tail off his shirt, folded it in quarters, and used a shoelace to hold the cloth against the wound. He looped his belt over her shoulders to make a sling.

There was a noise outside. The crunch of shoe leather against pebbles. Stopping and starting. Someone in no hurry. Someone tracking, hunting.

"Paul, he's coming. We have to hide."

"This way." They ran farther inside the cave. The air grew colder and carried an odor of charcoal and bat feces. They proceeded deep inside, following the light from the single flame. Blood oozed from the dressing on Alicia's arm. "Up there." Marcus pointed to an outcropping of rock. "You can hide up there. I'll draw this guy out and hope I'm better with a pistol than he is with a rifle."

"We should stay together—"

"Alicia, you're hurt, losing blood. I'm going to boost you up there. Once you're in the crevice, don't make a sound. Let's go." Marcus set the lighter on a rock. He laced his fingers together and knelt down. "Put your right foot in my hands. Hold onto my head or shoulders. Ready?"

"Yes."

She stepped in his hands and he hoisted her to the ledge. He picked up the lighter and walked deeper into the cave. A gust of air blew the flame, almost blowing it out. Marcus stepped back. He'd come within a few inches of walking into some kind of hole. He held the lighter closer to the gap. It was larger than a manhole, edges chiseled, as if it had been hand-carved by someone centuries earlier. Marcus picked up a small rock and dropped it. He counted the seconds to himself waiting for the rock to hit bottom. There was no sound. Then he had an idea.

— —

Alicia lay on her left side. She could hear the man enter the cave. He was less than one hundred feet away from her. She took deep, quiet breaths and slowly released the air. *Just breathe. Heart's pumping too hard. Cold. So damn cold.*

There was a strong light somewhere near the entrance. She knew the man was carrying a flashlight powerful enough to light most of the cave. She slid backwards, as far as possible. Her head bumped into something hard. She touched it with one hand. It felt like she was touching an urn, or vase—old clay hard as the rock.

The light died. Total blackness. She could hear the intruder's footsteps. Soft. Moving—the hunter stopping to listen. *Where's Paul? Will he be okay? This is not a place for dying.* Her mind racing, breathing shallow, the coppery smell of blood in her nose. Within a few seconds, she knew the man had come close, maybe less than ten feet from her. She could hear him inhale. She held her breath and prayed.

— —

Marcus lit the lighter, reached high as he could and set it on a rock outcropping thirty feet into the grotto, beyond the bottomless pit. He assumed the man was just around the bend, probably very near where Alicia was hiding. Marcus knew the Beretta had one bullet left. One shot.

Or one well-placed push.

The flashlight was on again. Three seconds and it was off. Marcus tossed a rock to the far left of where he thought the man may be.

Bam—bam—bam—

Three shots rang out. The bullets ricocheted around the stone walls. Sparks flying and rocks shattering. The noise of firepower echoed deep into the subterranean bowels of the cave. The odor of burned cordite drifted through black air.

"Drop the rifle!" Marcus ordered. "I have a gun pointed at your heart."

"You must have x-ray vision, asshole," came the gruff response.

"What do you want?" Marcus slid off his shoes and walked quietly closer to the shelf of rock between him and the man.

"You know what we want."

"Who are *we*?"

"People you don't want to mess with. Where's the spear?"

"If you'd checked my car, you'd know."

"I'll check your dead body first."

"You were tracking us...how?"

"Let's just put it this way, there's no place on earth you and the woman can hide."

The flashlight burst on, blinding Marcus as he tried to take aim.

Bam—

A bullet came within inches of Marcus's left eye. He returned fire, aiming directly at the light. The flashlight exploded. At once the cave was black. The only illumination came from the lighter perched at the far end of the cave.

Marcus could hear the man coming closer. Taking soft steps. Marcus bent down, picked up a pebble and tossed it to the far left. There was an immediate rifle shot. The man now was in the opening to the section of cave where Marcus waited behind the protrusion of rock. The man fired another shot and entered, rifle pointed at moving shadows. He looked up at the tiny flame burning on the other side of the rocky wall.

Marcus slammed his fist into the man's lower jaw. He went down, the rifle sliding across the stone floor. Then he came up with a knife in his right hand. Marcus dove for the rifle just as the blade entered his shoulder.

The man was thick with muscle across the chest, powerful arms. He roared and charged like a grizzly bear. Marcus grabbed the man's right hand and slammed it hard against a boulder, the knife falling from his grip. The attacker swung at Marcus's head, knuckles hitting just above the left eyebrow.

Marcus saw a flash of white. He stepped backwards, head woozy, a draft of cold air rising up from the dark pit.

"Where's the spear!" bellowed the man.

Marcus crept to the side, using one foot to feel for the opening to the hole, blood dripping down his arm. "You should have checked the car."

"You're lying!" The man attacked, seizing Marcus by the neck, big hands squeezing. "The spear! Where is it? And where's the flash drive?"

Marcus felt the bile and heat rise in his chest. He fought for a taste of air, the cave spinning.

Something slammed against the man's head. The blow brought him to his knees. Marcus stepped back, gulping in air. Alicia stood behind the man, a shattered object gripped in her hands. She saw the glint of the knife blade under the soft light. She reached for it, but the man grabbed her around the ankle and snatched the knife. He held it to her throat. Marcus ran to the rifle, picked it up and pointed the barrel straight at the man's face. "Let her go!"

"Or what? You'll shoot me?"

"Yes."

He laughed. "Don't you know I'm one of hundreds? You kill me and there will be another one in a few hours."

"Who are you working for?"

"I'm just a soldier ant. You'll never find the colony. But they'll always find you. Right now I'd say you're the most wanted man on earth. You give me the spear and the flash drive. I'll leave. I'll collect my bounty and tell them I killed you and the woman."

"Tell who?"

The man said nothing.

"How'd they know about the drive?"

"Even the best plumbing will eventually leak. Where your drip happened, I don't know. But these people have long taproots. The bounty: fifty million Euros for the spear and the flash drive. Now, put the rifle down or I'll cut her from ear to ear."

"Okay." Marcus lowered the rifle to the floor of the cave. He stood, reached in his pockets and produced the spearhead and the flash dive. "You want these? Come and get them."

"Kick the gun away from you!"

Marcus used his foot to kick the gun to the far right, parallel from where he stood. The man released Alicia, the knife in one hand, and he came closer.

Marcus held the drive in his left hand, the spear in his right. He stepped to his left a half foot, the open hole in the cave floor shrouded in dark and now directly between him and the approaching man.

"Stop!" Marcus ordered. "If you want to live, tell me who sent you. How'd you track us?"

"You think you can get to that rifle before I split your spinal cord with this knife? It won't happen." He took another step forward and fell into the center of the hole. The big man was quick. He reached out, grabbing the edge of the opening, his arms fully extended.

Alicia ran to the rifle. Marcus shoved the drive and spear back in his pockets. He stepped near the edge of the hole, the man struggling to pull himself up. "Gimme a hand!" yelled the frantic man. He fought to hold onto the damp rock, hands and fingers slipping. "Help me!"

Marcus stood over the hole. "Who sent you? Tell me!"

"Pull me up!"

Marcus reached out with a bloodied hand, the pain in his shoulder white-hot. He grabbed the man's hand. "Who sent you?"

"If I don't get outta here, you're coming with me."

Marcus couldn't get a firm grip with his bloodied hand. His grip began slipping. The man's eyes grew wider, his breathing fast. "You'll never escape them!"

"Who!"

"The Circle. If I'm going to hell, I'm taking you with me." The man let go of the edge of the hole and grabbed Marcus with both hands. He was dead weight. Marcus felt something pop in his wounded shoulder, pain searing, and the cave suddenly hot. His socked feet slid closer to the opening.

The man's lips sneered in a demonic grin. Alicia slammed the rifle barrel into his teeth. The impact knocked him back and he fell.

The falling man's screams seemed to go for a full minute before fading into a murmur, a whisper, and then silence.

NINETY-EIGHT

Fifteen minutes later, Marcus opened the trunk and found the first aid kit. He turned on the car's headlights and set Alicia down in front of the light so he could better treat her injury. Marcus used sterile gauze to clean the wound. "I have to stop the bleeding and need to get that bullet or bullet fragment out of there, but I don't have a knife."

Alicia's face dripped from perspiration. Her hair was damp in the cool desert air. "You're hurt, too, Paul. Maybe we can find help…a clinic… maybe."

Marcus pulled the spear from his pocket. He opened a plastic packet and removed gauze, damp with antiseptic. He folded a clean napkin. "Open your mouth and bite down hard on this. Look the other way." He placed the napkin between Alicia's teeth. Marcus used the tip of the spear to open the wound, causing blood to flow down her arm. Alicia's nostrils flared. She stared at the moon, neck muscles knotting in pain. Marcus dug in flesh a half-inch, found and removed the bullet fragment. Then he saw something else. It was about twice the size of a grain of rice. It was black with a tiny red tip. He removed it. "Now I know *how* they're tracking us. It's a sub-dermal microchip, and it's pinpointing our location via satellite to someone's monitor. Who the hell implanted it in your arm?"

Alicia's breathing was fast, her mind racing. "Oh my God…it was the mosquito bite that took a week for it to go away. I was drugged! That microchip had to have been injected into my arm a few days before I left to join you."

"Who drugged you?"

"A guy from the state department I'd met. We had lunch twice and dinner once. It was after the dinner, at an outdoor restaurant on the water called Captain Nemo's. I woke up in my bed and couldn't remember how I'd got there. And I'd only had two glasses of wine. Paul, they set me up. They set us both up. I might as well have been *sent* here, but they did it so they could track you." She turned her head to Marcus. "Jonathon Carlson has been watching everything we do."

"And we're going to let the world watch him."

Marcus cleaned the wound. He found a needle and thread in the kit, sterilized the needle and began stitching the wound, closing it. "Just rest. The worst is over. Lay down."

He ripped his blood-soaked shirt from his shoulder and used another piece of gauze to clean the deep knife wound. He applied pressure to stop the bleeding. A minute later, he closed his eyes and leaned against the bumper of the car, blood seeping through his fingertips.

Alicia turned her head toward Marcus. "We've got to stop your blood loss. She struggled to sit.

"No...you have to rest." Marcus folded another small towel and held it against his shoulder. He set the microchip on a flat rock and looked at Alicia. "The assassin's mission was to kill us. If this chip doesn't move, they'll believe he succeeded. If they don't hear from him in a few hours, they'll assume he didn't and come looking for us. This chip discovery will buy us some time, and we need it. It'll be dawn in a few hours. Let's get some rest, make sure the bleeding has stopped, and move on."

Alicia smiled. "You look like shit, Paul. Maybe an hour and we can get outta this place."

Marcus nodded and leaned back against the car, his clothes damp with sweat. Then he lifted his eyes to the heavens, the stars now on fire—the vast land around him flooded with serenity, the hills pocketed in deep shadow. Marcus felt as if the dark blue universe had poured down from the deepest reaches of creation to flood the desert with its quiet strength. He watched a meteor arc through the sky, carving a rooster tail of light across the cosmos. Sleep encircled him.

He saw Tiffany walking her horse at sunrise. She was in a meadow, leading the horse by its reins. She'd been crying, a single tear rolling down her cheek. Marcus wanted to reach up and wipe it away. Wanted to hold her one more time.

Seven other horses appeared at the top of the hill. Seven riders, all in silhouette, sitting quietly on horseback, a blood red sun rising in the sky behind them.

NINETY-NINE

When Marcus opened his eyes again, it was still dark, the morning sun was only a smoldering ash buried in the horizon across the Sinai Desert. He looked to his left where Alicia was standing up. She said, "We have to go."

Marcus glanced down at his shoulder, dried blood on the gauze. He touched the bandage, looked under it. The bleeding had stopped and the wound appeared better. The taste in his dry mouth was like copper, metal, and sand.

She glanced at her arm and lifted the gauze. "Paul, my arm...it's healed. I need to process this." She lifted her eyes to Marcus, her face filled with awe. "I need to wrap my mind around this."

"You can't process it in human terms. It's larger than anything we can even hope to understand." Marcus touched his injured shoulder. "Let's go."

He walked back to the car, sat in the driver's side and turned the ignition. Nothing. Marcus tried again. Nothing. "Battery's dead."

"Maybe we can hitch a ride."

"Look at us, Alicia. It looks like we've been through a war. Also, we're in the middle of the Sinai Peninsula. No one would stop." He pointed to the car the men used to chase them into the desert. "Let's see if we can find their keys." They walked to the abandoned car, stepping around the body of the man Marcus had shot. The dead man looked Middle Eastern. His chest was soaked with dried blood, eyes open, the corneas clouded, and a fly crawling near crusted blood in the corner of his mouth.

"Let's hope the car keys are on that guy and not on the one down the hole in the cave," Alicia said, bending down to search the body. "Bingo." She found car keys, a Jordanian passport and a cell phone. A wad of Egyptian cash was money-clipped to an America Express card. Alicia opened the passport and read. "Name's Amal Nasar, from Jordan."

"Let me see his phone." She handed it to him, and he scrolled through the last few numbers on the man's mobile phone. "Look, at this."

"What?"

"One of the last numbers this guy called was the same one Nathan Levy texted to me—the number of Andy Jenkins. What if Jenkins is the Lion?"

Alicia reached for the phone. She quickly removed the sim card, waving away a fly from her face. "Let's get our laptops and get the hell out of here."

On the outskirts of Cairo, Marcus and Alicia bought new clothes. He purchased a small box and packaging material. Then he placed the spear inside. They abandoned the car and took a bus to the airport.

They approached the gate and paid cash to ship the small package counter-to-counter from Cairo to Stockholm. Marcus used the rest of the dead man's cash to buy one-way passenger tickets to Stockholm.

ONE HUNDRED

STOCKHOLM, SWEDEN

*U*nder assumed names, Marcus and Alicia checked into the Lydmar Hotel. Their room overlooked the harbor and, under different circumstances, they would have taken time to appreciate the view. Instead, they quickly settled in and began setting up their laptops with audio recording capabilities. Using the private number to U.S. Senator Wyatt Dirkson, which Alicia had hacked, and a covert routing configuration, Marcus made the call.

Jonathon Carlson answered on the fourth ring. "Hello, Senator. Congratulations are in order. It looks like you have more than enough votes on the surveillance bill to pass it. It'll easily pass the House."

Marcus said, "Maybe that's because you've manufactured terrorist's attacks to justify passage of the bill. Blow up some buildings, capture a few American hostages, and you can scare people into thinking every man, woman and newborn baby will be safer with microchips planted inside them. Is that why you had The Post reporter, Al Weinstein, kidnapped and killed in Libya? Was it so you could justify mandatory sub-dermal GPS tracking and stick it in the surveillance bill?"

Carlson was silent more than five seconds. "Who the hell is this? How'd you get Senator Dirkson's damn phone?"

"I suspect you know who this is, Carlson. You've been tracking me for the last two months."

"What do you want, Marcus?"

"You're a clever fella. So clever, in fact, that you and your pals in your Circle of 13 really think the world is yours to use and destroy. Guess what—it's not. Those days are numbered—"

"Go to hell!"

"That might be a trip you'll take soon. You'll be able to say hello to your relatives—your great grandfather and grandfather. Your family inheritance, your sick legacy, will no longer include trying to rule the world. It's over. Your grandfather wanted the Spear of Destiny…wanted it enough to kill General Patton for it. He never got it, neither will you."

"I've heard you were a sick man, Marcus, a man with delusions. You need to be in a hospital, maybe shock therapy for starters."

"How many in your Circle of 13 are on the Kinsley Group payroll? A real circle has no beginning and no end. Your ring of misfits can't quite grasp that. You think you're invincible, but what you do has a cause and effect—way outside the circle. It's traceable if someone looks close enough. And, you know very well what we'd find, your fingerprints covering the edges of deceit. You won't get away with Kennedy Junior's death any more than you'll escape prosecution for starting the war in Syria under false pretenses, or dodge complicity in the kidnapping of journalist Al Weinstein. We can credit Syria to you and your robber barons, too. Don't forget the recent assassination of Prime Minister Meltzer; and before that, the murder of Yitzhak Rabin. You thought the sand in the Middle East was your sandbox, but it's mixed with way too much blood. What a tough love game you play, trying to leverage power between the Arabs and Jews. I'm leaving out some details, but I'll post those stories on my blog. It'll be required reading."

"I refuse to play *your* little game. Nothing you've said, of course, is accurate or attributable to me. However, I do look forward to meeting you, Mr. Marcus. It's going to be a pleasure to show you around the ranch. In the meantime, I'm hanging up."

"Is that where most of the bodies are buried? Enjoy the ranch with the little time you have left, Carlson. You're going to be indicted for war crimes against humanity and murder, just for starters. Maybe you'll spend the rest of your miserable life as a cell mate with known terrorist Zacarias Moussaoui."

The call disconnected.

Marcus felt sweat roll down his sides, his lips parched, heart hammering. He looked up at Alicia. She let out a deep sigh. "Wow…you definitely stepped on a fire ant hill. Let's see where they scatter. If he doesn't use a different phone, we'll turn his current phone into a one-way hidden microphone, and we'll record everything that comes out of Carlson's mouth. Beginning right now." She tapped her keyboard, used the audio software to adjust the controls, and put the volume on speakerphone.

There was the sound of a phone call going through, and then a woman answered. "Senator Rush's office, may I help you?"

"Madelyn, it's Jon Carlson. Is Wyatt in his office?"

"Yes, sir. I'll put you through to his private line."

"Thank you, dear."

"Hey, Jonathon. You lose my cell number?" Senator Dirkson laughed.

"No, but someone else found it."

"What do you mean?"

"Listen to me! Paul Marcus is onto us. He knows everything."

"*Everything*. What are you talking about…*us?*"

"Don't even go there. You wouldn't have that damn senate seat, and you wouldn't be in a position to run for president if it weren't for me. Marcus made the connections to Kinsley. He knows about Syria, maybe Libya. He's made the connection to Weinstein. The son-of-a-bitch, he knows about Meltzer's assassination…and the bastard even knows Kennedy Junior's death wasn't an *accident*—"

"Enough! We need to meet. I don't like this kind of conversation over the phone, even on a secure line."

"I'm calling a mandatory meeting tomorrow. Get your ass on one of my jets and get down here. We'll bring in Moscow through satellite." The lines disconnected.

Alicia glanced up and smiled. "Gotcha."

Marcus sat back in the chair. He looked out the hotel window to the bay, suddenly surprised by the beauty of the area as he watched an assortment of boats work their way across the sparkling water. "Moscow. In Patton's day, Stalin wanted to own the spear after Hitler and Patton lost it. Today, someone in Moscow is inside the Circle of 13. Yep, you're right. It's a small world after all."

ONE-HUNDRED-ONE

O ver the course of the afternoon and into the early evening, eleven private jets landed at the four-thousand-foot runway on the Circle M Ranch in Texas. Armed security driving Mercedes and Ford Expeditions, all black with dark, tinted windows, met each member of the Circle of 13. The members were escorted to a large meeting room that resembled an opulent hunting lodge with overstuffed couches and chairs. A slate and river rock fireplace took up half a wall. Trophy deer and elk heads were mounted to the heart-of-cypress paneling. A large conference table sat in the center of the room.

Waiters brought imported water, coffee, snacks. A few members sipped expensive scotch and bourbon, holding separate conversations waiting for the meeting to begin.

Jonathon Carlson entered the room precisely at 7:00 p.m. The service staff left the room; its doors were locked and armed guards were posted at every entrance and exit. A secure satellite feed filled a plasma monitor on the wall behind Carlson. On the monitor was an image of a man in silhouette sitting in a chair, smoke curling up from a Turkish cigarette in his left hand.

Carlson called the meeting to order, set his cell phone next to a legal pad in front of him, recognized the participants—all but the man in the monitor—and said, "Gentlemen, we have a situation, and it is a very grave one. Despite intense efforts to find them, Paul Marcus and NSA employee, Alicia Quincy, are still on the run. Their last known location was in the middle of the Sinai Peninsula. Somehow these two have managed to evade or eliminate our operatives. The microchip implanted in Quincy has been found and apparently abandoned."

— —

Alicia Quincy sat next to Marcus in the hotel room, adjusted the audio feed from Carlson's meeting, and then glanced at the healed area of her arm where Marcus had removed the microchip. She half smiled and watched the digital modulation scope on the laptop screen rise and fall each time Carlson spoke. She said, "You bastard. How dare *you* drug, tag and track me like an animal. Keep talking, because now you're on the endangered species list."

— —

Carlson touched the legal pad in front of him with the tips of his splayed fingers. He scanned the room, each man waiting for him to continue. "We have no reason to doubt that Marcus and the woman continue to travel with the spear and an information-packed flash drive. The latter, in and of itself, could prove detrimental or have enormous value to us. However, now that Marcus has somehow managed to open a deep hole into our businesses and the history of our businesses, his silence is of the utmost importance."

"What exactly do you think he knows?" asked Alexander Van Airedale, his ice blue eyes looking over the frame of his glasses.

"It's not what I think—it's what I damn well heard him say. He knows about our falsifying documents to build public and congressional support for wars in Syria and Libya. He knows we executed the two Israeli prime ministers, arranged Al Weinstein's kidnapping, and that we had Kennedy Junior removed."

"Jonathon?" the image in the monitor spoke. In silhouette, the others in the room could see the man gesture with his hands, cigarette smoke trailing near his left ear.

"Yes, Mr. President?"

"You said you heard him—heard Paul Marcus say these things?"

"I did."

"How did you *hear* him?"

"On the phone. Marcus used Senator Dirkson's private number to reach me."

"And did he speak to you on your mobile?"

"Yes."

"Where is that mobile right now?"

Carlson looked down at the phone on the table in front of him. "It's here. It's with me."

"Destroy it!"

"What?"

"Immediately! You are a fool!"

The monitor faded to black, and Jonathon Carlson felt the bile rise in his throat.

— —

Alicia turned to Marcus. "I recognize the accent. We have a former president of Russia and the other names. Yes! May the circle be broken!"

Marcus nodded and pushed back from the table. "It'll take me a little time to build the website and post this audio onto it. I'll see how many current pictures I can dig up of these guys and post their images, too."

Alicia folded her arms across her breasts. She glanced out the window to the boat traffic on the bay. "They're sending their invisible army for us. I'm not sure there is any place left on earth for us to go, Paul."

"That's why I have to get to the Nobel ceremonies. I'll have a huge international stage. If I can deliver the information on the flash drive and direct the world to the new website with the eye-opener of what we uncovered about the Circle of 13, we'll have made the first strike. If anything happens to us, authorities will know where to look."

Alicia turned to face Marcus. "Who, anymore, are the authorities?"

"One of them is Secretary of State Merriam Hanover. I'd made her a promise I'd attend the ceremony. We can trust her. Now is the time to RSVP. I'll call her."

Alicia smiled. "Maybe she can spare a formal dress. I have nothing here to wear."

"The hotel can make those arrangements, and I'm hoping Secretary Hanover can spare a security detail to get us safely to the Nobel ceremonies."

ONE-HUNDRED-TWO

The next day Marcus and Alicia rode the service elevator down to the loading dock in the rear of the hotel. He wore a tuxedo, and she was dressed in a long, black gown. Walking across the loading dock Alicia said, "Somehow, leaving from the back door of our hotel and standing next to a garbage dumpster takes a wee bit of the glamour out of attending the coveted Nobel Prize ceremonies."

"Forget the limo, our escort's going to be in a van. And that's probably him arriving right about now." Marcus looked toward the service entrance parking lot where a dark blue cargo van was entering.

The van stopped in a loading zone and the driver got out. He had close-cut blond hair, linebacker shoulders, and wore a black suit, dark glasses, and a flesh-colored radio receiver in his right ear. "Mr. Marcus, Miss Quincy. I'm Darryl Lawson. The Nobel ceremonies are not too far away from here. We should be there in plenty of time. I was just informed that the president would like to meet with you prior to the acceptance speeches."

Marcus nodded. "Okay." A red dot swept across his tuxedo jacket.

"Down!" yelled Lawson, pushing Marcus behind the van.

The rifle bullet hit the dumpster directly behind where Marcus had stood. The round punched a dime-sized hole through the metal. "Get in the van! Lie down!" shouted Lawson. He opened the side doors. Alicia dropped between the seats. Marcus crouched next to her. Lawson climbed over the seats, put the van into gear and sped off. A second bullet blew out one rear window in the van.

Hundreds of spectators and media from around the world converged on the Stockholm City Hall, a building inspired by the architects who designed Renaissance palaces. A BBC journalist looked into a live television camera and spoke. "This is the culmination of the world's most prestigious award ceremonies. Laureates and luminaries from around the globe are here tonight. Just a few minutes ago, we spoke with U.S. Secretary of State Merriam Hanover who confirmed rumors that Paul Marcus, the enigmatic American nominated for the Nobel Prize in Medicine, is indeed here. Marcus, as you may know, made international headlines for refusing to accept the nomination. It's not publicly known why he changed his mind. Security is tighter than ever before because this is the first time a sitting American president is accepting the Nobel Peace Prize Award."

Federal agent Darryl Lawson stayed behind in the Secret Service mobile command area of the building where he debriefed his superiors on the shooting. Another agent escorted Marcus and Alicia through the corridors where agents staked out positions in front of locked exits.

"The president will join you in a minute," said the agent, opening a door to the posh settings of a private VIP room. The walls were paneled with dark, rich wood. Antique furniture gave the large room a feel of Swedish antiquity. Five large chandeliers bathed the guests in a warm glow. Women in elegant, long gowns accompanied men in black jackets, white ties and tails. The professional wait staff served champagne from crystal glasses and carried silver platters filled with mounds of black sturgeon caviar and broiled prawns. His Majesty, the King of Sweden, held court in one area of the room, sharing stories with the laureates.

A woman, hair pinned up, wearing a dark blue business suit, approached Marcus and Alicia. "Mr. Marcus?"

"Yes?"

"I'm Liv Backlund from the concierge's office. I apologize for any intrusion, however, sir, there is a gentlemen on the phone who says he has an urgent message from his sister."

"Who is he?"

"He said his name is Laurent Fournier. He said his sister is Gisele Fournier."

Marcus said nothing for a few seconds.

Alicia said, "That's impossible. Gisele is dead."

"I'm sorry Madame," the woman nodded. She looked at Marcus. "Shall I tell the caller you can't be reached?"

"No, I'll take the call."

"Very good, sir. You may take the call in the hall outside. Please, follow me."

Alicia gave Marcus an anxious look. He said, "It's okay. I'll be right back."

In the hall, the concierge pointed to a white phone cradled on top of a polished marble and mahogany stand. As he lifted the receiver, the woman smiled and left. "This is Paul Marcus."

"Mr. Marcus, my name is Laurent Fournier. I don't mean to bother you. It's just that I saw all of the news coverage of your arrival in Stockholm, and I thought of my sister, Gisele. She spoke highly of you."

"I'm very sorry for your loss. Your sister was a fine and caring person."

"Thank you. When Gisele's body was being prepared for burial, the funeral director discovered a sealed note she had apparently hidden in her blouse either before her death from the car accident or as she lay dying. Your name was on the envelope."

Marcus felt his heart beat faster. "What does the note say?"

"It was written by my grandfather, and it appears to be some sort of communiqué to a nun, an assistant to the Pope at the end of World War II."

"Please, read the opening sentence."

"No problem. It says, '*Dear Mother Pascaline, please inform the Pope that we are praying for a swift recovery in France and the rest of Europe from the aftermath of such a terrible war.*'"

"Is there text at the bottom of the letter written in a different language?"

"Yes, but I can't read it."

"Give me your number, and I'll text you back mine. Can you send me a picture of it as soon as you get my number?"

"Yes, no problem."

As the man spoke, Marcus memorized the number. "Thank you, Mr. Fournier."

"Oh, one other thing. Gisele mentioned to me she'd told you that Paris Police Inspector Juneau said there was no Inspector Victor Roux when she'd called with the information warning of the possible assassination attempt on Israeli Prime Minister Meltzer. There is a story this morning in the news—the French DGSE has arrested Inspector Juneau because they believe he has connections to whoever killed Meltzer."

Marcus closed his eyes for a moment. "Thank you for telling me." Then he sent a text to the number and waited.

ONE-HUNDRED-THREE

A licia accepted a glass of champagne from a waiter. After he left, she turned to Marcus who arrived back inside the great room and briefed her on the call. "Is the postscript on the letter from Gisele Fournier's grandfather in Arabic?"

"No, it's Hebrew. Philippe Fournier wrote, *'My dreams do not allow me very much sleep anymore. I have premonitions without a real sign as to their ultimate meaning. Perhaps, Pope Pius, you can hear my sins, interpret my dark dreams and offer hope. Not for me, but for mankind. I have sinned. I have killed because of the atrocities of Hitler and the war. I have seen visions of an army of wicked, not unlike the last war, crawling over a dark land. And I've seen a multitude of angels, and then a single angel, his sword drawn high over his head. I believe the vision is that of Saint Michael. The Order of St. Michael, as you know was founded here in France in 1469. In A.D 539, the last of the three horns was removed recognizing the Pope as a civil leader. I have reason to believe Saint Michael will return to where he was last seen on earth as an advocate of the children of Israel. I'm not sure what this means, however, one angel who guards the bridge carries the passage of the prince who arises from Daniel.'"*

"You see a correlation, don't you, Paul? I do, too. And I think some of the stuff we found in the vase, on that scroll written by Daniel, is connected to this."

Marcus lowered his voice. "It could be our missing link...the actual date of the final day. Philippe Fournier mentions 1469 and 539 A.D. You add those and you get 2008, and that's past history. The numbers on the scroll were 1260 days. Daniel also wrote that Saint Michael returned five decades and one day after the third horn was plucked away. Fournier writes about a third horn being removed in 539."

Alicia keyed in her mobile phone and waited a few seconds for the information to appear on the screen. "It says Saint Michael, known as the Archangel, the angel who did battle with Satan, made his last appearance on earth atop the Castel Sant'Angelo, an old Roman mausoleum. The time was the triumph over the plague, and the year was 590 A.D."

The doors opened and two more Secret Service agents entered, followed by the president, first lady, Secretary Merriam Hanover, assistants and two additional agents. The couple slowly worked the room, handshakes, wide smiles and snatches of congratulatory conversation, making their way to the Swedish King.

Alicia said, "If we add five decades and one year, fifty-one years to 2008 we get 2059. But what does that mean?"

"There's still the reference in Daniel to 1260 days."

"Which is about three and a half years."

Marcus glanced around the room. The president's party was coming closer. "Alicia, let's tee up Daniel's reference to Saint Michael returning fifty-one years after the horn was plucked away. If we add that number to the year the horn was plucked away, we come up with 590 A.D, the last time Archangel Michael was seen on earth. We need to go to Rome, to the bridge Gisele's grandfather visited when he met with the Pope. I think that's where we'll find the last number to the puzzle, the missing link."

"Here comes the president. Listen, Paul, you don't have to be on the damn stage tonight. If one of Carlson's hit men got inside here—"

"I have no choice."

Secretary Hanover approached Marcus and Alicia. She introduced herself to Alicia and said to Marcus, "Thank you, again, for changing your mind. It means a lot for the president to have you here. That's what he wanted to tell you himself." She lowered her voice, eyes straying from Marcus and then returning to his face. "Paul, I was briefed on what happened outside your hotel. We have agents combing the area. Hopefully, we'll find the person or persons."

"The trail leads deep into America."

"What do you mean?"

"Here comes the president. You need to hear what I have to tell him. The world needs to hear it."

Merriam Hanover made the introductions. The president was gracious, making general conversation with both Alicia and Marcus. Then the president said, "Paul, your discovery will help fight heart arrhythmias for untold numbers of people for generations to come. It's an honor to share the Nobel stage with you."

"Thank you, Mr. President. The feeling is mutual. Your winning the Peace Prize is unprecedented. Congratulations."

"There are many others far more deserving of this award than me. I'm accepting it in their honor."

"I've admired how hard you've worked to bring about peace around the world. Unfortunately, there are others just as dedicated to undoing, stopping or preventing work like yours from succeeding."

"Sadly, I'm aware of that. It is my hope and prayers that the greater prevalence of ideas and ideals contribute to movements of compassionate human relations far beyond an ideology." The president paused, glanced around the room, lowered his voice and said, "Paul, I was told of what happened to you and Miss Quincy earlier today. Do you have any idea who's behind this attack?"

"Yes. Mr. President, I've spent the last two months researching papers from Isaac Newton and the Bible. What I've found, I'm convinced, is a code—a prophecy, if you will. It's a direct insight into the future of the world, and what we, as a global people can do about ensuring our future."

The president tilted his head, his eyes narrowing. "Please, go on."

"Most of it I'll say on stage, in front of the world. But privately, I wanted you to know about a group called the Circle of 13."

"What do you know about them?"

"These billionaires have controlled many of America's major event changers—game changers—both political and corporate. Most are associated with the Kinsley Group or some of the companies it manages. Some of their members include Jonathon Carlson, Alexander Van Airedale, Robert Kitchener, and Simon Yarborough. There are nine others including the former president of Russia. These men all have major vested interests into the world's biggest companies dealing in oil and gas, telecommunications, security, banking, insurance, and defense. Controlling Middle Eastern political agendas, ensuring oil and gas distribution from the area, is their top priority. Some of the original seeds were planted when Standard Oil married many of its assets with the German company, I.G. Farben. From direct investments made with Nazi Germany to investments made in the Middle East, these people have set the world's energy policies. To serve their interests, they've leveraged the Palestinian and Israeli issues, taking out prime ministers or heads-of-state at will…and even the only son of an American president."

"What do you mean?"

"John Kennedy Junior. I have reason to believe his plane crash was no accident. I think that Kennedy, his wife, and her sister were victims of a plot. Had he lived, Kennedy's emergence on the political stage could have been a game changer. Beyond that, under the journalistic banner, he was investigating the murder of Yitzhak Rabin, and he was opening the investigation into his own father's assassination."

"Why would he do that?"

"I think he had evidence of a deep conspiracy, and he wanted to reveal the facts in *George*, the magazine he owned at the time. He wanted to expose the corruption. I'm convinced that the same hidden group, those who were behind the Rabin murder, has now assassinated the Israeli prime minister because the interim prime minister has deep ties with Carlson and the Kinsley Group."

"Do you have proof? Do you have something tangible beyond a revelation you've deciphered from Isaac Newton's papers and the Bible?"

"Yes." Marcus reached in his jacket pocket and found the flash drive. "It's all on here—the heated conservation recorded from a meeting of the Circle of 13 yesterday. Carlson spells out some of their involvement. He admits the group's involvement in the things I mentioned to you. This and more are posted on a website I'm revealing today."

"If what you're telling me is accurate, there will be federal grand juries convened. I'll instruct the attorney general to begin an investigation, including joint house and senate investigations. Why put your life in danger to bring this to the public?"

"I believe you know that answer, Mr. President. Something you don't know is what else is on the website. It's a prophecy. It foreshadows a nuclear war. But most importantly, it gives us options and guidelines. If we, as a people, choose not to fix what's wrong with the world, we'll inherit the consequences of our inactions."

"The consequences, the penalty of our indecision, do you know what they may mean for us?"

"Yes, and I think I'm about to know when."

ONE-HUNDRED-FOUR

When Marcus was introduced, there was a noticeable shift of focus among the hundreds of people in the audience. They seemed to collectively sit a little straighter, ready to listen to each word, unsure of what the controversial Nobel laureate was going to say. Television cameras followed him across the stage, taking his place behind the podium.

Marcus looked at the large audience. The president and first lady sat in the front row next to his Majesty, the King of Sweden, the King of Norway and dozens of other dignitaries from more than fifty countries. Alicia stood in the wings, off stage, her heart pounding. She watched as Marcus began to speak.

"It is an enormous honor to stand before you tonight in a hall filled with the many people whose dedication, hard work and discoveries will make the world a better place. I'm, quite frankly, a little embarrassed to be here among such greats—those people far more deserving than I to receive this award. My original intent in mapping the electronic coding of the human heart and trying to find a better and more accurate way to prevent ventricular fibrillation wasn't as altruistic as it might sound. It was selfish. You see, I spent two years of my life working twelve-hour days to keep my daughter alive. She suffered from heart arrhythmias caused by ventricular fibrillation. It was her illness that propelled me to succeed to save her life. At the time, I wasn't thinking of, nor was I concerned about the lives of others with the same disease. And that's unfortunate, because today I realize the global ripple effects of what I discovered. I was so buried in my work I couldn't see what my work should have been all about—what it may have meant for others. Tiffany didn't live long enough to receive the treatment for her sick heart. She and my wife were murdered."

Marcus scanned the rows of people, many in the audience hanging onto his every word. Secretary Hanover shifted in her seat. Marcus looked up toward the balcony and continued. "After that, any faith I had in mankind, in God…in anything, for that matter was gone. Almost two years later, I received an invitation from the Hebrew University of Jerusalem to examine some very old notes. They were handwritten papers donated to the university, and the original author was Sir Isaac Newton. You see, Newton had spent most of his life studying the Bible. He was convinced of the Bible's accuracy and of its prophetic potential…noting that, if we, as humans, could learn to listen—we'd recognize and heed the voice of God found throughout the Bible. Newton began to map out various passages from the books of the Bible, and he did it looking at connective points-in-time, peeling back layers of history and literally tracking down the subtle voices that, when combined, spoke to him collectively, in a harmonic stratum. After more than fifty years of studying the Bible, Newton said he felt like a child standing by the sea, his knowledge of the universe no greater than the pebbles and shells around his feet. He said when he looked up, the vastness of the ocean, with its depth and horizon into infinity, God was everywhere."

Marcus paused and looked out at the audience. People shifted in their seats. The president nodded and Marcus said, "There is a message I've come here to deliver to you. What Isaac Newton did take away from his studies was this: we humans are our brother's keepers. Adherence to the word of God, which includes the giving of ourselves to others, is our most noble call. I believe that's what the Nobel Prizes are all about—giving of one's self to others. Each of us in this room, and the seven billon others walking this planet, can be just as effective as any Nobel laureate in our own circle of influence. We simply must care enough to do it."

There was a murmur from the crowd. The television director inside the control booth spoke into his headset. "Camera one! Get a close-up of the first lady and cut back to the speaker."

Marcus said, "After fifty years of studying the prophecies from the Bible, Isaac Newton believed that if mankind doesn't heed the warning signs, if we continue on a path of gluttony, power, greed and hate for one another, our world will come to an end. Newton calculated it might occur in the year 2060."

The audience fidgeted, each person visibly reacting to Marcus's words. "But, remember, in 1725 Newton didn't have a computer. I've crunched the numbers and fed in his findings and data. I don't believe 2060 is the year. God has made known enough of the puzzle pieces to paint the following picture: as nations, our actions must include the complete dismantling and removal of all nuclear weapons from earth. We must end hostile expansion at the suffering of other nations, because there will be consequences."

Marcus reached inside his jacket pocket and took out a flash drive. He held it up for a moment.

The TV program director squinted at the monitor inside the satellite broadcast truck. "What's in his hand? Move, camera two! Now! Get a close-up."

Marcus smiled. "On this small drive is a big picture. A small group of extremely wealthy people has leveraged their power, affluence and influence to literally rape Earth's natural resources, nations, and the people who call those countries home. They've created strife and deception to cause wars, which they finance and gain tremendous profit. To move their political agendas, to secure oil and gas exportation channels, they've assassinated heads of state, and they even took out the son of a former American president."

"Holy shit!" said the TV director. "Camera four—slow pan of the audience. Now!"

The president shifted in his chair, his face unreadable. A hush fell over the spectators. Alicia's heart was in her throat. She looked through a crack in the side curtains to watch the audience, fearful that Marcus would be shot dead where he stood.

Marcus glanced at the flash drive. "This group is called the Circle of 13. All of their names, corporations they own or control, and many of the unlawful activities they've created and continue to participate in and benefit from…are all on here—this flash drive contains proof. This information will soon be found on a website. It's revelation310.org. You'll hear the audio from a meeting that the Circle of 13 members held last night at Jonathon Carlson's ranch sixty miles west of Dallas, Texas. On the audio, you will hear how they are fearful the world will know they are complicit in the death of Prime Minister Meltzer, John Kennedy Junior, and others."

There was a collective gasp from the audience, the first lady touching her hand to her mouth.

Marcus said, "Jonathon Carlson is a principal with the Kinsley Group and the majority stockholder with Integrated Security Corporation, the multinational corporation that is financing Senator Wyatt Dirkson's bid for presidency. Some of the members include Alexander Van Airedale, Simon Yarborough, and others. Their goals are simple: to dominate the world and its people for their personal, financial and political ambitions. They'll try to achieve it by making a desperate and dark world—a world that will rise up in what will be known as Armageddon. One part of their plan is to know everything about *you*. It's a new world in which privacy is relinquished at birth. Some of their targets include the passage of the National Surveillance Bill that, if enacted into law, would mandate the sub-dermal implanting of micro-chips under the skin of American citizens. But remember, the Circle of 13 is global. The law is written with international rider clauses encouraging other nations, those with deep financial and political ties to the U.S., to enact time-lines adopting and adapting the law for their citizens. If the bill passes, there is nowhere on the planet for you to escape them. You lose your freedom, your privacy, and Jonathon Carlson alone stands to receive billions of dollars."

Jonathon Carlson sat alone in his private study at his ranch. A fire crackled in the river rock fireplace. He leaned back in a deep leather chair, nursed a fifty-year-old scotch from a crystal glass, and stared at the television monitor on the wall. Then he threw the glass against the rock fireplace. He picked up the phone next to his chair and made a satellite call. The former president of Russia answered the call, his voice flat. "How did *this* man get on the Nobel stage in front of the world?"

"He slipped through our net."

"Incompetent fools! Carlson, you're responsible for this. Now look at what we're facing. The information Paul Marcus has on that flash drive must never make it to the Internet."

"He won't leave Stockholm alive."

"Shut up! You listen to me because I will not repeat this again. Marcus and the woman with him must disappear tonight. No trace of their bodies. And, immediately, you need to create publicity that indicates Marcus is delusional, a man who has long suffered from mental trauma. He was and is a dangerous, paranoid schizophrenic. Create false doctors reports. Buy whoever needs to be bought. NOW!"

"I understand."

"I am putting a hundred million dollar bounty on his head for the immediate recovery of the drive before Marcus can upload his information. I expect you to match it."

Carlson said nothing.

The Russian yelled. "Two hundred million to the first person who brings me the head of Paul Marcus with the flash drive in his mouth!"

— —

Marcus concluded his speech by saying, "Our world, its resources, its very heart, lungs, and soul are all part of the essence of a higher power, a loving power that has given us our lease on life and on our planet. Now that lease is coming to term. Not because of an expiration date, but rather because of how we've abused or allowed the abuse of privileges we've been given; and, unfortunately, we continue to ignore the example given us. Isaac Newton thought the prophecies were pointing to the year 2060 as the day our earth stops its orbit. I will post new information that changes that date. The date I've been directed to, and one that appears more accurate than Newton's, will be on the website. It'll be there for the world to see, evaluate and hopefully heed. You all know Isaac Newton for his work on *gravity*. But, I believe, his greater mission was *destiny*. Now it's your chance to pick up the torch and make a difference. "

Marcus scanned the audience. "Thank you."

The audience sat stunned for ten long seconds. The president began clapping, followed by the First Lady, the King of Sweden, and the rest of the massive auditorium rose to thunderous applause. The King of Sweden stood. The president and first lady stood. Then the entire crowd, a sea of black formal clothing, rose and applauded as if their team had just won the World Cup.

Marcus nodded, turned and walked off the stage into the arms of Alicia. She held him tight. "You said what needed to be said."

"We have to get out of here quickly."

A woman stepped from an alcove and said, "Mr. Marcus, Miss Quincy. Secretary Hanover needs to have an urgent word with you. Please come with me." Jennifer Greene, Secretary of State Hanover's executive assistant smiled and led Marcus and Alicia through the backstage area. As they followed her, Marcus reached inside his pocket and hit the audio record settings on his cell phone.

One minute later, they entered a private room.

ONE-HUNDRED-FIVE

Secretary of State Merriam Hanover stood alone, beneath a sixteenth-century Renaissance oil painting of a winter scene in Stockholm. She smiled when Marcus and Alicia entered the room. "Thank you, Jen. You may return to the Nobel speeches."

"Okay," the woman said, iPad in one hand and her mobile in the other. She smiled and left.

Secretary Hanover lifted her purse from the ornate table in front of her. Within seconds, her face melted from a smile to a mask of hard porcelain. She reached in the purse and pulled out a small pistol, pointing it straight at Marcus. "Paul, I hate to do this. Really, I do. I've actually become very fond of you. But you have given us no choice."

"*Us?* So you're with them. You're one of Carlson's followers."

"You have no idea who we really are and what we represent."

"Yes we do," Alicia said. "And, you made no real effort to free Brandi and Adam. They were nothing more than pawns in some freaking chess match with your people and Iran."

"Shut up! Paul, you're going to put the flash drive on the table. Then you're going to remove the encryption on that revelation310.org website so we can take it down now. After that, I'll make a call and you and Miss Quincy will be escorted off the premises."

"Merriam...put the gun down. There is still time for you to—"

"To do what? You haven't a clue as to what will happen in the next five years. Give me the drive...now." She raised the pistol.

"I can't do that."

"Then you are forcing me to kill you and your girlfriend. Take the flash drive out of your tuxedo pocket. I can't afford to hit it with a bullet. Paul, this is all about national security. Nothing, and I mean nothing, trumps that."

"Bullshit!" Alicia said. "It's all about power and greed."

To the far right, an exit door quietly opened an inch. NSA Deputy Director, Bill Gray, raised his Glock and stepped inside. "Drop the gun, Merriam!"

Secretary Hanover turned toward him and pointed her pistol.

"Bill, I didn't know you made the invitation list."

"The president invited me. Drop the gun! Drop it!"

She fired a shot. The bullet hit the wall to the left of Gray's head.

He squeezed the trigger, the round entering Secretary Hanover's head just above the left eye. Blood sprayed across the snow scene in the painting, and Merriam Hanover fell dead to the floor.

Gray holstered his gun. "She was the one who knew about the Russian physicist, Abromov, and his defection to Israel. And she tried to prevent it. But there *is* no Abromov."

Marcus nodded. "I need to get Alicia and I out of here. Can you get us to the airport?"

"I'll have one of the agents drive you while I take care of this mess." He touched his forehead with one finger and blew out a deep breath. "What a damn breach...an internal conspirator...dear God..."

As Alicia and Marcus started for the door, she turned back to Gray. "Thank you, Bill."

He nodded. "You two need to vanish...you need to make the world believe you've died. Trust me, there is no other option if you want to live."

— —

Marcus didn't feel the adrenaline drain from his nerves and muscles until the Alitalia flight had been in the air more than an hour and was cruising at thirty-five thousand feet over Germany. He sat in coach with Alicia, the spearhead in one pocket and the flash drive in another. Alicia touched his hand. "Are you okay?"

446

"I keep thinking about Merriam Hanover. How'd they get to her?"

"How do they get to anyone who craves power? They feed the narcissism with appetizers and promise them a meal ticket for life." Alicia looked across the aisle to a woman who held a sleeping baby in her arms, and then she glanced back at Marcus and squeezed his hand. Something through the window of the plane caught her eye. "Paul, what's that?"

Marcus stared out the window for a few seconds. He could see a fighter jet in the distance gaining on the plane. "It's a T-50 fighter jet."

"Looks like it's too close for comfort."

Inside the Alitalia cockpit, the co-pilot watched the radar. In Italian, he said, "Aircraft approaching on starboard. He's in violation of safe airspace."

"Call Munich tower," the pilot said. "Who is this crazy bastard?"

For a few minutes, the pilot of the T-50 fighter jet followed the commercial airliner. In Russian, he spoke into his radio mouthpiece. "Visual established. Permission to take down aircraft. The aircraft should be out of municipality areas within two minutes."

"Permission granted. Fire when ready."

Marcus watched the fighter jet keep a close flying distance. He whispered to Alicia. "They're here because of us." Marcus glanced around the plane. "Must be at least two-hundred people on this flight, and there's not a damn thing I can do."

Alicia held his hand. She licked her lower lip, her heart rate climbing.

Marcus reached in his pocket and pulled out the spearhead. *If we go down, maybe the fire will be hot enough to destroy this.* He closed his hand around the blade.

Alicia's eyes widened. "Paul, look—there's another jet."

Marcus shielded his eyes from the sun streaming through the airplane window and watched a second jet approach.

"They've sent two," Alicia said.

"No, no they haven't. It looks like some sort of F-22, America-made, but it's more aerodynamic."

Three seconds later, the pilot in the F-22 fired a single rocket into the side of the T-50 fighter jet. The blast from the explosion rocked the commercial jetliner. Passengers screamed in horror as the sky around them turned into a white vapor followed by a fiery orange ball. The T-50 fell to earth somewhere over Germany.

Directly behind his seat, Marcus heard a woman vomit. People openly cried. Babies wailed and Marcus silently prayed they'd touch down in Rome before they were blown out of the sky somewhere over Europe.

ONE-HUNDRED-SIX

Marcus and Alicia caught a taxi out of Rome Fiumicino Airport and instructed the driver to take them to the Castel Sant'Angelo. "No, problem," said the driver. "You have luggage?"

"No," Alicia said. "How far is the Castel Sant'Angelo?"

"Not too far. It is even more beautiful in December because the sky is bluer. You can really see the old castle and the statue of Saint Michael on top of it."

In the backseat of the car, Marcus closed his eyes and visualized the various mathematical connections and combinations to the numbers left behind by Daniel and Philippe Fournier. He reached for his cell and pulled up the letter Fournier had written to the Pope, and then he re-read the words written by Daniel and sealed in the old vase. *'Behold and seek the angel whose lance guards the passage to Michael. Know that the day of Michael's return marks the season of the beast and the slaying by the prince.'*

"I'm not sure what this means," Marcus mumbled, then continued reading… *'one angel who guards the bridge carries the passage of the prince who arises from Daniel.'*

Marcus turned towards Alicia. "I believe I know where to look for the missing link!"

"The sign, I think, will be somewhere on or near one of the statues of the angels on the bridge leading to the Castel Sant'Angelo…or maybe on the statue of Saint Michael."

The taxi driver pulled up in front of the Castel Sant'Angelo. "There it is," he said. "During the seventh century, the bridge was used to expose the bodies of the executed. They stuck decapitated heads up on the posts. In those days, the leaders of Rome believed the public display of an execution was a good deterrent. Now, it is the bridge of angels; however, I believe some of the sinners of Rome's earlier times still cross the bridge at night." He grinned.

"Very funny. Is the bridge pedestrian-only?"

"Yes, this is a destination for tourists from all over the world. Each angel carries an instrument of Christ's passion. The Pope commissioned the statues in 1598. The master, Bernini, was the head sculptor or designer, who assigned eight of them to other sculptors, many of them his pupils, reserving two of them for himself to do. He designed all ten angels when he was seventy years old, devising them from three points of view so that they could be seen from a frontal view and also a forty-five-degree angle. Historians say it took the old man seventy weeks to sculpt the angel that represents the crown of thorns."

"*Thank you,*" Marcus nodded and paid the driver who then drove away.

They stared at the ancient bridge leading across the Tiber River to the massive, round fortress. The design of the bridge incorporated five wide arches. The river, reflecting the blue sky, flowed silently through the arches.

"I've never seen a castle quite like that one," Alicia said. "The taxi driver said it was built to be a mausoleum but it turned out to be everything from that to a torture chamber."

"I'm not concerned as much with the castle as I am with the bridge and one single statue. Gisele Fournier mentioned that her grandfather spoke of one statue here that, in a way, reminded him of the Weeping Angel in the UNESCO Garden of Peace."

They walked to the bridge and stepped to the center. Dozens of tourists crossed the bridge, each snapping photos of the statues of angels. Alicia watched them. "This is very impressive. I don't see the angel with the lance."

"Maybe it's closer to the Castel Sant'Angelo. The driver said each angel is representative of Christ's passion. There's the angel with the sponge. And over there is the angel with the crown of thorns."

"Each one has an inscription at the base."

They walked to the far end of the bridge. The angel closest to the Castel Sant'Angelo held the lance over her head. Her face was turned away from the fortress, looking toward the east. Staring at the tip of the lance, Marcus felt the quiver of the scar in his chest. The inscription at the base of the statue read: *Vulnerasti cor meum.* Marcus said, "The words are Latin and they mean, *thou has ravished my heart.*"

"In the taxi, you mentioned the similarities between what Daniel wrote before the birth of Christ and what Philippe Fournier wrote after World War II."

"The one constant in both is the mention of the angel who *guards the passage*. That's the way Daniel put it. Fournier wrote that one angel *who guards the bridge carries the passage of the prince who arises from Daniel.*"

Alicia looked up at the statue with the lance. "The words *guards* and *passage* are the same in what Daniel and Fournier wrote. Passage and guards... well, this is definitely the passage to the castle. The angel with the lance is the last one before you get to the castle. Maybe she's the guardian angel." Alicia smiled. "Sorry, it's been so long since I felt like smiling."

"I know." Marcus touched the base of the statue. The wind blew across the Tiber River, and pigeons rose from the old fortress, turning around over the bridge and flying back toward the Vatican. "Philippe Fournier made a connection we didn't see."

"What?"

"He specifically mentioned Daniel...Daniel the prophet in his letter to the Pope. He said, *'Who guards the bridge carries the passage of the prince who arises from Daniel.'* The *passage* of the prince..." Marcus used his mobile to find the Internet. He keyed in information, looked back to the angel with the lance and then read from his screen. "In the Book of Daniel, chapter twelve verse one, he writes, *'At that time, Michael, the great prince who protects your people, will arise. There will be a time of distress such as has not happened from the beginning of nations until then. But at that time, your people—everyone whose name is found written in the book—will be delivered.'*"

"What was he saying?"

"Let's look at the numbers." Marcus felt the adrenaline pumping, his hand trembling.

Alicia stared up at the statue of Saint Michael. "So the word *passage* has nothing to do with this bridge or a passage to the fortress where a bronze of Saint Michael stands. It has to do with a *passage* in the Bible."

"Yes! Specifically Daniel 12:1, which makes reference to Saint Michael and reuses some of the words Daniel wrote and sealed in the vase. Let's add chapter twelve and verse one. That gives us the number thirteen. Revelation 13 deals with the end of times as does Daniel 12:1. We can add the number thirteen to what we already have: begin with 1469, the date the secret Order of St. Michael was founded in France. Add the date to 539, the year the third horn was removed and the Pope became a civil leader. That adds up to the year 2008. When we factor in the other number from Daniel and mentioned by Fournier, 1260 days or three-and-a half years, we go from the year 2008 to the year 2011."

"We're beyond 2011."

Marcus stared at the statue, the lance a silhouette. "I'm wondering if the last part of the equation is the addition of the twelfth chapter and first verse in Daniel, added together is the number thirteen, and when that's in the equation, factoring in all that Daniel and Philippe Fournier corroborated, we have the year 2024…"

Alicia let out a low whistle. "So the year 2024 might be the final days of earth."

"I don't know. I'd like to find something to corroborate that."

"Maybe we'll find it."

"Right now we have to upload everything on the flash drive to the website and include the year 2024 unless we can find—"

"Excuse me."

Marcus and Alicia turned around to see a tourist approaching them. He walked with a slight limp coming from his left leg. The man was less than six feet tall, early sixties, steel blue eyes that captured the sky's reflection off the river. "Do you mind taking a picture of me for my daughter? She's back in England. I'm here in Rome for a couple of days on business. Her church youth group told her this was one of their favorite places. They're very much into angels." He smiled and held out a small camera.

"Sure," Alicia said, glancing at Marcus, giving him the camera.

The man backed up and stood next to the statue of the angel with the lance. He smiled. "When you focus the camera you need to focus on this." The man opened his coat and displayed a pistol strapped to a holster. Then he wrapped his hand around the pistol grip. "Now, Mr. Marcus and Miss Quincy, here's what we're going to do. We're going to walk back across the bridge, and we'll get in my car. From there we're going to a private room where you will remove the encryption on the revelation310.org website and you will give me the flash drive in your pocket along with that spear point. I bet the spear point looks like the spear the lovely lady above me is carrying. Too bad she isn't on your side. Now, move."

Marcus glanced up at the statue of Saint Michael high above the fortress. Then he looked directly at the man. "When did you breach?"

"Pardon me?"

"Breach. You know, crossed the line from working for the U.S. Government to working against it. When did you go from protecting the constitution to working for those hell-bent on destroying it? Hello, Andy Jenkins."

The man said nothing for a moment. "How did you know?"

"I didn't. You do fit the profile, though. Right age. Slight limp from your left leg. You sold out the people of Israel, America, and much of the world, for that matter. Tell me Jenkins, was it you who personally took down Kennedy's plane, or did you sit back on the sidelines and call the shots. Or did you and your cronies have a cigar and a scotch after one of your assassins did it?"

"Shut up and start walking."

Marcus and Alicia turned and started toward the far side of the bridge, Jenkins, hand inside his jacket, following right behind them. When they were in the center of the bridge, Marcus gripped the camera in his right hand. Without hesitation, he turned and threw the camera directly at Jenkins's head. The impact caught him on the lower jaw, dazing him for a second.

It was enough time for Marcus to grab Alicia by the hand. "Jump!" He tossed her over the railing and followed right behind her. Within two seconds they splashed into the Tiber River.

Jenkins leaned over the railing, firing two shots. The bullets cut through the water right between Marcus and Alicia. "Dive!" Marcus ordered. They dove down, two more bullets slicing through the water.

A police officer, coming from the side of the bridge closest to the Castel Sant'Angelo, drew his pistol and ran toward Jenkins. Jenkins fired, hitting the officer in the shoulder. The impact knocked him to the ground. Jenkins turned and jogged off the bridge, limping, glancing back over his shoulder to see where Marcus and Alicia had surfaced.

A fisherman in a small boat was coming under the bridge just as they popped to the surface. Marcus waved down the fisherman. The man in the boat cut the engine and leaned over, extending a hand to lift Alicia from the river. Marcus followed, flopping into the center of the boat. "Go!" Marcus said. "Go! Bullets!"

"Andiamo rapidamente!" shouted the fisherman. He leaned back and gunned the engine. He had unkept brown hair, dark eyes and a tanned, raw-boned face. He looked at Marcus and Alicia and smiled. Within seconds the boat was moving on plane down the Tiber River, cutting a V across the dark and ancient waters.

ONE-HUNDRED-SEVEN

*T*en minutes later the fisherman pulled his boat up to the side of a concrete walkway, a wall near it covered with green ivy. He slowed the engine approaching the dock. "Como il suo italiano è?"

"Not very good," Marcus said. "How is your English?"

The man smiled. "It's fine. There is a cleat to tie the rope."

"I see it." Marcus stepped from the boat and extended a hand to Alicia.

She got out of the boat and turned back to the fisherman. "Thank you for pulling us out of the river."

He smiled. "You are very welcome."

Alicia looked at him a long moment. Never had she looked into eyes as kind as this man's eyes. She felt vulnerable but safe.

Marcus said, "Thank you. We need to find a hotel."

"Why was that man shooting at you?"

"Because we found information that's very damaging to the people he works for."

"What will you do with this information?"

"Give it to the world." Marcus pulled his phone and flash drive from his wet pants. "These may be ruined."

The man smiled. "Perhaps not. Many say the waters of the Tiber are blessed. If you are in need of a safe haven I know of one."

"Where?"

"It is on the island of Panarea near Sicily. There is a small house on a center hill north of the town. It has been in my family for many generations. No one is physically there now. You may use it. The door is always unlocked."

Marcus nodded. "Why are you doing this? You don't even know us."

The man glanced across the river and then up to Marcus and Alicia. He smiled. "What is there to know that I do not recognize?"

Alicia asked, "Who are you?"

The sound of police helicopters and the wail of sirens came from near the Vatican. The fisherman said, "You both must leave now.."

Marcus nodded. "Thanks." He turned to Alicia. "There are some steps by the wall."

Alicia wanted to say something to the fisherman, but was at an odd loss for words. She simply stared at him for a few seconds and then continued with Marcus down the walk to the long set of concrete steps leading up to the inner city. They climbed the steps and turned back to the river. The boat bobbled in the current, still tied to the dock, but the fisherman was nowhere to be seen.

Marcus and Alicia ran up to an intersection and caught a city bus. They paid the fare and took a seat in the back of the bus, tourists and Italian workers watching them in their wet clothes.

Once the bus pulled away from the curb, Alicia glanced through the back window toward the river. "Paul, that man who pulled us from the water, he seemed so at peace. I felt like…I don't know…"

They were quiet a minute, the Roman Coliseum to their right out the window. Marcus finally said, "They won't stop until they're stopped."

"I know," Alicia whispered.

"Once we get the last of the information on the website, once we incinerate the Spear of Destiny…maybe things will change for the better…for the world."

"Only if the world wants to change itself."

"I have to upload information, including the image of the text on the scroll Daniel wrote and sealed. We'll trace the connections from William Chaloner in Isaac Newton's day to Andrew Chaloner in the thirties and forties. And we'll expose Jonathon Carlson today and the Circle of 13 tied to World War II up through the Kennedy assassinations, the Israeli prime minister murders, to the prophecies of the Middle East and the rest of the world. We'll explain the connection to the year 2024."

Alicia shook her head. "But we don't know for certain 2024 is the year."

"Maybe we never will, or maybe we will before this is done."

"Let's find some dry clothes, a laptop or a tablet."

"We need something else."

"What?"

"Some kind of disguises. They'll be watching every terminal. We have to change our appearances a lot."

— • —

Andrew Jenkins drove down Via della Rotonda and whipped his car into the parking lot of the Hotel Abruizzi. He parked and began making a series of calls to his contacts in Rome. To the last one he said, "I want people at every ticket counter at the airport, train and bus terminals. You catch these two, and you'll have more money than the Pope."

"I understand the urgency," said the voice of a man.

Jenkins disconnected and called Jonathon Carlson. "I'd found them, on a bridge over the Tiber River in Rome. I was bringing them into our custody when they escaped by—"

"By what? An act of God?" Carlson shouted.

"They jumped off the damn bridge! Right in the middle of the river. I had to shoot a cop who was in the vicinity."

"You had them in your grasp and you lost them? You lost the flash drive? The spear, too? You know what's next don't you? Russia will send their own to retrieve what Marcus is carrying. That revelation310 website already has more than fifty million views in one day. Find that bastard and the woman with him. Don't fail us again, Jenkins."

— • —

Deep in the heart of the Kremlin, in a safe room, the Russian picked up a secure line and punched a phone number to which only he had access. The man who answered the line spoke with an Arabic accent. In Russian, Heydar Kazim said, "Yes?"

"We have another job for you."

"What is it?"

"You, no doubt, know of the current situation with that revelation310.org website and the Circle of 13. My credibility has been severely compromised, too. The two Americans, Paul Marcus and Alicia Quincy, are believed to be somewhere in Rome. I want them dead. Send visual proof. You must bring me the flash drive Marcus carries, and you must find it before he uploads the other things he implied were there. Also, we think he still is carrying the Spear of Destiny. Stalin almost had his hands on it after the war. The Motherland would be better today had he acquired it. Bring the spear directly to me."

"What is the bounty?"

"Two hundred million Euro."

"You will have it within forty-eight hours." The assassin disconnected. He quickly broke down his Giat rifle. He placed each part into a specially designed carrying case, left his apartment in Venice, and slipped quietly into the cool December evening.

— —

It was dark when the Arabic couple arrived at the train terminal and paid cash for two tickets. The woman wore a veil over her face, just beneath her eyes. She looked as if she was just days from giving birth. The husband, a man with a full beard and walking with stooped shoulders, held his wife by her forearm, approaching the steps leading to the railcar.

The conductor came up to them. "Per favore, mi ha lasciato l'aiuta." He helped the pregnant woman up the two steps. Her husband nodded to the conductor and said, "Molti ringraziamenti."

The couple entered the Euro-Italian liner and walked two cars forward toward their assigned seats. They moved down the aisle in the railcar, which was about half filled with commuters and tourists bound for the first stop, Naples.

The man helped his wife sit slowly in her seat and then sat beside her. She opened a Suduko book and began working a puzzle. Her husband unfolded a copy of the La Repubblica, spread it neatly on his lap, and started reading. After they were settled in, when Marcus could feel no one was looking, he whispered to Alicia, "They have a dining car on this train. Maybe we can eat, and I can use a table to work."

Thunder and lightning cracked and rain began to fall. Alicia looked out the window. She could see one person approaching the ticket booth before rain obscured her view.

—▪—

Three minutes before the train left the terminal station in Rome, a man bought a ticket. Walking under his umbrella, he boarded the last railcar, and Andrew Jenkins took his seat in the rear of the car as the train pulled out of the station.

ONE-HUNDRED-EIGHT

The tall, thin conductor with a pronounced Adam's apple came down the aisle taking tickets and checking passports. When he got to Marcus and Alicia, he said, "Lei parla l'italiano?"

"Sì," said Marcus. "Siamo in grado di parlare inglese troppo."

The conductor smiled. "Ah, yes. Very good. I speak a little Arabic, too. I don't know if you and your wife care for an upgrade. We had a few no-shows on the train, and there are some sleeper compartments available. I just thought it might be more comfortable for your wife."

Alicia smiled. "Thank you. My back is aching." She turned to Marcus. "Do you mind if we upgrade?"

"Of course not."

The conductor smiled. "Very good, please follow me." He led them through two cars until they came to the sleeper cars. The aisle narrowed and numbered compartments were on either side. "You will occupy suite thirteen. We have already turned down the two beds. There is one on the bottom and one on top, plus a small desk and chairs." He opened the door and ushered Marcus and Alicia inside the suite. "How would you like to take care of the extra charge?"

"How much is it?" Marcus asked.

"Seventy-five Euros."

Marcus pulled out money and counted the amount. "Thank you."

"Good evening. Please let me know if there is anything more that you should need. The dining car serves until ten." He nodded and backed out of the room, ducking his head at the eve of the door.

Marcus opened his laptop and logged online, ready to begin uploading from his flash drive to the website.

— —

Andrew Jenkins left his seat and walked less than a dozen steps to the back of the train. Studying the schematics of the train's online operating system, he knew a single antenna receiving a KU-band satellite signal fed the Internet server, and that the server was kept under lock and key in an alcove in the rear of the last railcar. Jenkins found the locked panel. He looked back toward the front of the railcar. All the passengers were turned in the opposite direction. The conductor was nowhere to be seen. Within twenty seconds, Jenkins picked the lock and opened the panel.

His idea was to render the server useless without causing smoke or fire damage. He knelt down and used the blade of a knife to cut wires. The lights on the server blinked twice and faded.

— —

Marcus logged on to the site he'd built, revelation310.org. He let out a low whistle.

"What is it?" Alicia asked.

"There are more than one-hundred and twenty million views. Let see what happens when I collate this information. We'll show the way Carlson and the Kinsley Group killed presidents, prime ministers, and tens of thousands of people in a dozen countries by fueling unjustified wars. All done to fatten their stocks, margins, and bank accounts—accounts that are nothing but money-laundering operations. For good measure, we'll add the recorded statement made by Merriam Hanover right before she tried to kill us. This is more than enough to hand down at least thirteen indictments for crimes against humanity. "

"When you add the pictures of Daniel's scroll from the sealed words along with the history of how we discovered the possible date of earth's last days, there'll be a billion views in forty-eight hours."

The image of the website turned to a black screen. Marcus hit the refresh button. Nothing. "Something's wrong."

Alicia leaned closer. "What?"

"We're offline."

"Maybe we're going through a tunnel and lost the satellite signal."

Marcus stood. "I'll go look. Stay here. Guard the flash drive with your life."

Alicia smiled. "I thought that's what we've been doing these last few days."

"I'll be back in a minute. The dining car is one car up. Do you want something?"

"Straight vodka would be great."

"You're pregnant, remember?" Marcus joked.

"Ha, ha," Alicia said.

Marcus smiled and left.

— • —

Andrew Jenkins relocked the panel and started walking from the last railcar through the train. He casually strolled, glancing at some of the occupied seats, his eyes never locking with anyone. He sauntered all the way to the head railcar, turned around and began walking back through the train, the passengers now mostly facing him. Some were sleeping. Some people played games on smart-phones or tablets. A few people were turning their electronic devices back on, trying in vain to find an Internet signal. One man, with a black fedora pulled down over his face, slept in his seat, a disheveled newspaper on his lap.

"Prego, il signore," said the conductor, walking around Jenkins.

"What's happened to your Internet?" asked an American tourist.

"I'm going to check, sir." The conductor continued walking.

Jenkins approached the serving counter in the dining car.

Marcus stepped into the dining car and stopped. He looked down the length of the car to the man whose back was facing him. The man walked with a slight limp to his left leg. Marcus froze. He watched the man shuffle up to the bar to order something from the bartender. Marcus backed out of the dining car and rushed to Alicia. He locked the door to the sleeper compartment. "We have trouble."

"What do you mean, Paul?"

"The guy who tried to take us from the bridge, Andrew Jenkins, is on the train. He's in the dining car."

Alicia stood from sitting on the bottom berth. "Did he see you?"

"I don't think so."

"How the hell did he find us?"

"I don't know. I hope Carlson didn't have a second GPS implant put inside you."

"We've got off get off this train."

"First stop is Naples. Until then, it's more than one hundred fifty kilometers per hour."

"Now I know what happened to the Internet satellite signal. Jenkins did something to sabotage it. Probably found the server and damaged or disengaged it." Marcus disconnected the flash drive from the laptop.

"That man, Jenkins, doesn't know we're in here. We didn't buy space in here when we bought tickets."

"No, but all he has to do is walk through the train. If he doesn't see us out there, he'll know we're in here."

"But he won't know which berth. There are twelve more."

"Unless he gets that information from the conductor."

—▪—

Jenkins walked back to the last rail car as quickly as he could, trying to keep his pronounced limp to a minimum. He entered the alcove where the conductor was opening the lock. Jenkins said, "Do you lose Internet service often?"

"Rarely. I'm sorry sir. Passengers are not permitted in this area of the train."

Jenkins smiled. "If it's your server, I'd be happy to take a look. I worked for Siemens. We're the same folks who build these trains and program them with the computers. I know my way around the inside of any computer."

"Okay. Maybe you know where to kick it." The conductor stepped aside.

Jenkins knelt down and pretended to investigate the source of the trouble. He said, "I can easily unscrew the front panel and see if the motherboard shook loose. That can happen."

"I hope you can fix it quickly. People on these routes love their Internet. Me, not so much."

Jenkins chuckled. "I'm beginning to think I caught the wrong train. My cousin and his wife are traveling to Naples. I was supposed to join them tonight. I got caught in traffic, the rain, and bought a ticket late at the station. I walked through the train and didn't see them."

"There is a second train leaving Rome in less than a half hour. Perhaps they are on that one."

"No, they were definitely boarding this one. He's about forty, broad shoulders. Tall. She's a little younger. Dark hair. Very pretty."

"I've checked all the ticket holders. Don't recall a couple like that. The only couple not seated in the general area that was supposed to be there, well, they don't match that description. She's pregnant. He's a little stooped over, has a beard. The lady must be Muslim. She's wearing a veil."

"Oh, I didn't notice them."

"That's because I put them in a sleeping suite. How are you coming?" The conductor leaned in closer. His eyes squinted in the lower light, and he pointed to the server. "The wires are cut! Couldn't you see that?"

Jenkins smiled. "Yeah, I guess I could." He grabbed the man's head, viciously twisting. The conductor's neck snapped. Ticket stubs fell from his hand, scattering across the alcove. He dropped to the floor with his eyes wide open.

ONE-HUNDRED-NINE

Alicia stood in the sleeping compartment and pulled the pillow from under her dress. She ripped the veil off the snaps and tossed it on the bed. "He knows we're here. We don't need this stuff now. Besides, I can't run very well with a pillow strapped to my stomach."

Marcus removed the fake beard. "He no doubt has a gun. Maybe we should make a fast break and run into the dining car. With so many people around, he'd be stupid to do anything."

"What if the sick bastard is standing in the hall? He's got orders to eliminate us. He doesn't care where he does it. He could shoot his way out of the damn train."

"We have something on our side?"

"What?"

"He doesn't know that we know he's here." Marcus held a finger to his lips. He heard a soft knock at the door across the hall. A man said, "Biglietto, per favore. Tickets, please."

Alicia whispered. "The conductor. We can tell him."

"What if it *isn't* the conductor?"

"He speaks with a perfect Italian dialect. If it's not the conductor, don't open the door then. The conductor would have a key."

"Jenkins can probably pick a lock."

"But if he tries that, it's going to take longer, and we can hear him."

The voice came closer. A soft knock on the door of the next compartment. "Biglietto, per favore...tickets, please."

Marcus and Alicia could hear the adjacent door open. A woman's voice answered. "È qui il mio biglietto."

"Grazie, signora."

Alicia leaned near Marcus's ear and whispered. "It has to be the conductor. The woman in the next compartment thanked him. Open the door."

"No." Marcus pulled the spearhead from his pants pocket.

"What are you doing, Paul?"

"It's all we have to defend ourselves. It's sharp and can do some damage to a throat if I can strike first."

There was a knock at their door. "Biglietto, per favore…tickets, please."

Marcus held his finger to his lips and looked at Alicia.

Another knock. "Biglietto, per favore…tickets, *please.*"

There was the sound of someone trying to pick the lock.

Marcus whispered in Alicia's ear. "It's not the conductor. Lie down on the floor. When I open the door, crawl out into the hallway and run like hell to the dining car."

"What are you going to do?"

Marcus said nothing. He took the Zippo lighter from his pocket and ignited the newspaper, allowing the paper to become engulfed in flames before he threw the pillow over it. The room filled with smoke.

The door swung open and smoke billowed into the hall. Andrew Jenkins, wearing the conductor's jacket, thrust his pistol into the blanket of smoke. He fired two quick shots. Marcus charged and hit Jenkins hard, pushing him backwards into the door across the hall. He bounced and hit the floor with a thud, knocking the wind from his lungs. Alicia dove beneath the smoke, rolling into the hall in the opposite direction from Jenkins.

Jenkins grabbed her leg and pointed the pistol at her head. "Back off!" Jenkins stood. "I'll kill her on the spot! Give me the flash drive and the spear. Do it now!"

A woman in one of the berths opened the door slightly and slammed it, locking the door.

"Let her go!" Marcus said, holding his hands out. "The drive, computer and spear are in the suite."

Smoke drifted from the room into the hall, dimming the lights. A silhouette, a man wearing a fedora, appeared at the end of the hall. He said, "Drop the gun, Andy."

Nathan Levy appeared through the smoke. He held a pistol pointed directly at Jenkins. "You betrayed me, you betrayed Israel, and you betrayed America. Was it always about the money?"

"Take another step, Nathan, and I'll put one through the girl's brain."

A smoke alarm in the hall blared. Jenkins pushed Alicia and fired at Levy. The bullet hit Levy in the gut. He returned fire, connecting a single shot to Jenkins throat, snapping his spinal cord in the back on his neck. He fell onto the floor, blood pumping from his mouth. He stared at Levy through the haze of smoke, his eyes dimming.

Levy held his stomach, blood seeping from his shirt through his fingers and onto the mauve carpet. He looked at Marcus. "Go! Leave now!"

"Lie down. We'll get you a doctor. Save your strength."

Levy shook his head and leaned against the wall. He glanced at Alicia and smiled. "You both must leave the train as it pulls into Salerno. That's in a few minutes. Don't go through the normal exit doors. Go out the opposite side of the train through the emergency exits, through a window if you have to." Levy coughed, his eyes closing in pain. He opened them and stared at Marcus for a moment, the smoke swirling in the air conditioning. "They have a huge bounty on your head. The information on the flash drive and the spear are what they want, and they want to silence you before you can add more to the website. They won't stop. You'll be hunted to the ends of the earth unless you can find a way to stop them."

Alicia said, "I'm going to get help."

"No!" Levy shook his head, the sweat beading on his face. "It's not safe. Trust no one. Get off the train and disappear." He looked up at Marcus. "Paul, you were right. What you said, I know now, is true. The conspiracy, the assassinations of Rabin and Meltzer, Kennedy. You also succeeded in shutting down some of Iran's nuclear progress. Two of their nuclear centrifuges self-destructed. The Iranians are hunting you, too."

The train began to slow. Levy held his stomach with both hands, the blood dripping across his shoes. With his back to the wall, he slowly lowered himself to the floor. He glanced up at Marcus. "In my office, I have a photograph of my father standing next to a burial trench in Nazi Germany. Many bodies are in the mass grave. A Nazi officer pointed a Luger at my father's face. He stared at death and didn't shy away. My father was a good man who did his best to protect his family. I did my best to protect the family of Israel. I can only pray that I have been my father's son." He glanced over at Alicia. "Take care of this man. You may be the last person on earth he can ever trust."

Alicia nodded and said, "I will."

Levy coughed, his eyes moving back to Marcus. "Paul…there is something else you must know. They have hired the devil himself to hunt you down—the Lion. He is unstoppable. God be with you. The assassin's name is…" Levy coughed, his eyes opening wide, trying to focus on something above Alicia's head. Nathan Levy touched Marcus's hand, closed his eyes and died as the train pulled into Salerno.

Marcus felt stomach acid burn in his throat. He opened his hand and stared at the spearhead. He looked at Alicia. "We have to go." Marcus took the pistol from Levy's hand and tucked it under his shirt.

ONE-HUNDRED-TEN

They didn't wait for the train to come to a complete stop entering Salerno station. Marcus kicked open the emergency door exit and turned to Alicia. "Ready?"

She shook her head. "Yes."

The train slowed to a crawl. Marcus jumped from the steps leading out the emergency door. Alicia followed. She rolled once on the concrete and got up. They ran through the perimeter of the station, ignoring the dozens of passengers sitting on bus-stop benches in the passenger arrival areas.

Marcus flagged down a taxi. He and Alicia jumped in the backseat and he said, "Parli inglese?"

"Of course. Salerno is the number six most popular Italian city to the tourists. Many from England and America."

"How far is the port?"

"Twenty kilometers. Not far."

"Good. Take us there."

"No problem. However, I am almost off the clock. Because my home is not far from the port, I will take you there. But, on the way, I must stop for a pizza I ordered. It will take only a few minutes. I used my mobile to call...how you say in English...a *take-out*. It is small restaurant downtown, so we go by there."

"Do you happen to know the ferry schedules?"

"Some. Where you want to go?"

Alicia glanced at Marcus. He said, "We're still undecided. Maybe in the area of the Aeolian Islands, Messina or maybe even Palermo."

"Some leave at eleven or closer to midnight, and you wake up in Sicily in the morning. However, most ferries do not operate to the islands in this month. All ferries operate to Sicily. More go to Palermo. Some to Messina and one will go to Catania. I am not certain of all their schedules."

"Please, take us to the port."

The driver nodded and pulled away from the rail station.

Another car left and kept a good distance behind the taxi.

Within minutes, the cab driver was driving through the streets of Salerno. Gesturing toward the peaks of the mountains, which were lit by the moon to the east of the city, he said, "It is beautiful, no? Good wine comes from those mountains." The driver slowed in front of a downtown restaurant. The word PIZZA flickered from a neon sign in the window. There was a large bell tower protruding from the adjacent building, the light from the moon coming through the massive arched portals on all sides of the tower.

"What's that?" Alicia asked.

The cab driver grinned. "It is the Duomo of Salerno. It's a cathedral—the final resting place of the Apostle Matthew. I'll be right back." He got out of the taxi and disappeared into the restaurant. Marcus stared at the bell tower, watching moonlight float through the arched portals. At that moment, the single bell began chiming: *dong...dong...dong...*

Marcus counted the rings. "Eleven...twelve." He stared at the belfry, the light of the moon streaming through the old stone porticos.

"Paul, what are you thinking?"

Marcus whispered, '*...about that day or hour no one knows, not even the angels in heaven, only the Father.*'"

Alicia looked from Marcus up to the bell tower. "What did you say?"

"I'm remembering something I read in the Book of Matthew that Isaac Newton mentioned in his notes."

"What?"

"Something Newton was trying to link to a passage from Daniel. Matthew wrote a direct quote from Christ that said, '*...about that day or hour no one knows, not even the angels in heaven, only the Father.*'"

"What are you saying?"

"Newton knew there was some connection between Revelation 12:12 in the year 2012 and some passage in Matthew. Now I know *what* that is…"

"What?"

"Thirty seconds ago, it just turned midnight, December twelfth. Add the twelfth day of the twelfth month and you get twenty-four…as in Matthew twenty-four. If you add the twelfth year, 2012, to twenty-four, you get thirty-six. Matthew 24:36 says, '…*about that day or hour no one knows, not even the angels in heaven, only the Father.*'"

"It sounds like Matthew was writing about the end of days."

"He was quoting Jesus. In Revelation, 12:12, John was quoting God."

"Do you remember what the passage in Revelation says?"

Marcus closed his eyes for a moment. '*Therefore rejoice, your heavens and those of you who will dwell in them. But woe to the earth and the sea because the devil has gone down to you. He is filled with fury because he knows that his time is short.*'

Alicia lowered her eyes from the bell tower to Marcus. "Paul, this is being *revealed* to us in layers…maybe in a way we can fully grasp it."

"There is a woman mentioned in Revelation twelve, who is described as clothed with the sun and the moon under her feet. On her head is a crown of twelve stars. Alicia, there is a similarity that Joseph gives of his father Jacob or *Israel*, his mother and their children. What if the stars refer to the twelve tribes of Israel…what if the woman in Revelation twelve is *Israel*… the *place* of Christ's birth?"

"The metaphor, the woman, is really a *nation*…Israel?"

"When Revelation speaks of the woman fleeing into the wilderness for 1,260 days, maybe it means the future time some have called the Tribulation. Twelve hundred sixty days is forty-two months of thirty days each. Forty-two months is three-and-a-half-years. In Daniel's prophecy, he mentions time, times and half a time…the seven-year week, may be divided into two periods of three-and-a-half-years each."

"Okay, Paul, what if we go back to what we found on the bridge over the Tiber River? We'd reached the year 2011 with some certainty—the year 2024 is still iffy. If we factor in Daniel's prophecy, a seven-year-week or what is really seven years, if the seven years is added to 2011 we come to the year 2018."

Marcus watched a large bat circle the bell tower three times and fly inside the belfry. "The bat flew in a perfect circle…and that's it!"

"What"

"The Circle of 13. Alicia, remember that Daniel 12:1 and Revelation 13 both deal specifically with the *end of times*. Add Daniel 12:1 and you have the number thirteen. That's the *common* factor, the number *thirteen*. That's our key and it points directly to the Circle of 13 and what those people have done to fulfill a prophecy of evil."

Alicia looked up at the bell tower, the moonlight iridescent in her pupils. She whispered. "Add thirteen to the year 2011 and it's the year 2024…the same number, the same year we reached on the bridge over the Tiber River. Paul, I have goose bumps all over my arms."

"We may know when…and we may know where…the *woman*, is the *place* of Christ's birth…"

"We need to get out of here. I wonder what's taking the taxi driver so long. Maybe I can pick up the Internet here." She used her mobile to find a signal. "It's weak at best."

"All I need is a half hour and I can finish and upload everything. See if you can find the ferry schedules from Salerno in Messina. Maybe there's an Internet connection on the ferry boats."

Alicia looked up the information. "Some of the ferryboats leave port at night so they'll be in places like Messina in the morning. Our shuttle leaves in one hour, and we can buy tickets up to departure time."

— —

Heydar Kazim braced his rifle on the open door of the rental car he parked in the dark under a cypress tree with low-hanging limbs. He stood in the shadows within fifty meters of the Cathedral of Salerno. He waited. Twenty seconds later, the taxi driver walked out of the restaurant carrying a paper bag. Kazim followed him for three seconds, the rifle cross-hairs in the center of the man's chest. Kazim squeezed the trigger. A bloom of red popped across the man's T-shirt. He toppled on his back to the sidewalk. The assassin set his rifle in the front seat and started the car. He raced to the taxi.

"Oh God!" shouted Alicia, watching the driver collapse in a pool of blood.

"Stay down!" Marcus yelled, crawling in the driver's seat. He started the taxi just as a car pulled in front of him, blocking the way forward. A rifle bullet exploded the passenger window above Alicia's head.

Marcus pulled the pistol from his belt and fired directly at the front windshield of the car. He backed up, put the taxi in drive and slammed into the rear section of the man's car before pulling out onto the street. He floored the accelerator. Marcus drove through the city square, tires screeching, a pedestrian running for the safety of a tree.

Alicia didn't move from the rear floorboard. "Did your bullets stop him?"

Marcus looked in the rearview mirror. The car was stationary. Two seconds later, the car was on the street, high-beam headlights reflecting from the mirror and burning into Marcus's eyes.

"No! He's coming. Stay down!"

ONE-HUNDRED-ELEVEN

*T*here was the approaching sound of emergency vehicles coming from all directions in the city. Marcus drove down one-way streets and back alleys, through ancient cobblestone and brick streets. He drove through a medieval cemetery where gothic tombstones and mausoleums cast shadows of stone under the moonlight.

Marcus looked in the rearview mirror. "I think we lost him."

Alicia rose from the backseat and crawled to the front. She pointed down the hillside to the bay and a lighted waterfront about two miles from them. "It looks like that's the port down there." She glanced at her phone. "My battery's dead."

— —

The ticket office was less than one minute from closing when Marcus pulled the taxi into the lot. The ticket agent, a woman with dark circles under her eyes, face flaccid and rubbery, glanced at Alicia in the maternity dress, no sign of pregnancy.

Marcus asked, "How much? Quanto per due biglietti al messina?"

"I speak English. You want a cabin or seats?"

"Cabin, thanks. How much"

"One hundred fifty Euros per person."

Marcus counted the money and handed it to the agent. She printed the tickets and said, "The ferry to Messina leaves from pier seven."

They boarded the ferryboat, approached the purser's desk and got directions to their cabin. Alicia asked, "Does the boat have Internet service?"

The purser shook his head, face flat. "Not yet. We'll have that service in the spring."

They found a small bar, ordered two sandwiches, and took the food to their cabin to eat. "Well, it's a little bigger than what we had on the train," Alicia said, sitting at the small table in the room. She unwrapped the sandwiches. "Try to eat, Paul."

He set the laptop on the table with the flash drive and spearhead. "In Messina, we'll have Internet service again. That's when it all comes together. Then we'll see if we can hire a helicopter pilot to take us to the mouth of Mount Etna. We don't even know if the eruptions have subsided."

"It's hard to catch the news when we are the news. I'd love to get in touch with my sister and mother…just to let them know I'm okay."

Marcus said nothing. He bit into the sandwich and chewed quietly, the food tasteless.

Alicia said, "We don't even know if the killer chasing us is from Carlson or Iran…or from somewhere else."

"Can we trust Bill Gray?"

"I don't know anymore. I'd like to think so. He saved our lives."

"We both worked for him, and I'd like to think he always worked for America, what it stands for…a constitution…a nation under God. But, then I look at the back of the dollar and see that eye staring at me. Our founding fathers were, I always believed, good men. Now, good men, and good women, for that matter, are a vanishing species. I trusted Merriam Hanover. Before Nathan Levy died, he said we could trust no one. After all of this is online, we have to vanish…literally. I have a bounty on my head, wanted dead or alive, large enough to float most small nations."

"It's not you. It's what you've found, and it's what you're doing with it." She reached across the table and touched his hand. "You, Paul Marcus, are a good man." Her eyes searched his face. "Did anywhere in those prophecies…did you see anywhere in there where I'd fall in love with you?" She squeezed his hand. "Because I have…I love you, Paul. I love you with all my heart."

Marcus looked at the moon through the porthole. "Alicia…I…"

"Shhh…you don't have to say anything. You don't even have to love me. But I can't help but to love you. I just wanted to tell you in case…in case I don't get a chance to tell you. You mean that much to me."

Marcus kissed her lips.

— —

Heydar Kazim drove his car slowly though the Port of Salerno parking lot. Within minutes, he found the abandoned taxi behind a building. He drove to the closed ticket office where he saw a posted schedule in the window that indicated the last ferry sailed thirty minutes earlier. Kazim used his mobile to make a call. "I need to charter a private jet to Messina immediately."

ONE-HUNDRED-TWELVE

The sun was rising above the Sicilian coastline when the ferryboat churned through the aquamarine blue waters into the Port of Messina. A gold Madonna statue, its arm and hand held up like a crossing guard, stood at the top of a white pedestal that elevated the icon more than eighty feet above the harbor. In the distance, Mt. Etna, a white collar of snow around its crest, belched smoke and steam into the pale blue sky.

Alicia looked out the cabin window and turned to Marcus. He sat at the table, formatting the text, photographs, and audio for the website. "Paul, take a break for a minute. Look at the bay. The water is so blue it almost hurts my eyes. I can see the volcano, Mt. Etna, in the background. There's smoke coming out of it."

Marcus stood; his back ached. He stepped to the porthole. "So that's Mt. Etna. We have to find a helicopter."

Alicia scanned the port area, the cars and people moving about the bustling harbor, ships loading and unloading people and cargo. "No matter where I look out there, I wonder if someone is looking back at us…looking to kill us."

"At this point, we need to go ashore with the rest of the passengers, blend in the best we can, use the crowds for safety, and then break away. Maybe we can hail a cab quickly, rent or even steal a car if we have to." Marcus sat back in front of his laptop and stared at the screen.

"How are you coming, Paul?"

"Getting very close. I've detailed the Circle of 13's connections to the assassinations, bank fraud, non-compete contracts with taxpayer money, political corruption, and how the Kinsley Group and Carlson's companies are defrauding the government in violation of SEC laws. I've provided proof that ties Jonathon Carlson's family to the investment in Hitler's buildup of the Third Reich, followed by Andrew Chaloner, Carlson's grandfather, using his bank and influence to launder Nazi money while they alleged it was profits from Dutch imports. A half billion buys a lot of wooden shoes. I've added the audio from Merriam Hanover. I've also included some of the prophecies from Daniel. As soon as we can get on the net, I'll upload it."

A voice came on the ship's public address system in English and Italian. "All passengers please prepare for docking and disembarking in Sicily. If you do not have a vehicle on the ferry, please report to the main seating area. If you do have a vehicle on board, please prepare to drive it onto the dock. Thank you for your business."

Marcus stood and lifted a pillow from one of the births. "Maybe there's a better way. Can a woman be pregnant two separate times within twenty-four hours?"

— —

Heydar Kazim sat in his rental car in the parking lot of the Port of Messina and watched the passengers leave the ship. He used a pair of high-powered binoculars and looked at the face of each passenger who walked down the gangplank. He was prepared for disguise, keeping in mind that odds were the man would not separate from the woman. Most likely, they would stand out from the rest of the passengers because they would lose the natural gait of travelers on holiday. The clues would be self-imposed, faces and eyes compromised from fear and suspicion. When prey knew they are being hunted, it is something he always can see, like wrinkled clothes or shadows they couldn't outrun.

This will be his most prized hit. The killings of the man and woman will deliver the largest bounty in history. The significance meant nothing to him. Perhaps it would rank up there with the killing of Osama bin Laden. It was a conquest that his employers placed enormous stock in seeing to the end. He felt the strange tingle in his chest he always got before a clean kill. It was sexual, a sensory response that he felt from his gut deep into his loins and testicles. The greater the challenge, the harder the hunt, the more magnified the feeling became. Toward the end, the moment before a well planned and executed kill, he would have an intense and pulsating erection that, afterwards, would require the services of a prostitute. *Death, the ultimate aphrodisiac.* The last time was after the hit on the Israeli prime minister. Kazim thought about the French prostitute he'd enjoyed after that kill.

Focus.

He shook the thoughts from his mind and concentrated on finding his prey.

— —

Marcus and Alicia entered the area of the ferry where more than fifty cars were parked, drivers flowing in and opening their cars. Marcus scrutinized the drivers, picking out one young man who seemed to be by himself. He stood next to his parked Fiat Punto. He wore his long-sleeve shirttail out, khaki shorts and sandals. A week's worth of black stubble grew from his face. Marcus approached with Alicia and said, "Come stai?"

"Sto buono."

"Parli inglesi?"

"Hell yeah, man. I lived in New York City for six years."

"New York cabbies are the only guys who can compete with Italian drivers. Look, I'm a little hesitant to rent a car here. You know the area?"

"I was born in Cantina, right down the road. Grew up in an orphanage there." He paused and studied Marcus's face. "Dude, you sure look familiar. Maybe we met in New York or someplace."

"Sure, it's a small world."

He looked at Alicia, his eyes lowered to her stomach. "When's the baby due?"

"Not soon enough." She smiled.

Marcus said, "If you could drive us to an Internet café, I'll fill your tank up for three months."

The man smiled, "No shit, three months?"

Marcus smiled. "Yeah, three months."

"Get in."

The ferry came to an abrupt halt, gears whined and the massive door in the bow area began lowering. "You mind if we take the backseat?" Alicia asked.

"You mean like I'd be your taxi driver?"

She smiled. "Chauffer sounds better. Just until we get to the Internet café."

"Pile in the back."

They got in his car and he started the ignition. A ferryboat worker, red baton in his right hand, waved the drivers off the ship.

＊＊

Kazim watched the faces through his binoculars. The stream began to slow to a trickle and there was no obvious sign of the Americans. *They didn't have a car.* They have to be looking for a taxi. He set the binoculars down on the seat next to his rifle. He watched the drivers steer their cars from the gaping mouth of the ferryboat. The vehicles looked like a disorganized road rally, drivers jockeying for positions that would allow them to get to the open road faster.

Kazim felt the quiver in his lower chest fade when the last of the cars emptied from the ship's belly. Maybe they were still on board. Hiding somewhere. He could stay and monitor the ship, knowing it would refuel, reload with passengers and cars and begin the return trip in two hours.

Something caught his eye.

One of the cars, a black Fiat Punto, had an anomaly. Kazim craned his neck to see. The car was in the middle of the pack, the road less than fifty meters away.

There it was—a piece of cloth, maybe the hem of a dress. It was caught in the door, flapping in the wind. Kazim put his car in gear, cursing the tourists, the passengers walking in front of him in search of taxis.

His chest tightened, the sensation returning, a radiance building through his belly and loins.

ONE-HUNDRED-THIRTEEN

*B*efore they sat up in the rear seat, Marcus and Alicia waited for their driver to pull away from the Messina harbor area and drive a few blocks into town. The man looked at them in his rearview mirror. "Name's John Gravina."

"I'm Alicia. This is Paul. Damn it, I caught my dress in the door." She opened the door and pulled her dress inside the car.

John glanced in the mirror. "I know it's none of my business. It's just odd that you're crouching down there in the backseat like someone is going to take your head off, especially since you're pregnant. I'm not in any deep shit sitting up here by myself, am I?"

"We just need to be cautious," Marcus said. "It's a long story."

"No problem." John slid the dark glasses down from the top of his head and pushed them up on the bridge of his nose and drove faster though the ancient streets of downtown Messina.

—■—

Heydar Kazim shifted gears in the Alfa Romeo Spider through the square in the heart of Messina. He scanned all oncoming vehicles, cars parked on the side of the road and cars in front of him, searching for the black Fiat Punto.

The mobile phone buzzed in the seat next to him. The caller was unknown. In Russian, Kazim said, "I'm in Messina."

"Where are the Americans?"

"They are close by. I know the car they're driving and—"

"And what! They should have been eliminated by now. Do you know what's happening while you're trying to find them? The Chinese smell blood. They know the Circle of 13 has been compromised severely. They're moving in, recalling debts, making inquiries and acquisitions, and they are in constant communications with Iran and Syria, the nations I have plans for. Find the spear! Find and destroy that flash drive!"

The former president of Russia slammed down his phone.

•—

"Can you drive faster?" Marcus asked.

John glanced up in the rearview mirror. "I don't want to drive too fast and cause your wife to go into labor." He chuckled.

"Trust me. I'm fine," Alicia said.

John downshifted around a city block and sped up. He flew though a school zone. Within seconds, he saw the lights of a police car in his mirror, the siren blaring. "Oh shit! The cops. I didn't see that school crossing. That's about the only reason the police in Sicily will stop you for speeding. You gotta be blowin' through a school zone. Damn!"

He pulled to the side of the road. The officer approached the car. He looked at John and then stared at Marcus and Alicia. In Italian, he asked, "Why the rush? And who are your passengers?"

John grinned. "My friend's wife is close to giving birth."

The officer raised an eyebrow. "I can offer you a police escort to the hospital."

Alicia shot a quick glance at Marcus.

•—

Heydar Kazim saw the police emergency lights. He recognized the black Fiat that the officer had pulled over. This gave him a plan. Kazim reached in the glove box and found a map of Messina. He shook the map open, covered his pistol and silencer with the map, and pulled up behind the black fiat. He watched the officer look at him curiously for a moment. Kazim smiled and got out of the car. Holding the open map, he approached the officer. In Italian he said, "Excuse me, sir. I'm terribly lost. I'm supposed to meet my friend at the Museo Regionale. Can you show me on the map?"

The officer raised his sunglasses and reached out. Kazim fired a single bullet through the map, hitting the officer in the center of his forehead.

"Oh shit!" shouted John in the front seat.

"Drive!" Marcus yelled, drawing the pistol from inside his jacket. Kazim pulled hard on the rear door handle. Locked. He fired a shot into the window. The bullet blew a hole through the laptop computer on the seat between Marcus and Alicia. Shards of glass rained down on them.

Kazim reached through the shattered window, his hand searching for the lock. "Give me the spear!" he ordered.

"Drive!" Marcus yelled. He opened the car door with force, slamming the door into Kazim's legs and groin.

John squealed the tires pulling away from the curb. Kazim stood. He fired three quick rounds into the speeding car. One round shattered the rear window. The other two hit the trunk and taillight.

"SHIT!" John yelled. "Who the hell *are* you two?"

Alicia shook pieces of glass from her hair. "Paul, he shot through the computer."

Marcus looked down at the laptop, the hole the size of a nickel through the center. He reached in his pocket and took out the flash drive. "Doesn't matter. It's all backed up here. We just need to get to any computer with an Internet connection to upload it."

John downshifted and flew through the old streets, past the crowds lined up to watch the noon performance of the astronomical clock near the Messina Cathedral. He looked up in the rearview mirror. "Now I know who you are. You're the dude who won the Nobel Prize and gave the speech about those guys you called the Circle of 13 and what crap the world's facing. And you're in my car...holy freakin' shit..."

Marcus could hear the sound of police sirens around the city. "John, please get us to a computer and the Internet. Time's running out."

"I don't even like the *way* you say that. Who was that dude? What did he mean about the spear?"

"It's a long story," Alicia said. "We have to find a computer and the Internet."

"There's a coffee shop, Café Messina, on Market Street. Somebody's always online in there. "

Marcus nodded. "How far?"

"One block. There's an alley behind the café."

John drove around slower cars, popping through the gears, pulling to an abrupt halt in the alley. They got out of the car. Alicia reached under the maternity dress and removed the pillow, tossing it in a garbage can in the alley.

John shook his head. "Damn! You're not even pregnant."

"No." With John following a few seconds behind, she and Marcus ran down the alley, turned left on Market Street and stopped when they reached the neon espresso sign where they entered the small café. Less than a dozen people sat at tables. Most were sipping coffee and eating pastries or salads. One heavyset man sat alone in the corner, eyes glued to his laptop computer screen, earplugs in his ears. He was playing a video game, the light from the screen bouncing in his eyes.

Marcus and Alicia walked over to him. "Perdonarci."

The man looked up just as John entered and approached them. "Che?" the man asked.

John said, "Devono prendere in prestito il computer."

The man shook his head. "No sono nel—"

Marcus reached in his coat and drew the pistol. "Get up! Spiacente. Alzarsi!"

The man raised his hands and stood. Marcus handed the gun to Alicia. "All I need is one minute."

Two people in the shop screamed and ran for the door. The storeowner picked up the phone and dialed the police.

Marcus inserted the drive in the side of the computer, found a strong Internet connection, and punched the keyboard. He uploaded data from the drive to the website, watching the bar in the bottom of the screen begin to fill. Ten percent...twenty-five percent...the solid colored line gradually loading.

Police sirens were coming closer. "Come on!" Alicia whispered, her eyes cutting from the terrified man to the computer screen, the pistol in her trembling hands.

John asked, "What is it? What the hell are you uploading?"

Marcus watched the bar. "Done," he said, ejecting the flash drive. "It's information that will either help prevent the end of earth…or cause it to happen. Let's go!"

Alicia lowered the pistol. She followed Marcus and John, all three bolting from the store, running down the alley and back to the car. Police converged at the front of the store, weapons drawn, snipers arriving and taking cover behind parked cars.

Heydar Kazim kept at a distance, following the sirens of the police and emergency vehicles to the small café. Officers began barricading the street. Kazim drove around the huge police presence on Market Street to the next block. Tourists on the streets pointed in the direction of the lights, sirens and confusion. Some readied mobile phone cameras, not knowing what to expect. Kazim honked his horn, scattering passersby, driving quickly down alleys and backstreets.

The black Fiat.

It was a blur in the distance. The car was speeding, moving down Via del Vespro, toward the port. Kazim followed. He reached for the Makarov under his coat and set the pistol in the seat beside him. His order was to kill, and he wasn't going to miss this time.

ONE-HUNDRED-FOURTEEN

*M*arcus sat in the front seat beside John, Alicia in the back. John said, "I'm in deep shit."

Alicia said, "No you're not. Tell the police we held a gun on you. You had no choice."

Marcus lowered the car's visor. "We have to find a helicopter."

John glanced in his rearview mirror, his vision obscured because of the dozens of cracks that ran through the safety glass from the point of the bullet's impact. "I know a place. We have to catch the A20. The place is north of Catania. They have a couple of helicopters. They do sightseeing tours, flying tourists around Etna and other places."

"Great. That's where we need to go."

John pulled onto the A20 and headed south. "I don't know if they're doing the flights now because the volcano erupted recently. It's always smoking, but a few days ago, there was some fire and lava flow. Geologists are saying Etna is too dangerous, too unpredictable to get very close. I'm almost afraid to ask, but why do you want to go there?"

Marcus was quiet a moment. "We're following some instructions."

"What do you mean?"

"I'm not completely sure."

"But you know that you need a chopper to fly over Etna. So, what the hell are you going to look for up there?"

"I don't know, John. We have no choice, really. We have to drop something in it."

"In Etna? You're dropping something in the freaking volcano?"

"Yeah."

"Hail Mary." He made the sign of the cross. "Who's the guy chasing you? Why's he trying to kill you?"

"He's a contract assassin. I imagine he's taking orders from some people we've pissed off, people who spent lifetimes—generations pillaging others for personal wealth and power."

"Look at that!" Alicia stared out her side window. "Paul, the volcano, it has a huge smoke ring rising out of it."

Marcus turned to his right and watched in disbelief at the large, white ring rising from its mouth and floating skyward.

John said, "I've lived here most of my life. I've never seen a smoke ring like that come out of the volcano. It's like those skywriters, a perfect circle."

Marcus watched the ring drift from the summit of the mountain toward the east, the ring growing wide and slowly dissipating, soon only a faint trace of the circle against the blue backdrop. *The Circle of 13,* he thought…*gone.* All of the information was now online, the secret brotherhood exposed for who and what they are.

They drove in silence for a few minutes, John constantly checking his mirrors. He touched a gold crucifix hanging from his neck. "Another hour, we'll be there. I don't know how or why you two picked me out of all those people on the ferry with cars. Even though my car's all shot up, this is history. I'm part of it. Maybe it's all for a reason."

Alicia smiled. "You said you grew up near here."

"About thirty kilometers south from here. The town is Cantina. It is beautiful."

"Are your parents there?"

"I don't know. I grew up in a Catholic orphanage. Those people were and are my family. The took care of me. One day I want to build orphanages in Sicily and run them like big families, because that's all the family some kids have…and it gives them something to return to. That's where I was going today. It's Sister Josephine's sixtieth birthday."

— —

Heydar Kazim drove far enough behind the black Fiat to prevent him from being spotted. He heard a short buzz indicating a text came across his phone. Kazim picked it up and read the screen: *You failed on one of two tasks. Marcus uploaded the information. Severe damage is occurring. Find the spear! If not, you will die slowly from the inside out!"*

— —

The network news anchorman took his seat behind the news desk at studios in New York City. He listened in his earpiece and the producer said, "Stand by Brian…three…two…one…you're up."

"We interrupt programming to report enormous repercussions around the world today by new information uploaded to revelation310.org, a website that made international news when Nobel Prize winner, Paul Marcus, gave his much talked about acceptance speech. The president held a news conference earlier and said the justice department is indicting and plans to prosecute Jonathon Carlson and six of the alleged members of a group called the Circle of 13. The justice department is requesting international prosecution for the remaining members, those living and working in other nations. The information Marcus added today provides evidence of a vast network of dummy corporations laundering billions of dollars. Those companies are reported to have ties to ownership of legitimate companies run by some members of the secret group. The information Marcus added to the site, if accurate, points to something that is not a conspiracy but rather a carefully orchestrated series of events that literally changed the course of history. These range from the deaths of President John Kennedy and his son, who Marcus says was assassinated, along with two Israeli prime ministers by people within the Circle of 13. These disclosures are connected to the stockpile of hidden fortunes by three current American and British oil and banking companies who allegedly made tens of millions from financing the buildup of Nazi Germany."

A hush fell over the lunch crowd dining in a Boston tavern where they watched the newscast on a wide-screen TV. "Turn it up!" shouted one businessman, opening his phone to make a call.

The news anchorman continued. "The U.S. Senate has voted by a two-thirds margin, to expel Senator Wyatt Dirkson for his involvement with

Carlson and the Kinsley Group. This is the second Senate expulsion since the Civil War. Senator Dirkson admitted his role, but says he's a victim of entrapment and blackmail. Perhaps the biggest part of this story is information Paul Marcus left on the website. We learned today that Marcus, who worked, at one time, with the National Security Agency, was a top cryptographer—a code breaker before turning to medical research. Marcus had been analyzing information that connects passages from the Bible to information brought forth in recently discovered papers from Isaac Newton's biblical research three hundred years ago. Newton reportedly indicated earth could end in 2060. But Paul Marcus, with the aid of today's super computers and his cryptography skills, says it might be closer to 2024. At this point, Marcus vanished right after his Nobel speech. It's assumed he's in hiding somewhere and alive because of the latest information uploaded to the website he'd created. That new information was uploaded just a little while ago—today. Authorities are looking for Marcus and the woman he's traveling with, Alicia Quincy, also a NSA computer expert. FBI director, Robert Edwards, said the bureau is searching for the couple to take them into *protective* custody. It's speculated that hired assassins are in pursuit of the couple in retaliation for exposing the Circle of 13 and their accomplices, all of whom are now under indictment for those revelations."

From neighborhood bars to boardrooms, people around the globe watched the stories unfold on televisions and websites. Facebook, Twitter and a dozens of the world's most trafficked social networks were on fire with tens of millions of people exchanging comments and speculating as to what the information on the website really meant.

Bold headlines in print and digital formats read: **2024 the Real Apocalypse? Are Isaac Newton and Paul Marcus Wrong? Doomsday Countdown?**

John drove the car from the main road, through a series of back roads and pulled into the open lot where two helicopters sat with Mount Etna in the background, white smoke billowing from its summit.

Marcus touched the spear in his jacket pocket, and felt a palpitation from the beaded scar across his chest.

ONE-HUNDRED-FIFTEEN

*T*here was one car in the gravel parking lot. It was parked near a small trailer. In English, Italian and Japanese the signs read: *See the Summit. Twice Daily Trips to the Summit of Mt. Etna.* Marcus and Alicia got out of the car and John said, "Whatever it is you have to toss in our volcano, I hope your aim is dead on."

Marcus smiled. "Me, too. That gas money I promised you—"

"Don't worry about it."

"Hey, your car's all shot up, too. I'd like to pay to fix it. Trust me on this…write down a bank account number where I can transfer the money."

"Are you sure?"

"Yes, please hurry."

John wrote the number on a slip of paper, folded it and handed the paper to Marcus. "Thanks, brother, but it's on the house."

"John, don't leave here the way you brought us in, okay? We might have been followed. I don't want you facing whatever or whoever is coming."

John nodded. "You guys take care of each other."

Alicia smiled, leaned down and kissed John on his cheek. "Be careful."

"I will. If you need a ride back…"

"We'll take the chopper back," Marcus said. "Now go on and get out of here."

They ran to the trailer, Alicia holding up the maternity dress so she could run easier. Marcus heard a BBC broadcast on the radio when he opened the office door of the flight service. A man wearing a baseball cap, polo shirt and jeans, stood from behind the desk. He was tall and athletic with a wide smile. "Welcome, folks, looking for a tour?" His accent was British.

"Yes," Marcus said, glancing out the window.

"I'm Steve Waterton. Where'd you like to go?"

"Can you fly us over Etna?" Alicia asked.

Waterton smiled. "I can fly you fairly close. The old volcano has been in a slight snit as of late. To be honest, it's like the mountain's got a big damn bee in its bonnet."

Marcus looked at the large aerial photographs of Mount Etna on the office wall, the crater wide, white gases trailing toward the camera lens. "Did you take these?"

"Photography is my hobby. Flying is my bloody passion. In this job, I can combine them both. I've always been keen to do that. After my time in the Royal Air Force, I came here. Never looked back. It's been thirteen years now."

An announcer on the BBC radio broadcast said, "No one has spotted the American, Paul Marcus, since his Nobel speech. His website, however, is an entirely different story. It's been visible to more than a billion people."

Alicia shot a glance to Marcus. She said, "Can you fly us over Mount Etna? It will be the highlight of our honeymoon in Sicily."

Waterton smiled. "I can fly you close, but not over the crater. The sulfuric gases and smoke can play hell with the intakes on the helicopter. The last thing you'd want on earth is to have our bird get its wings clipped over an active volcano, especially this one. Temperatures in Etna's belly are more than two-thousand degrees Fahrenheit."

"Can we go now?" Marcus asked.

"You seem pretty anxious. Doesn't appear that you or she brought a camera for sightseeing, and your wife is wearing a maternity dress. Whatever your reason for wanting to see Etna, that's your business, I suppose. If you got the price of admission, you can fly."

"How much?"

"It'll be two-hundred-twenty-five U.S. dollars each. The trip is a little more than an hour. We'll fly the north side of the volcano, around the perimeter circle, and then head back."

Marcus counted the money. The BBC radio broadcast continued. "The pope has commented, as have many religious scholars and heads of state around the world. Theologians seem split on the probability of what Paul Marcus presents on the website about the end of days on earth. Sir Isaac Newton, whom Paul Marcus traces through Newton's days in the Royal Mint, apparently left little known, yet vast quantities of biblical research. The results are a combination of Newton and Marcus. A formidable team separated by three centuries. Here in London, Prime Minister Singleton says he will be attending the funeral for U.S. Secretary of State Merriam Hanover. It is not certain who shot Secretary Hanover or why, but we are getting bits of information, allegedly, connecting her to the Circle of 13. As of the whereabouts of Paul Marcus and NSA employee, Alicia Quincy, no one seems to know."

Waterton put the money in a small, steel box filled with checks and a few Euros. "We'll lock the office on our way out. My partner is on holiday. I have a feeling you'll be my last customers of the day anyway." He led them across the lot to the helicopter. At the helicopter doors, he said, "There are three sets of headphones and mouthpiece microphones. We'll be able to chat, and I'll point out some of the more remarkable artifacts in and around the volcano. Ladies first...go on and climb in the bird. There's plenty of room for both of you in the back, that way you can experience Etna together."

Alicia boarded the helicopter. Waterton walked around and opened the door to the pilot's side. Marcus stepped up to the pedal on the skids to enter the helicopter. A stir caught his eye. It was a reflection from the dark window of the helicopter capturing something moving behind him.

A man. Running. Fast. Silent.

Before Marcus could turn around, the man said, "Arms up in the air! Now or I'll shoot you in the back of your head."

Marcus raised his arms and turned to face Heydar Kazim. He held the Makarov in one hand, aimed directly at Marcus's chest.

The face.

Marcus had seen it. *Where? Think.*

The man who killed his family.

The Lion

Kazim said, "Either you do what you're told, or I shoot you and search your dead body. Then I shoot the girl in the gut so she can wander off in the woods and die slowly."

Alicia watched in terror, fearful that the man she loved was going to die in front of her. She looked over to Waterton in the pilot's seat. He was reaching for something in the console next to him.

Kazim said, "With one hand, slowly reach into your pocket and set the spear on the ground. If you move quickly, you will die, and so will the girl and the pilot."

Marcus did as ordered, taking the spear from inside his sports coat pocket and setting it on the ground in front of him.

Kazim glanced down. "Good. Now step back."

Waterton shoved open the passenger door next to him in the cockpit. He pointed the pistol and squeezed the trigger. The bullet hit Kazim in the upper stomach, knocking him to the ground, the gun flying from his hand. Marcus picked up the spear and jumped in the helicopter. He shouted, "Go! Go! Go!"

Waterton started the engine, the rotor blade swinging into motion. Alicia looked out the window. "He's going for his gun!"

Kazim crawled painfully toward his gun, trailing blood. The helicopter blade gained fast rotation, building lift. Kazim reached for his gun. He grabbed it just as the helicopter rose into the air, the prop blowing dust and grit into Kazim's face, obscuring a clear shot. He fired three shots, one bullet striking the skids. Waterton flew above the office trailer, climbed over the tree line and set a course for Mount Etna.

Marcus said, "Thank you."

Waterton nodded. "When you fly for the Royal Air Force, you fly armed. Who the hell is that bloke?"

"I don't know."

"What's this spear? What is it so important to him?"

"It has a long history."

"Would the history go back two-thousand years?"

Marcus was silent.

Alicia said. "Yes. Two thousand years. You knew all along. How?"

"Your faces have been on the tube and all over the Internet. Now, do you two want to tell me the real reason you want to fly to Etna?"

Marcus looked at the horizon, the volcano growing closer. "The spear has to be thrown into Mount Etna."

"What! Why?"

"I was told to do it."

"Who told you and why?"

"I don't know all the reasons. I may not know any of the reasons. Look, I truly believe I was told by God to do it."

Waterton nodded, the volcano reflecting from his dark glasses. "That's bloody good enough for me."

Marcus looked at Etna growing closer. He said, "That's the largest volcano in Europe. Some people believe when it blew up seven or eight thousand years ago, the explosions, quakes and energy sent a massive tsunami creating a flood of epic proportions over the entire Middle East and Europe. Maybe this spearhead will somehow keep that from happening right now."

Waterton kept his eyes straight ahead, the volcano now a mammoth mountain in front of them. Smoke drifted eerily from the summit and trailed high into a flat cloud.

— —

Kazim stood and walked to the trailer door. He fired a shot into the lock then kicked the door open. He went behind the counter and picked up a set of keys from one of two hooks on a bulletin board. Above the keys was a note held into place with a thumbtack that read: *chopper two.*

He pulled a bungee cord from a shelf next to the bulletin board, opened the door to a bathroom and found a clean, white towel. He lifted his bloodied shirt and placed the towel to his wound then used the bungee cord to hold it in place. He limped to his parked car and removed the rifle. Then he walked to the remaining helicopter, opened the door, and started the engine, the rotor blade whining. Within one minute, Kazim was in the air and flying the helicopter toward Mount Etna.

ONE-HUNDRED-SIXTEEN

*M*arcus watched Waterton work the helicopter controls, using his feet in unison with one hand on the cyclic stick. Marcus could feel the physics of lift and propulsion. "You ever fly a chopper?" Waterton asked.

"No. You make it seem easy."

"Nothing to it that practice won't conquer."

Mount Etna was less than a mile away. It rose more than ten thousand feet above Sicily. The neck of the old mountain wore a scarf of snow. Silvery smoke drifted from its crater. Alicia said, "It's breathtaking. Etna is fire and ice together on a podium high above the rest of earth."

Waterton nodded. "No matter how many times I fly Etna, she always looks a little different. Sometimes it's the light, the weather, or the mood Etna's in at the time."

Marcus said, "Maybe Etna's in a cooperative mood. It looks like the wind is blowing the smoke to the north. Maybe we can get closer than what you thought."

Waterton studied the smoke for a moment. "Like I was saying, Etna always looks different, but as many times as I've flown people up here, I've never seen the smoke sort of bow down like somebody's pulling it in a near straight damn line north. Wish I'd brought my camera."

Alicia glanced back to the west. Her eyes opened wide. "Paul, we've got company. A helicopter is coming behind us."

Waterton looked to the west. "That's my second bird! Who the hell's flying it?"

Marcus watched the helicopter in the distance. "Get us over the summit! Fast as you can! Whoever it is wants to stop us. We're so close."

Waterton accelerated, banking into the wind and turning the helicopter to approach the volcano from the south. "Hold on. You never know what the winds will be like when you fly above her throat. God help us if the mountain decides to burp. Our uninvited guest will be here in less than a minute."

Marcus removed the spear and the flash drive from his pocket. "Just a little closer...we're almost there."

— —

Kazim held his bleeding stomach with one hand and worked the controls with the other. Blood soaked the towel, seeping between his fingers. Sweat poured from his ashen face. He lifted the rife from the seat next to him, used his feet to control the rotor blades, and held the helicopter stationary in one position near Mount Etna. With his pistol, he shot out the window next to him. The noise from the rotors was deafening. Wind blew hard through the open hole. Kazim rested the rifle on the hole in the window. He aimed, centering the cross hairs in the scope over his target, the helicopter now approaching the mouth of Etna.

He fired.

— —

The bullet blew apart the windshield closest to Marcus. The round hit Waterton in his arm and entered the side of his chest, destroying ribs and collapsing a lung. He lost control of the helicopter for a brief moment.

"I'm shot!" he said, his face tightening in pain. "I'll try to set her down."

"No!" Marcus shouted over the prop noise. "We're almost there."

Waterton said nothing for a few seconds, his jaw line popping. He glanced down at the spearhead Marcus held in his hand. "You say that spear goes back two thousand years?"

Alicia said, "Yes!"

Waterton nodded. "Let's make that delivery!" He pushed the controls and flew the helicopter over the crater. Marcus looked down. He could see the orange glow of molten lava bubbling, crawling inside the volcano like a life form, its gases and smoke swirling from the caldron.

"Get me to the center!" Marcus shouted, cracking open the side door, the wind rushing against his face.

Alicia looked behind them. "He's catching us! Paul, hurry! Drop it!"

Marcus held the flash drive and the spear in one hand. He opened the door all the way and leaned out, beyond the skids. He felt instant heat, as if he'd opened the door to a blast furnace. Marcus dropped the flash drive and spear, both falling far below and into the seething red and orange lake of fire. "Let's go!"

Waterton accelerated, moving quickly across the wide mouth of Etna. He could see the chase helicopter was less than three hundred yards behind him.

Kazim gripped the pistol with one hand and flew the helicopter over the lip of the crater. He pointed the barrel in the direction of his target and fired two shots. Both missed as he dipped the helicopter to adjust the trajectory with his speed.

Waterton cleared the other side of the crater, his breathing labored, stomach filling with waves of nausea. "Hang in there!" Marcus shouted."

"I'm bloody trying! We're clear from Etna's blowhole!"

Kazim's helicopter was in the center of the volcano's mouth. He cursed Marcus and tried to accelerate faster, sweat dripping from his face, the hot wind howling through the hole in the windshield.

Alicia and Marcus looked back just as Etna exploded. An enormous ball of orange fire blew up from the crater. The heat and force of the explosion disintegrated Kazim's helicopter. The blackened shell dropped into the mouth of the volcano.

The energy from the scorching blast rocked Waterton's helicopter like a leaf caught in a tornado. The helicopter bucked and pitched, almost rolling end over end in midair, the powerful kinetic force against the rotors pushing the helicopter far away from Etna. There was a second, larger explosion spewing fire, red lava and rocks a half mile above the summit. Etna disgorged flames and lava as if it were an enormous fountain of fire, the blast witnessed for more than a hundred miles in any direction.

Marcus glanced over at Waterton. Blood trickled from the pilot's mouth. He was losing consciousness. He looked back at Marcus and said, "Use your feet for the blades…they have to work together. The controller in the center is the gas…like the throttle on a motorcycle…and this…the cyclic is how you aim her." He smiled. "How'd we do?"

Marcus blinked, his eyes watering. "We did fine…and you did great." He touched the top of the man's hand.

Waterton nodded, pressed the button to unbuckle his harness, and died in his seat. The helicopter started a slow spiral.

Alicia looked at Marcus. "Can you fly it?"

"I don't know. I have to get behind the wheel." Marcus gripped the cyclic as the helicopter began spinning faster. He pulled Waterton's body from the pilot's seat and climbed in fighting to bring the helicopter under control. It pitched violently in the air. Alicia saw blue sky then the earth rush up. More sky. Then the enormous fire from Etna in the distance. Then the sea. They were close to the sea.

Marcus fought the controls. He worked the pedals with his feet, trying to find a balance. He gripped the cyclic to stabilize his direction. He was dizzy and disoriented from the spinning. It was as if the helicopter was caught in a vortex he couldn't break.

"Paul…" Alicia reached up from the back seat and placed her hand on his shoulder. She closed her eyes and prayed—prayed harder than she ever had in her life. Through tearing eyes, she said, "I love you, Paul."

Seconds later, the helicopter crashed into the blue waters of the Mediterranean Sea. The force threw Alicia into the front of the helicopter, her head slamming violently against the console. Blood poured from a large gash. Marcus grabbed her, pressing one hand to her bleeding forehead. She was unconscious. Marcus could smell fuel mixing with seawater, and the sound of hot engine parts touching the incoming water. "Alicia!"

No response.

"It's going to be okay. Breathe! Damn it! Breathe!"

The sea poured into the cockpit. Alicia was still, like a ragdoll in Marcus's arms. "Don't die! Please!" He tried to wipe the blood from her face, the water rising, covering his waist. He reached for the radio, keying the microphone. "Mayday!" he shouted. "Mayday! We need help!" No signal. The radio was dead. He dropped the mic and held Alicia as the water swirled around them. Marcus tried to move. He looked around, scanning the front and back area of the helicopter, looking for life preservers. Nothing but rising water. Marcus held Alicia's head above the water and tried to kick out the door.

Within seconds, the helicopter tilted, cantering to the far left. Marcus looked up through the shattered window at the hard blue sky. "Please! God! Don't let her die. Please! I can't lose her...not now...not again." Marcus wept, holding Alicia's head to his chest, the water swirling around them as the broken helicopter shuddered and sank into the emerald sea. "No!" Marcus used both legs, now kicking at the splintered glass, in one final attempt to free them as the sunlight dimmed beneath the surface of the ocean.

ONE-HUNDRED-SEVENTEEN

*P*aul Marcus could see only black. He heard the crackle of police and emergency radios in the distance. When he opened his eyes, it was still dark. The stars were so close a man could reach out and touch them. So bright and alive with light. He was cold, lying on his back, looking into the heavens when a meteor cut a blistering path in the inky sky.

"Damn shame," he heard one of the medics say. "The whole family murdered. The woman and little girl probably first…and then the man. If we could have been here five minutes earlier…maybe it would have made a difference, at least for the husband. Looks like he bled out from the stab wound on the right side of his chest."

No! I'm not dead! Marcus wanted to say. But he could not form any words. Only thoughts, visions…visions of places he'd never been. People he'd never met. How long had he been lying here, in the cold and rain? Why did he pull over to help the man? *Why! Why! Why!* Tiffany and Jen would be home in bed if…"

They pulled something over him—a white sheet. The stars were gone. Black enveloped him, and then there was a single light in the distance cloaked in absolute quiet. He free-fell through a dimension with no traceable reference to time and place. He was drenched in light, naked, his entire being an open book. He felt no fear.

Paul Marcus felt absolute love.

His grandmother stood next to him, hand extended, smiling. She spoke without moving her lips. *"You did it, Paul…you did it…I love you."* He reached for her just as she smiled again and faded away, the light growing stronger. Then he could see the compassionate face of Bahir, eyes warm and reassuring. Marcus tried to say something. He couldn't talk. His thoughts seemed to transmit with no need to speak them.

The light slowly faded, and the cries of sea gulls seemed far away. Someone lifted a cool, damp cloth over his face.

Marcus was on his back, the sound of breakers, the smell of the sea, the scent of olive blossoms and hibiscus in the breeze. He opened his eyes and used one hand to remove the cloth from his face.

Alicia was lying next to him twenty-five meters inland from the beach.

Please be alive, Marcus thought, crawling to her. *God, let her be alive.* He lifted her head, gently, using one hand to wipe the wet sand from her lips and forehead. He could feel a pulse, slow but strong. Her eyes fluttered a second, and then opened. Her head and face were bruised and cut.

Alicia tried to smile. "Paul, what happened? Where are we?" She glanced to the left and right. There were islands in the distance, volcanic cliffs jutting up from the sea. "How'd we get here?" Her voice was raspy.

Marcus looked around the area. "I don't know. Maybe we're on an island."

"The last thing I remember was the helicopter hitting the water." She sat up and focused on Marcus, gently touching his forehead. "You're cut, and you've got a bump there. How do you feel?"

"A little woozy." Marcus shielded his eyes from the glare of the sun off the water. "Maybe we're somewhere near the coast of Sicily. Look, there's a small harbor down there." He pointed to a few fishing boats and sailboats anchored in the calm harbor. "I see one small boat moving. A fisherman, maybe."

Alicia stared at the small boat in the distance. Marcus stood and stepped to the beach. There was an indentation where a small boat had come ashore. He stared back at the spot on the beach where they had been. "Maybe someone carried us from a boat to up here. We might be…"

"Might be where?"

"Maybe the Aeolian Islands. North of Sicily."

Alicia's face filled with hesitation, her eyes taking in the island and the harbor. "I have goose bumps all over. Are we alive or is this some come kind of death dream we're sharing?"

"We're alive, I think." Paul smiled and added, "But a lot can happen in a dimension where time itself means nothing... *for the things which are seen are sequential, but the things which are not seen are eternal.'* "

Alicia looked down at the maternity dress, ripped and still damp from the sea. She laughed. "I didn't dress very well for heaven." She looked around her. "It's beautiful here. Maybe this *is* paradise...let's climb a little higher."

They walked a rocky path that led them to a cliff that overlooked the sea. The island had a natural curve to its south face, the cliffs jutting straight down into cobalt blue waters. Marcus studied the terrain, his eyes drifting across the pastoral hills, down to the old-world harbor and the quaint seaside village. The air smelled sweet, pink heather cascading from the slopes, lemon and orange trees planted in nearby fields.

"I could grow to like this place," Alicia said, the wind teasing her hair.

"Maybe we could call this home. We'll be the nameless couple who drifted in with the tide one day and decided to stay."

"You think?"

"Yes." Marcus looked across the immense indigo blue ocean. He could see smoke from Mount Etna in the sky. "At this moment in time, I feel so much alive. For such a long time, I felt dead inside. Should I trust this new feeling? What do we really see, Alicia?"

"Maybe the world will listen and hear what you found...what you shared with them. Love between people is what we can see and feel...maybe we commit to that."

"Maybe. That hope is about all we have left."

"I disagree, Paul." She took his hand in hers. "We have much more left. For whatever reason, you were picked. I don't know for sure how or why. I don't even know why I'm standing here on this beautiful windswept island with you. For a concise moment, we had the chance to experience the things eternal. You, Paul Marcus...you and Isaac Newton...had the window to the universe opened for a brief period. You recognized the patterns of the universe...and of human nature. You found some of the unseen links. With guidance from God, you showed your fellow man what it is...and most importantly...you showed them what it can be."

Marcus watched the smoke from Etna on the horizon, and then his eyes met Alicia. He could hear the roll of the breakers on the beach below them.

The breeze was blowing through her hair; and even in her disarray, she was beautiful. He reached out to her, took her face in his hands, and leaned in to kiss her gently.

She looked up at him, her blue eyes searching his face.

Marcus used his thumb to push a lock of hair from her eye. "I'm not the same man I was when this started. I could never be that man again. I've found what I didn't know even existed. I love you, Alicia." He kissed her again. Alicia's eyes sparkled, catching the light off the sea. Marcus cupped her face in his hands and kissed her tenderly, the sound of breakers rolling, tears spilling from her eyes.

She smiled and said, "I love you, too, Paul."

He took her hand, and they walked a small path through the verdant green of the island.

Twenty minutes later they came to a cottage on a small hill. Marcus said, "I bet the door's unlocked."

"You think so?"

"Somehow I don't think it's ever been locked."

ONE-HUNDRED-EIGHTEEN

WASHINGTON, DC

*I*t was almost 9:00 p.m. when Bill Gray stood from his desk in the NSA complex and walked three doors down the hall to the media room. Half a dozen analysts sat behind computer monitors and read data. Seven widescreen television monitors were at the far end of one wall. Network and cable newscasts were recorded and archived. Gray watched a live feed from CNN. "Could you turn it up, Ben?" he asked one man.

"Sure."

The CNN newscaster said, "Authorities in Sicily say they've called off the rescue and search for the bodies of a man and a woman believed to have been Paul Marcus and Alicia Quincy who apparently died in a helicopter crash into the Mediterranean Sea. Paul Marcus, as you probably know, became a global household name in the last few days after he accepted the Nobel Prize for medicine and issued a warning to the world. Marcus's website has words he says he photographed directly from prophecies that where sealed by the prophet Daniel more than four hundred years before the birth of Christ. Mysteriously, the information seems to make connections to many of today's largest companies and the people who run them. Federal indictments have been handed down against six of the wealthiest people on earth. The last person known to have seen Marcus and Quincy is John Gravina, a thirty-five year old Sicilian who was shot by an unknown assailant and left for dead. From his hospital room, Gravina told police he drove Marcus and Quincy to the Adventure Flight Helicopter Service where the couple had made plans to fly over Mount Etna. A pilot from the flight service is missing and presumed dead as well. The helicopter was pulled from thirty feet of water. Its doors had been ripped off in the crash. There were no human remains found in the helicopter, and officials believe the bodies of the pilot, Paul Marcus and Alicia Quincy are lost at sea."

— —

Jonathon Carlson sat by himself in the dark. One small lamp was on near the overstuffed leather chair in his library. A few yellow flames licked at the split oak logs in the fireplace. Carlson's cell phone buzzed softly. He looked at it on the lamp table next to his chair, ignoring the call from Russia for the third time in the last hour. Carlson lifted a bottle of sixty-year-old Macallan Scotch and poured the remaining portion into a crystal glass, the ice partially melted.

He raised the glass in a toast to a framed photograph on the wall of his grandfather taken inside the I. G. Farben building in Germany. His grandfather was frozen in time, shaking hands with two other men, an American and a German. Dozens of workers, mostly women wearing smocks, were out of focus, blurred images in the background. The German in the picture wore a fedora hat and trench coat, his face turned in profile, looking directly at Andrew Chaloner. A close observer could make out the dark of a small moustache above the German's top lip.

Jonathon Carlson stared at the photograph, softly lit by a single low-wattage bulb above it. "I raise my glass to you Grandfather, and to your circle of friends. My circle is broken...as is this inheritance I've tried to build upon. I personally may have been defeated, but our cause will never die." Carlson lifted an antique Colt .45 pistol. Without hesitation, he placed the end of the barrel next to his temple and pulled the trigger. Blood and brain matter splattered on the screen of his cell phone, which buzzed for the fourth time within the hour.

— —

The former president of Russia cursed Jonathon Carlson. He threw his phone against the wall in his office directly under a photograph of Joseph

Stalin, who was dressed in uniform at the Potsdam Conference in 1945. In the picture, Stalin sat next to Prime Minister Winston Churchill and President Harry Truman. The purpose of the meeting was to decide how to administer punishment to defeated Nazi Germany.

In the background, almost out of focus, a keen observer could make out the image of a man staring at the back of Stalin's head. The man was David Marcus.

ONE-HUNDRED-NINETEEN

(CATANIA SICILY - SIX MONTHS LATER)

John Gravina looked across the desk at the woman and asked, "Are you sure?"

The assistant bank manager leaned forward and nodded. Her dark hair was pinned up, a single strand of pearls around her slender neck. She lowered her voice. "Yes, Mr. Gravina. The deposit was wired into your account three days ago. Here is a printout of the statement. I almost forgot. She reached inside a drawer and handed John an envelope. This is addressed to you. It arrived yesterday by messenger."

John nodded, looked at the sealed white envelope, and opened it. He took out a single page and read:

Dear Mr. Gravina:

This is an anonymous donation to you. The benefactor, although deceased, instructed me to transfer funds into your bank account. The request was that you will use the money to build a new orphanage and have sufficient operating capital for a number of years. The total bequeath is twenty million Euros.
The only stipulation of you is that you never try to locate the estate of the deceased and that you name the orphanage the Mohammed Zaki Home for Children.

Most respectively,

Andrew James Thomas
Executor, Royal Bank of Scotland
Cayman Islands

—◆—

Marcus and Alicia stood at the dock on Panarea Island two hundred miles north of Sicily and watched the hydrofoil approach the harbor. Alicia wore a white cotton sundress, flip-flops, and her hair was pulled back in a ponytail. Her skin had tanned auburn, leaving a sprinkling of freckles across her bare shoulders. Marcus wore shorts, boat shoes and a T-shirt. He hadn't shaved in a week. The breeze off the water tossed his thick hair.

"Are you just a little nervous?" Alicia asked.

"More anxious than nervous. Unless he broke his promise, Bill Gray is the only human left on planet earth who knows we're still alive."

Alicia smiled and touched Marcus's hand. "Well, Bill is not alone on the trip over here. I'm sure they've talked."

The hydrofoil shuttle boat slowed entering Panarea's San Pietro harbor. The eighty-foot water taxi pulled up and docked parallel to the main pier. Porters and guides from nearby hotels helped passengers unload and carry their luggage to waiting golf carts. The only other form of transportation on the island were bicycles.

The last passenger to walk off the hydrofoil was the deputy director of NSA, Bill Gray. He carried a single file folder and no luggage. He smiled stepping up to Marcus and Alicia, kissing her on the cheek. "Alicia, the islands have been good to you. You look relaxed."

"I am, Bill, finally. How have you been?"

"Good. Retiring in fifty-seven days." He turned to Marcus. "Paul, it's good to see you. Beautiful place you've picked."

"We didn't really pick it. It sort of chose us."

Gray nodded. He glanced back at the boat. Two deckhands carried an animal kennel by its handles. Through the wire mesh, Marcus could see his dog Buddy. "Thank you," Gray said to the deckhands. "Please, just set it there."

"Buddy!" Marcus said, bending down to unlock the kennel. Buddy ran out, barked and almost climbed in Marcus's lap trying to lick his face. "I've missed you so much. Have you been keeping an eye on the farm?" Buddy barked, wagging his tail in a blur.

Alicia squatted and petted the dog. "Hi, Buddy. Welcome to your new home. There's plenty of water for you to splash in on an island. I think you'll like it here." He licked her cheek.

Gray said, "I imagine Buddy could use a patch of grass. It's been a few hours since he saw land. Let's take a walk."

They walked up a winding cobblestone path that wound its way around white homes, purple and blood-red bougainvillea cascading over very old stone terraces, the scent of citrus in the gentle wind. Gray stopped and looked at the sea below them, the islands rising out of the sea like volcanic leviathans roosting on the edge of earth. "This beauty has a feel of antiquity here," Gray said.

Marcus smiled. "Panarea is the smallest of the Aeolian Islands.

"You both look happy. Are you?"

Alicia said, "I'm sad I can't tell my family where I am. I can't even tell them I'm alive."

"In time you will. Right now, it's still too dangerous for them if they know where you can be found."

"I worry about my mother. I don't know how my niece is doing since she was released from Iran."

Gray tilted his head. "All indications are she's fine. Alicia, if you want to let them know you're alive, I understand…that's your choice. I just wouldn't tell them where to find you. Not now. Not yet." He looked at Marcus. "Paul, your farm, your horses are fine. We've been paying to maintain it. For the sake of legal discourse, we can mock-up a property sale to give the appearance that it has fallen into the hands of county government for a probate sale to a fictitious owner. The real deed, of course, will remain secured in your name when, and if, you choose to return home."

"Thank you, Bill."

He nodded. "I don't know how well you've kept up out here with what you did, but you've sent the nearest thing to a human tsunami around the world that's ever been seen in modern times. Charges ranging from murder to fraud, theft, conspiracy to defraud the U.S. Government, war crimes against humanity, and a whole list of charges have been leveled at most of the Circle of 13. The International Criminal Court is involved. Carlson blew his brains out. Some of the others are asking for plea bargains by turning into government witnesses, bartering for reduced time in jail and paying hefty fines. Fines so big they could almost offset the budget deficit. There's something else I need to tell you?" Bill looked at the sapphire sea and deeply inhaled, searching for the right words.

"What?" Marcus asked.

"The man who murdered Jennifer and Tiffany was, as you know, the Lion. His real name was Heydar Kazim, and he's been killed."

Marcus said nothing, looking at the dark blue sea, his eyes cutting over to Gray.

"Before Jonathan Carlson put a bullet through his skull, he admitted to Van Airedale, one of the thirteen that Kazim—the Lion, was closing in on you. It was Kazim who was vaporized over Mount Etna. Another thing, Van Airedale admitted that the person who originally authorized the kill order on you and your family was Secretary Hanover. I'm so damn sorry, Paul."

Marcus said nothing. He looked over to Buddy as a horn sounded from one of the boats in the harbor. Buddy raised his ears. Alicia took Marcus's hand in hers and said, "Thank you, Bill, for telling us."

Gray nodded. "What you two did has great historical consequences… and, in time we'll learn the extent of the impact. It will be big. But you'll have to stay in seclusion—in the ultimate witness protection program, right here, for the foreseeable future. We set up new identities for you—birth certificates, records, credit reports, passports. Everything you'll need. It's all in this file folder. " He handed the folder to Alicia.

Marcus said, "It was worth it. I hope Israel isn't too angry with me."

Alicia shot Marcus a curious look.

Gray said, "They know what you did was to bring the Iranian nuclear effort to a screeching halt. It'll take them years to rebuild, if ever. Too bad you had to go through such a charade to pull it off."

"Charade?" asked Alicia. "What charade?"

Marcus said nothing, his eyes following Buddy.

Bill cleared his throat. "Paul agreed to take this on after he received the invitation from Professor Jacob Kogen to go to Israel. It was the perfect cover and opportunity."

Alicia pulled a strand of hair behind her ears, her eyes incredulous. "So this whole thing was covert from the beginning...Paul used as a field agent to stop the Iranians?"

Marcus said, "It was to free Brandi and Adam, too, Alicia. After you told me about them, I contacted Bill and agreed to go to Jerusalem. Everything else became part of the cover—one that turned into a vortex no one could have predicted. And we, you and I, did the planet a lot of good by bringing down the Circle of 13."

"How about the Bible codes? The prophecies? It all made perfect sense!"

Bill said, "That got the world's attention more than anything. Everyone is wondering if it's real. You have to admit, it certainly created a hell of a diversion to what was really going on. Also, the public's outrage at what these billionaires did is what's moving the prosecutions through the World Court."

Alicia looked out to sea, her eyes following a gull over the marina. "Why didn't you tell me, Paul?"

"To protect you. After Brandi and Adam were freed, I tried to keep you out of the rest of it. You wanted to stay, and by then I didn't want to let you go."

Bill smiled and said, "It can't hurt if some people believe the world will end in 2024...it might propel change in the self-centered direction we're heading. I have no illusions about mankind as a whole. But you have the world talking...and listening. If you two somehow stumbled upon some truths from Bible prophecies, even a hint that suggests a possibility the earth will end in 2024, issuing a warning to mankind to stop its greed, that's a damn good thing. It would mean there'd be less need for guys in my line of work. And that's just fine." He cut his eyes from Alicia to Marcus. "You really didn't, I assume, discover something concrete that I should know about, did you?"

Alicia glanced down at Buddy, and then met Gray's eyes. She tilted her head, almost like she was trying to look into his mind. "What if everything Paul told you and the rest of the world is true, Bill? You know the dirty little secrets of millions, the places they try to hide their indiscretions, their greed.

Would they change? Will they change? On a personal level, what would you do if you knew these prophecies were true?"

There was a second blast of a boat horn. Bill said, "I think I have changed, and I'd like to believe much of the world has taken notice, maybe become more tolerant and more compassionate of each other, and who knows…maybe a little more virtuous, too. We can only hope so. I guess I'd better be heading back. I don't want to miss the boat."

Marcus said, "Thank you for coming out here, and thank you for coming to my farm when you did. All of what we've been through was damn well worth it because what we've been given in life, I've learned is worth fighting for."

Alicia bit her bottom lip. "Bill, I believe, no, I absolutely *know* what we discovered is very real—especially the big picture of it all. We were led to it. We may have discovered it in the context of performing something else, but that's the way some things happen. The year 2024 isn't that far away. It may not be the exact date, but who really knows? Perhaps we still have time to get things right."

Bill nodded. "Maybe. Thank you, Alicia for all you did."

Alicia smiled and unsnapped a gold-chain necklace that held a small gold cross. "Take this back to Virginia. Please, give this to my mother. That's all you have to do. She'll know." Alicia dropped the necklace in the palm of Gray's hand.

"Okay. I'd best be going. Oh, while I'm thinking of it, I was intrigued by something I read in the news recently."

"What's that?" Marcus asked.

"The Hebrew University Library where *you* spent time, Paul…that library received an anonymous gift for a half billion dollars to set up a foundation trust fund. The apparent benefactor had only a few stipulations. One, a professor in the university, Jacob Kogen, was to be the head trustee; the second condition was that the money is to be used solely for the purpose of war reparations. The reparations are to go to families of people killed or robbed of their fortunes and homes by Hitler and Stalin during the period before and through World War II."

Marcus said nothing.

Alicia hid a smile and watched Buddy chase a leaf.

Gray said, "That was quite a gift. Do you know anything about that, Paul? Alicia? Never mind, I really don't want to know the answer to that."

There was a loud blast from the shuttle boat. "Marcus glanced down to the harbor. "Looks like your ride is about to leave."

Gray released a deep breath from his lungs. "Yeah, I guess it is."

Alicia leaned in and kissed Gray on his cheek. "Can't you stay for dinner? Spend at least one night? It'll do you some good."

He shook his head, turning to leave. "I wish I could stay. I don't know how you two did everything you did. Damn remarkable. Too bad you can't take the credit for something truly good. Then again, maybe it's a shared secret credit between you and Isaac Newton. Yeah, we really shouldn't need people in our line of work."

"Oh, that reminds me...I suppose I need to officially resign from my job," Alicia said. "I quit."

Gray smiled, buried his hands in the pockets of his trousers, turned, and walked back to the harbor.

EPILOGUE

licia watered the roses and hibiscus that grew on both sides of their small house on the hill. Buddy lay in the shade of a large olive tree and closed his eyes in the late afternoon. Soon, he heard Marcus walking up the gravel path to their home.

"Hey, Buddy, look what I brought you from town." Marcus held up a Frisbee he'd hidden behind his back. Buddy barked and paced. Marcus tossed the Frisbee over the yard. Buddy bolted across the grass, catching the Frisbee before it could hit the ground.

Alicia stood and smiled. "What a team you two make. Does Buddy ever miss a catch?"

"Only if I do a lousy throw."

"Maybe we could find a bat and a softball and hit Buddy a few grounders."

"You should see him clear the bases."

"Oh, he bats, too?"

"He's more of a catcher and an outfielder."

"Could you use somebody on first base?"

"The three of us would make a pretty cool team?"

"Imagine if there were four of us?"

Marcus said nothing for a moment. "*Four* of us?"

Alicia smiled wide, the setting sun across the Mediterranean dancing in her eyes. "Yes, four of us."

Marcus grinned. "A baby?"

Buddy dropped the Frisbee at Marcus's feet and barked once.

Marcus raised his eyebrows. "How long have you known?"

"Just a little while. Are you okay with—"

"Yes…absolutely. I'm not just okay, I'm thrilled." He stepped over to Alicia, took his hand in hers and led her onto the terrace beside the house, overlooking the sea. He laced his hands behind the small of her back and gently pulled her closer to him. "I'm thrilled beyond words."

Alicia nodded. "I was so worried that the timing was all off. I didn't know how to tell you…I'm so happy…" she paused, her eyes tearing.

"It's okay." He used his thumb to wipe away a single tear from her cheek. "I think we're off to a good start for a team, Mrs. Marcus."

"Start?"

"Yeah, you know, a team could be three or more—"

"Or less." She laughed. "The only condition I'm evoking in round one is that I never have to wear that maternity dress I had to wear for three long days and nights."

"Sounds like a deal."

Buddy sat quietly on his haunches, directly behind them, a Frisbee in his mouth. Marcus laughed and took it, tossing the Frisbee far across the yard. Buddy ran after it, jumping high in the air, defying gravity just for a moment. It was at that same moment the sun slipped into the coppery sea. A gull rode the trade winds above them and laughed. Buddy seemed to smile in midair with the Frisbee caught between his teeth. Time soon dissolved into a full moon rising over the darkening ocean, the tide ebbing its way over rocks and barnacles.

The wind picked up bringing the scent of the night-blooming heather. "I'm cold," Alicia said.

Marcus stood behind Alicia and reached his arms over her, pulling her closer to him. They watched the yellow moon rise higher, the islands now mammoth silhouettes ascending from the depths of a golden sea.

Beyond the horizon, an ancient volcano slept quietly while the moon climbed high over the summit and cast light deep into the unblinking eye of Etna.

The End

CPSIA information can be obtained at www.ICGtesting.com
Printed in the USA
LVOW06s1635230715

447375LV00019B/1271/P